The Adventures of Kung-Fu Robot

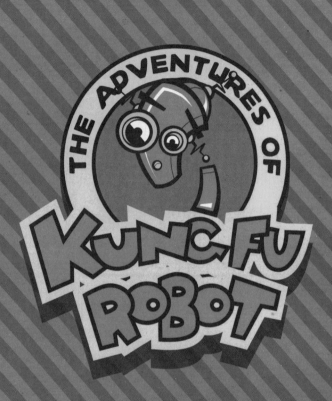

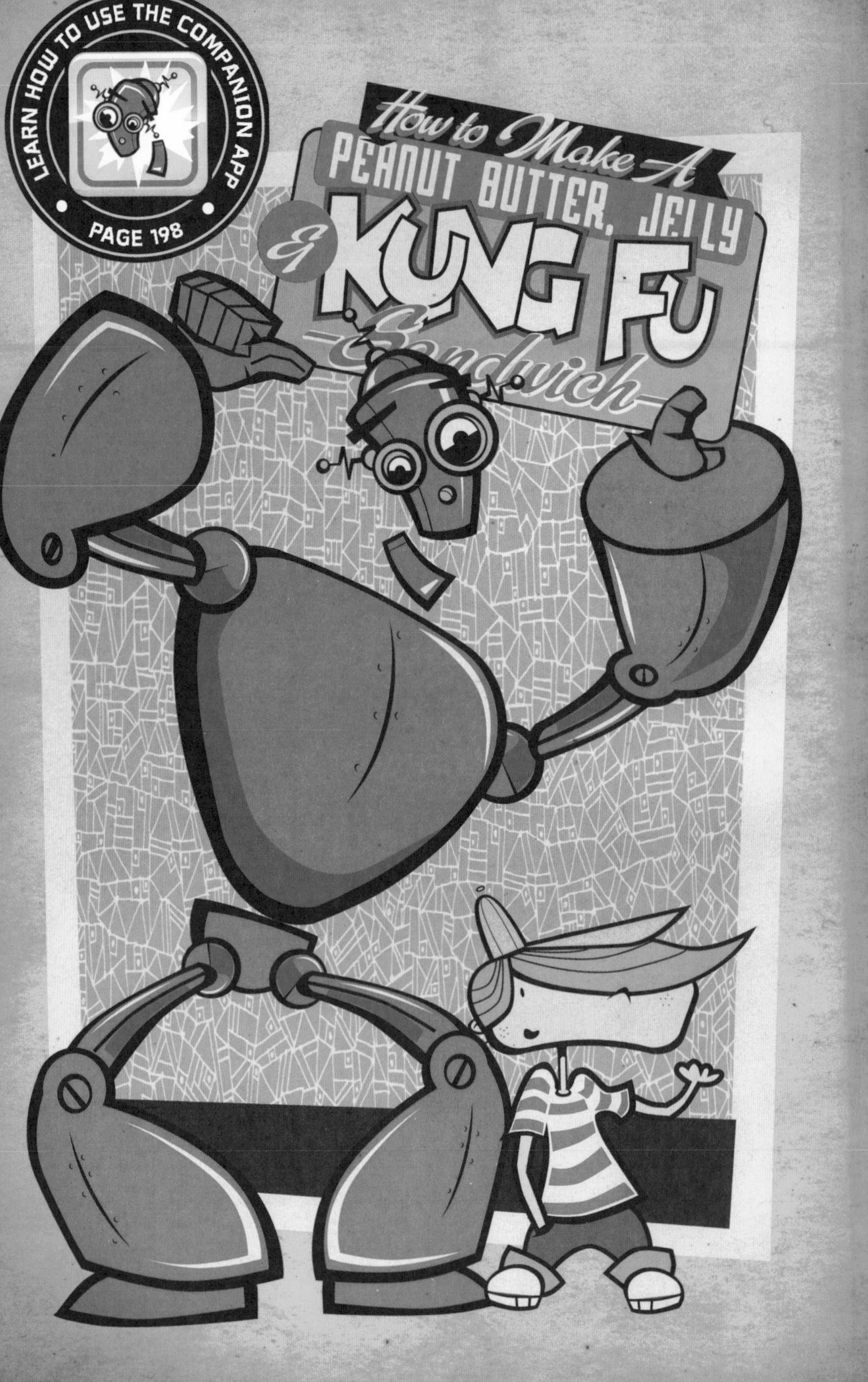
LEARN HOW TO USE THE COMPANION APP
PAGE 198
How to Make A
PEANUT BUTTER, JELLY
& KUNG FU
Sandwich

The Adventures of
KUNG-FU ROBOT

HOW TO MAKE A
PEANUT BUTTER, JELLY & KUNG FU SANDWICH

ART & STORY by
JASON BAYS

Andrews McMeel
Publishing®

a division of Andrews McMeel Universal

FOR ASHBY, ASHTON, OLIVER, DOMINIC, ANDREW, AND GRACE

"IMAGINATION IS MORE IMPORTANT THAN KNOWLEDGE. FOR KNOWLEDGE IS LIMITED TO ALL WE NOW KNOW AND UNDERSTAND, WHILE IMAGINATION EMBRACES THE ENTIRE WORLD, AND ALL THERE EVER WILL BE TO KNOW AND UNDERSTAND."

—ALBERT EINSTEIN

CHAPTER 1

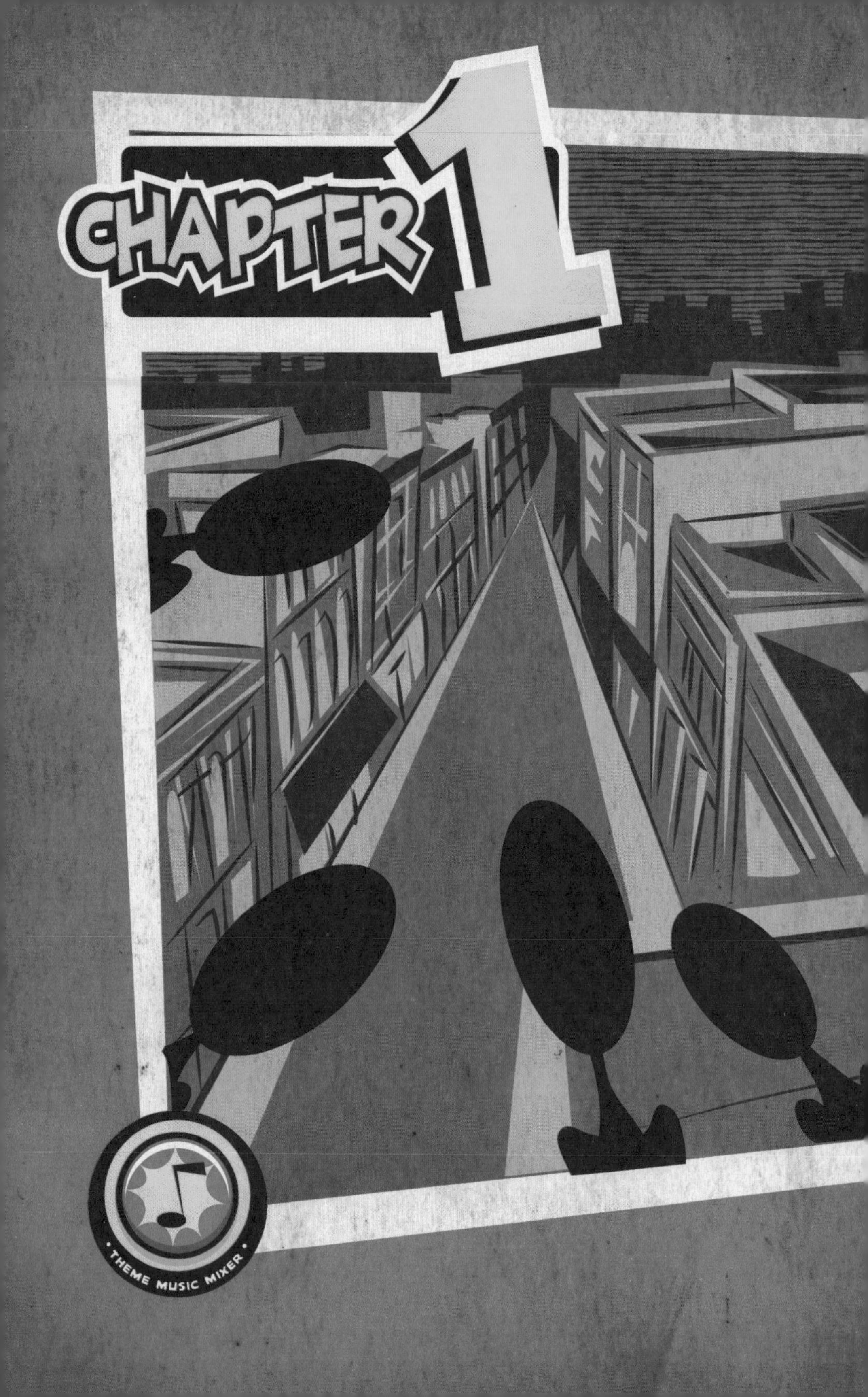
THEME MUSIC MIXER

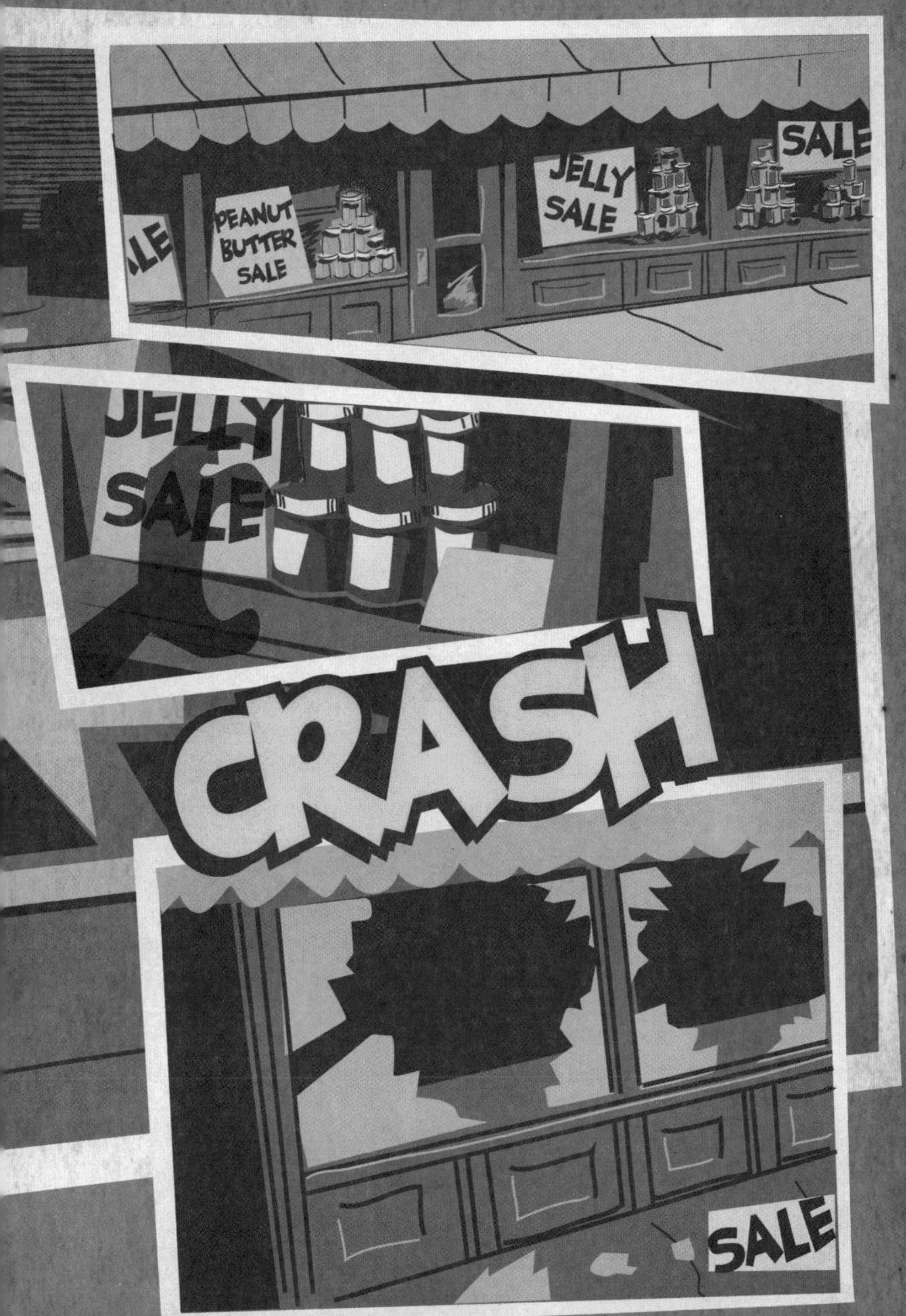
LE
PEANUT BUTTER SALE
JELLY SALE
SALE
JELLY SALE
CRASH
SALE

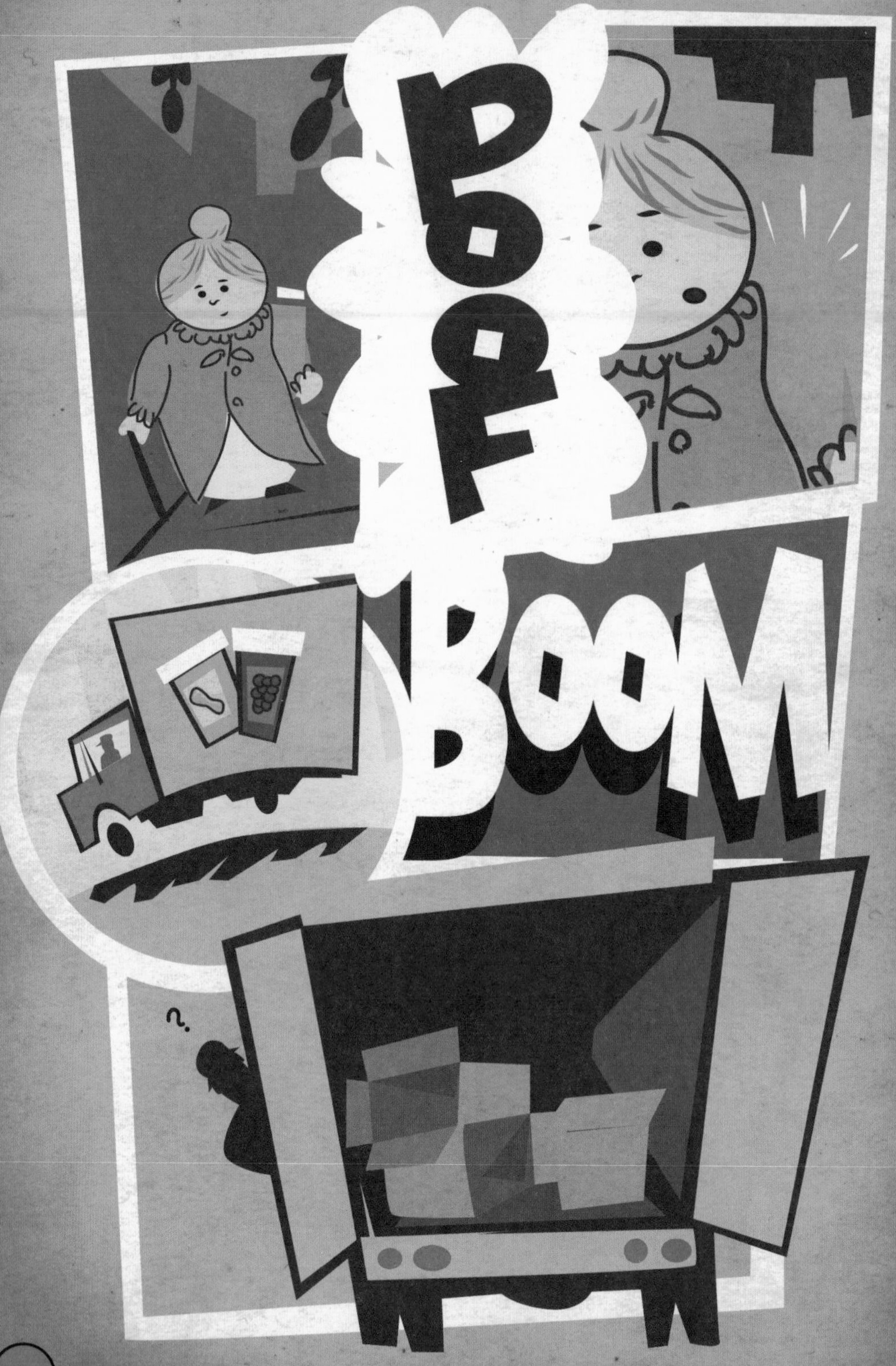
POP
BOOM
?

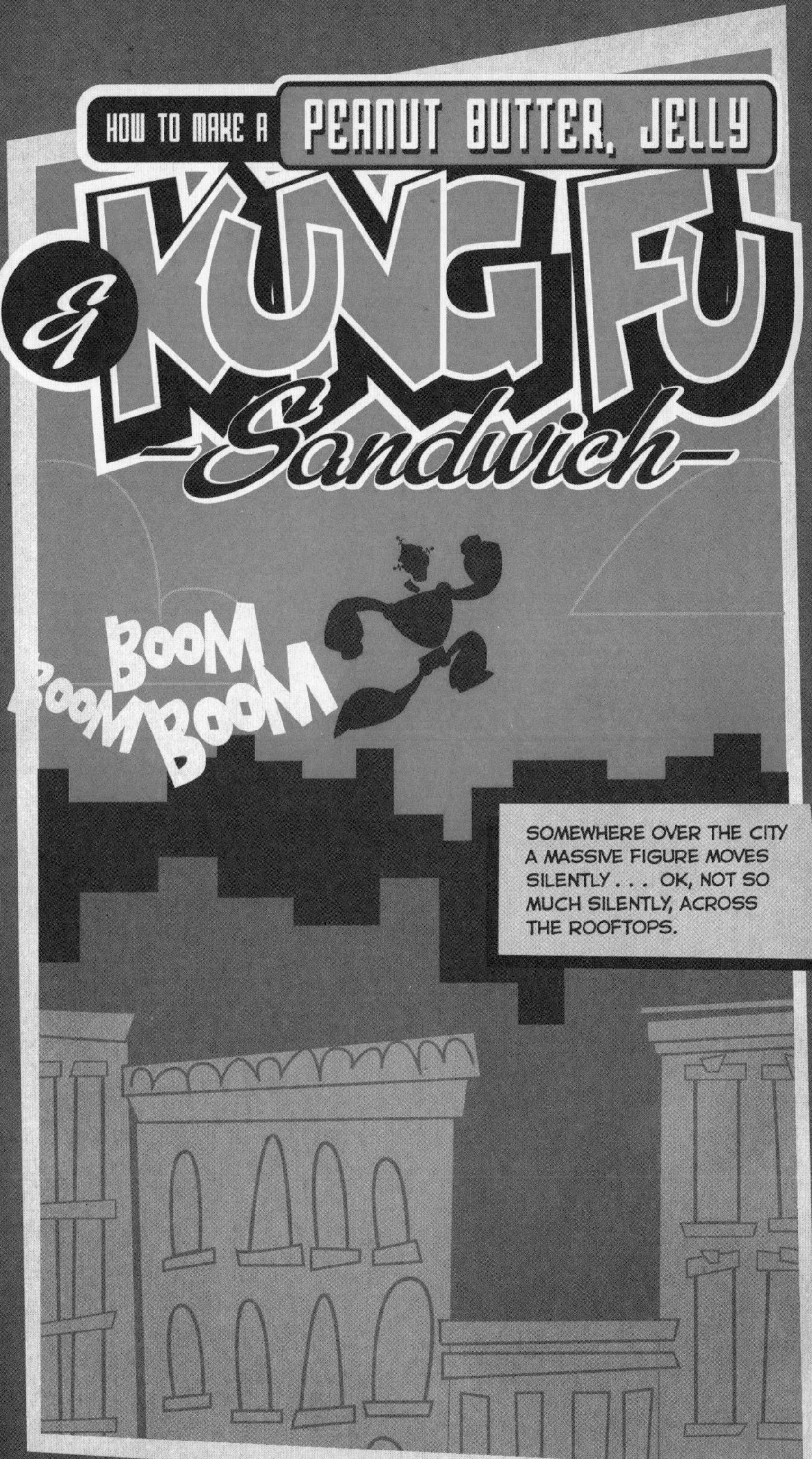
HOW TO MAKE A PEANUT BUTTER, JELLY
& KUNG FU
-Sandwich-
BOOM
BOOM BOOM BOOM
SOMEWHERE OVER THE CITY A MASSIVE FIGURE MOVES SILENTLY . . . OK, NOT SO MUCH SILENTLY, ACROSS THE ROOFTOPS.

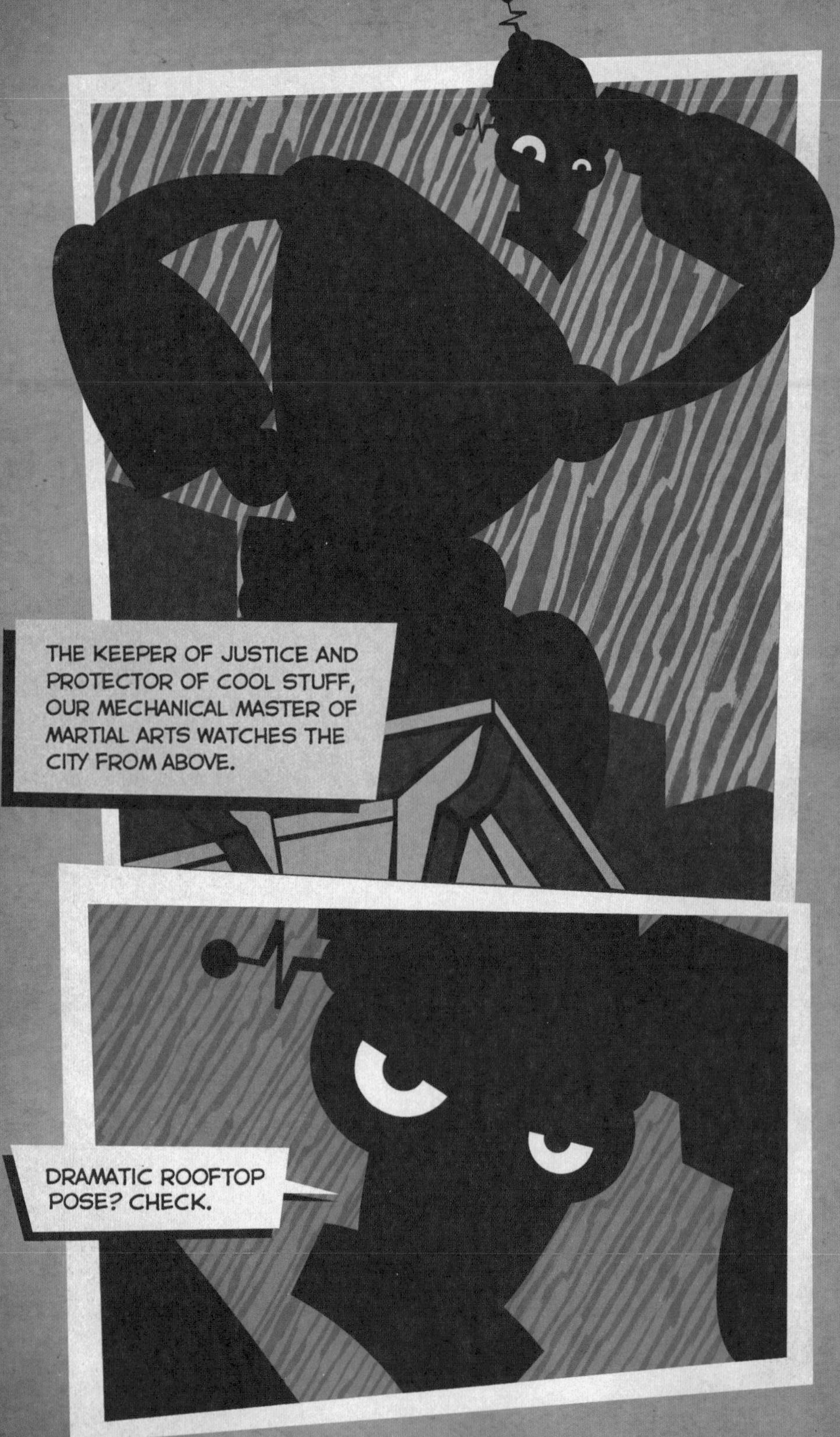
THE KEEPER OF JUSTICE AND PROTECTOR OF COOL STUFF, OUR MECHANICAL MASTER OF MARTIAL ARTS WATCHES THE CITY FROM ABOVE.
DRAMATIC ROOFTOP POSE? CHECK.

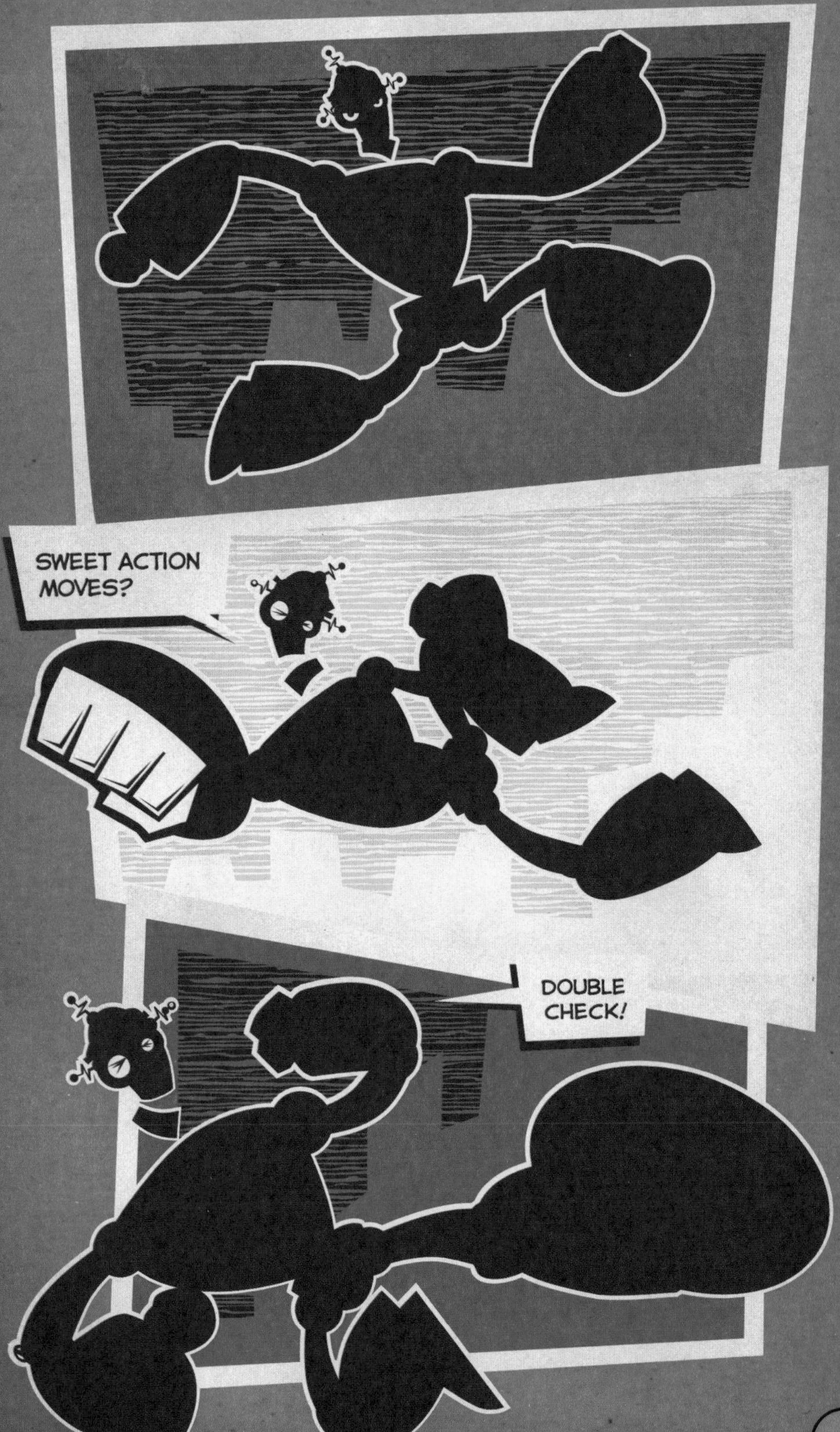
SWEET ACTION MOVES?
DOUBLE CHECK!

INTRODUCING KUNG FU ROBOT!

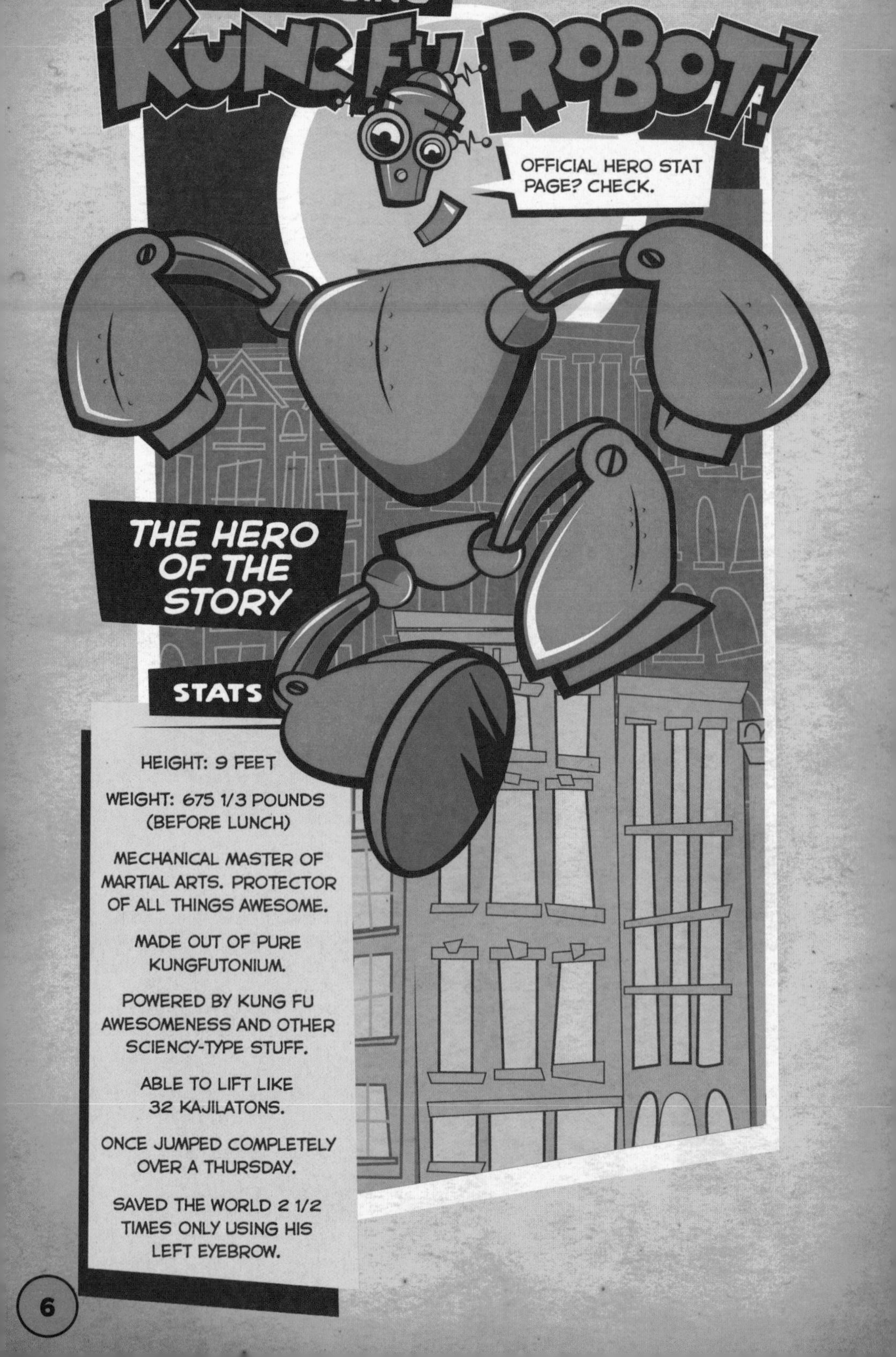
OFFICIAL HERO STAT PAGE? CHECK.

THE HERO OF THE STORY

STATS

HEIGHT: 9 FEET

WEIGHT: 675 1/3 POUNDS (BEFORE LUNCH)

MECHANICAL MASTER OF MARTIAL ARTS. PROTECTOR OF ALL THINGS AWESOME.

MADE OUT OF PURE KUNGFUTONIUM.

POWERED BY KUNG FU AWESOMENESS AND OTHER SCIENCY-TYPE STUFF.

ABLE TO LIFT LIKE 32 KAJILATONS.

ONCE JUMPED COMPLETELY OVER A THURSDAY.

SAVED THE WORLD 2 1/2 TIMES ONLY USING HIS LEFT EYEBROW.

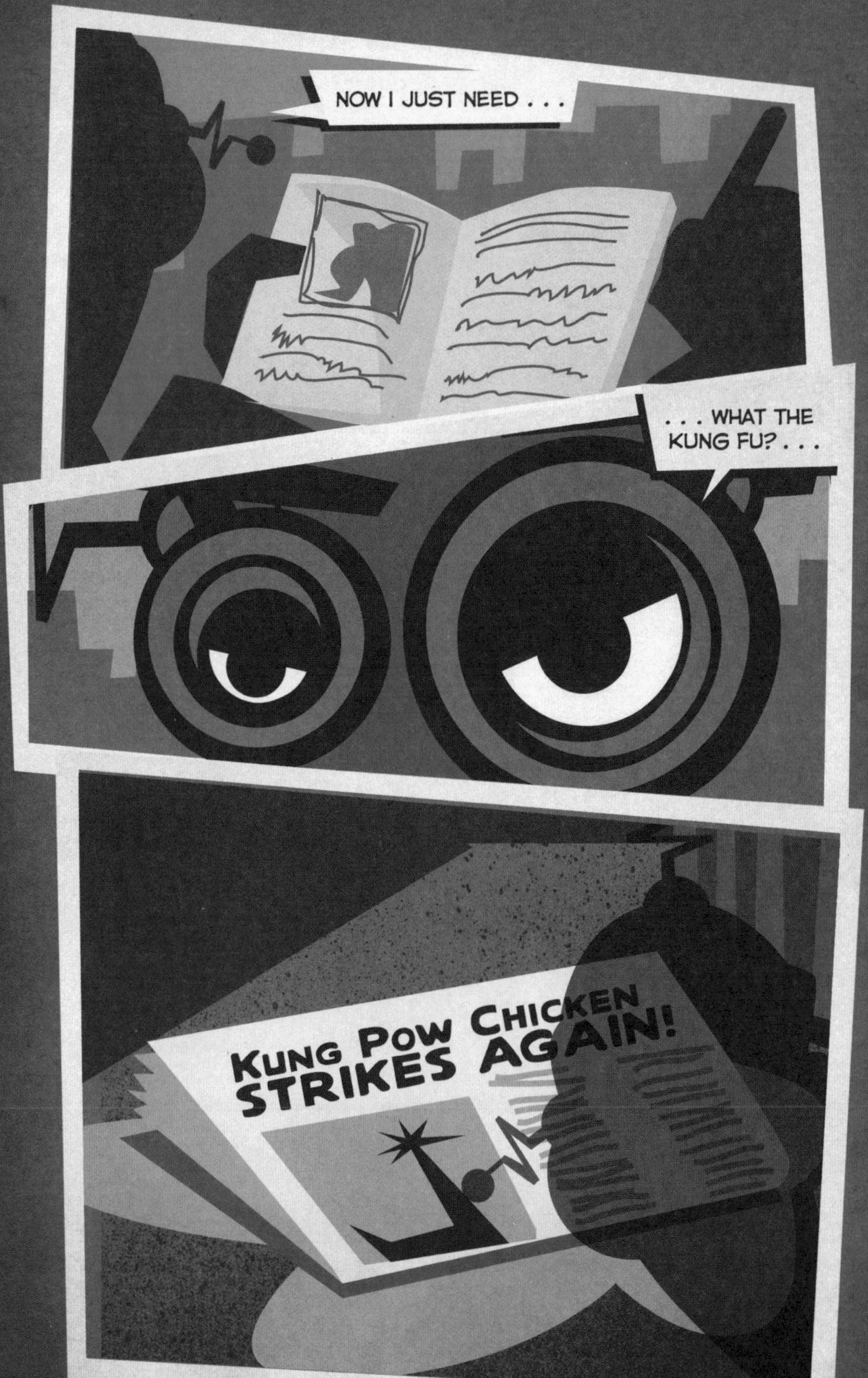
NOW I JUST NEED . . .
. . . WHAT THE KUNG FU? . . .
KUNG POW CHICKEN STRIKES AGAIN!

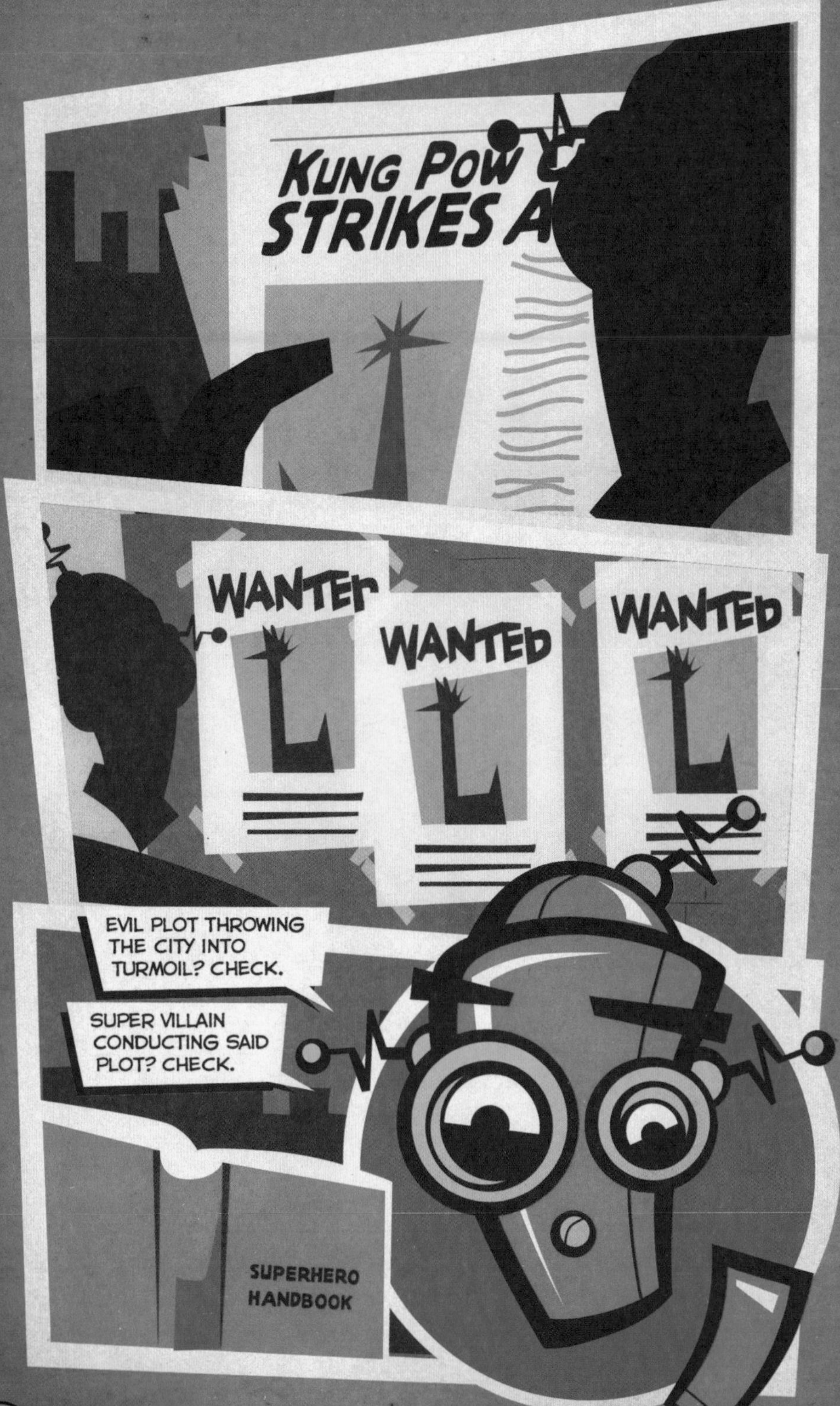
KUNG POW
STRIKES A
WANTED
WANTED
WANTED
EVIL PLOT THROWING THE CITY INTO TURMOIL? CHECK.
SUPER VILLAIN CONDUCTING SAID PLOT? CHECK.
SUPERHERO HANDBOOK

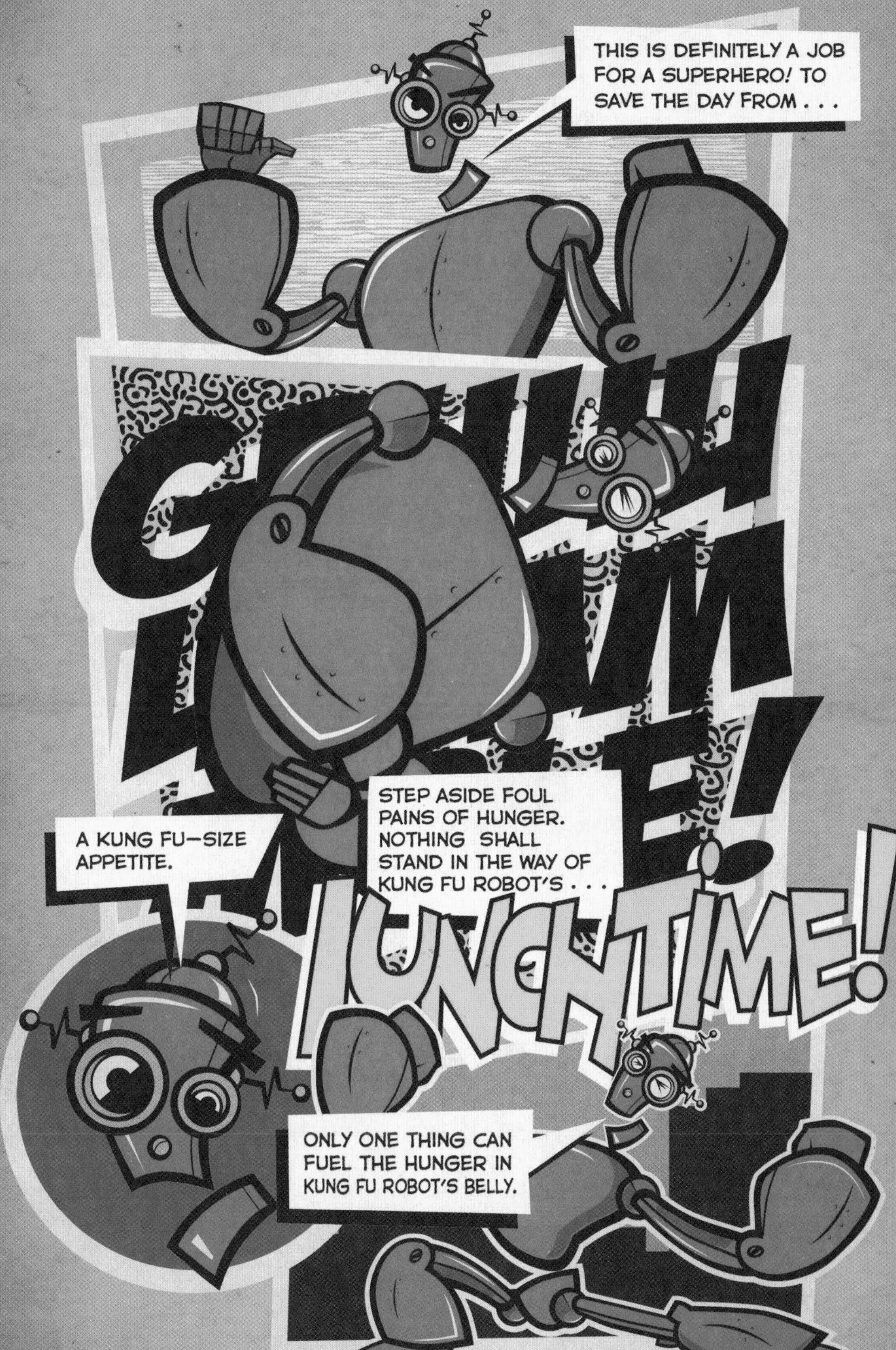
THIS IS DEFINITELY A JOB FOR A SUPERHERO! TO SAVE THE DAY FROM . . .
A KUNG FU—SIZE APPETITE.
ONLY ONE THING CAN FUEL THE HUNGER IN KUNG FU ROBOT'S BELLY.
STEP ASIDE FOUL PAINS OF HUNGER. NOTHING SHALL STAND IN THE WAY OF KUNG FU ROBOT'S . . .
LUNCHTIME!

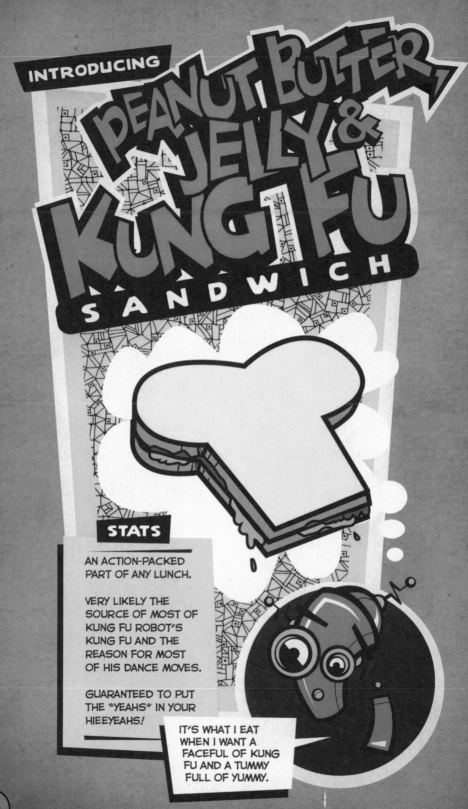

INTRODUCING

PEANUT BUTTER, JELLY & KUNG FU SANDWICH

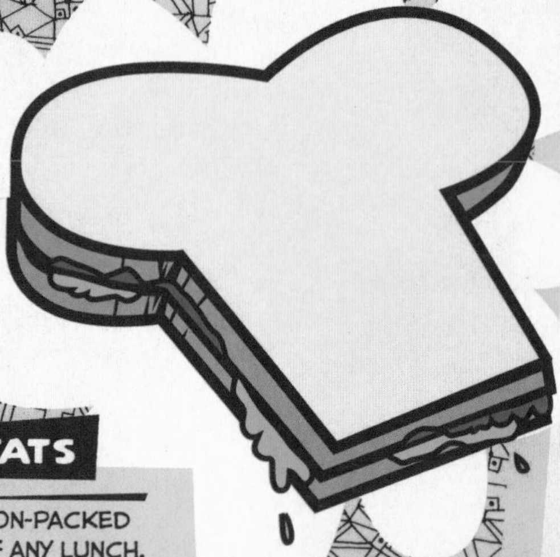

STATS

AN ACTION-PACKED PART OF ANY LUNCH.

VERY LIKELY THE SOURCE OF MOST OF KUNG FU ROBOT'S KUNG FU AND THE REASON FOR MOST OF HIS DANCE MOVES.

GUARANTEED TO PUT THE "YEAHS" IN YOUR HIEEYEAHS!

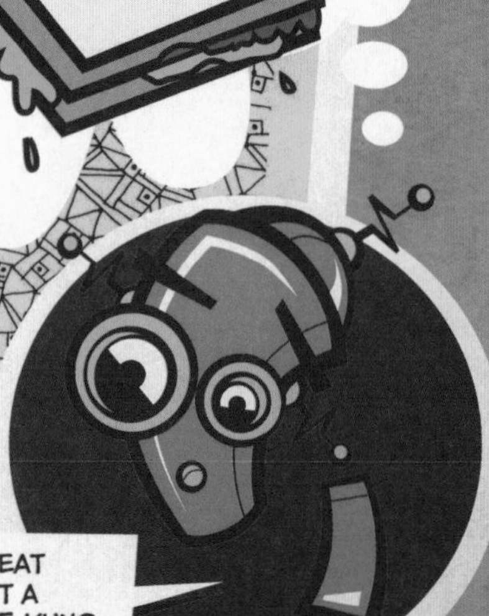
IT'S WHAT I EAT WHEN I WANT A FACEFUL OF KUNG FU AND A TUMMY FULL OF YUMMY.

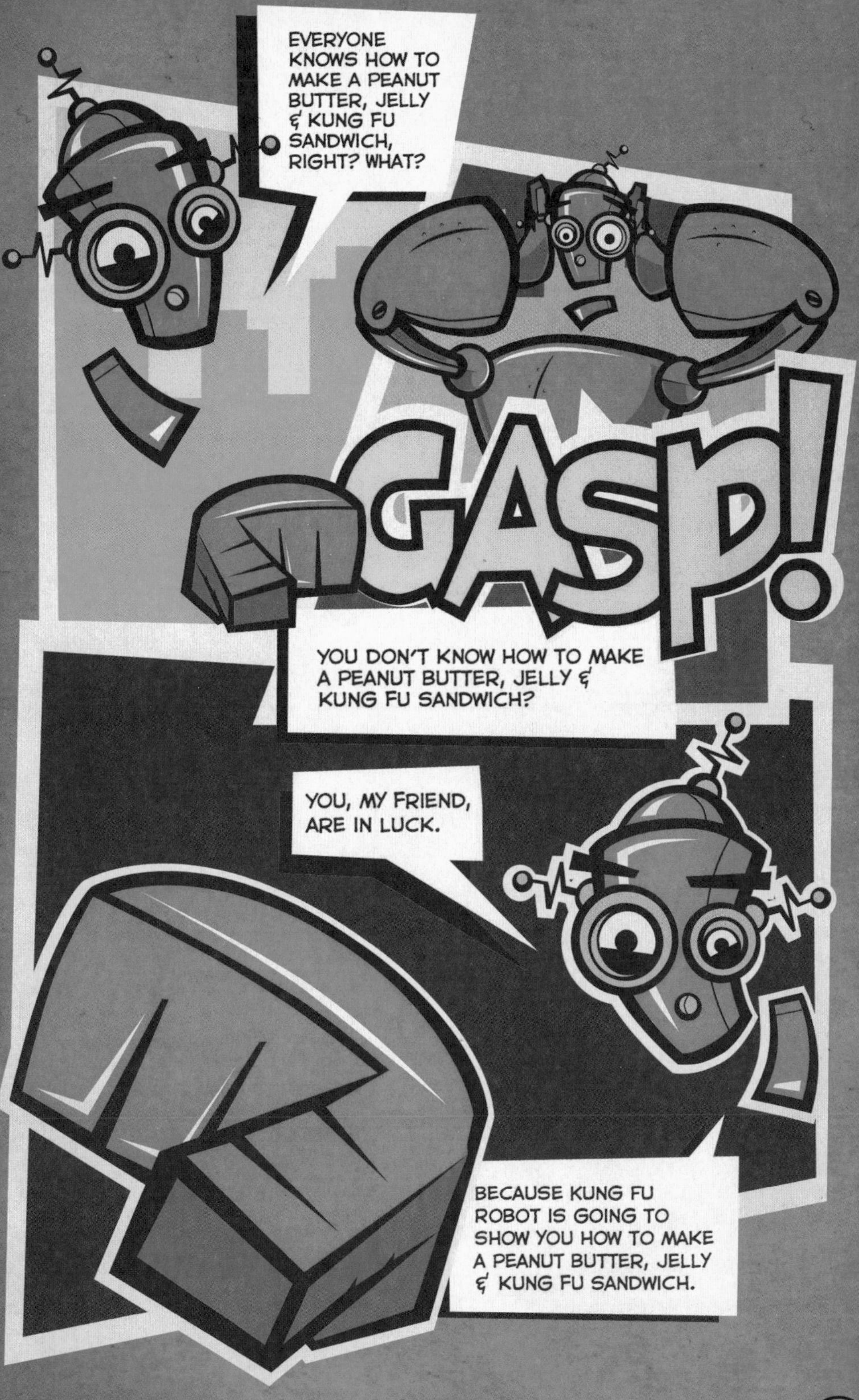
EVERYONE KNOWS HOW TO MAKE A PEANUT BUTTER, JELLY & KUNG FU SANDWICH, RIGHT? WHAT?
GASP!
YOU DON'T KNOW HOW TO MAKE A PEANUT BUTTER, JELLY & KUNG FU SANDWICH?
YOU, MY FRIEND, ARE IN LUCK.
BECAUSE KUNG FU ROBOT IS GOING TO SHOW YOU HOW TO MAKE A PEANUT BUTTER, JELLY & KUNG FU SANDWICH.

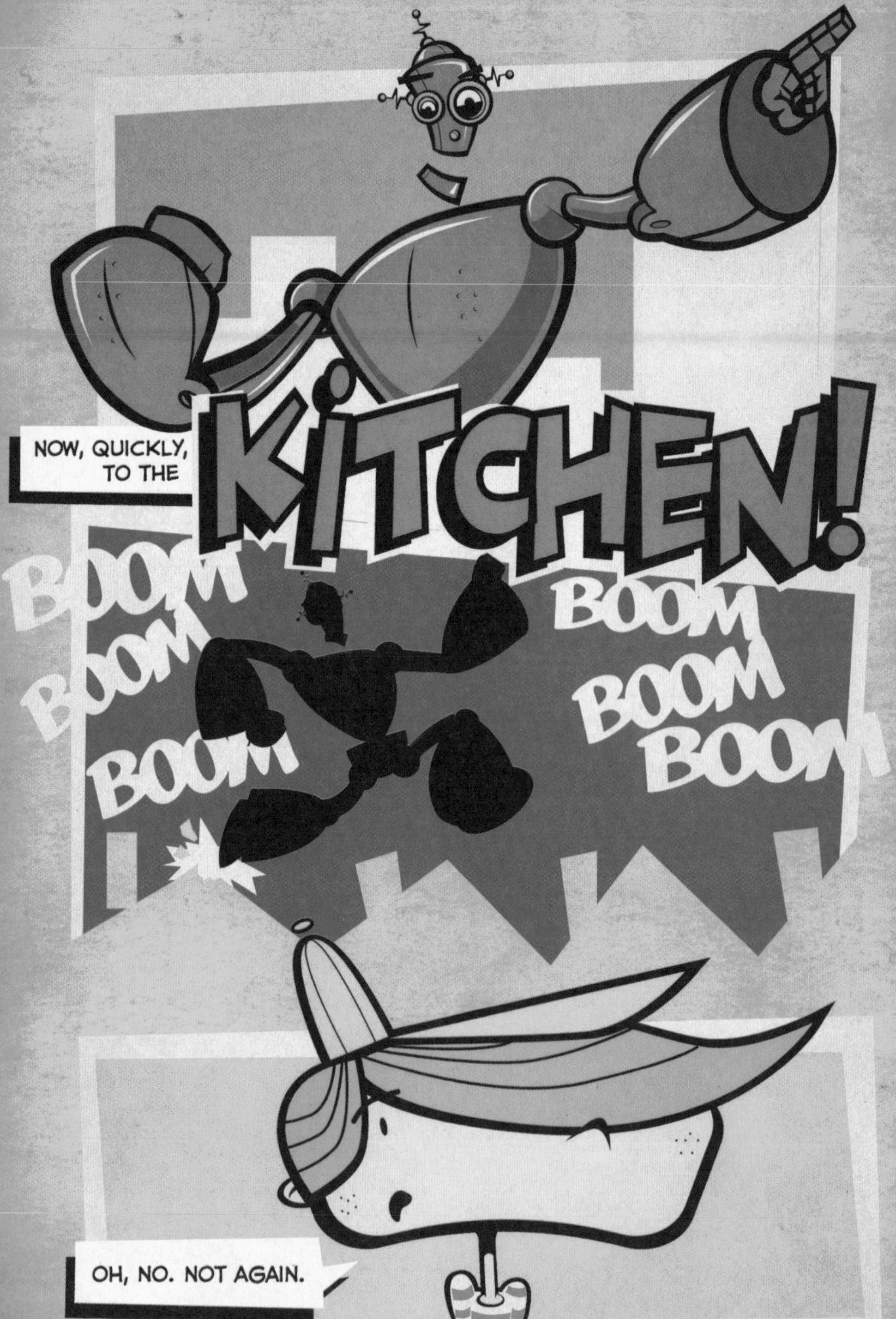
NOW, QUICKLY, TO THE KITCHEN!
BOOM BOOM BOOM BOOM BOOM BOOM
OH, NO. NOT AGAIN.

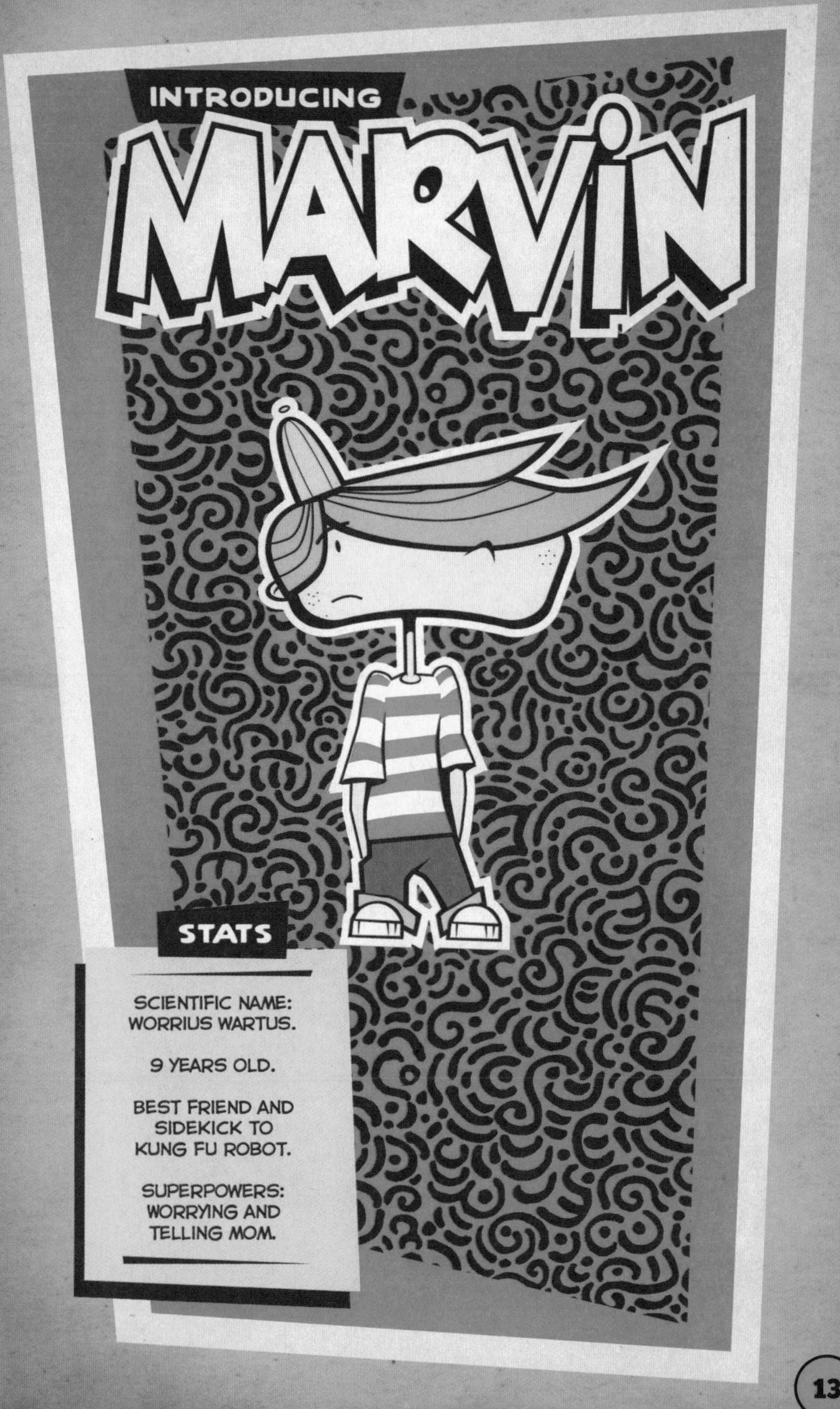
INTRODUCING
MARVIN
STATS
SCIENTIFIC NAME: WORRIUS WARTUS.
9 YEARS OLD.
BEST FRIEND AND SIDEKICK TO KUNG FU ROBOT.
SUPERPOWERS: WORRYING AND TELLING MOM.

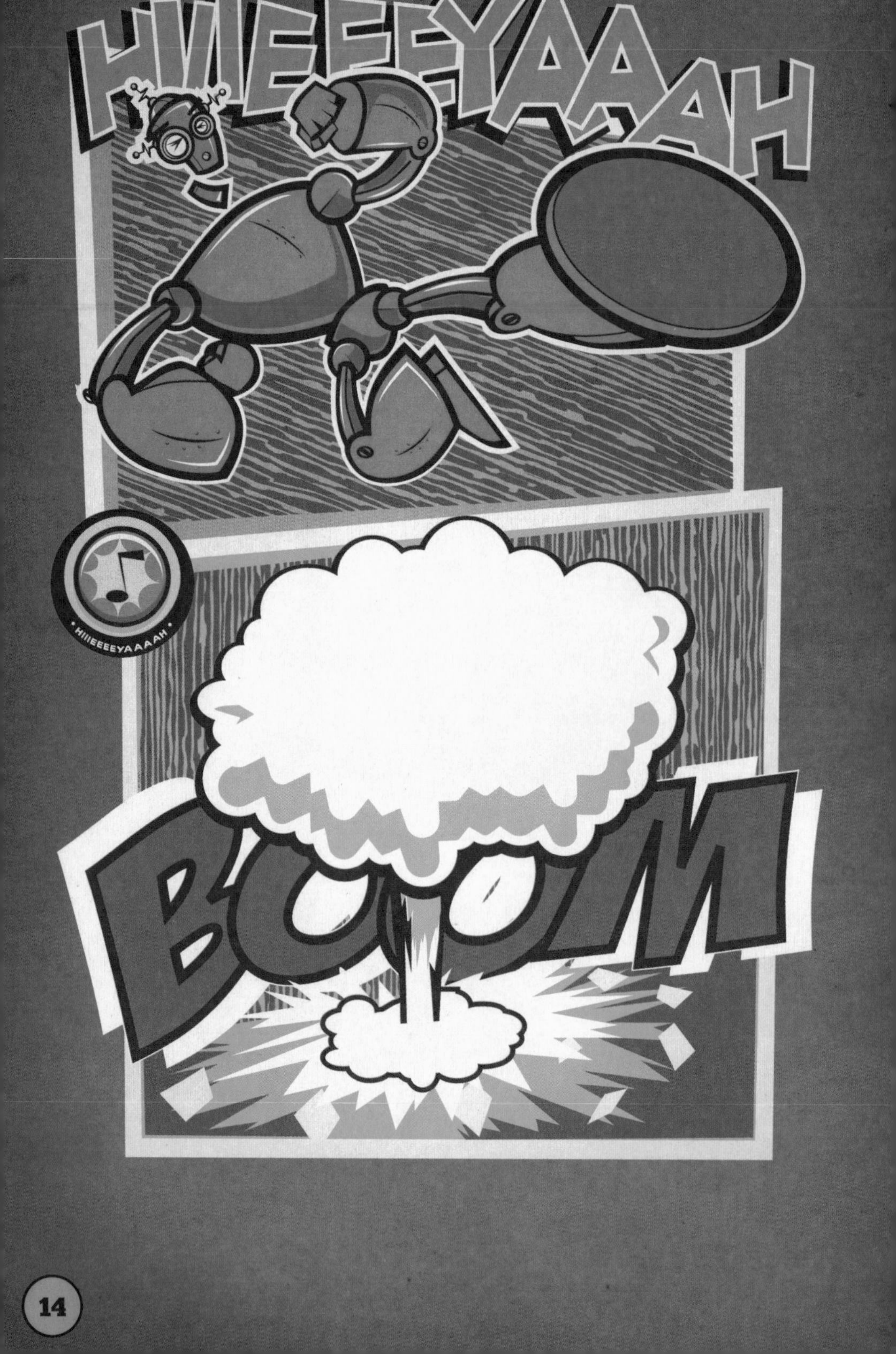
HIIIEEEEYAAAAH
HIIIEEEEYAAAAH
BOOM

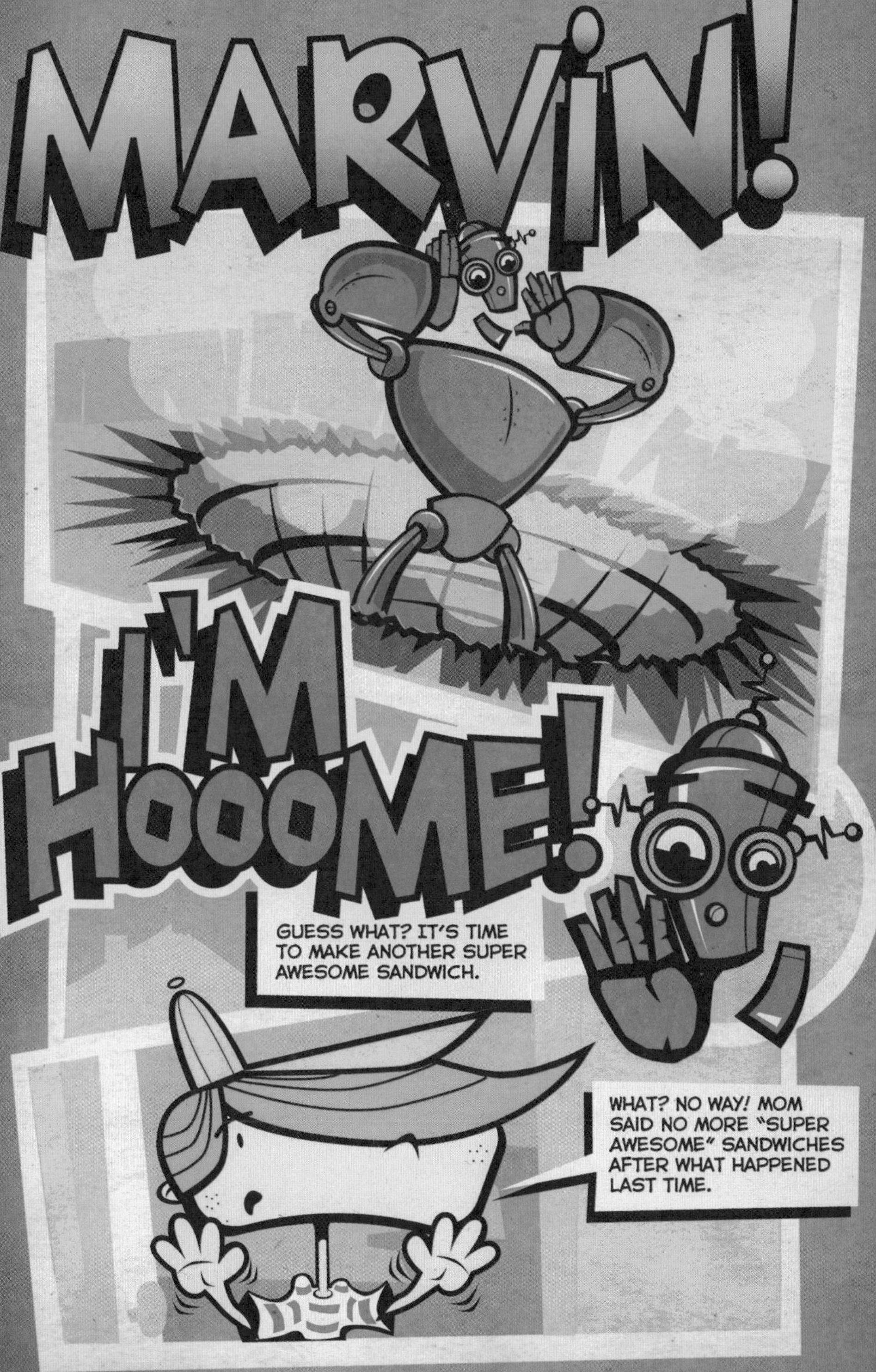
MARVIN!
I'M HOOOME!
GUESS WHAT? IT'S TIME TO MAKE ANOTHER SUPER AWESOME SANDWICH.
WHAT? NO WAY! MOM SAID NO MORE "SUPER AWESOME" SANDWICHES AFTER WHAT HAPPENED LAST TIME.

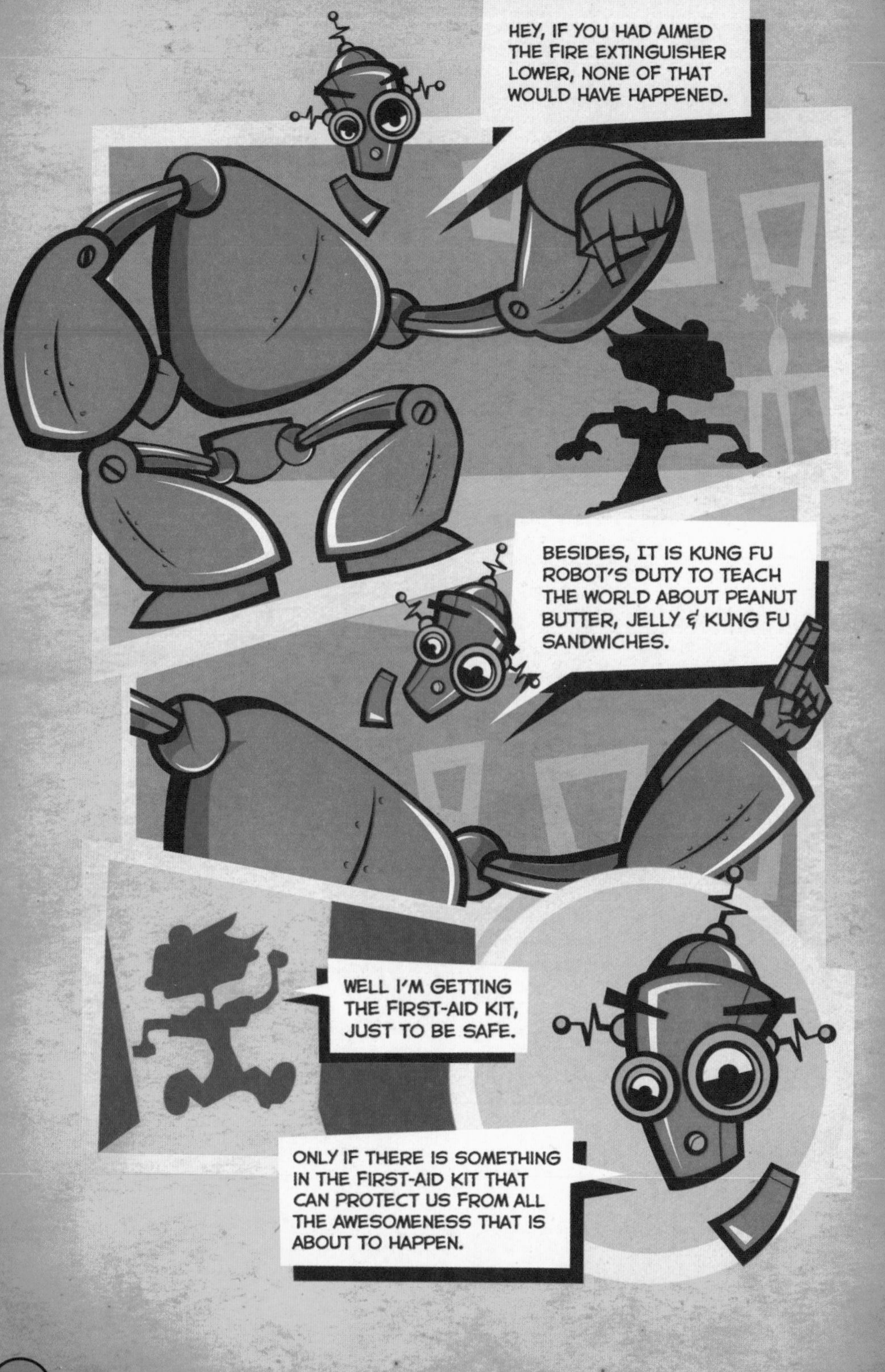
HEY, IF YOU HAD AIMED THE FIRE EXTINGUISHER LOWER, NONE OF THAT WOULD HAVE HAPPENED.
BESIDES, IT IS KUNG FU ROBOT'S DUTY TO TEACH THE WORLD ABOUT PEANUT BUTTER, JELLY & KUNG FU SANDWICHES.
WELL I'M GETTING THE FIRST-AID KIT, JUST TO BE SAFE.
ONLY IF THERE IS SOMETHING IN THE FIRST-AID KIT THAT CAN PROTECT US FROM ALL THE AWESOMENESS THAT IS ABOUT TO HAPPEN.

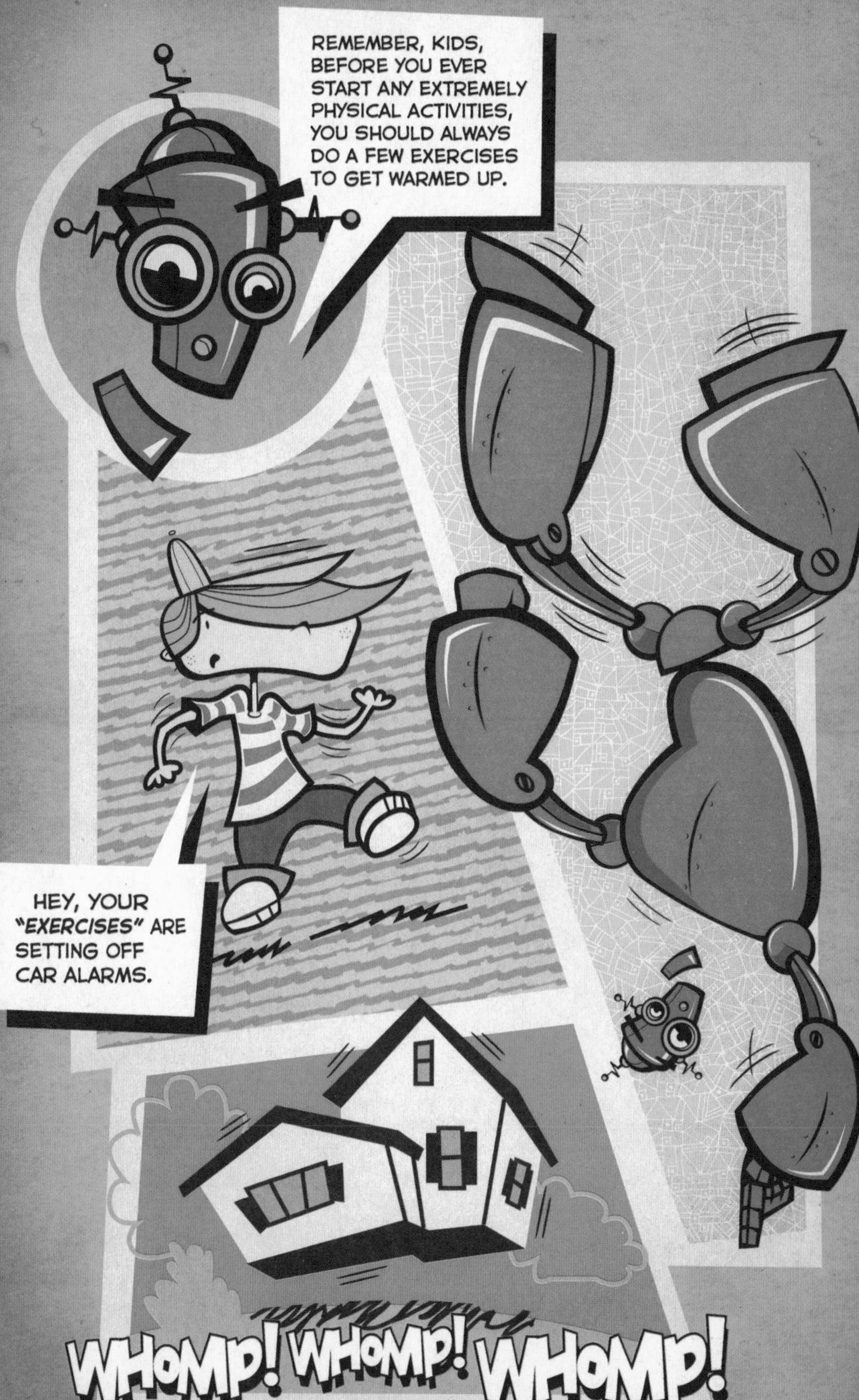
REMEMBER, KIDS, BEFORE YOU EVER START ANY EXTREMELY PHYSICAL ACTIVITIES, YOU SHOULD ALWAYS DO A FEW EXERCISES TO GET WARMED UP.
HEY, YOUR "EXERCISES" ARE SETTING OFF CAR ALARMS.
WHOMP! WHOMP! WHOMP!

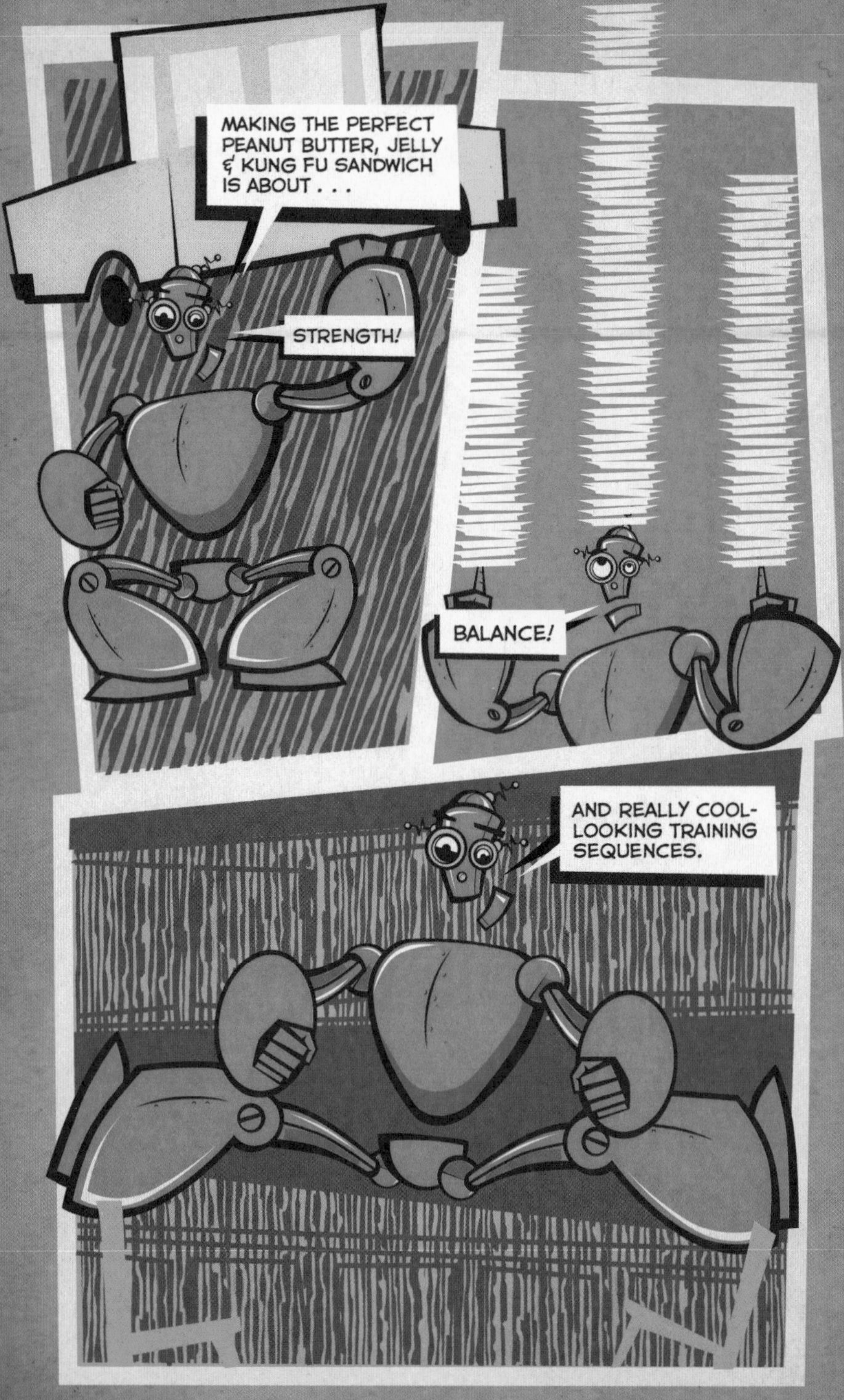
MAKING THE PERFECT PEANUT BUTTER, JELLY & KUNG FU SANDWICH IS ABOUT . . .
STRENGTH!
BALANCE!
AND REALLY COOL-LOOKING TRAINING SEQUENCES.

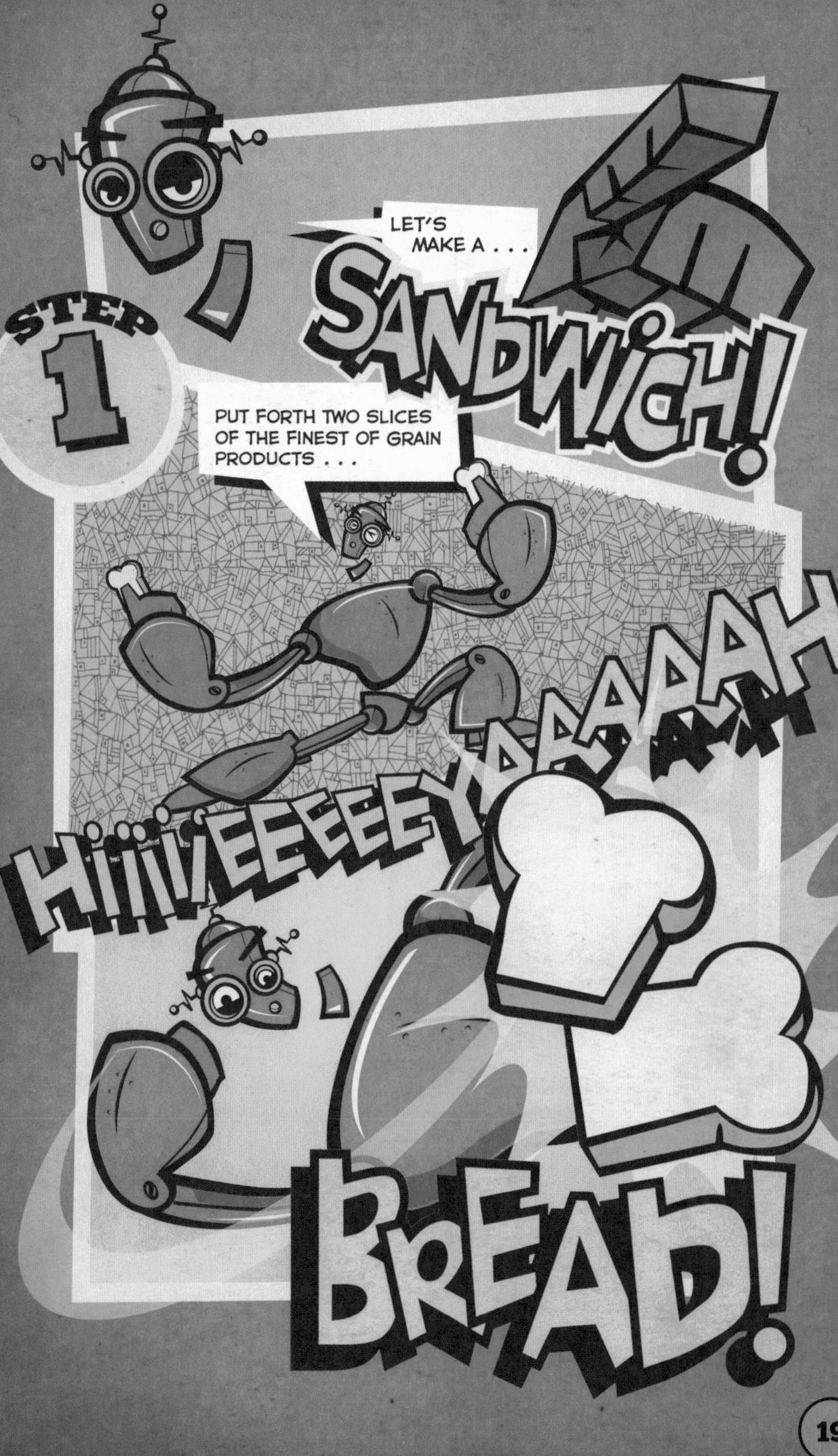
LET'S MAKE A . . .
SANDWICH!
STEP 1
PUT FORTH TWO SLICES OF THE FINEST OF GRAIN PRODUCTS . . .
HiiiiiEEEEEEYAAAAAAH . . .
BREAD!

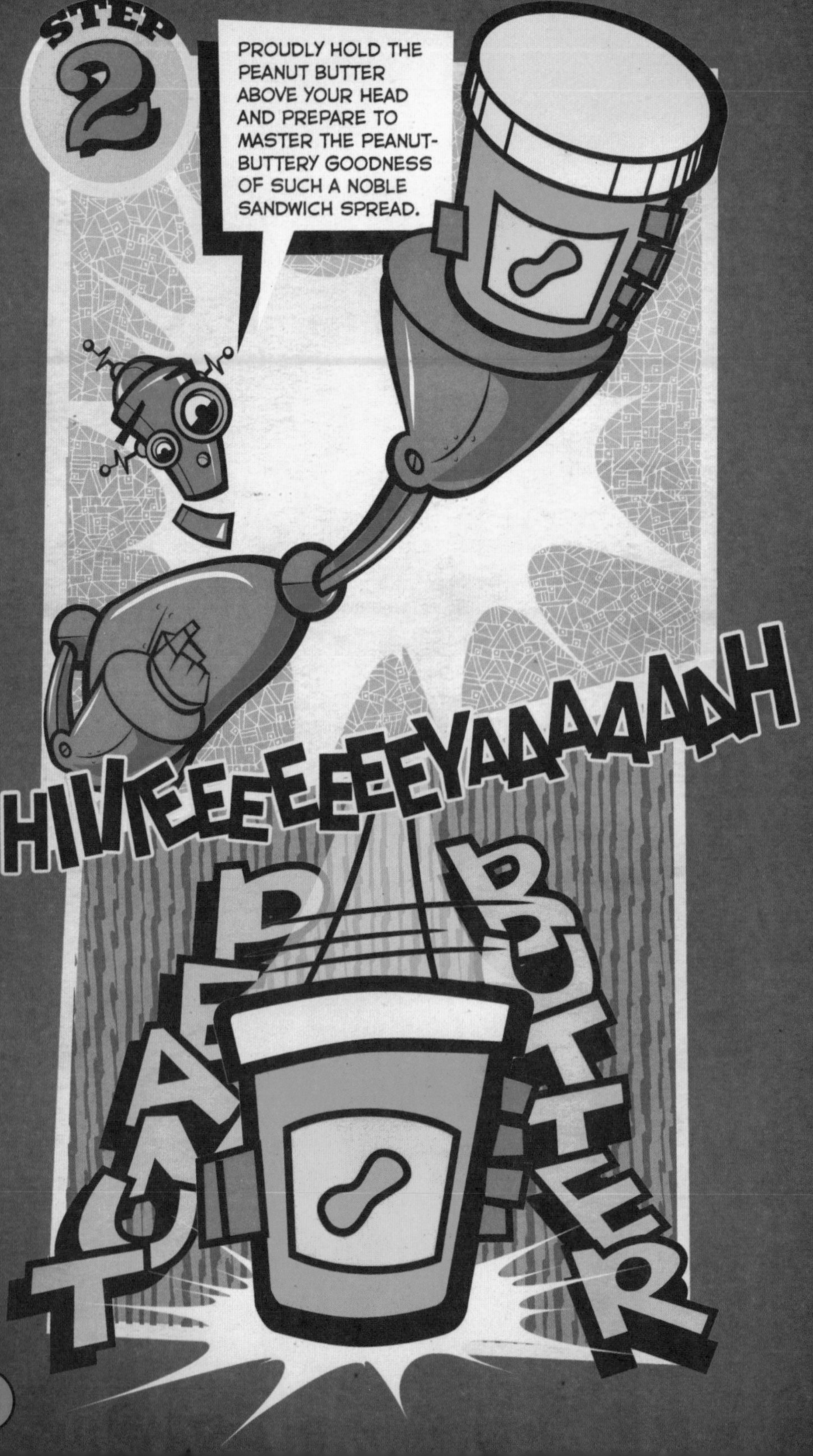
STEP 2
PROUDLY HOLD THE PEANUT BUTTER ABOVE YOUR HEAD AND PREPARE TO MASTER THE PEANUT-BUTTERY GOODNESS OF SUCH A NOBLE SANDWICH SPREAD.
HIIEEEEEEYAAAAAAH
PEANUT BUTTER

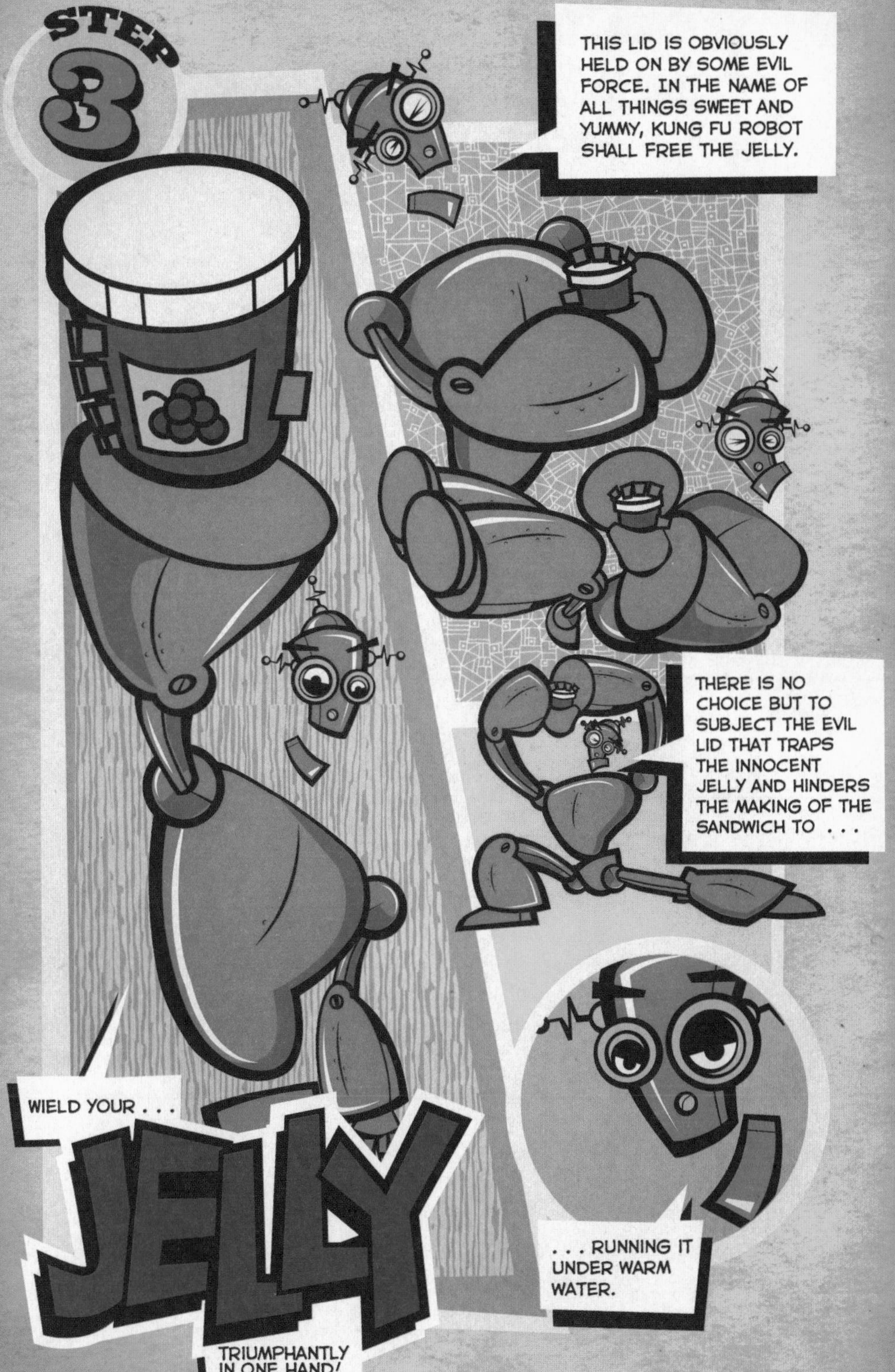
STEP 3
THIS LID IS OBVIOUSLY HELD ON BY SOME EVIL FORCE. IN THE NAME OF ALL THINGS SWEET AND YUMMY, KUNG FU ROBOT SHALL FREE THE JELLY.
THERE IS NO CHOICE BUT TO SUBJECT THE EVIL LID THAT TRAPS THE INNOCENT JELLY AND HINDERS THE MAKING OF THE SANDWICH TO . . .
WIELD YOUR . . .
JELLY
TRIUMPHANTLY IN ONE HAND!
. . . RUNNING IT UNDER WARM WATER.

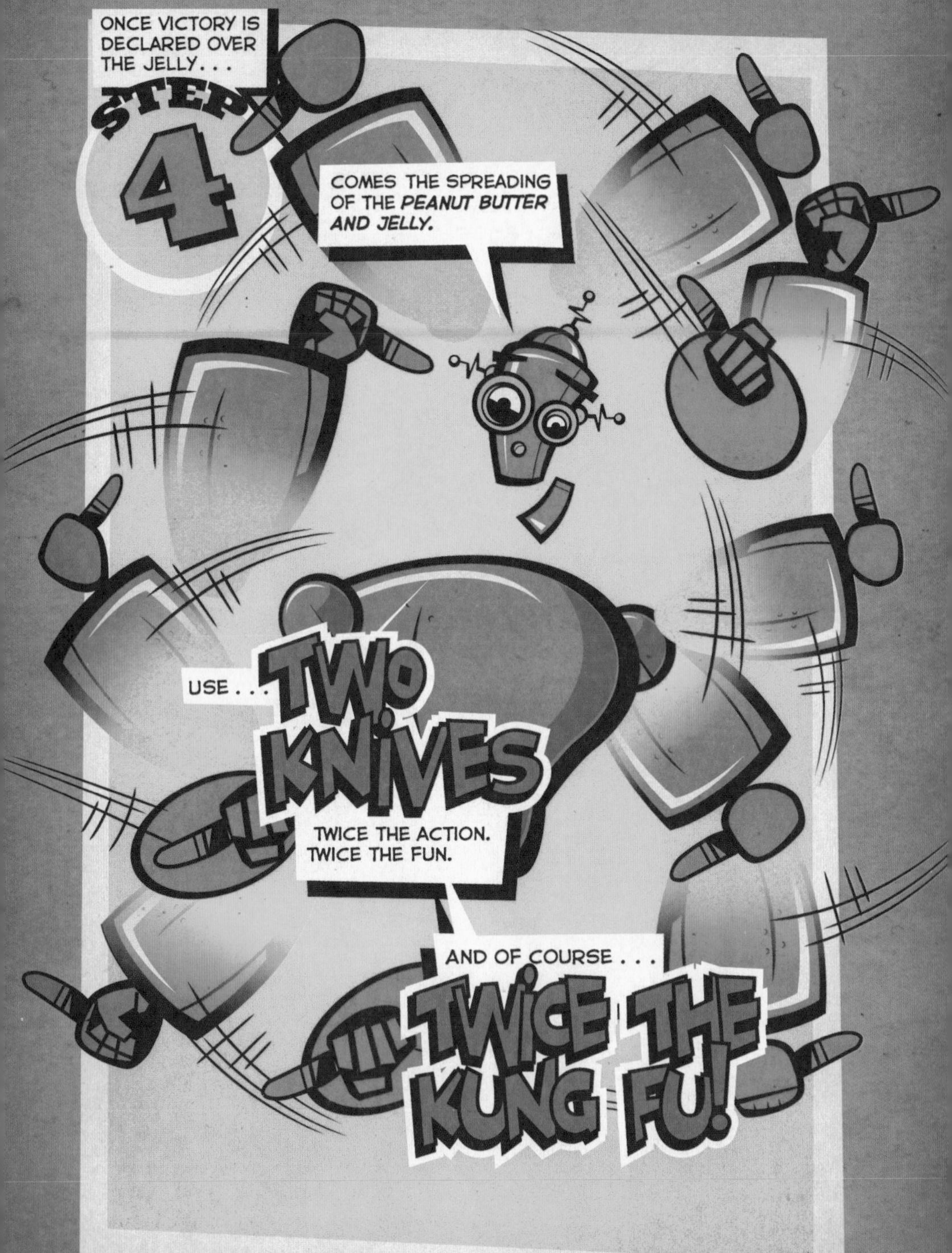
ONCE VICTORY IS DECLARED OVER THE JELLY . . .
STEP 4
COMES THE SPREADING OF THE *PEANUT BUTTER AND JELLY.*
USE . . . TWO KNIVES
TWICE THE ACTION. TWICE THE FUN.
AND OF COURSE . . .
TWICE THE KUNG FU!

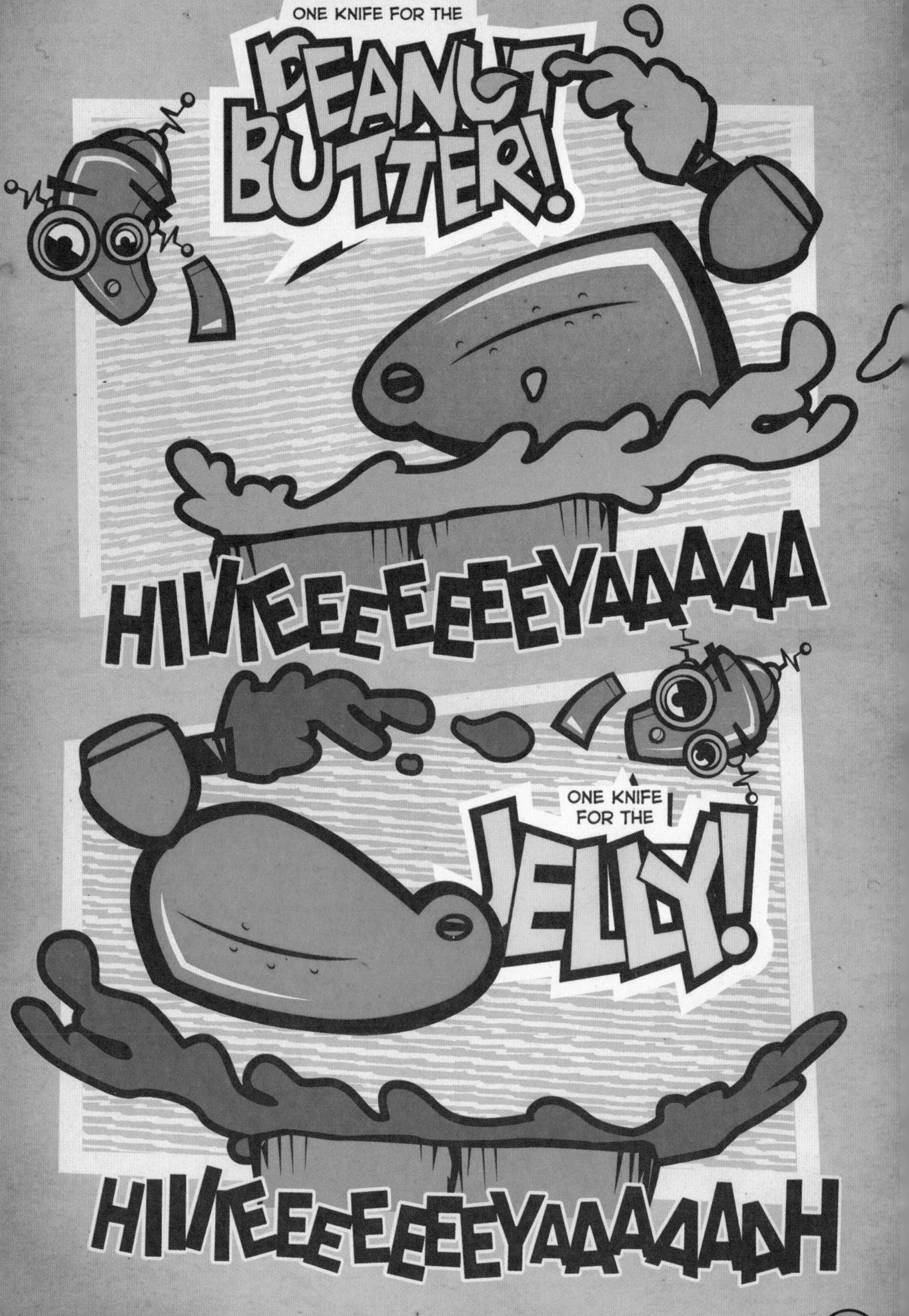
ONE KNIFE FOR THE
PEANUT BUTTER!
HIIIEEEEEEEYAAAAAA
ONE KNIFE FOR THE
JELLY!
HIIIEEEEEEEYAAAAAAH

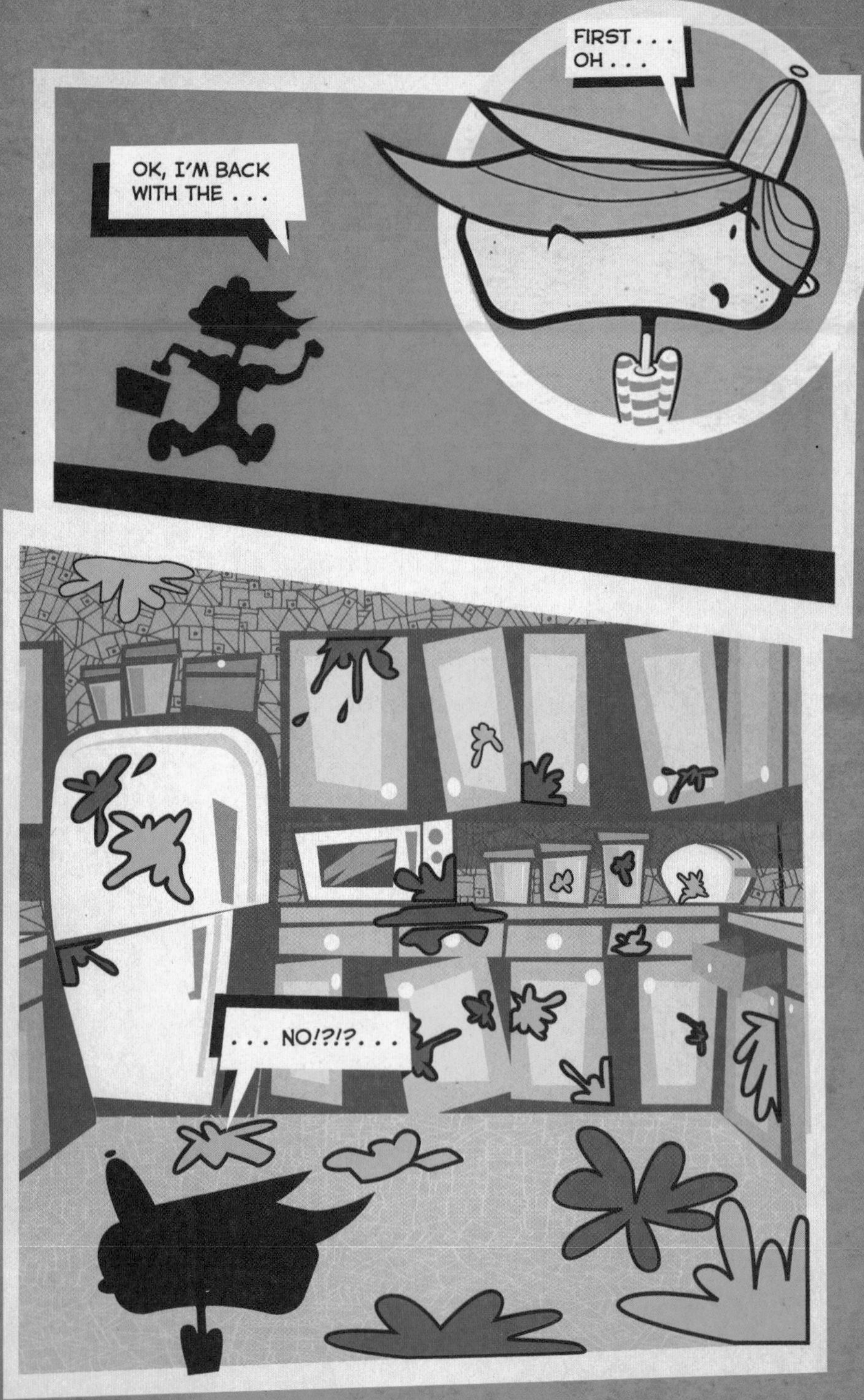
OK, I'M BACK
WITH THE . . .
FIRST . . .
OH . . .
. . . NO!?!?. . .

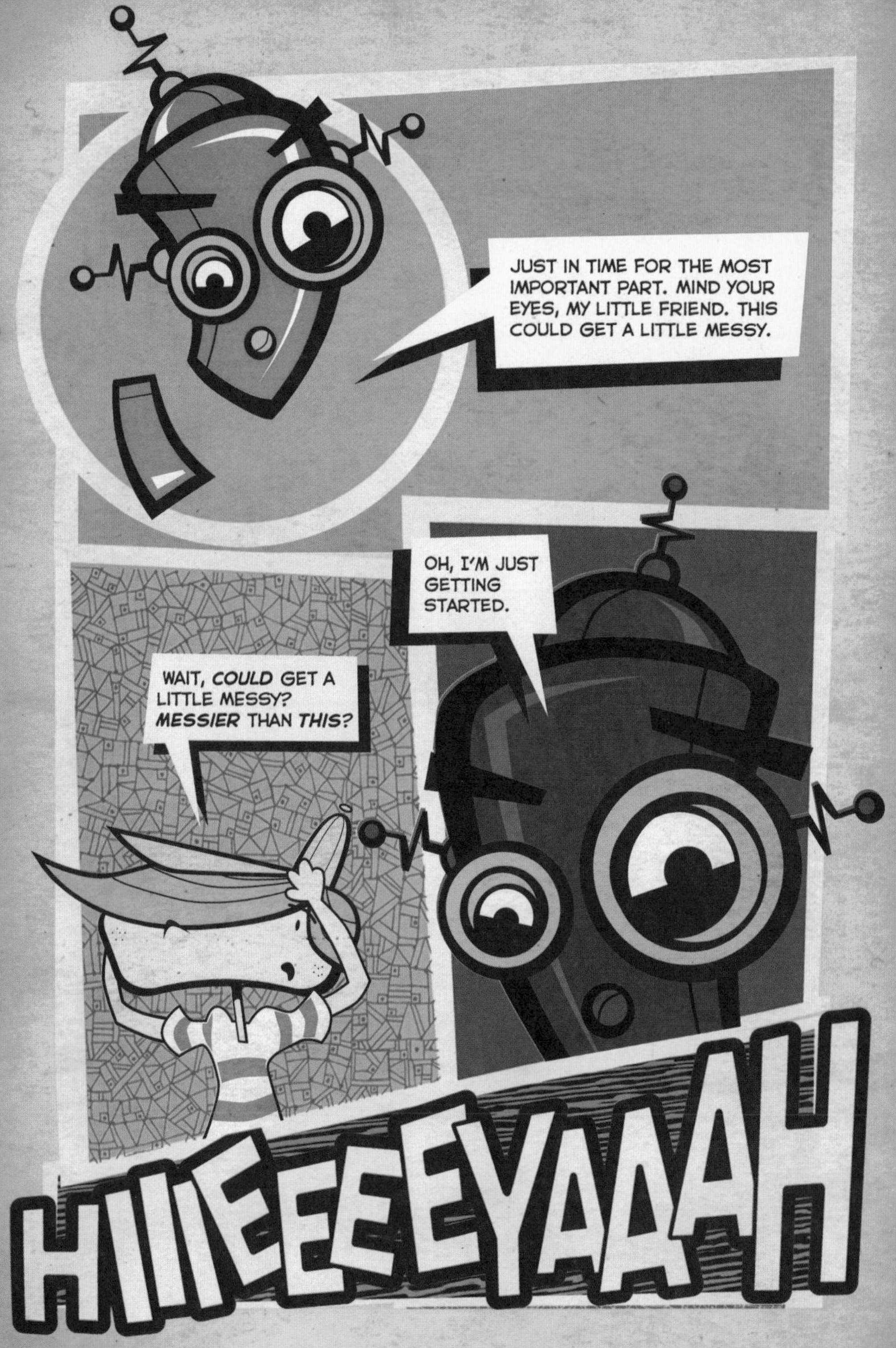
JUST IN TIME FOR THE MOST IMPORTANT PART. MIND YOUR EYES, MY LITTLE FRIEND. THIS COULD GET A LITTLE MESSY.
OH, I'M JUST GETTING STARTED.
WAIT, *COULD* GET A LITTLE MESSY? ***MESSIER*** THAN ***THIS***?
HIIIEEEEYAAAH

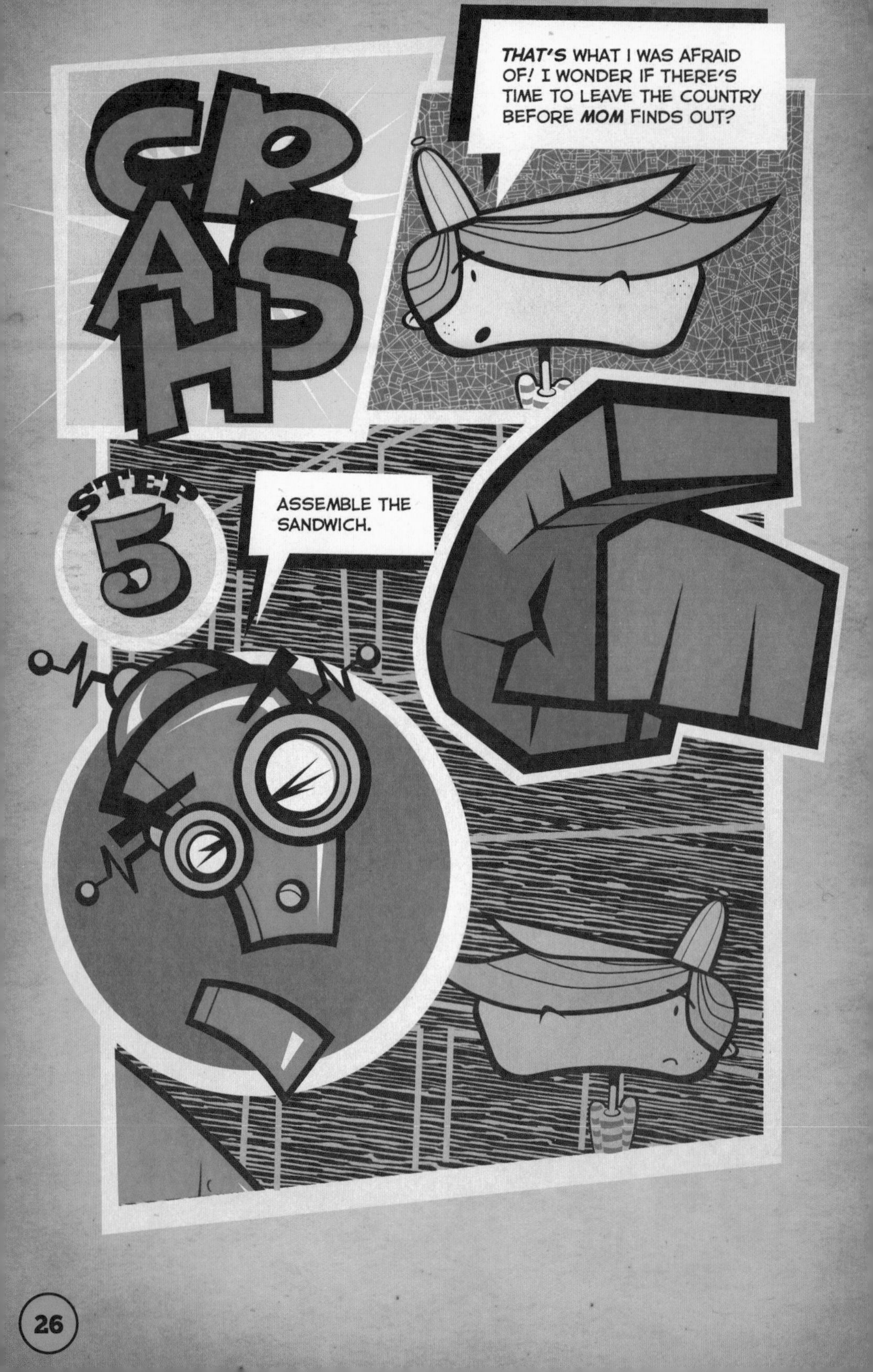
CRASH
THAT'S WHAT I WAS AFRAID OF! I WONDER IF THERE'S TIME TO LEAVE THE COUNTRY BEFORE MOM FINDS OUT?
STEP 5
ASSEMBLE THE SANDWICH.

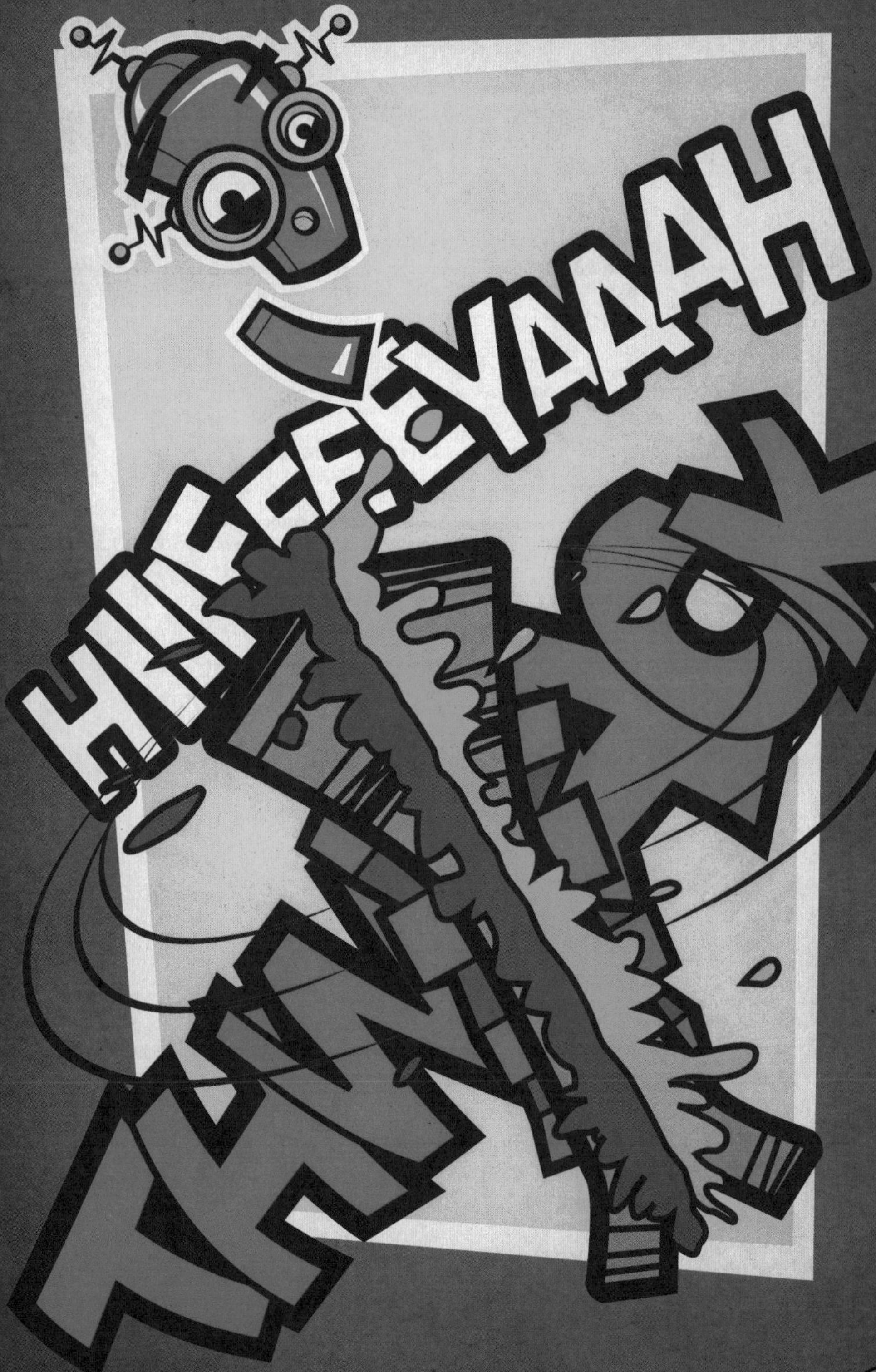
HIIEEEYAAAH

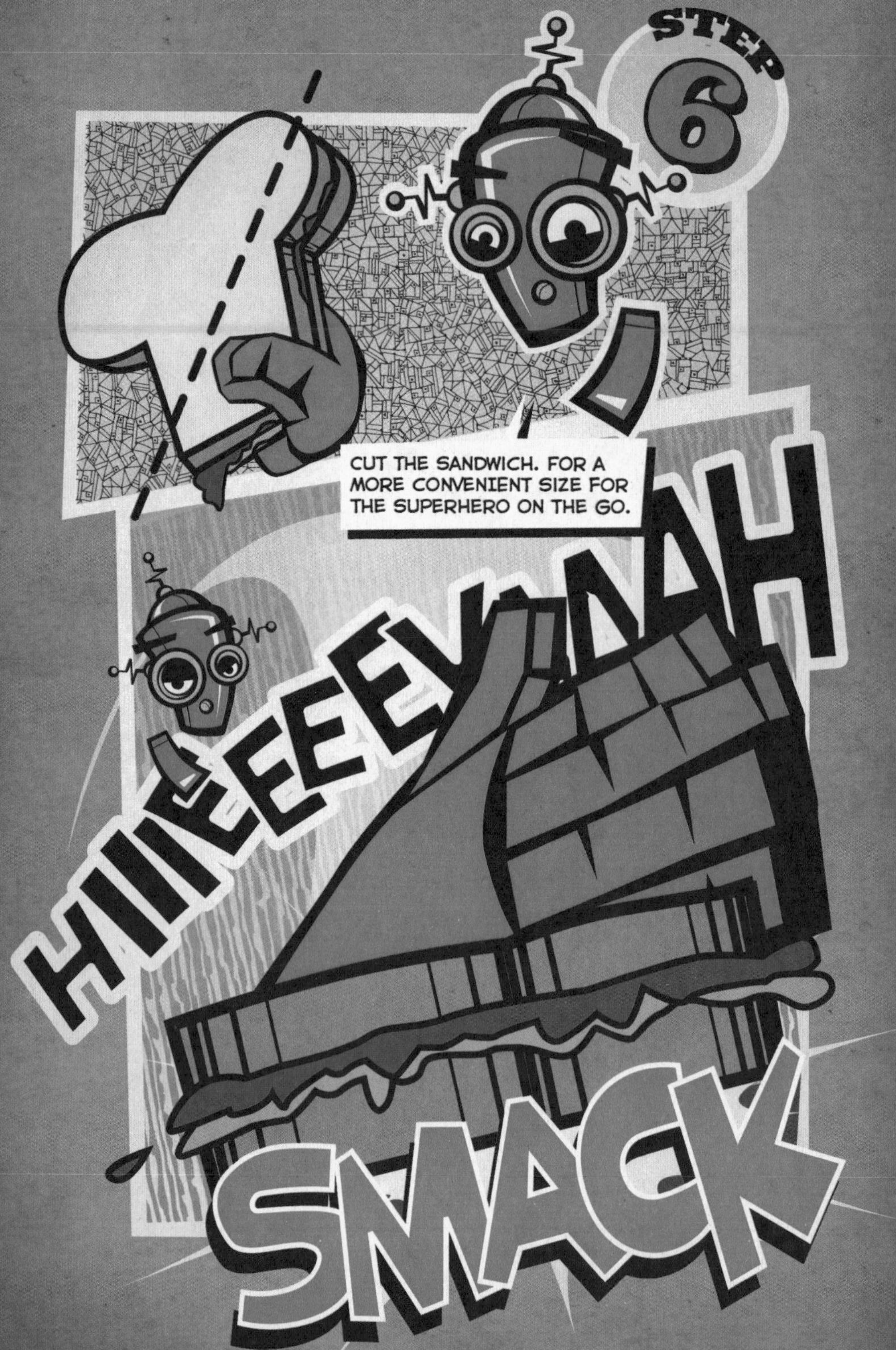
STEP 6
CUT THE SANDWICH. FOR A MORE CONVENIENT SIZE FOR THE SUPERHERO ON THE GO.
SMACK

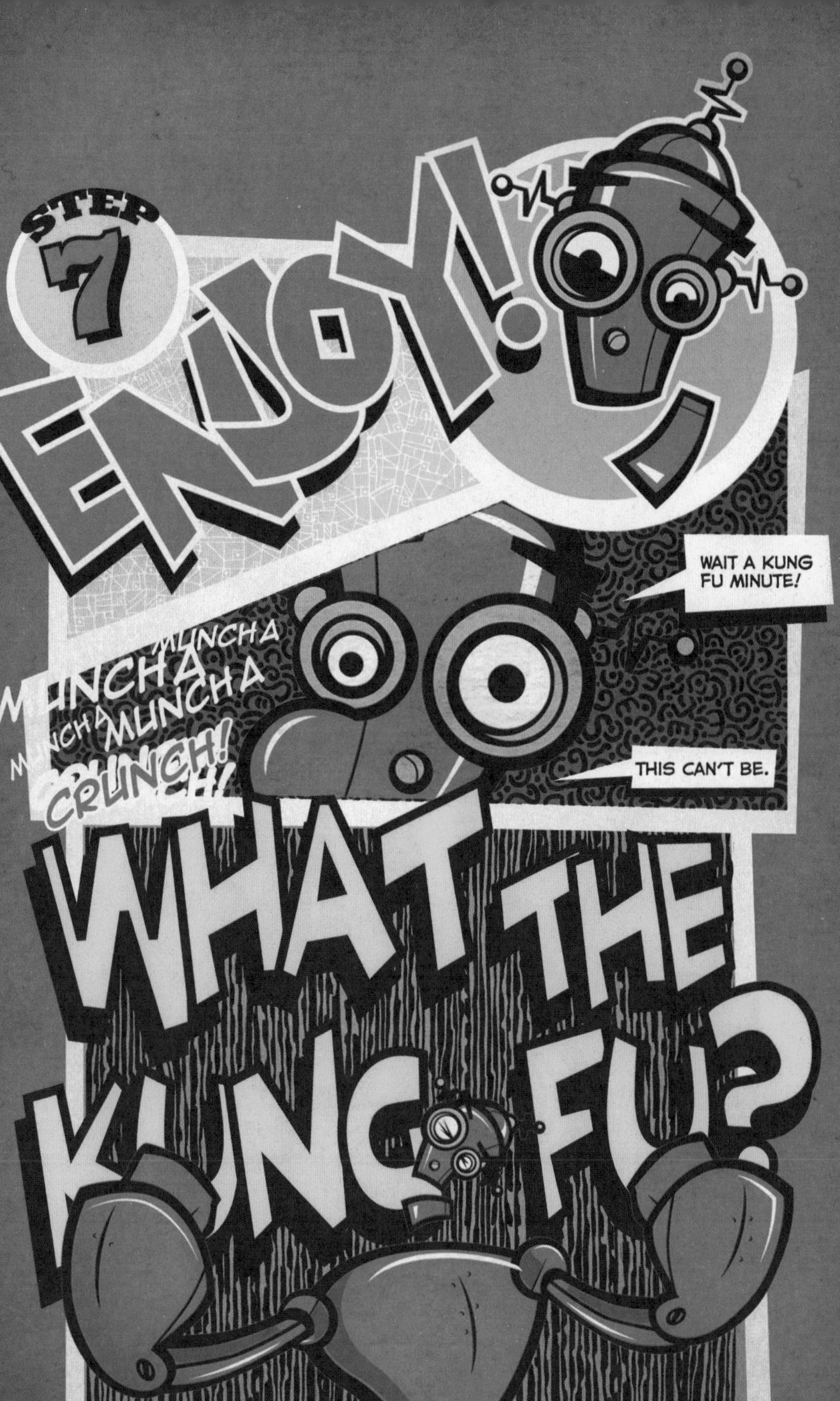

STEP 7
ENJOY!
WAIT A KUNG FU MINUTE!
MUNCHA MUNCHA
MUNCHA MUNCHA
CRUNCH!
THIS CAN'T BE.
WHAT THE KUNG FU?

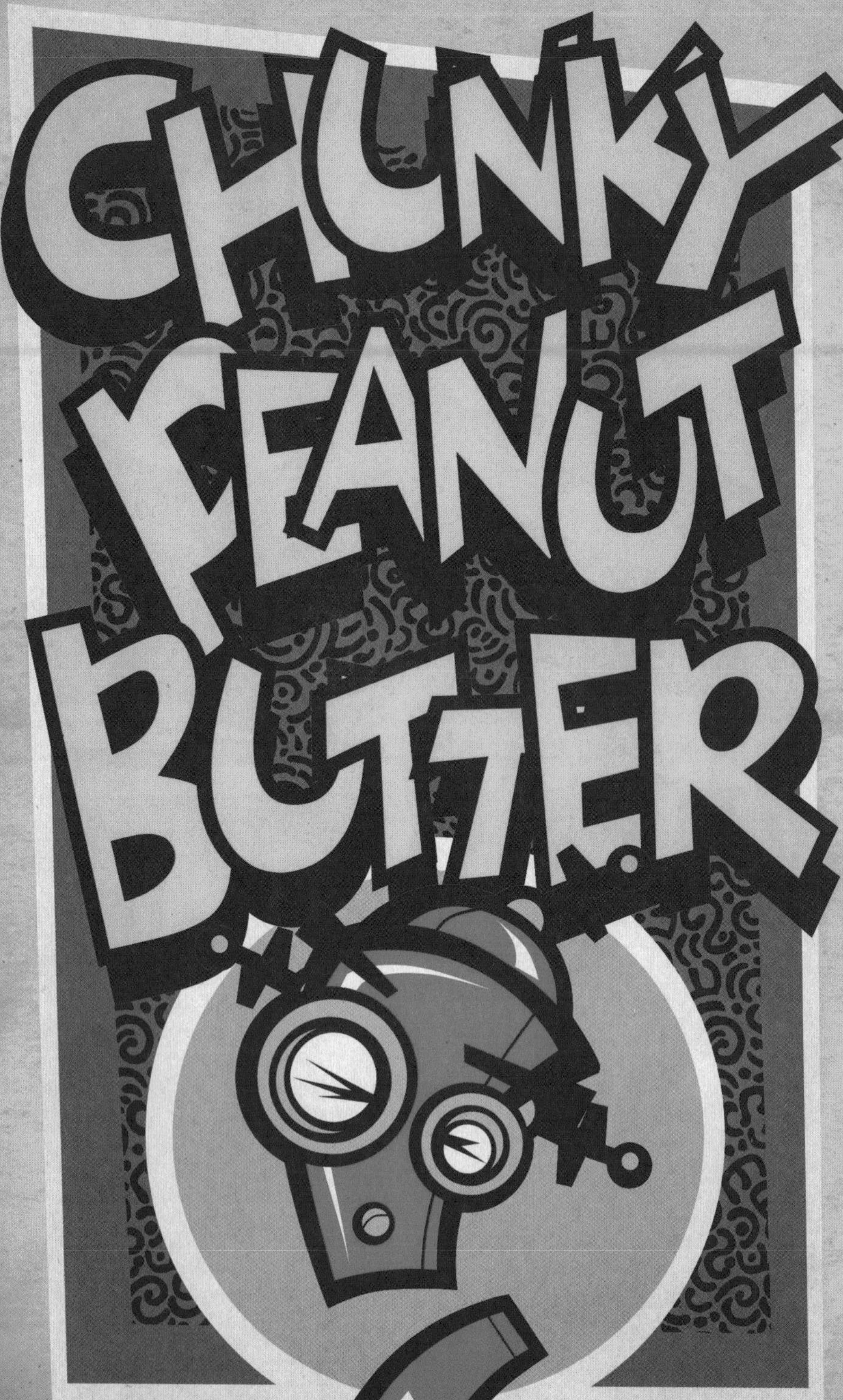
CHUNKY
PEANUT
BUTTER

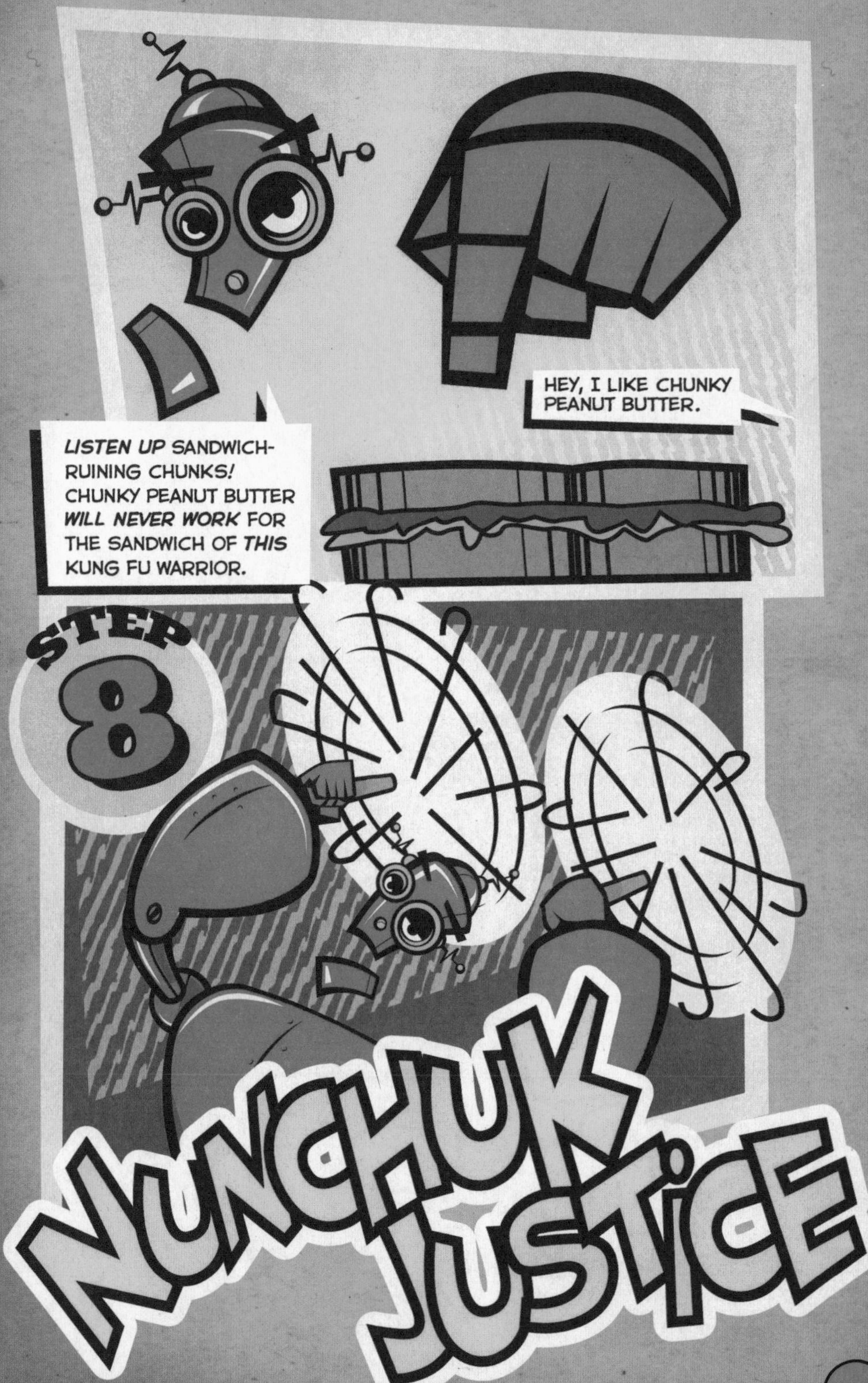

LISTEN UP SANDWICH-RUINING CHUNKS! CHUNKY PEANUT BUTTER WILL NEVER WORK FOR THE SANDWICH OF THIS KUNG FU WARRIOR.
HEY, I LIKE CHUNKY PEANUT BUTTER.
STEP 8
NUNCHUK JUSTICE

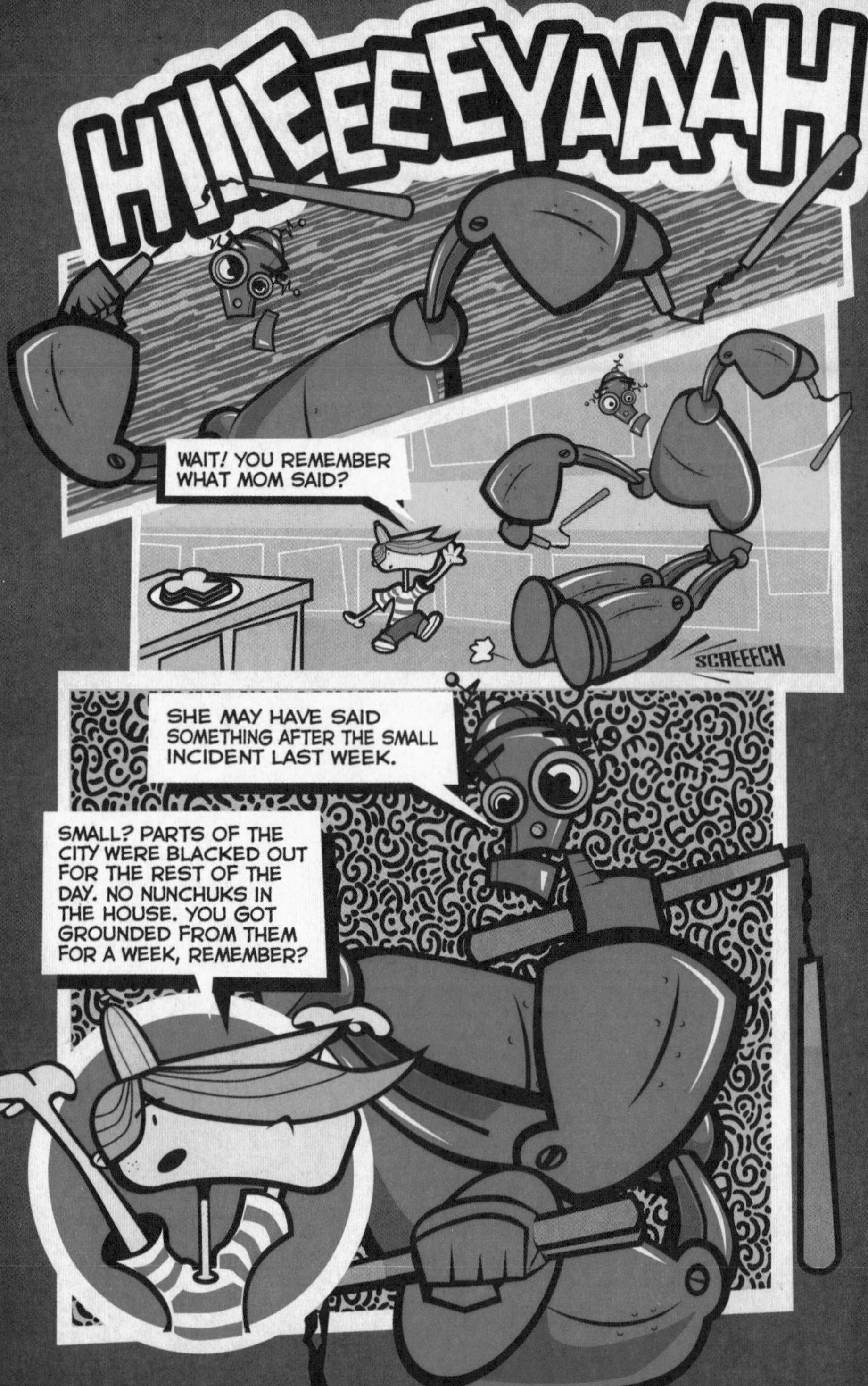
HIIIEEEEYAAAH
WAIT! YOU REMEMBER WHAT MOM SAID?
SCREEECH
SHE MAY HAVE SAID SOMETHING AFTER THE SMALL INCIDENT LAST WEEK.
SMALL? PARTS OF THE CITY WERE BLACKED OUT FOR THE REST OF THE DAY. NO NUNCHUKS IN THE HOUSE. YOU GOT GROUNDED FROM THEM FOR A WEEK, REMEMBER?

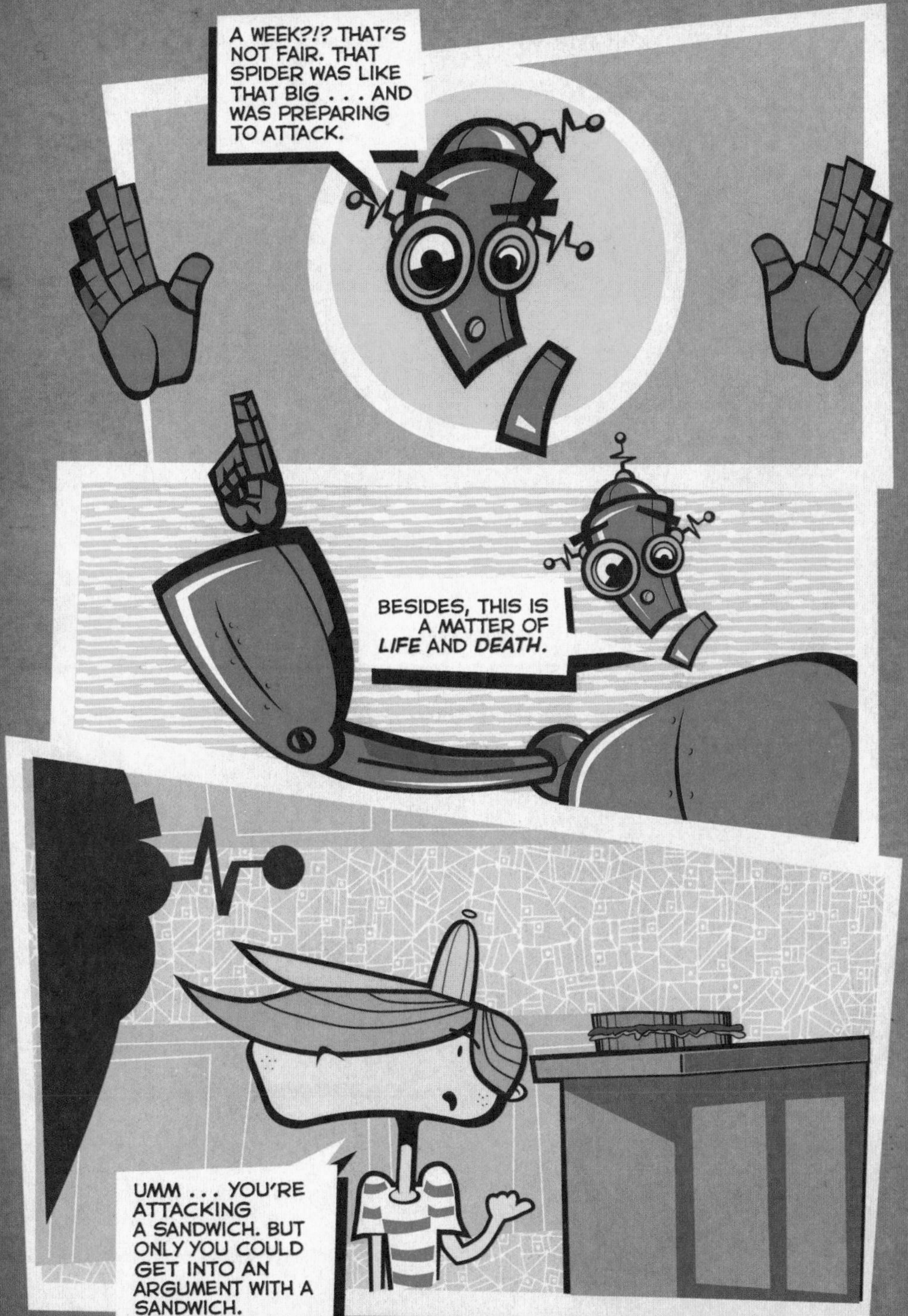
A WEEK?!? THAT'S NOT FAIR. THAT SPIDER WAS LIKE THAT BIG . . . AND WAS PREPARING TO ATTACK.
BESIDES, THIS IS A MATTER OF *LIFE* AND *DEATH*.
UMM . . . YOU'RE ATTACKING A SANDWICH. BUT ONLY YOU COULD GET INTO AN ARGUMENT WITH A SANDWICH.

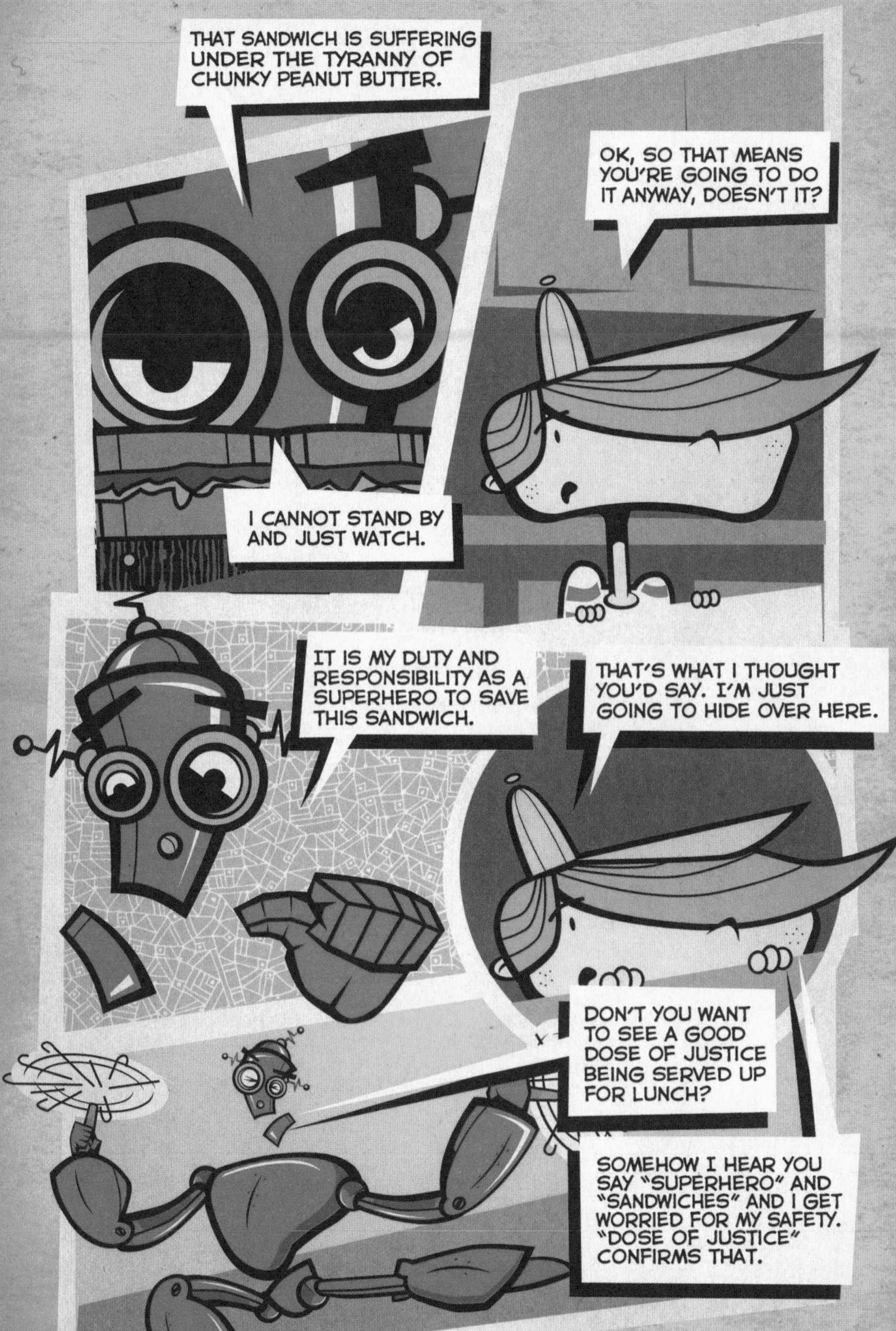
THAT SANDWICH IS SUFFERING UNDER THE TYRANNY OF CHUNKY PEANUT BUTTER.
I CANNOT STAND BY AND JUST WATCH.
OK, SO THAT MEANS YOU'RE GOING TO DO IT ANYWAY, DOESN'T IT?
IT IS MY DUTY AND RESPONSIBILITY AS A SUPERHERO TO SAVE THIS SANDWICH.
THAT'S WHAT I THOUGHT YOU'D SAY. I'M JUST GOING TO HIDE OVER HERE.
DON'T YOU WANT TO SEE A GOOD DOSE OF JUSTICE BEING SERVED UP FOR LUNCH?
SOMEHOW I HEAR YOU SAY "SUPERHERO" AND "SANDWICHES" AND I GET WORRIED FOR MY SAFETY. "DOSE OF JUSTICE" CONFIRMS THAT.

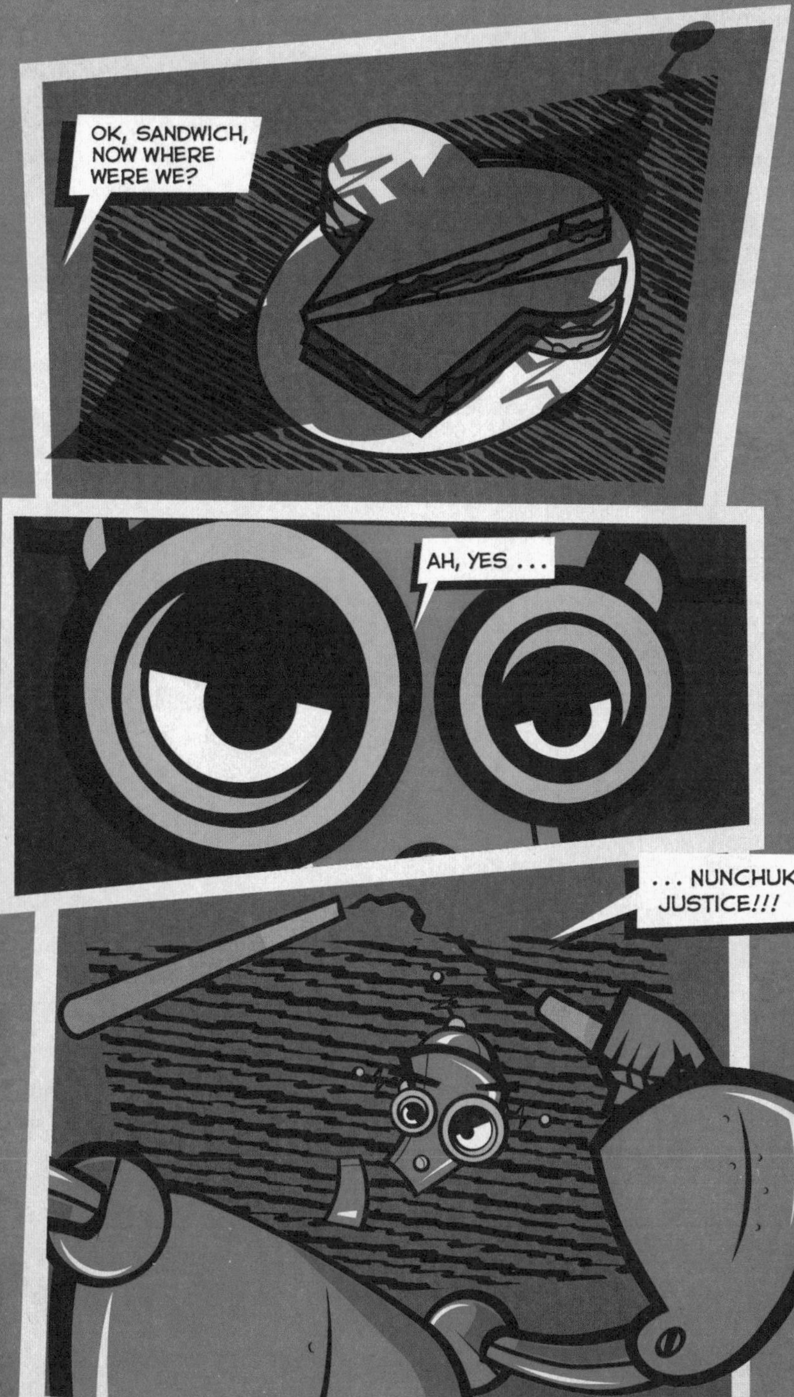
OK, SANDWICH, NOW WHERE WERE WE?
AH, YES . . .
. . . NUNCHUK JUSTICE!!!

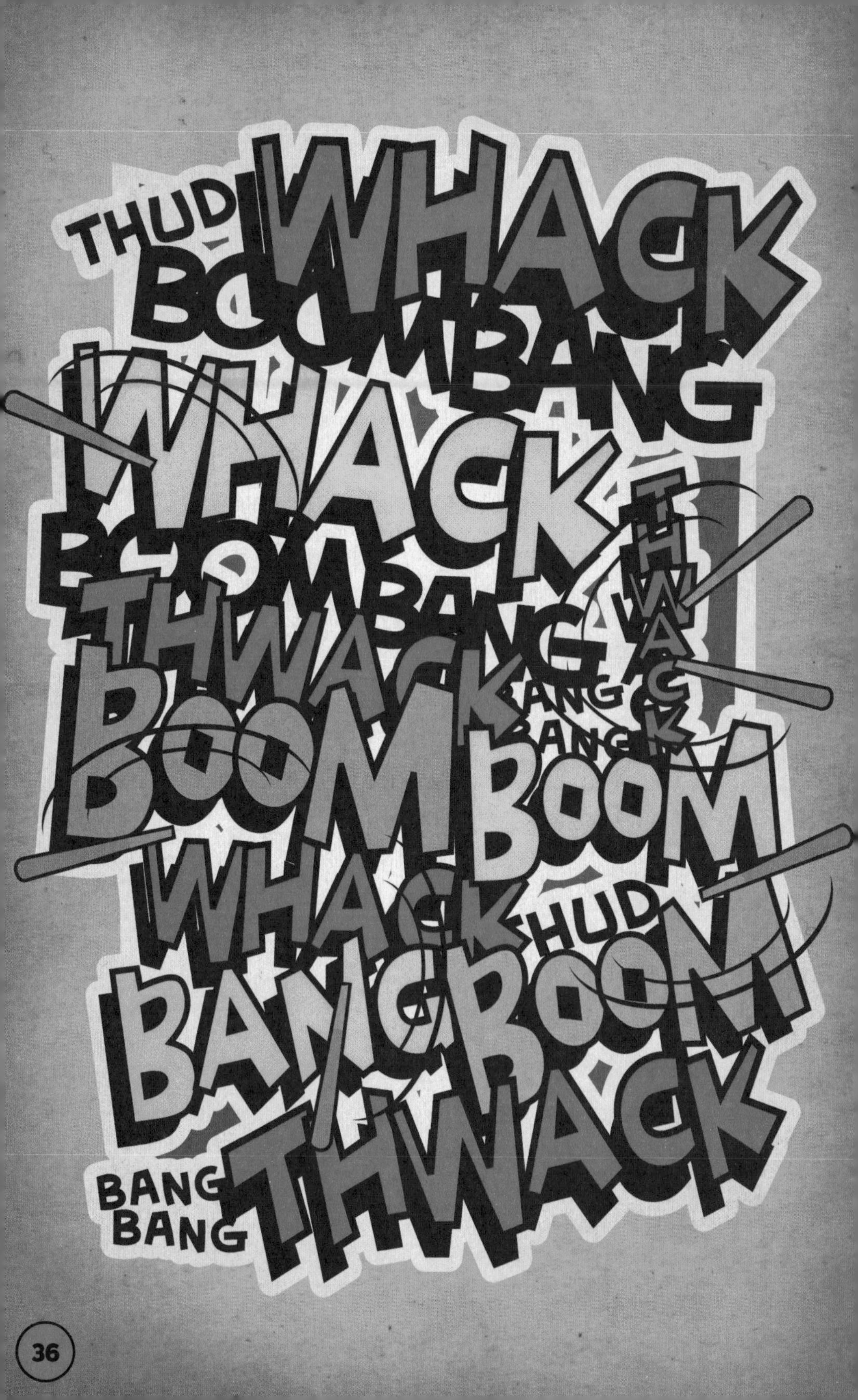
THUD
WHACK
BANG
WHACK
BANG
THWACK
THWACK
BANG
BANG
BOOM
BOOM
WHACK
HUD
BANG
BOOM
BANG
BANG
THWACK

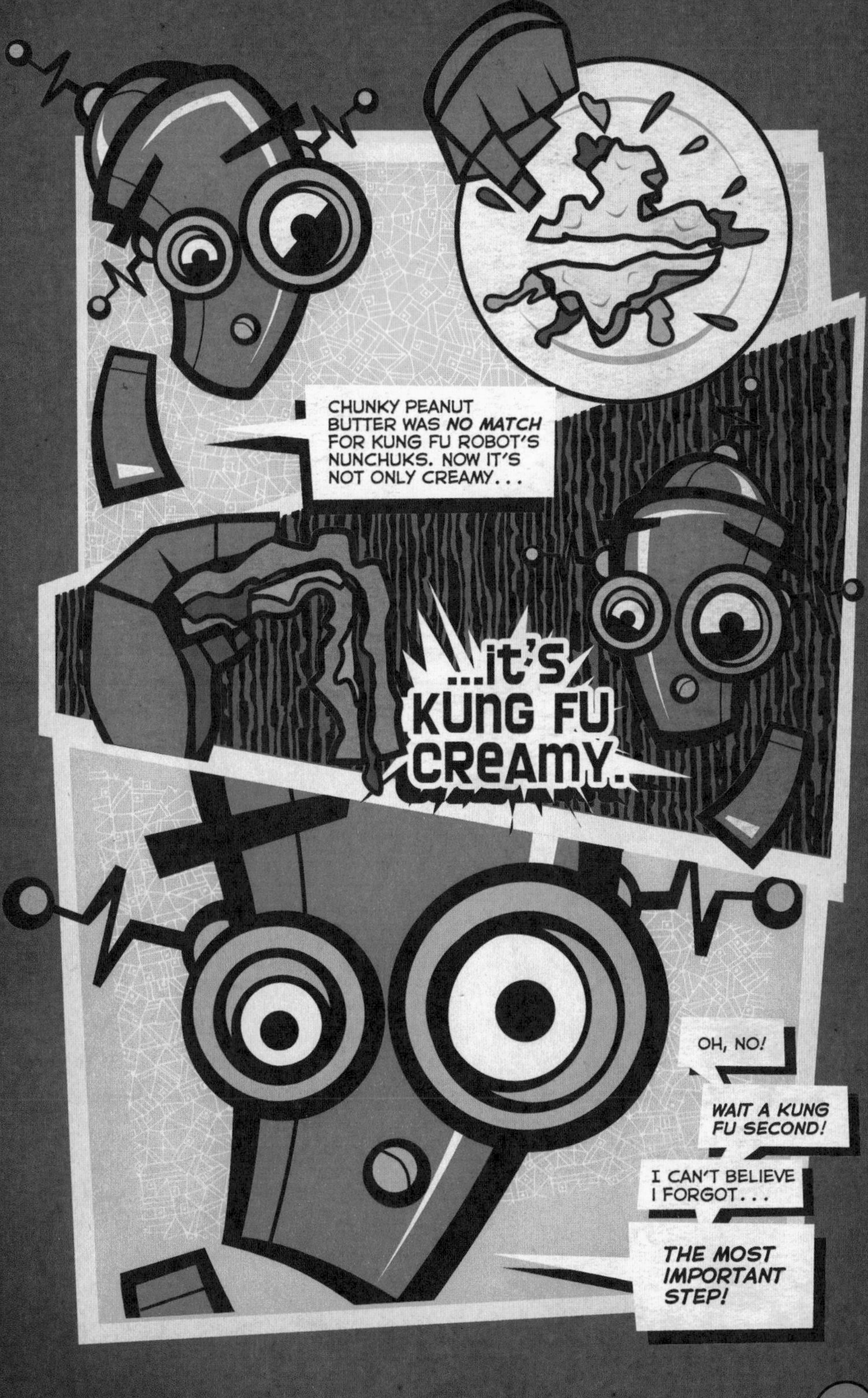
CHUNKY PEANUT BUTTER WAS *NO MATCH* FOR KUNG FU ROBOT'S NUNCHUKS. NOW IT'S NOT ONLY CREAMY . . .
...it's KUNG FU CREAMY..
OH, NO!
WAIT A KUNG FU SECOND!
I CAN'T BELIEVE I FORGOT . . .
THE MOST IMPORTANT STEP!

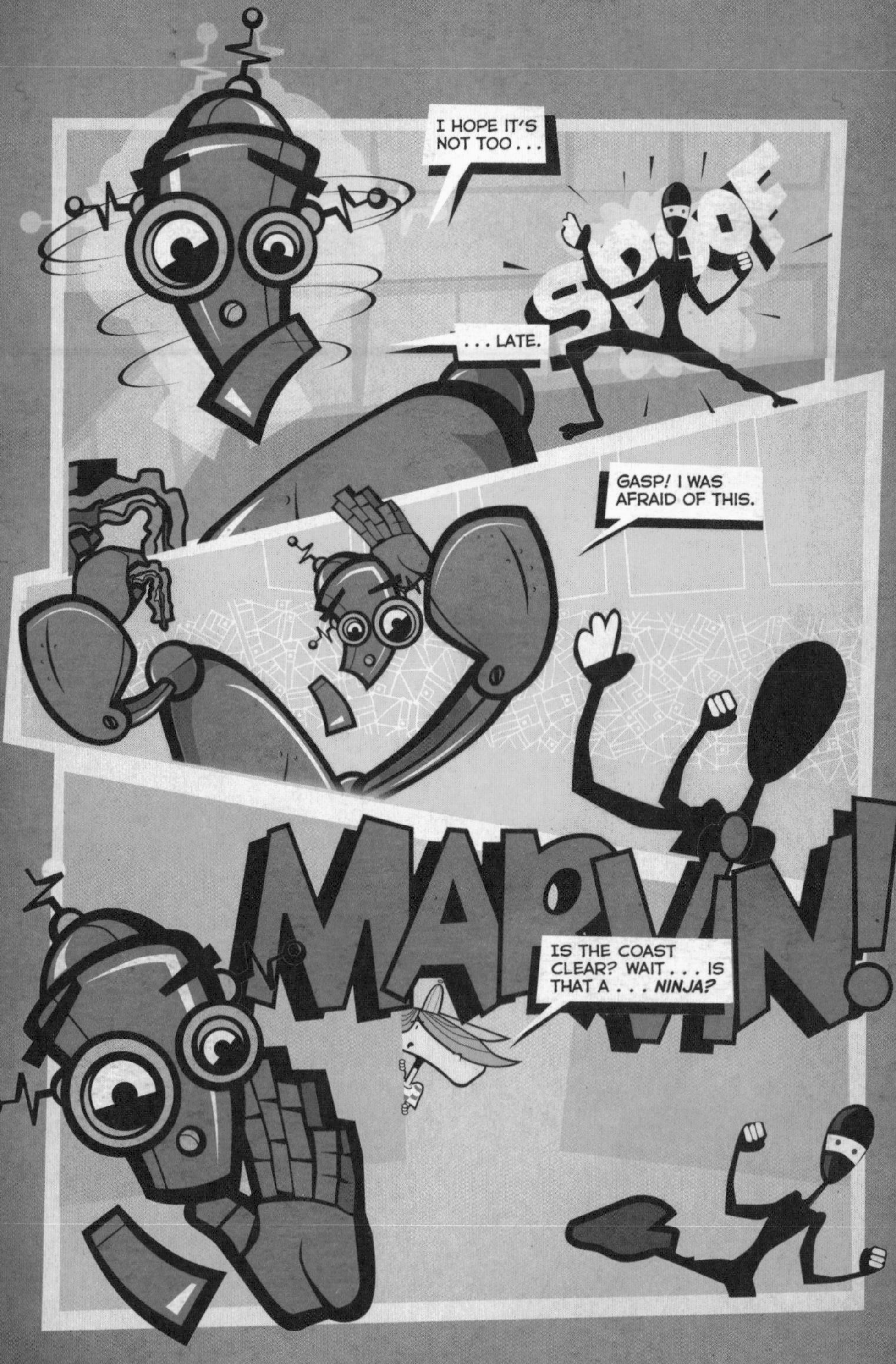
I HOPE IT'S NOT TOO . . .
SPOOF
. . . LATE.
GASP! I WAS AFRAID OF THIS.
MARVIN!
IS THE COAST CLEAR? WAIT . . . IS THAT A . . . *NINJA?*

STEP 9

WHAT WAS STEP 9?

WATCH FOR NINJAS!

INTRODUCING

NINJAS

OVERALL RUINER OF MOST THINGS FUN AND AWESOME, LIKE PEANUT BUTTER, JELLY & KUNG FU SANDWICHES.

ALWAYS SNEAKY AND HIDING IN SHADOWS.

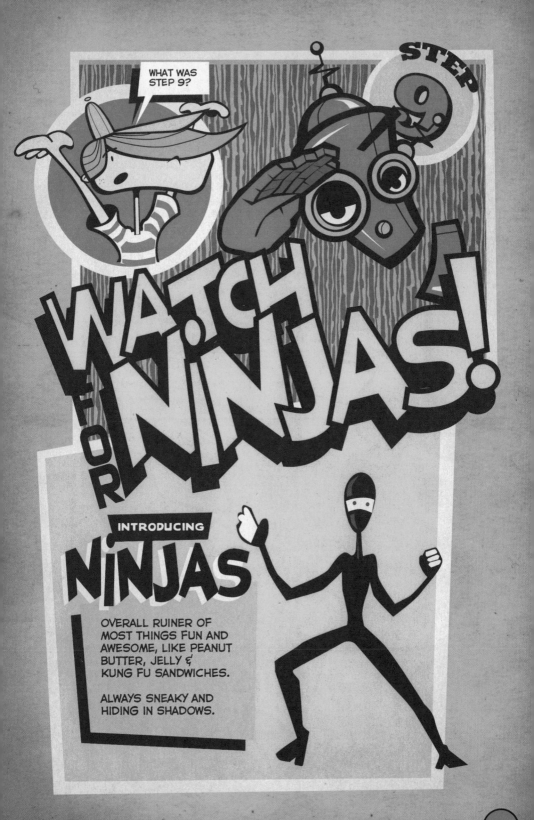

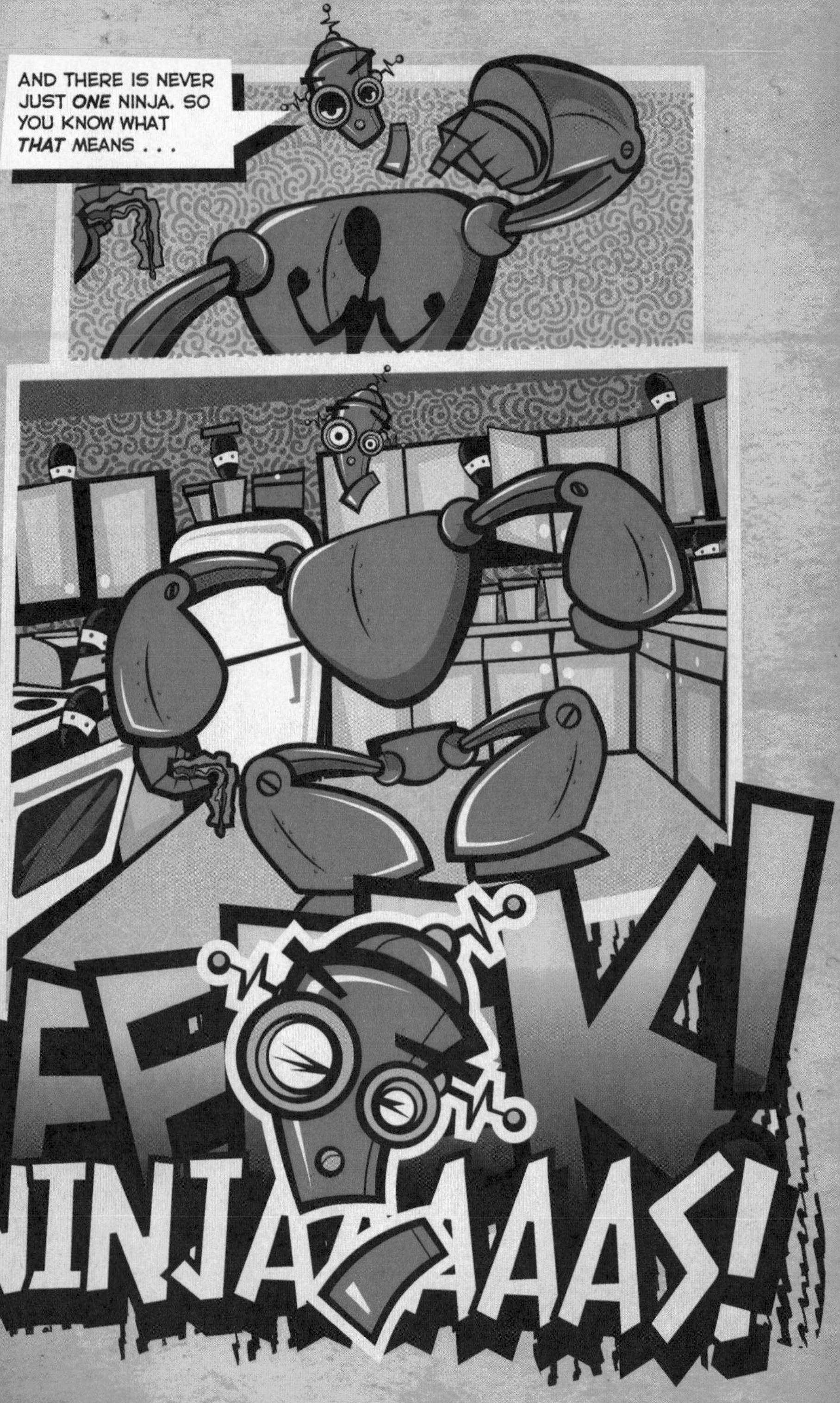
AND THERE IS NEVER JUST *ONE* NINJA. SO YOU KNOW WHAT *THAT* MEANS . . .
NINJA AAAS!

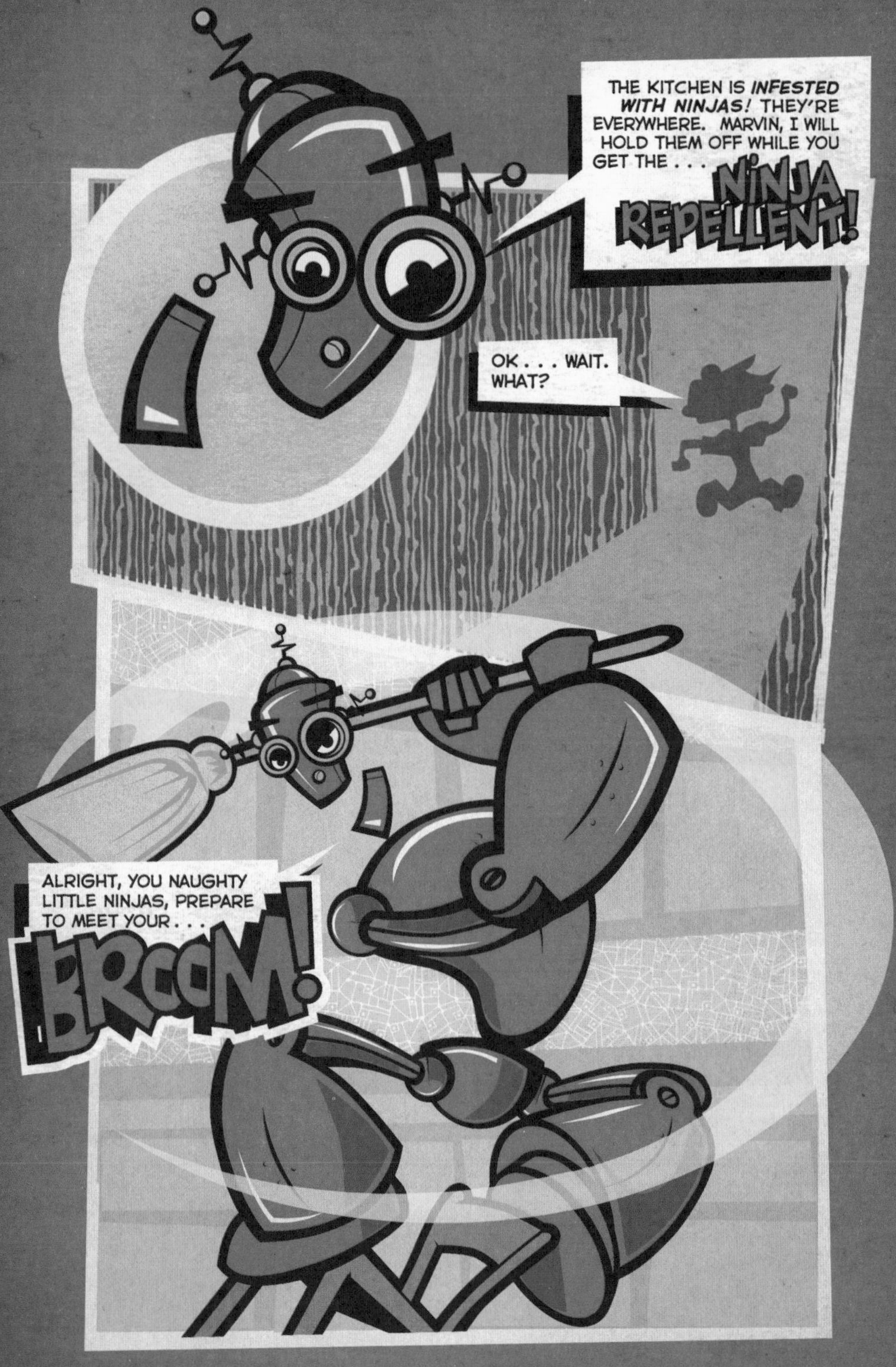
THE KITCHEN IS *INFESTED WITH NINJAS!* THEY'RE EVERYWHERE. MARVIN, I WILL HOLD THEM OFF WHILE YOU GET THE . . . NINJA REPELLENT!
OK . . . WAIT. WHAT?
ALRIGHT, YOU NAUGHTY LITTLE NINJAS, PREPARE TO MEET YOUR . . . BROOM!

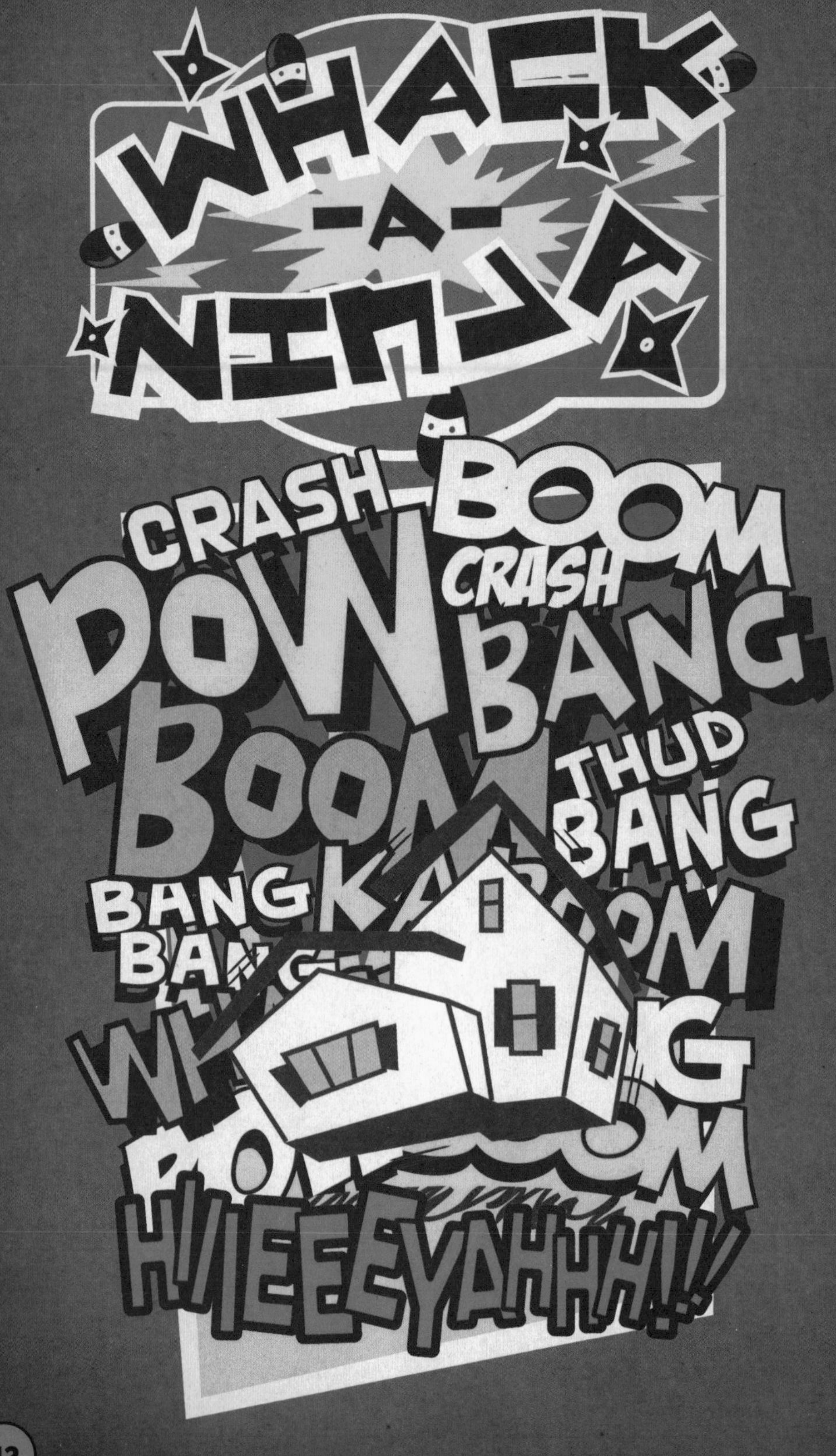
WHACK
-A-
NINJA
CRASH
BOOM
POW
CRASH
BANG
BOOM
THUD
BANG
BANG
HIIEEEYAHHH!!

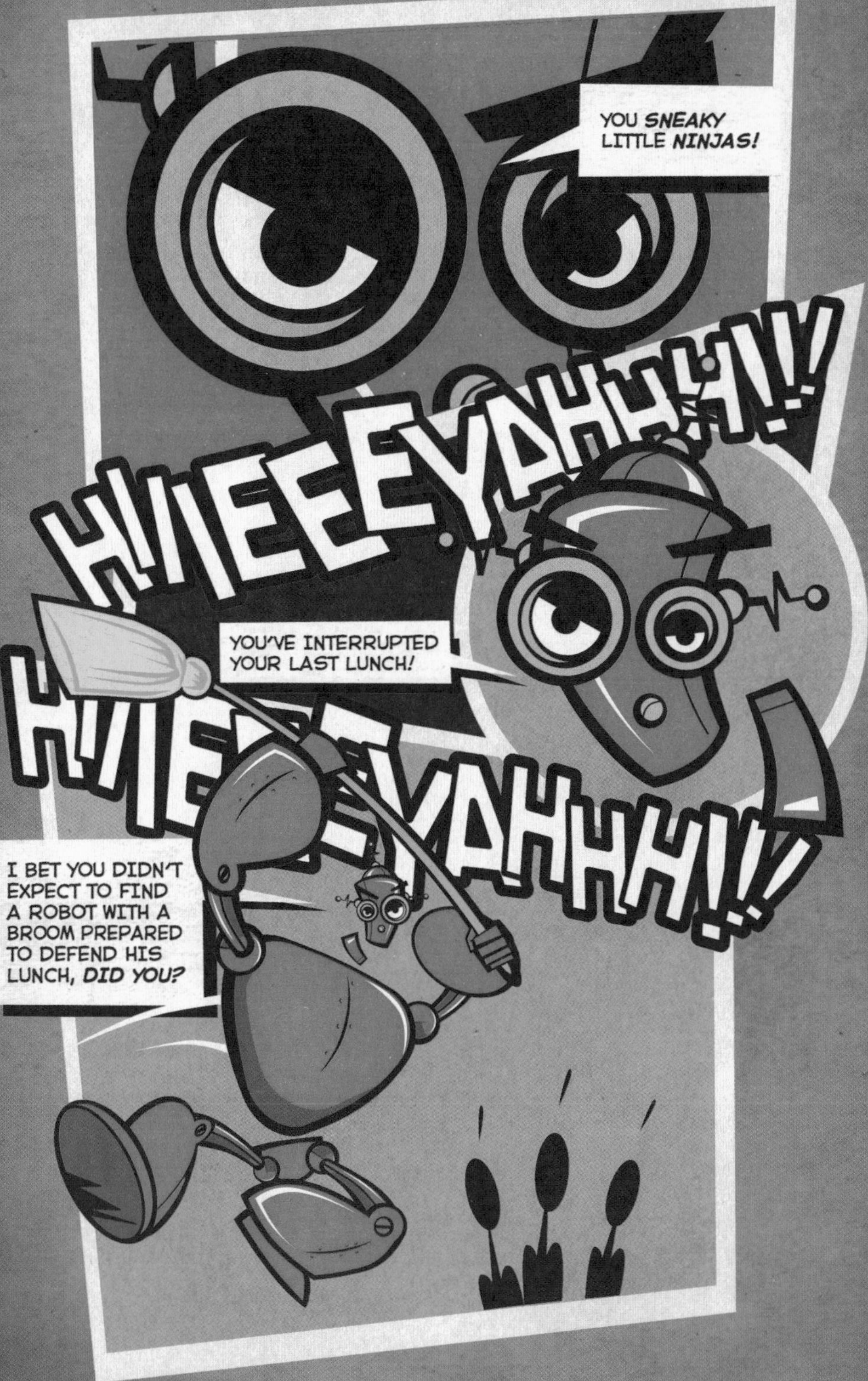
YOU *SNEAKY* LITTLE *NINJAS!*
HWIEEEYAHHHH!!
YOU'VE INTERRUPTED YOUR LAST LUNCH!
HWIEEEYAHHHH!!
I BET YOU DIDN'T EXPECT TO FIND A ROBOT WITH A BROOM PREPARED TO DEFEND HIS LUNCH, *DID YOU?*

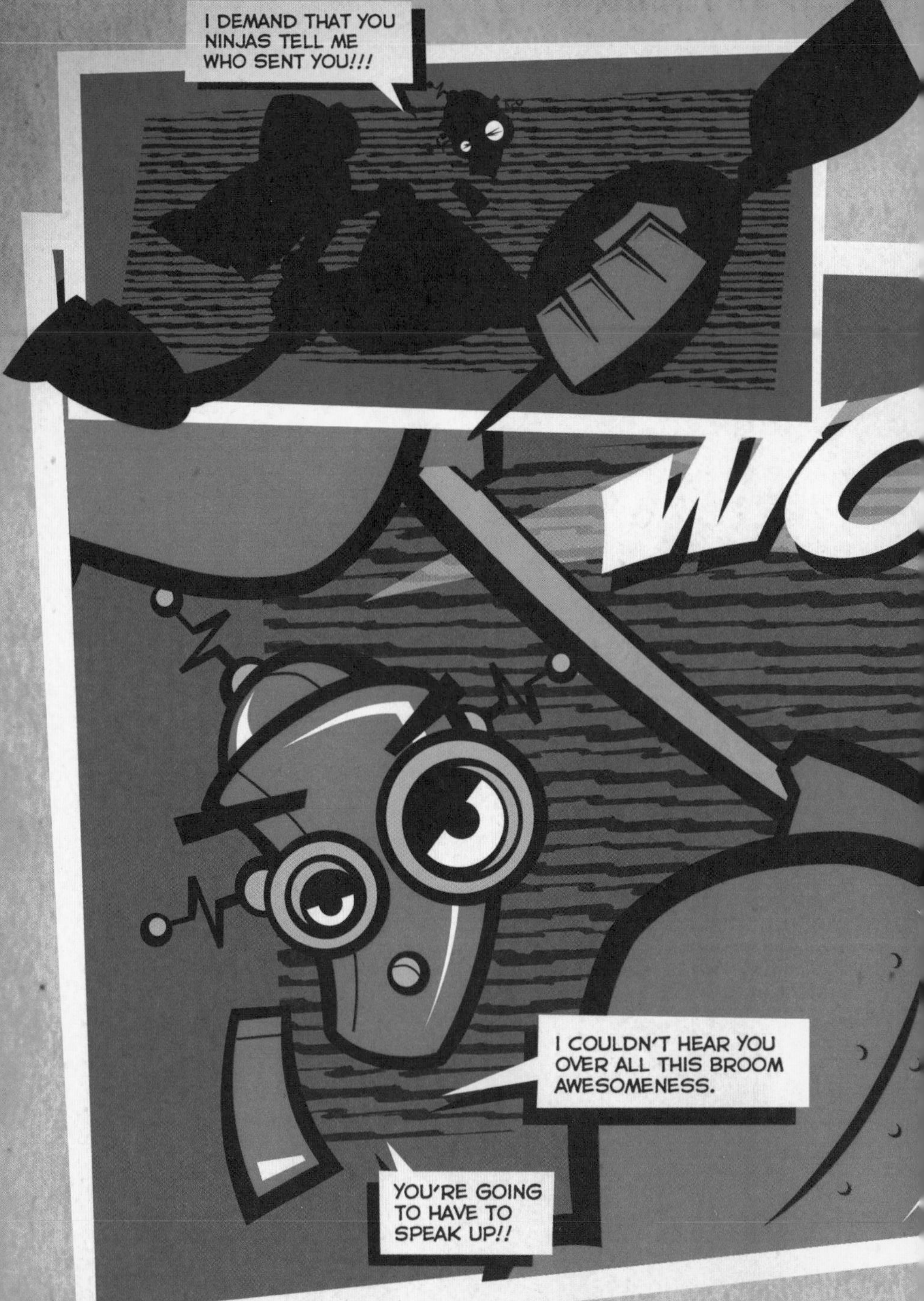
I DEMAND THAT YOU NINJAS TELL ME WHO SENT YOU!!!
I COULDN'T HEAR YOU OVER ALL THIS BROOM AWESOMENESS.
YOU'RE GOING TO HAVE TO SPEAK UP!!

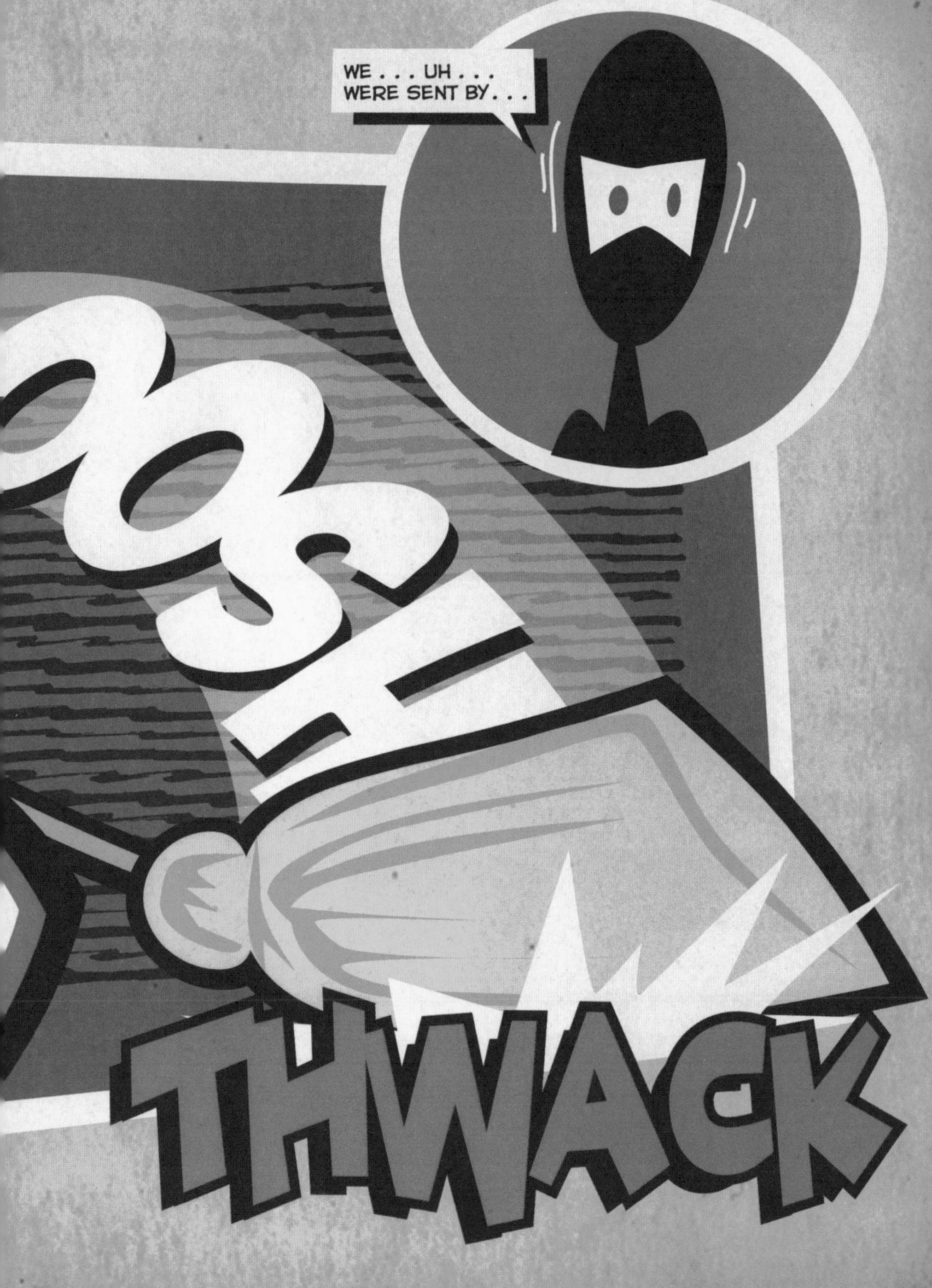
WE . . . UH . . .
WERE SENT BY . . .
OOSH!
THWACK

WHIFF WHIFF WHIFF WHIFF WHIFF

LISTEN UP, NINJAS!! YOU BETTER START TALKING . . .

KABOOM POW BANG POW CRASH CRASH POW ANG BOOM THUD WHACK BANG

. . . OR I'M GOING TO HAVE TO START GETTING ROUGH!

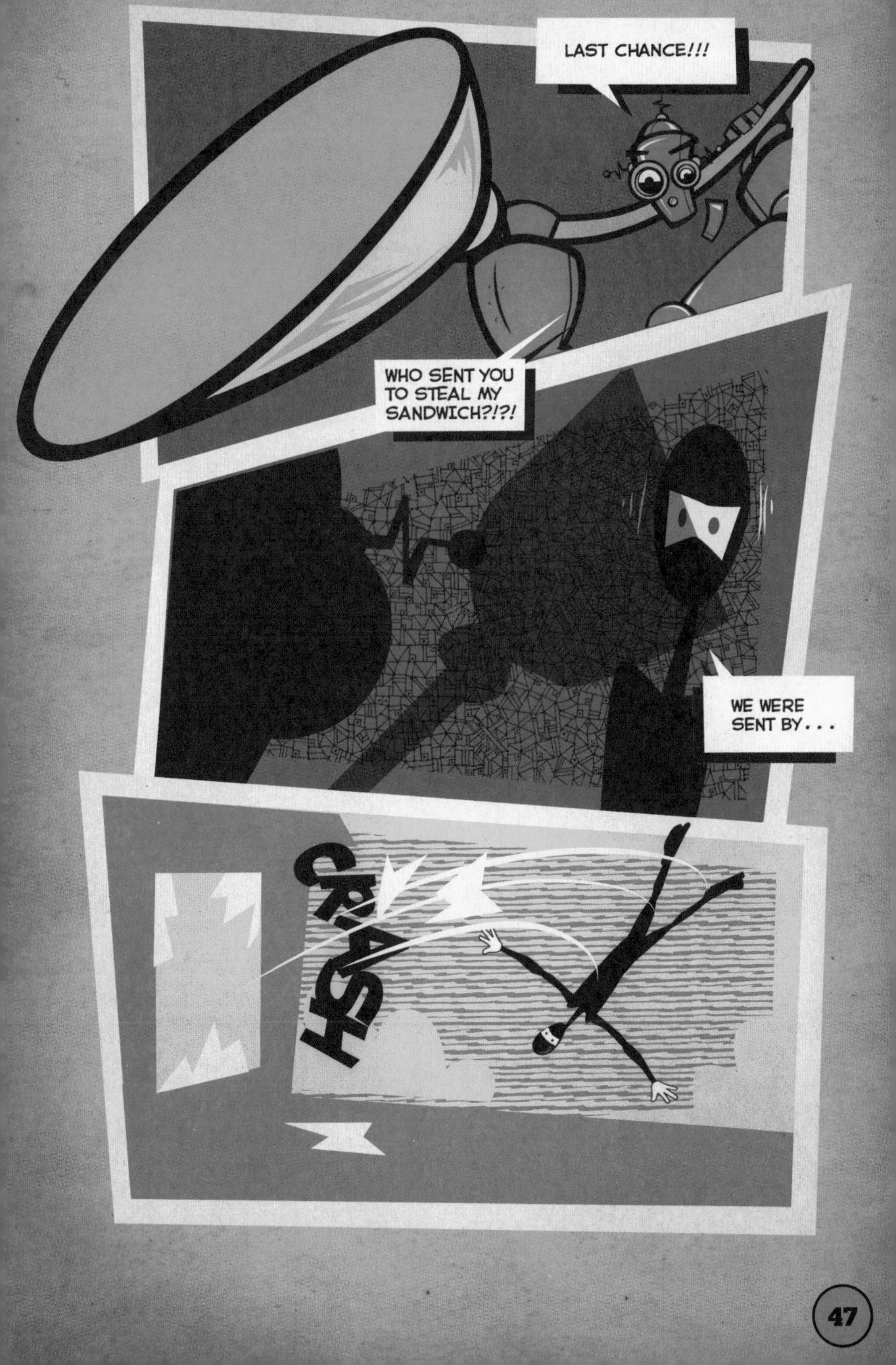
LAST CHANCE!!!
WHO SENT YOU TO STEAL MY SANDWICH?!?!
WE WERE SENT BY . . .
CRASH

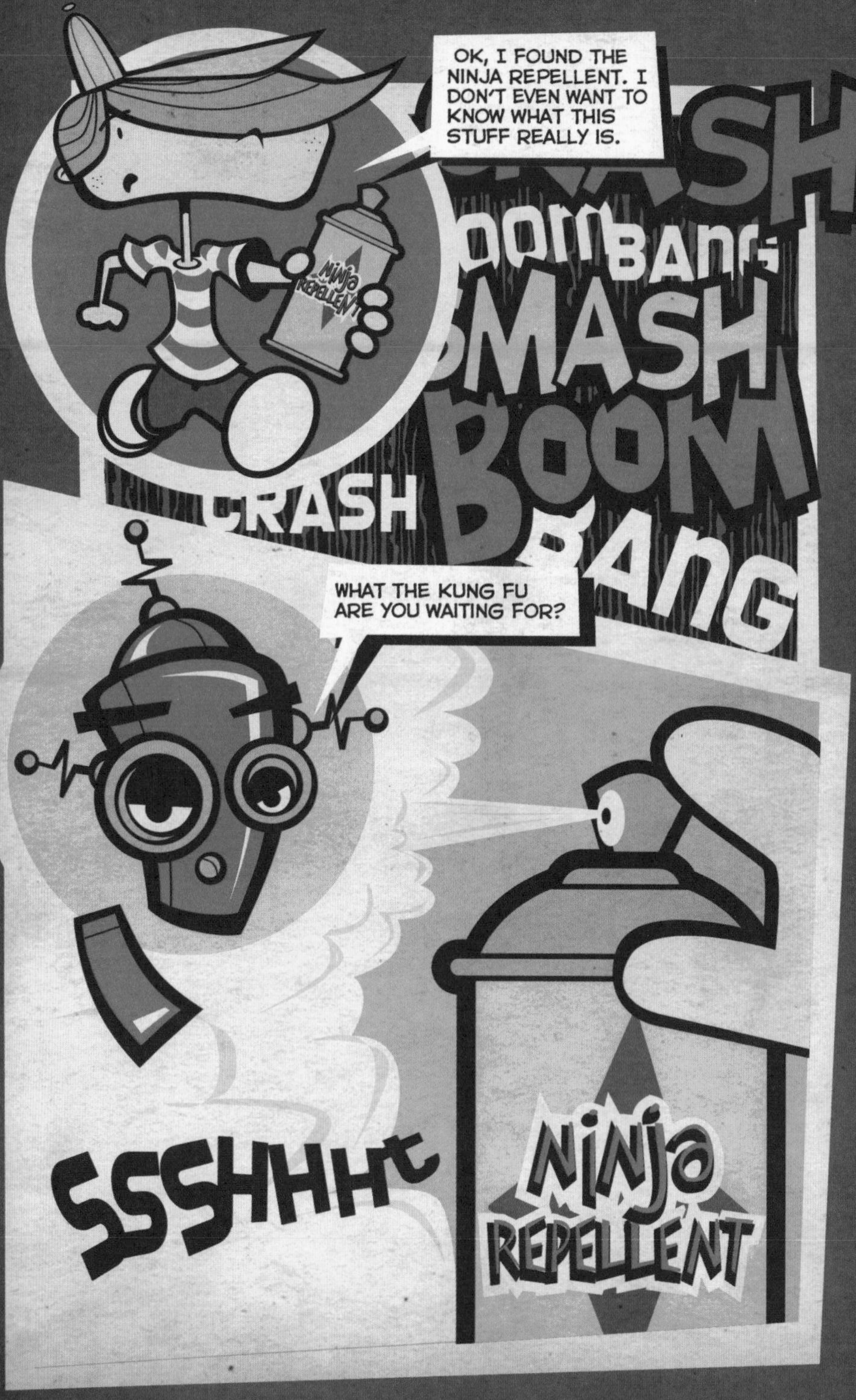

OK, I FOUND THE NINJA REPELLENT. I DON'T EVEN WANT TO KNOW WHAT THIS STUFF REALLY IS.
NINJA REPELLENT
BANG
CRASH
BOOM
WHAT THE KUNG FU ARE YOU WAITING FOR?
BANG
SSSHHHt
NINJA REPELLENT

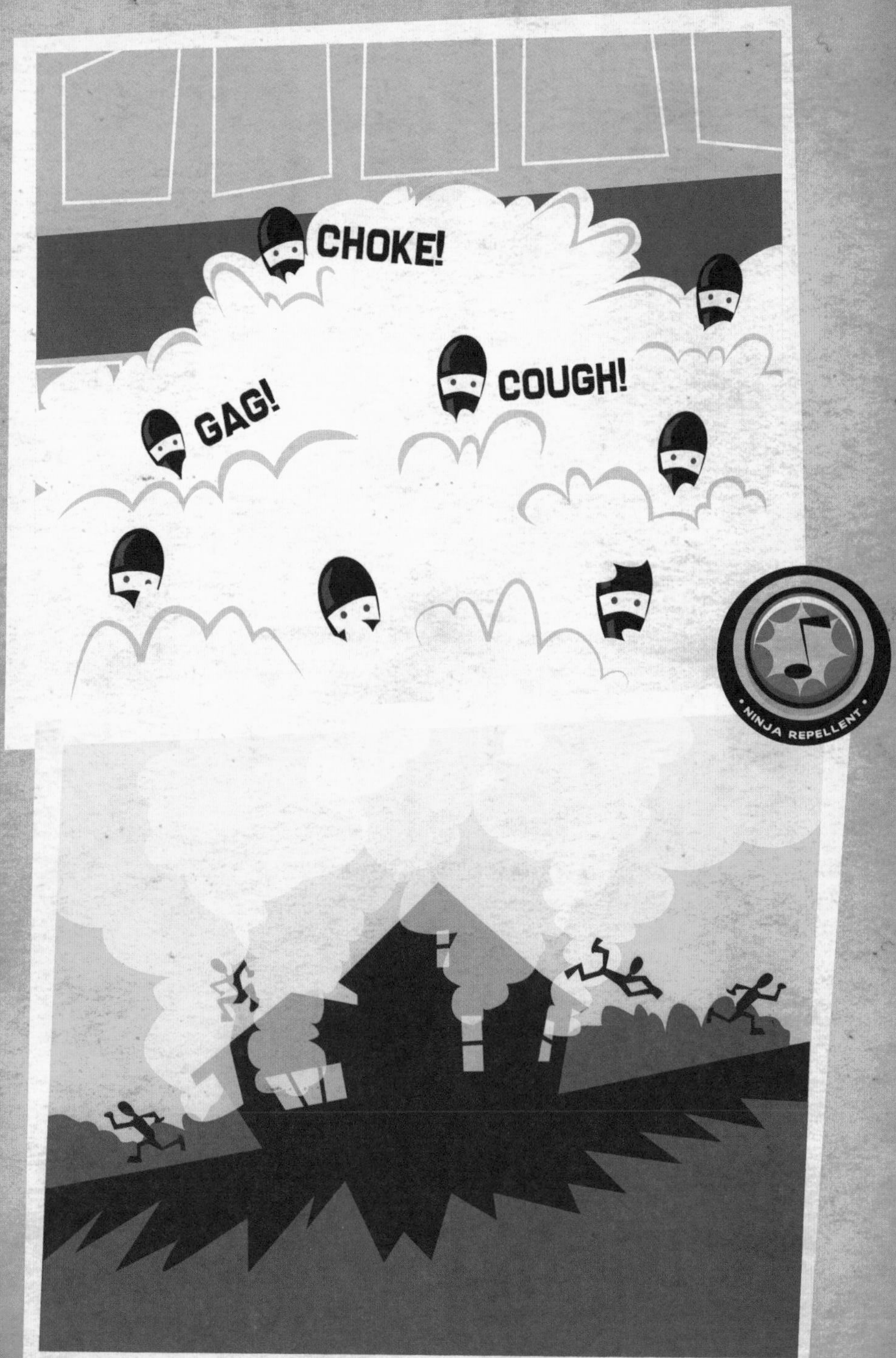
CHOKE!
COUGH!
GAG!
NINJA REPELLENT

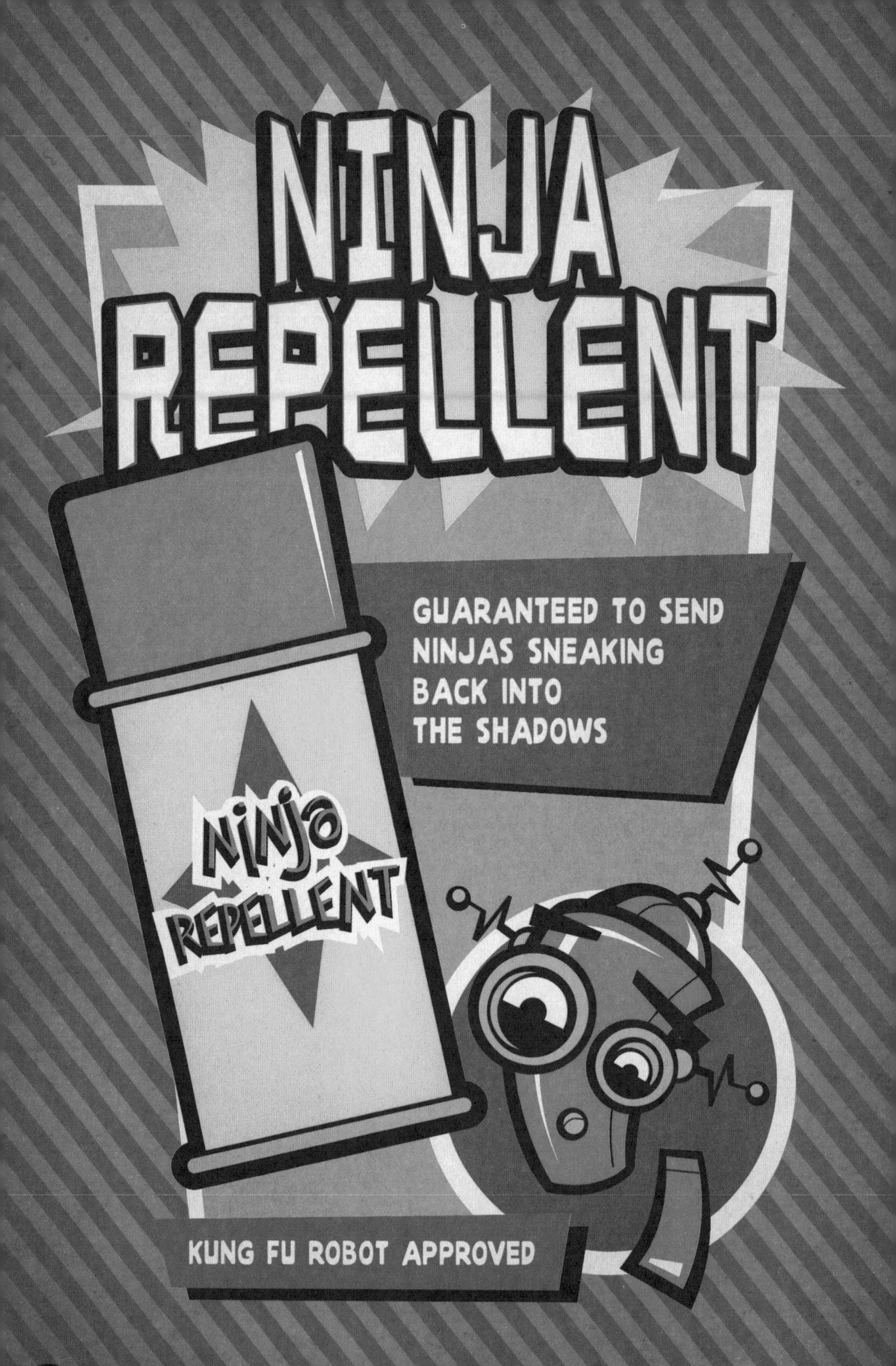
NINJA
REPELLENT
GUARANTEED TO SEND
NINJAS SNEAKING
BACK INTO
THE SHADOWS
NINJA
REPELLENT
KUNG FU ROBOT APPROVED

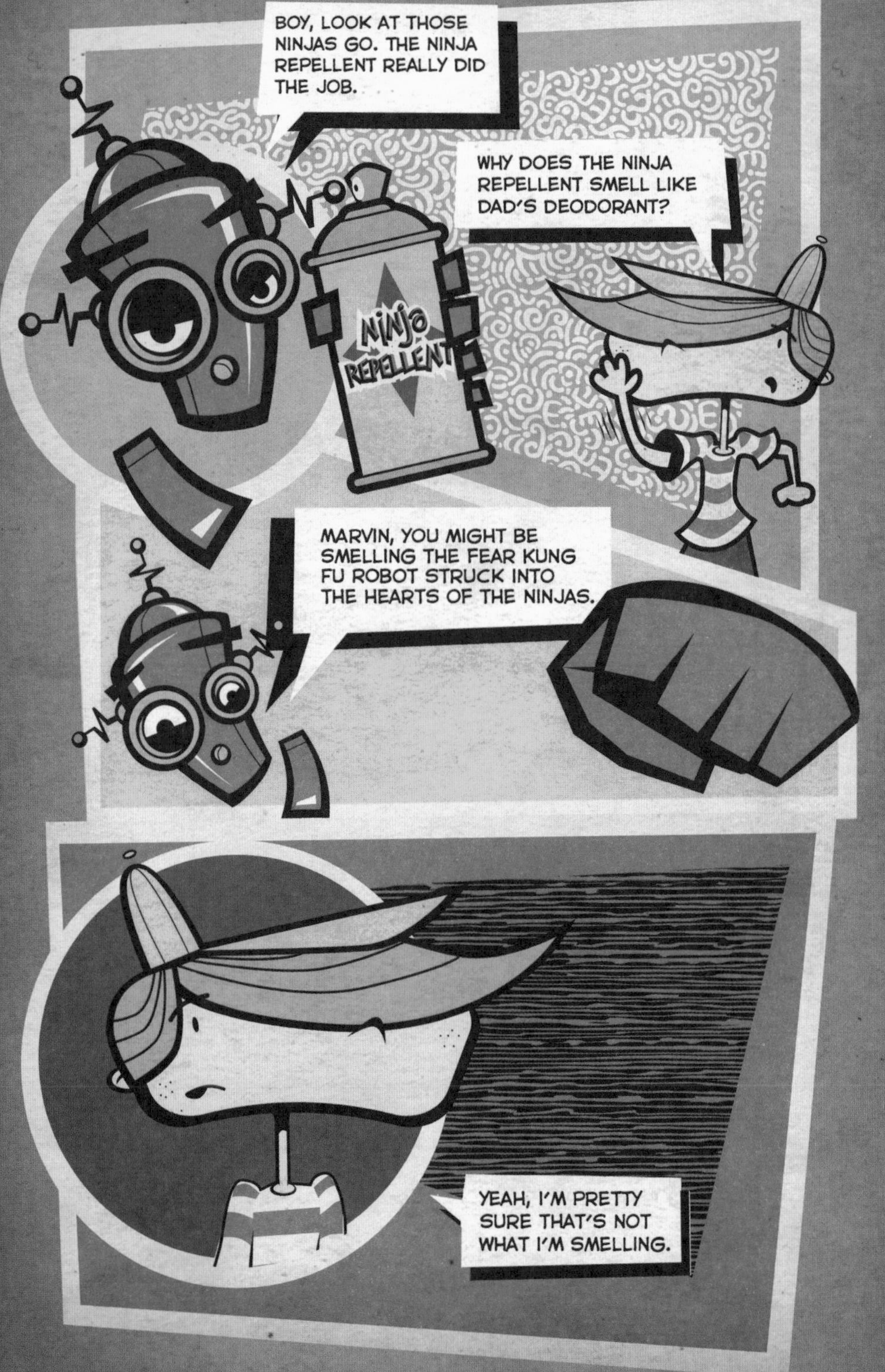
BOY, LOOK AT THOSE NINJAS GO. THE NINJA REPELLENT REALLY DID THE JOB.
WHY DOES THE NINJA REPELLENT SMELL LIKE DAD'S DEODORANT?
NINJA REPELLENT
MARVIN, YOU MIGHT BE SMELLING THE FEAR KUNG FU ROBOT STRUCK INTO THE HEARTS OF THE NINJAS.
YEAH, I'M PRETTY SURE THAT'S NOT WHAT I'M SMELLING.

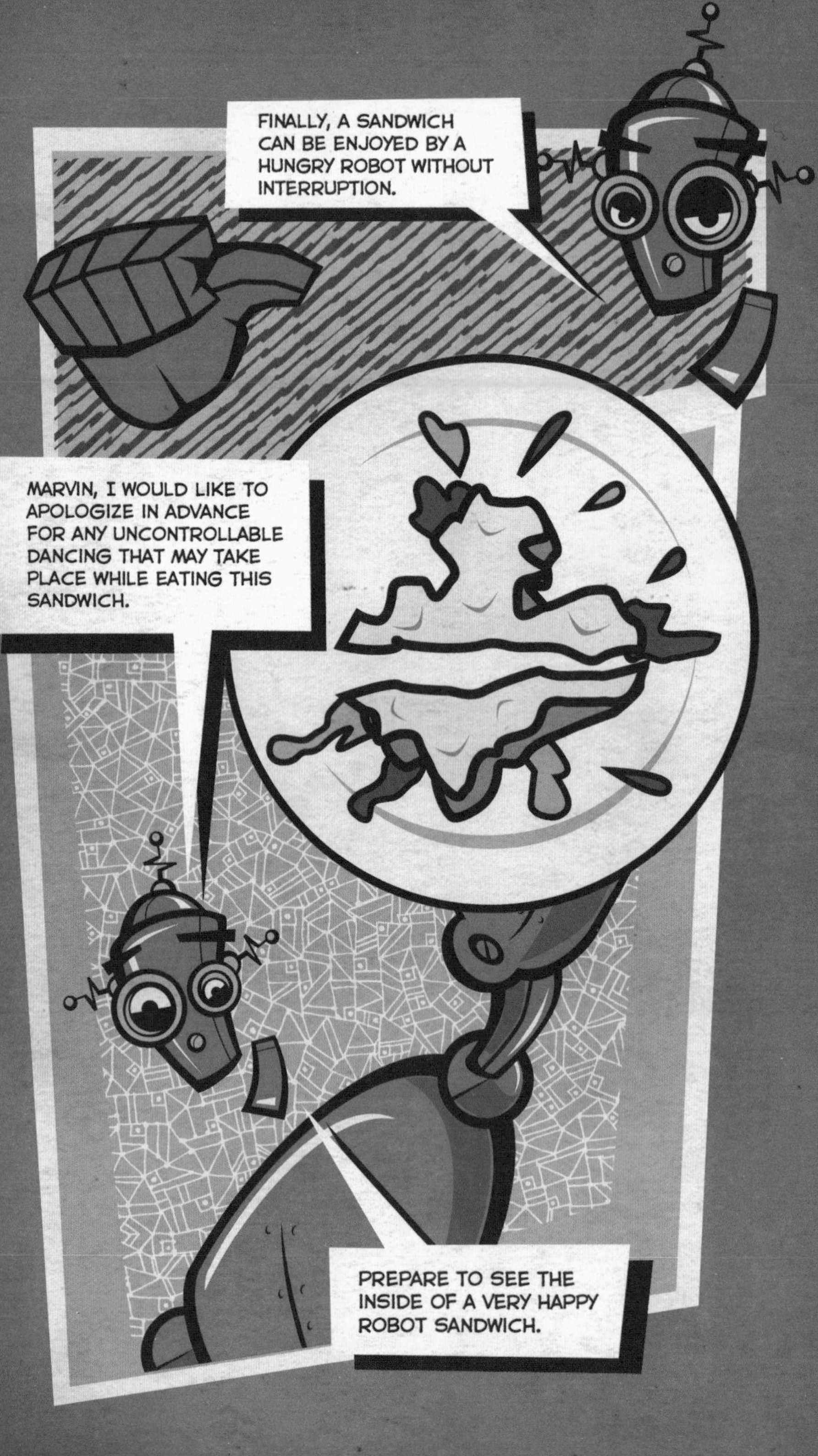
FINALLY, A SANDWICH CAN BE ENJOYED BY A HUNGRY ROBOT WITHOUT INTERRUPTION.
MARVIN, I WOULD LIKE TO APOLOGIZE IN ADVANCE FOR ANY UNCONTROLLABLE DANCING THAT MAY TAKE PLACE WHILE EATING THIS SANDWICH.
PREPARE TO SEE THE INSIDE OF A VERY HAPPY ROBOT SANDWICH.

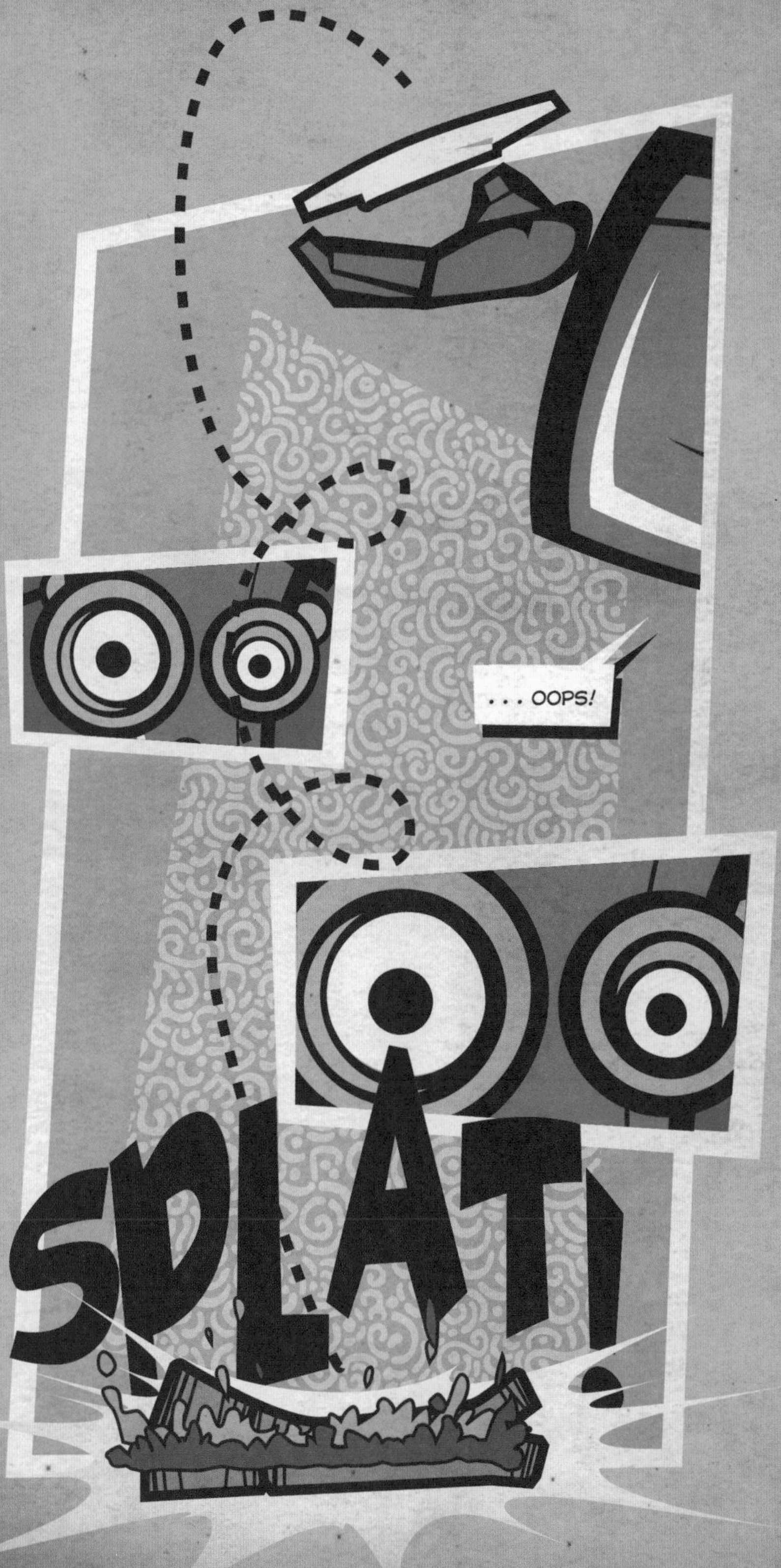
. . . OOPS!
SPLAT!

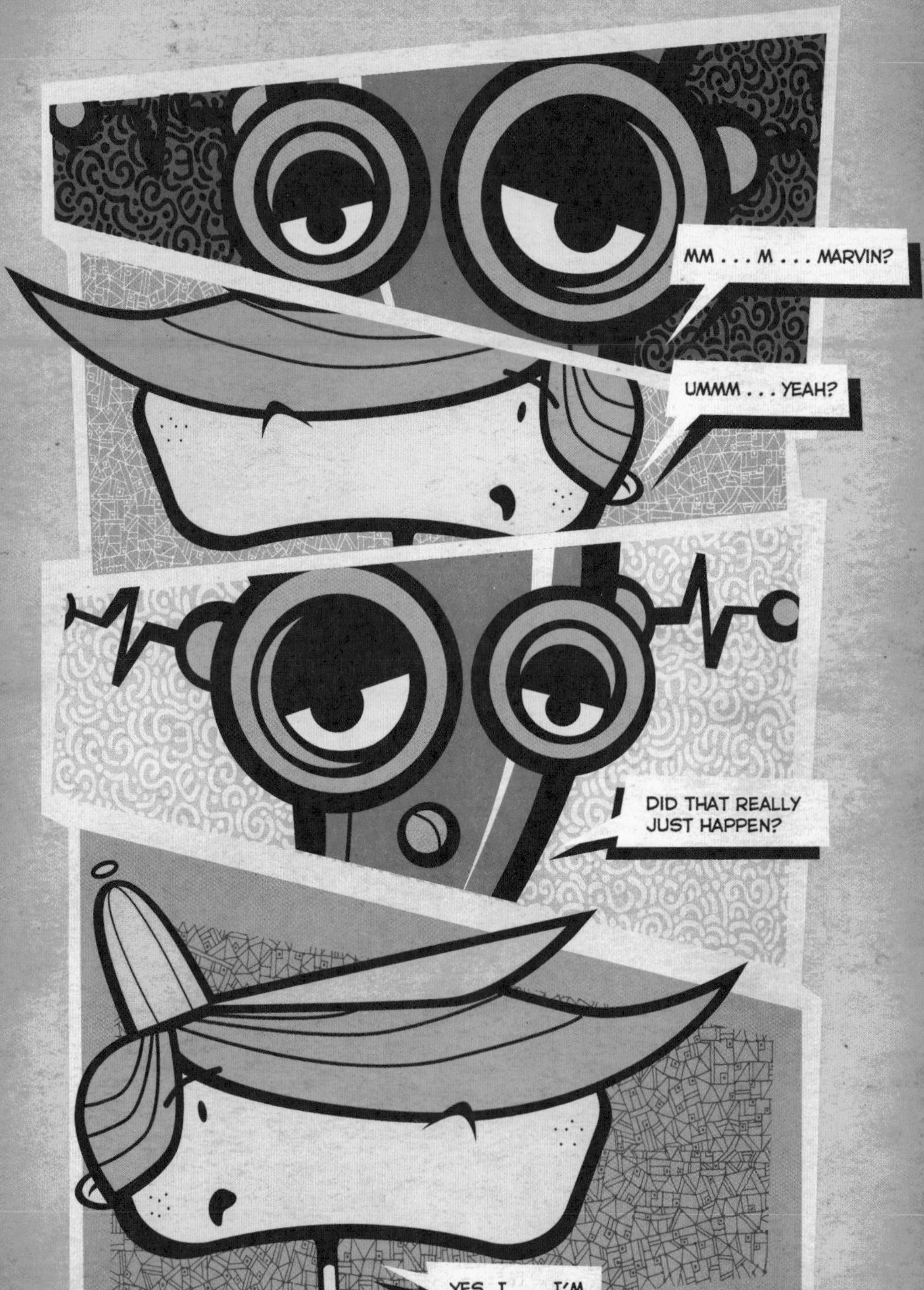
MM . . . M . . . MARVIN?
UMMM . . . YEAH?
DID THAT REALLY JUST HAPPEN?
YES. I . . . I'M AFRAID IT DID.

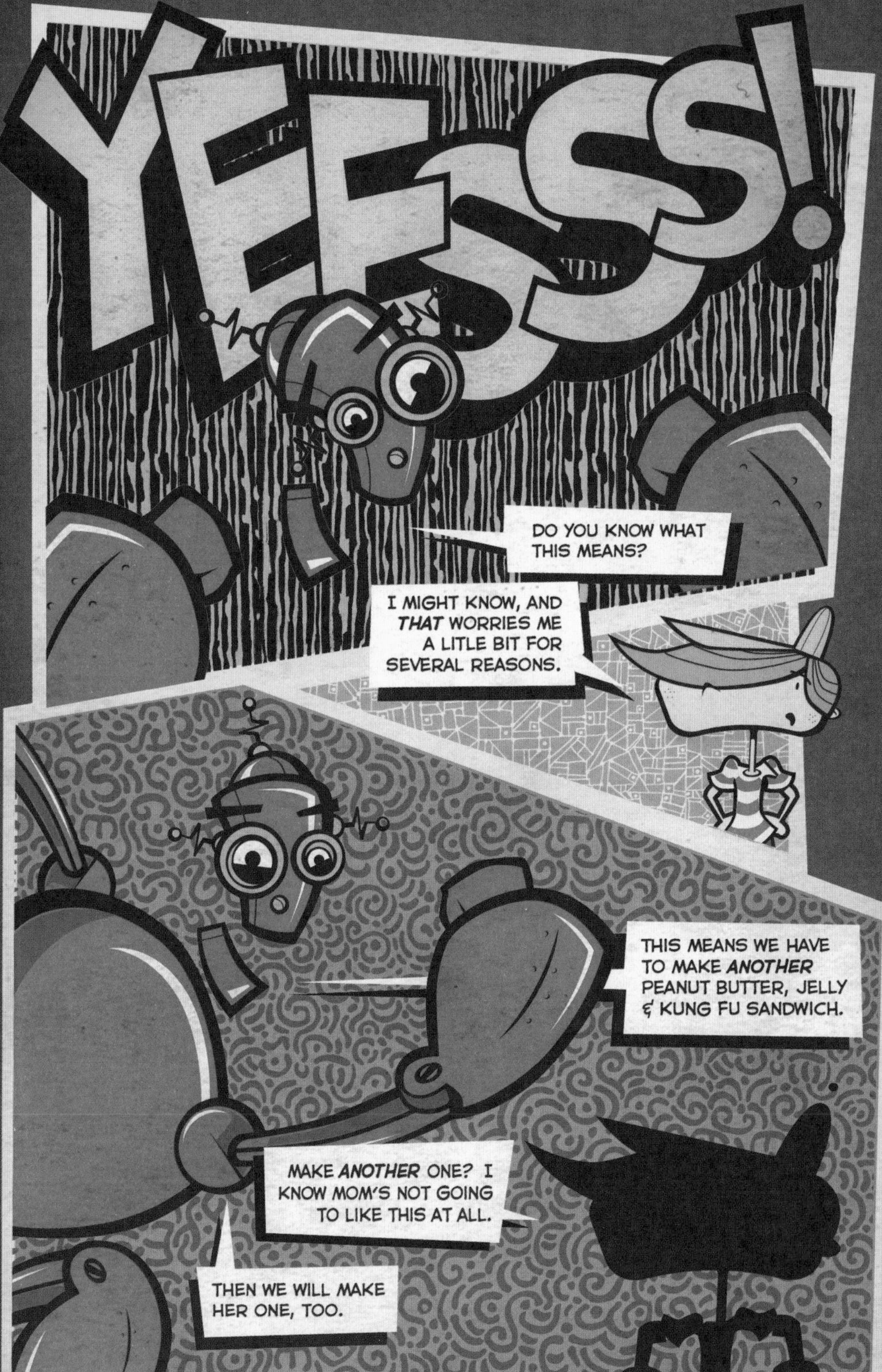
YEESS!
DO YOU KNOW WHAT THIS MEANS?
I MIGHT KNOW, AND *THAT* WORRIES ME A LITLE BIT FOR SEVERAL REASONS.
THIS MEANS WE HAVE TO MAKE *ANOTHER* PEANUT BUTTER, JELLY & KUNG FU SANDWICH.
MAKE *ANOTHER* ONE? I KNOW MOM'S NOT GOING TO LIKE THIS AT ALL.
THEN WE WILL MAKE HER ONE, TOO.

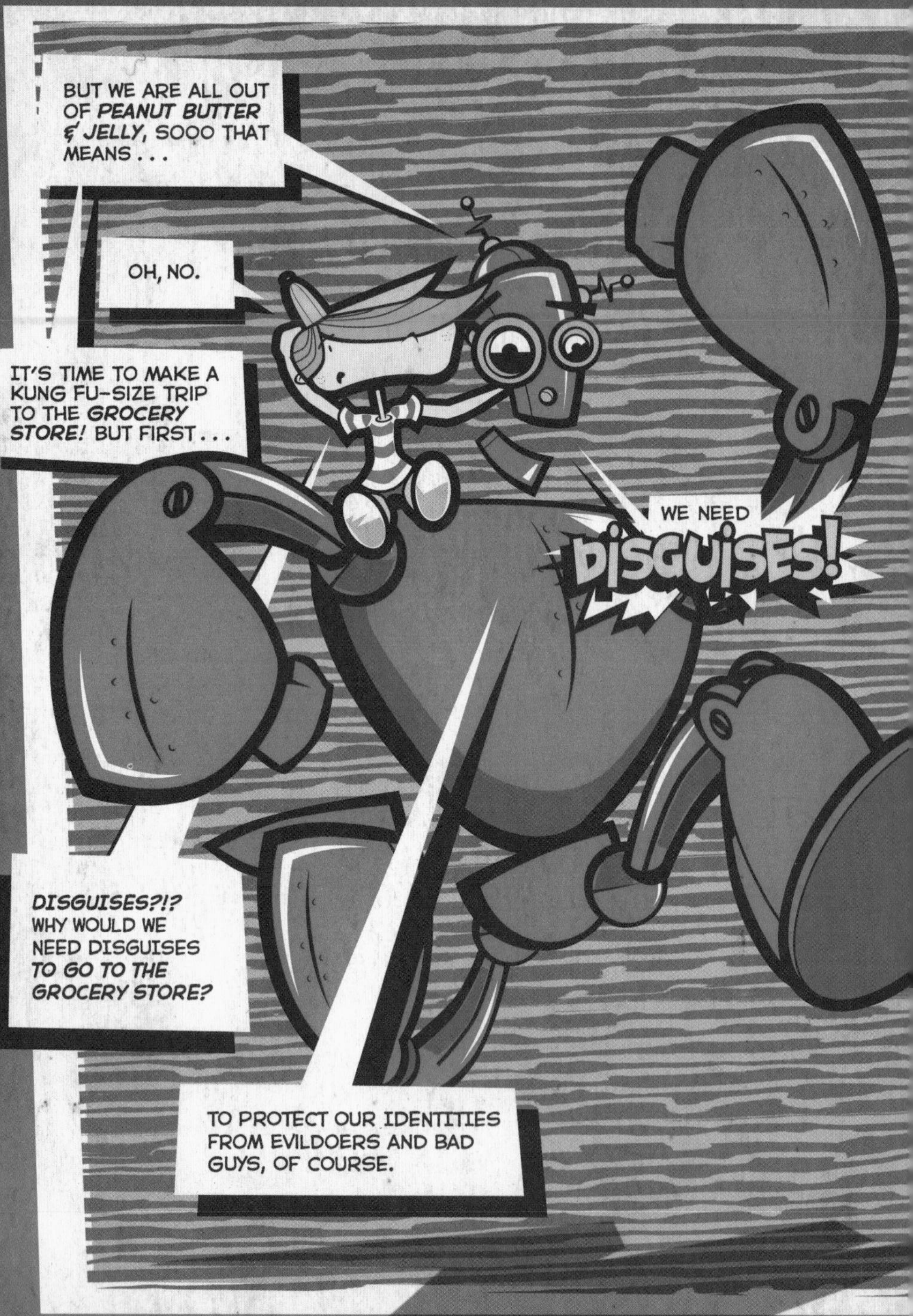
BUT WE ARE ALL OUT OF *PEANUT BUTTER & JELLY*, SOOO THAT MEANS . . .
OH, NO.
IT'S TIME TO MAKE A KUNG FU-SIZE TRIP TO THE *GROCERY STORE!* BUT FIRST . . .
WE NEED
DISGUISES!
DISGUISES?!? WHY WOULD WE NEED DISGUISES *TO GO TO THE GROCERY STORE?*
TO PROTECT OUR IDENTITIES FROM EVILDOERS AND BAD GUYS, OF COURSE.

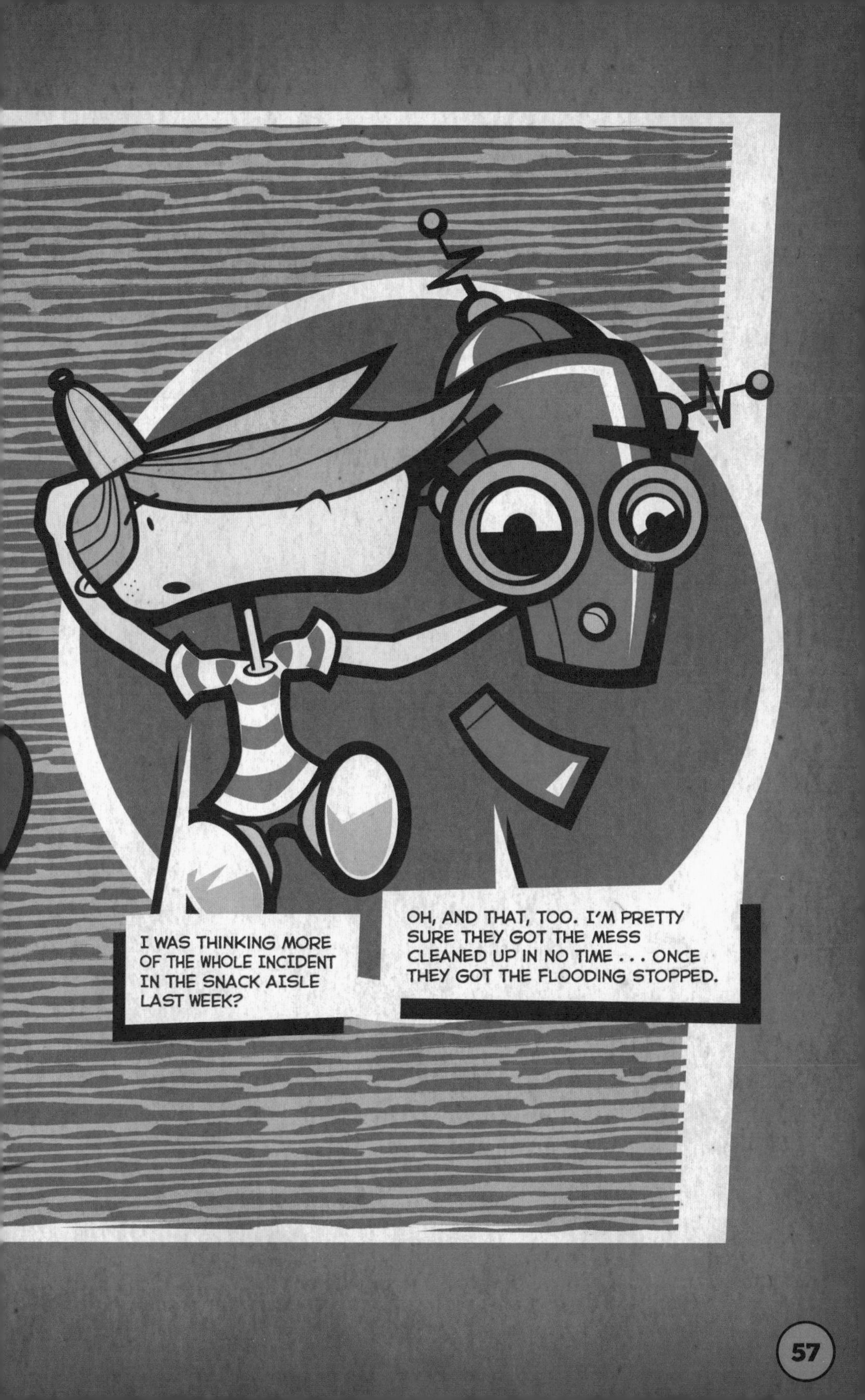
I WAS THINKING MORE OF THE WHOLE INCIDENT IN THE SNACK AISLE LAST WEEK?
OH, AND THAT, TOO. I'M PRETTY SURE THEY GOT THE MESS CLEANED UP IN NO TIME . . . ONCE THEY GOT THE FLOODING STOPPED.

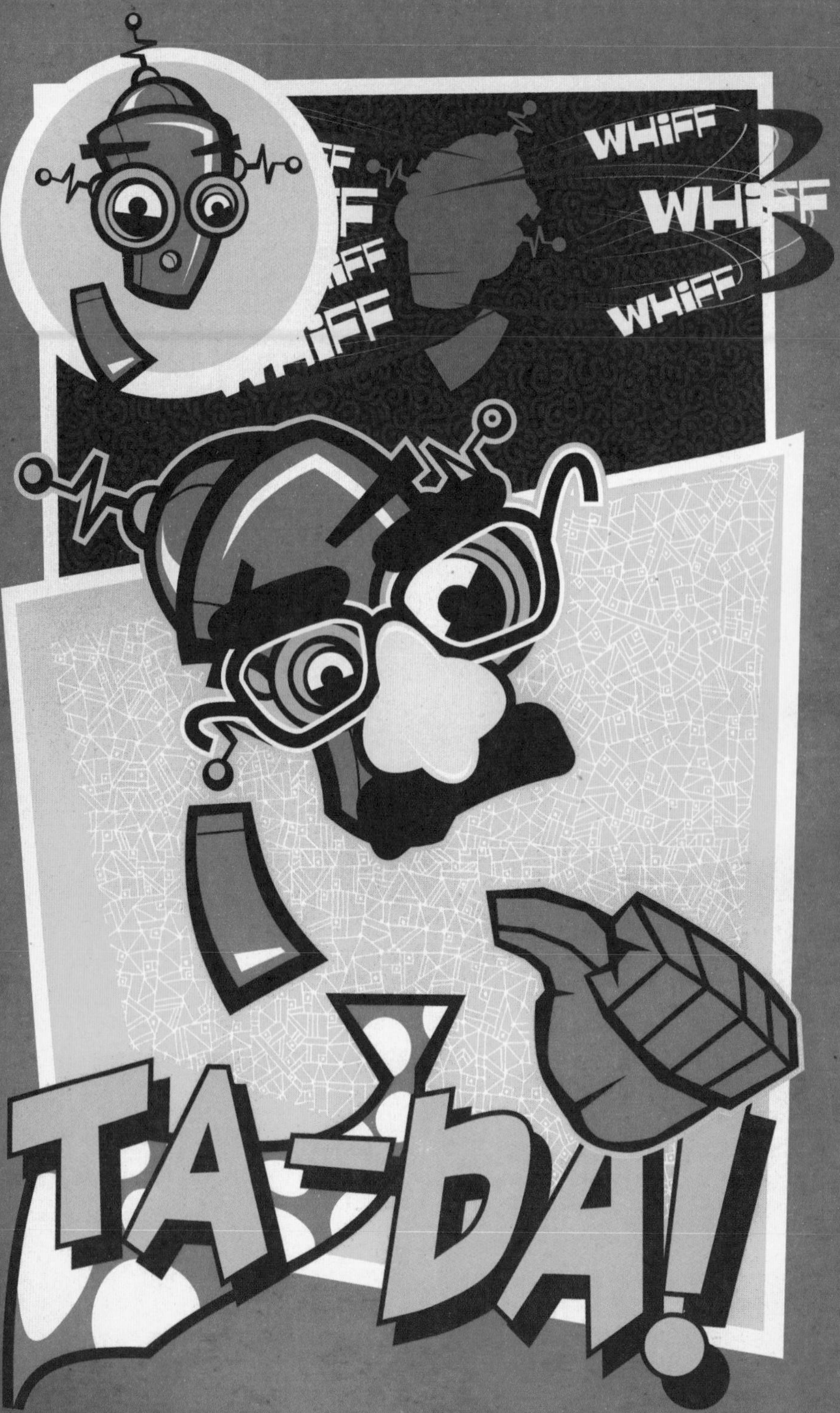
WHIFF
WHIFF
WHIFF
TA-DA!!

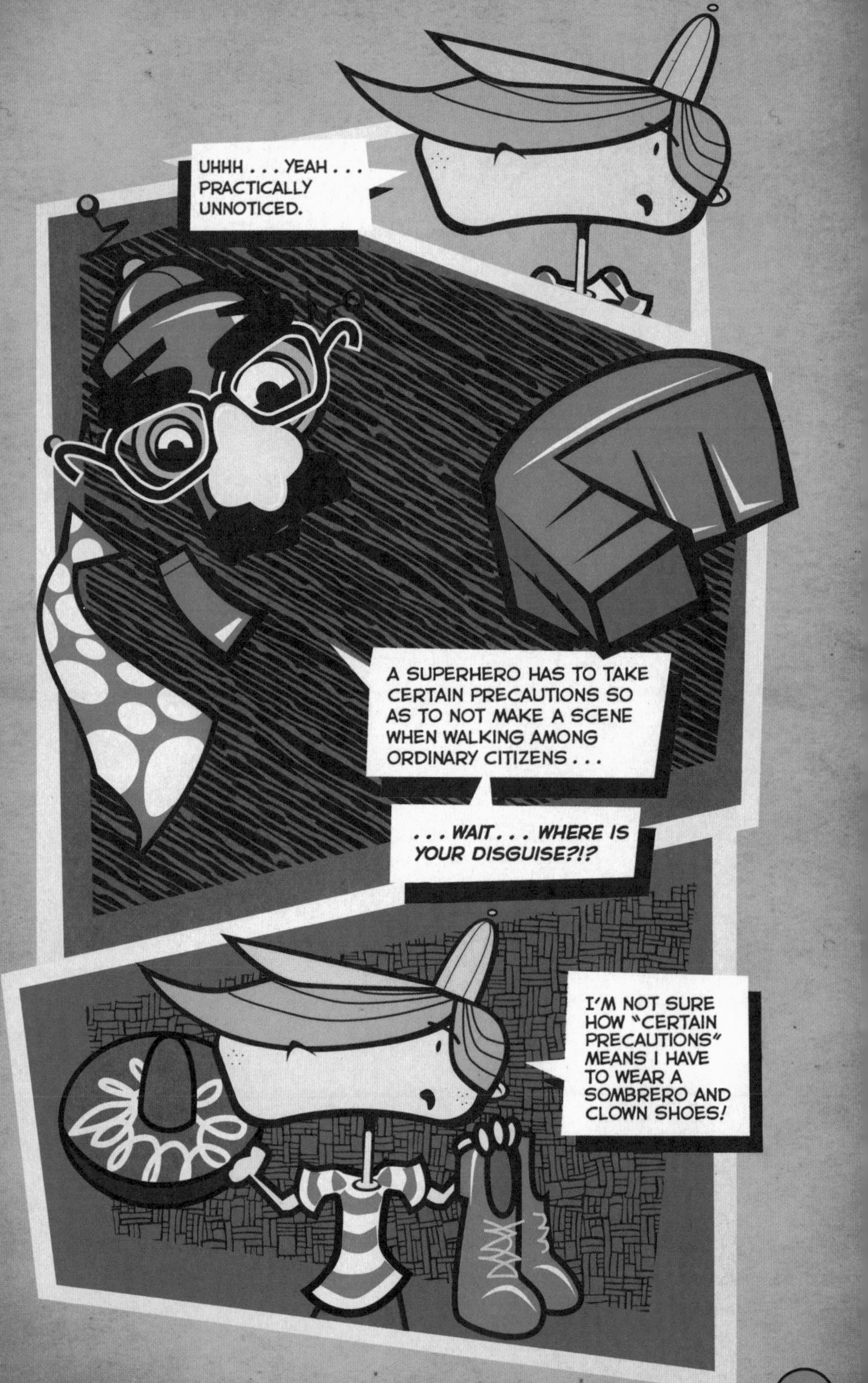
UHHH . . . YEAH . . . PRACTICALLY UNNOTICED.
A SUPERHERO HAS TO TAKE CERTAIN PRECAUTIONS SO AS TO NOT MAKE A SCENE WHEN WALKING AMONG ORDINARY CITIZENS . . .
. . . WAIT . . . WHERE IS YOUR DISGUISE?!?
I'M NOT SURE HOW "CERTAIN PRECAUTIONS" MEANS I HAVE TO WEAR A SOMBRERO AND CLOWN SHOES!

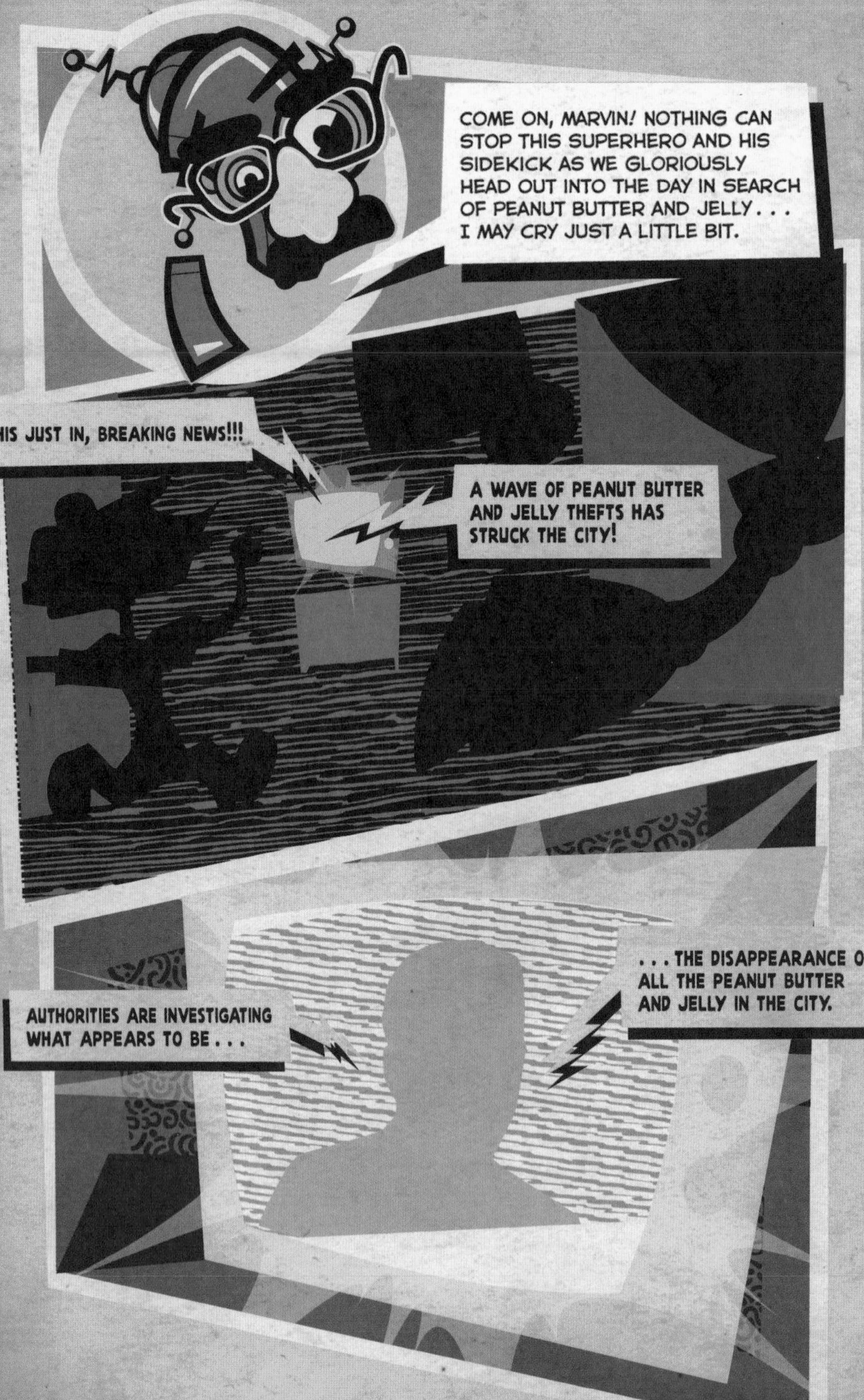
COME ON, MARVIN! NOTHING CAN STOP THIS SUPERHERO AND HIS SIDEKICK AS WE GLORIOUSLY HEAD OUT INTO THE DAY IN SEARCH OF PEANUT BUTTER AND JELLY . . . I MAY CRY JUST A LITTLE BIT.
THIS JUST IN, BREAKING NEWS!!!
A WAVE OF PEANUT BUTTER AND JELLY THEFTS HAS STRUCK THE CITY!
AUTHORITIES ARE INVESTIGATING WHAT APPEARS TO BE . . .
. . . THE DISAPPEARANCE OF ALL THE PEANUT BUTTER AND JELLY IN THE CITY.

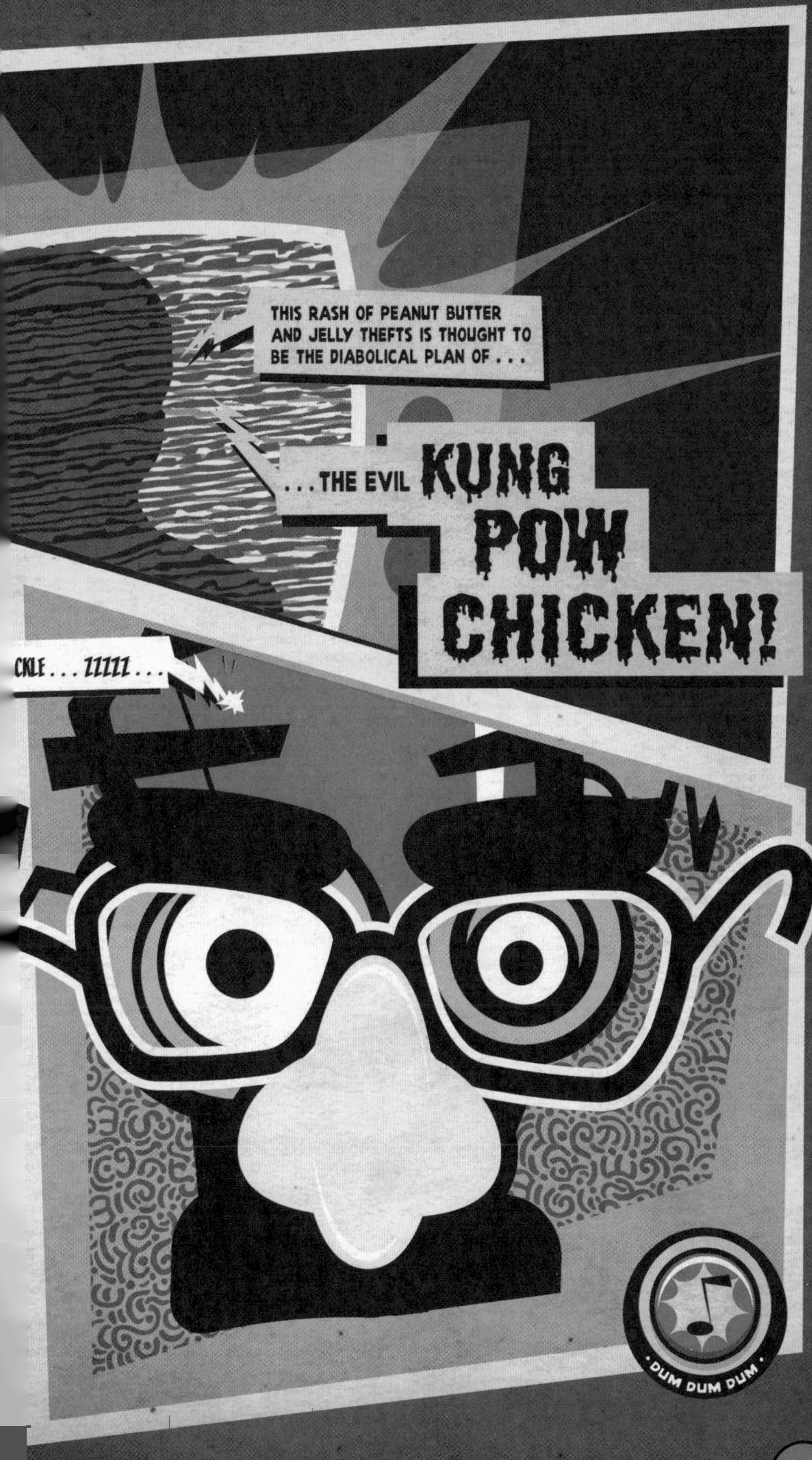
THIS RASH OF PEANUT BUTTER AND JELLY THEFTS IS THOUGHT TO BE THE DIABOLICAL PLAN OF . . .
. . . THE EVIL KUNG POW CHICKEN!
CKLE . . . ZZZZZ . . .
DUM DUM DUM

CHAPTER 2

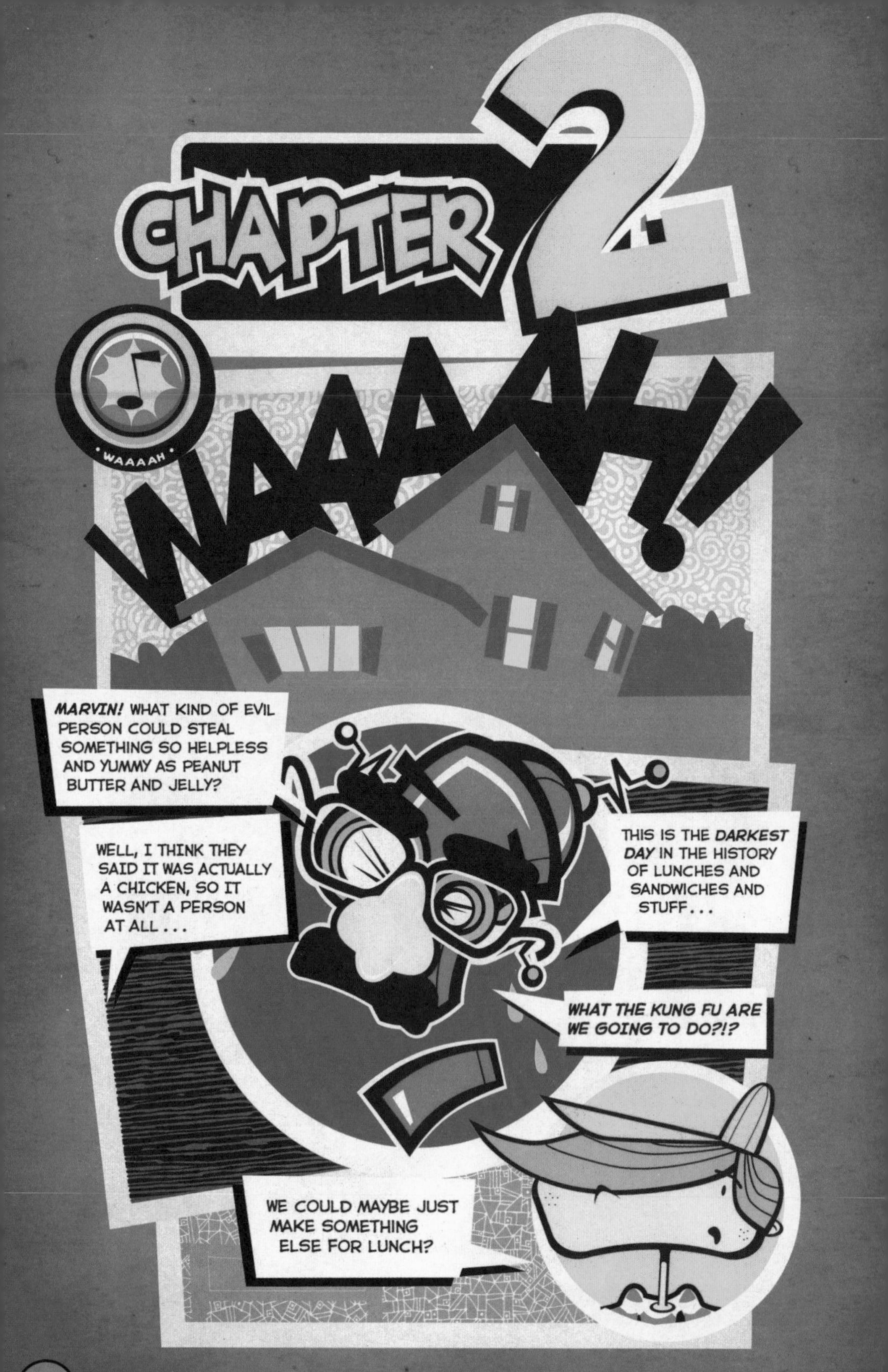
WAAAAH
WAAAH!
MARVIN! WHAT KIND OF EVIL PERSON COULD STEAL SOMETHING SO HELPLESS AND YUMMY AS PEANUT BUTTER AND JELLY?
WELL, I THINK THEY SAID IT WAS ACTUALLY A CHICKEN, SO IT WASN'T A PERSON AT ALL . . .
THIS IS THE *DARKEST DAY* IN THE HISTORY OF LUNCHES AND SANDWICHES AND STUFF . . .
WHAT THE KUNG FU ARE WE GOING TO DO?!?
WE COULD MAYBE JUST MAKE SOMETHING ELSE FOR LUNCH?

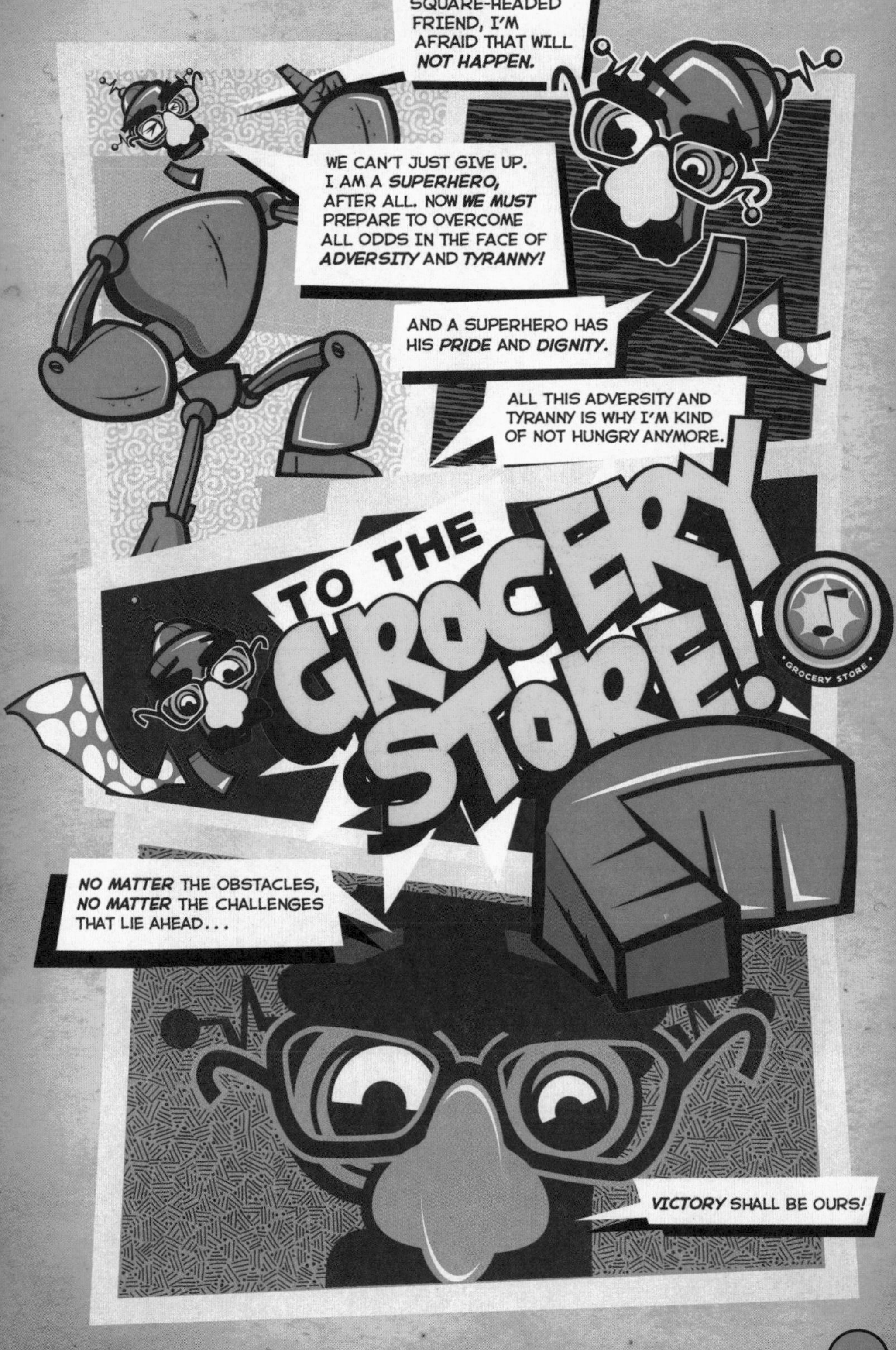
MARVIN, MY SQUARE-HEADED FRIEND, I'M AFRAID THAT WILL NOT HAPPEN.
WE CAN'T JUST GIVE UP. I AM A SUPERHERO, AFTER ALL. NOW WE MUST PREPARE TO OVERCOME ALL ODDS IN THE FACE OF ADVERSITY AND TYRANNY!
AND A SUPERHERO HAS HIS PRIDE AND DIGNITY.
ALL THIS ADVERSITY AND TYRANNY IS WHY I'M KIND OF NOT HUNGRY ANYMORE.
TO THE GROCERY STORE!
GROCERY STORE
NO MATTER THE OBSTACLES, NO MATTER THE CHALLENGES THAT LIE AHEAD...
VICTORY SHALL BE OURS!

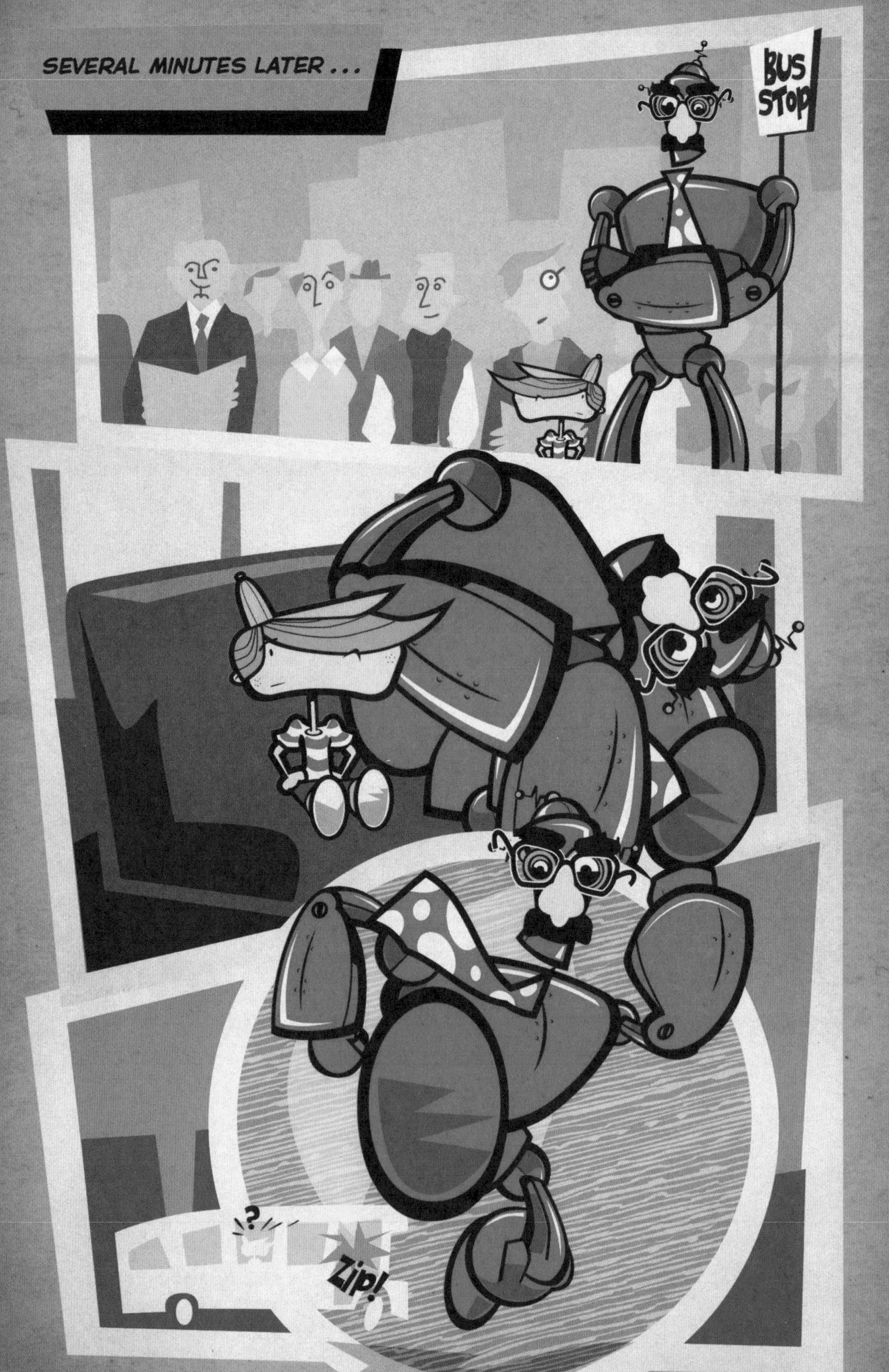
SEVERAL MINUTES LATER . . .
BUS STOP
?
ZIP!

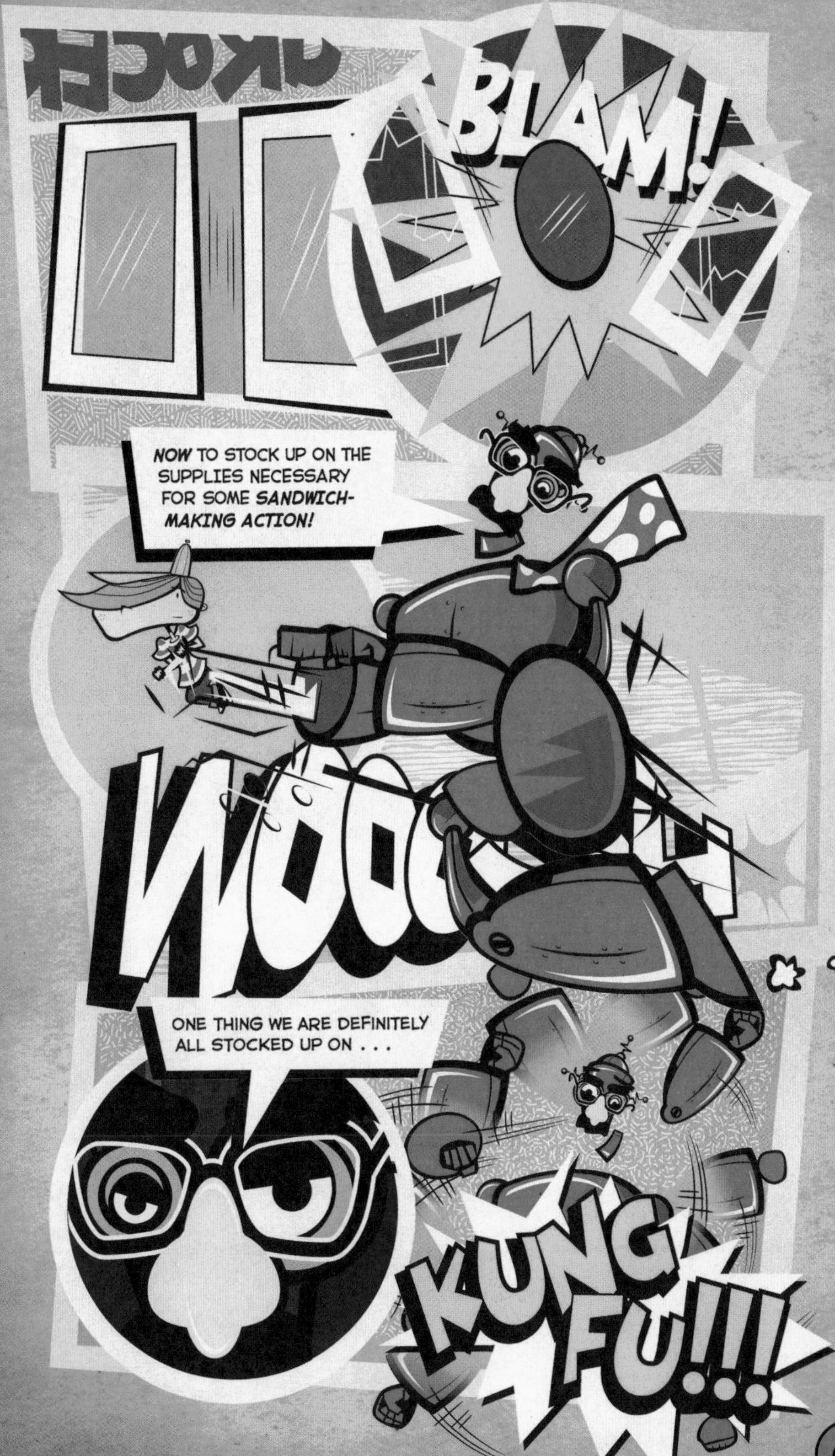
BLAM!
NOW TO STOCK UP ON THE SUPPLIES NECESSARY FOR SOME *SANDWICH-MAKING ACTION!*
ONE THING WE ARE DEFINITELY ALL STOCKED UP ON . . .
KUNG FU!!!

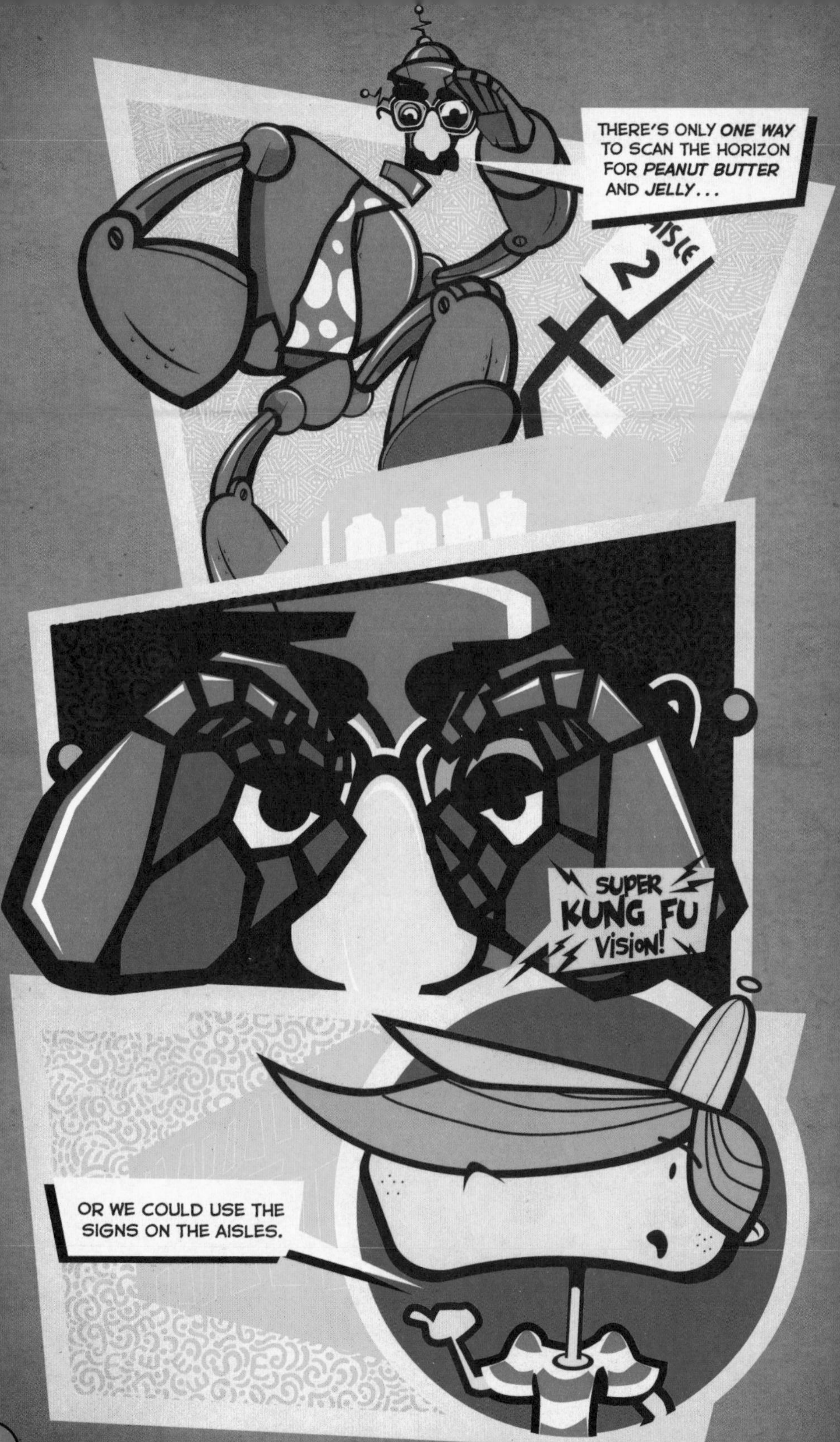
THERE'S ONLY ONE WAY TO SCAN THE HORIZON FOR PEANUT BUTTER AND JELLY...
AISLE 2
SUPER KUNG FU VISION!
OR WE COULD USE THE SIGNS ON THE AISLES.

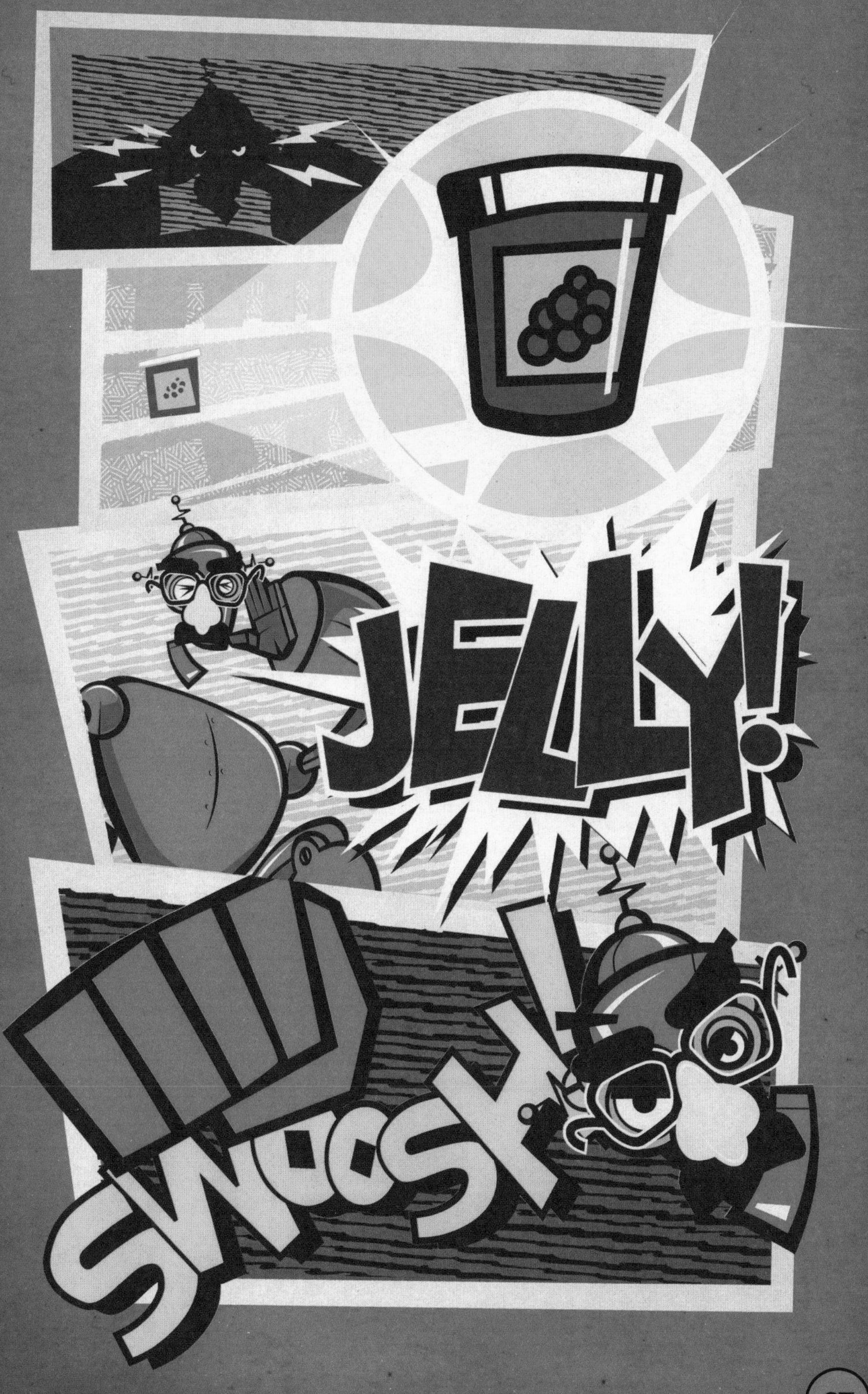
JELLY!
SWOOSH!

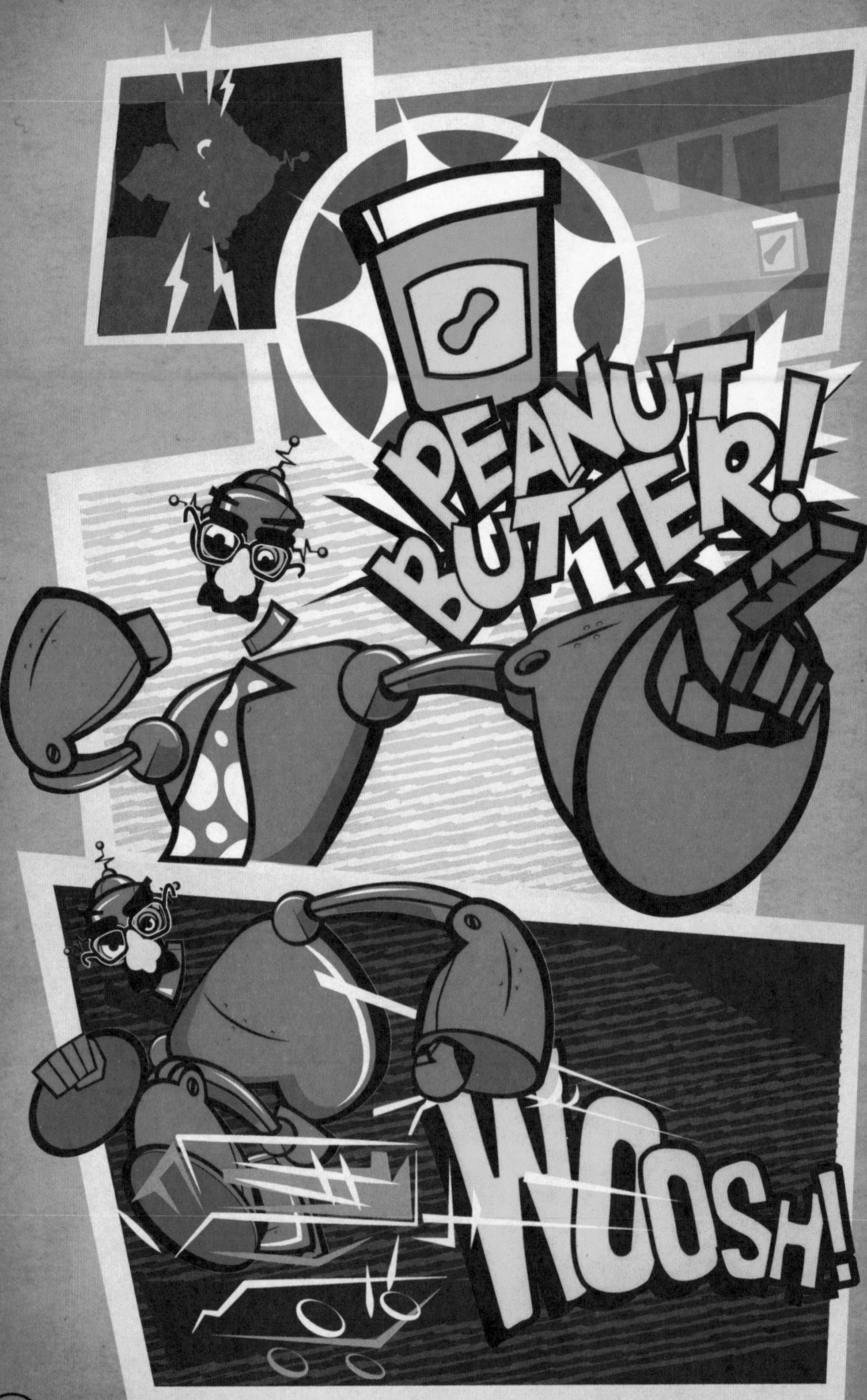
PEANUT BUTTER!
WOOSH!

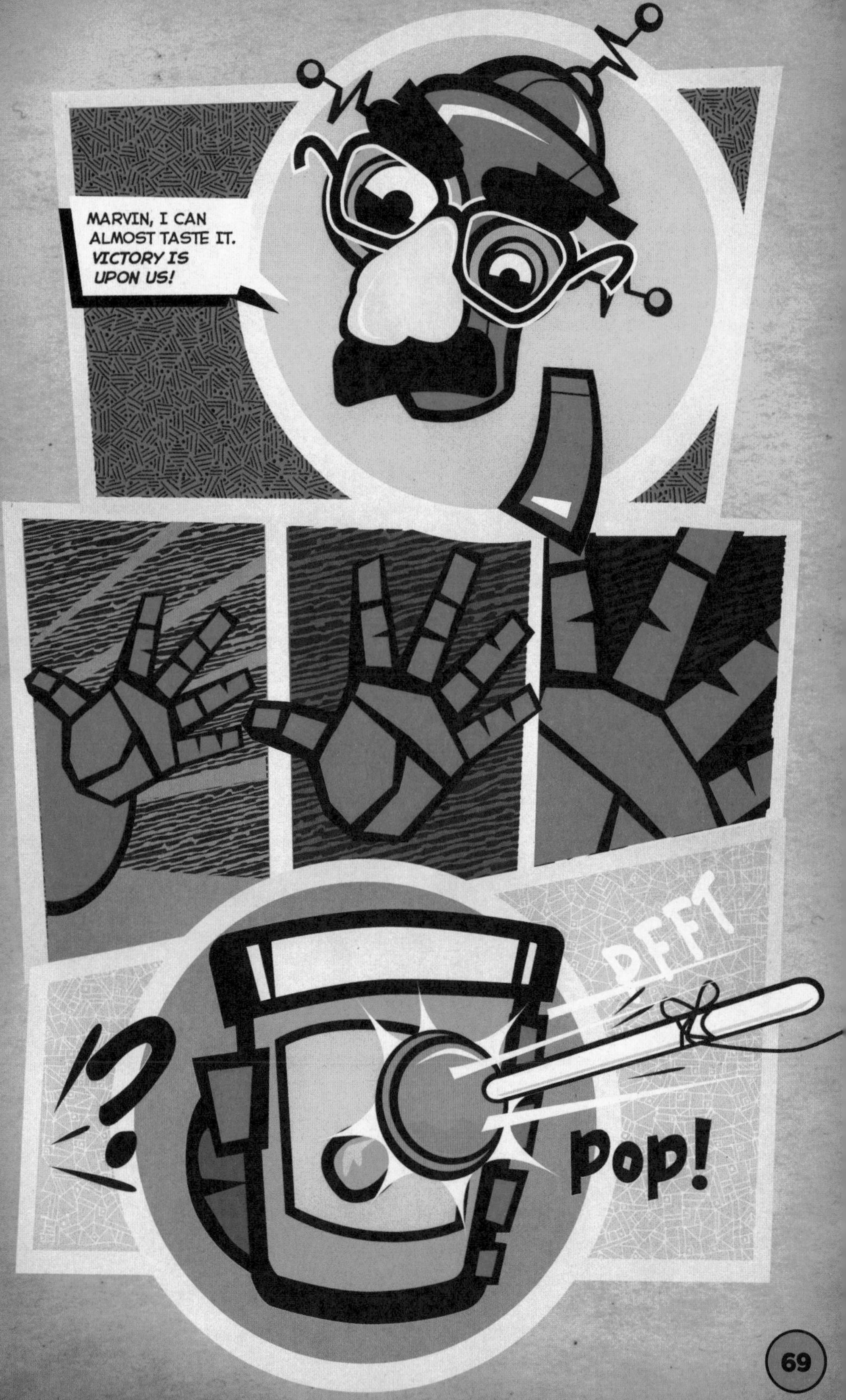
MARVIN, I CAN ALMOST TASTE IT. *VICTORY IS UPON US!*
PFFT
pop!

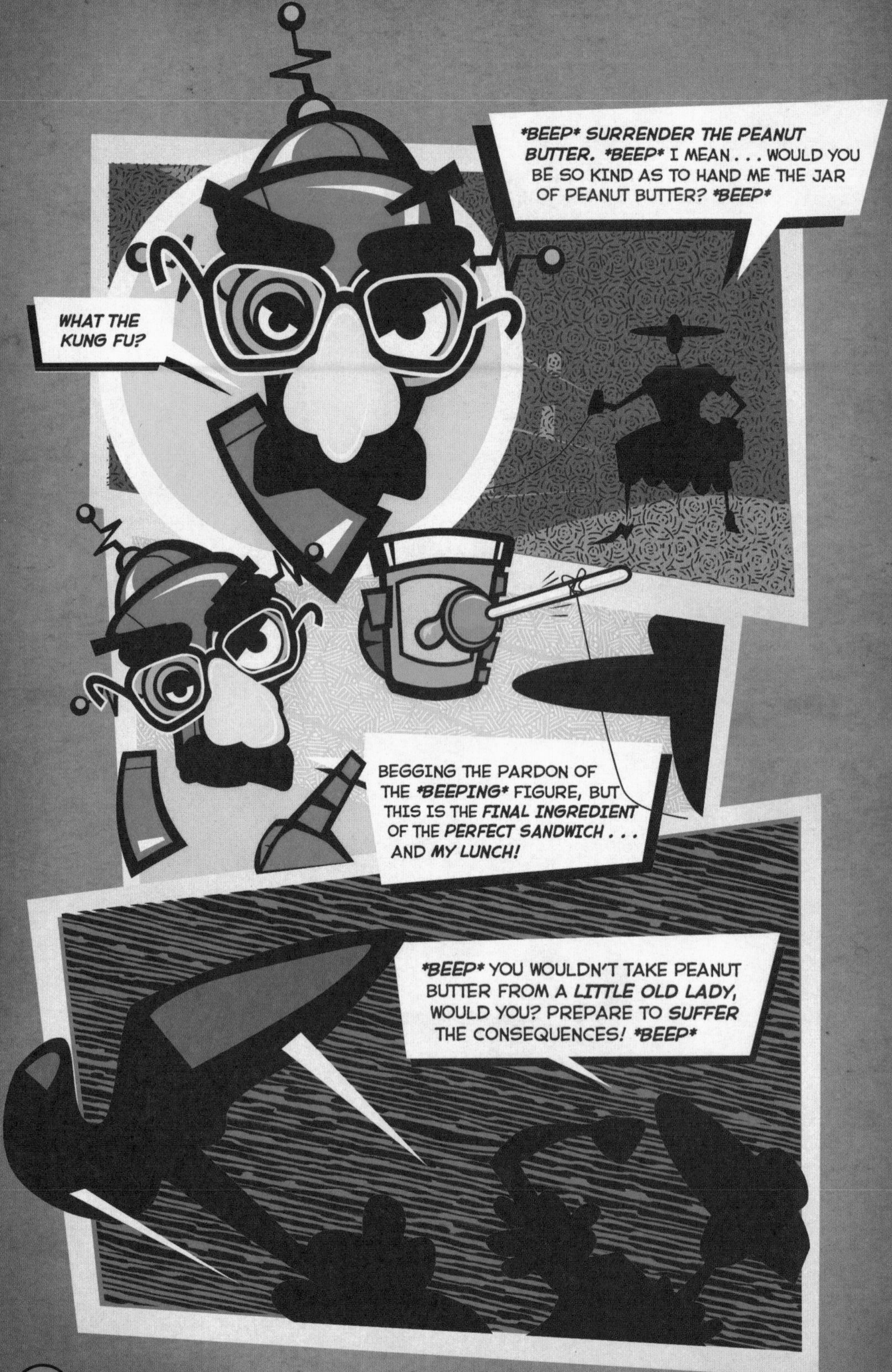
BEEP SURRENDER THE PEANUT BUTTER. *BEEP* I MEAN . . . WOULD YOU BE SO KIND AS TO HAND ME THE JAR OF PEANUT BUTTER? *BEEP*
WHAT THE KUNG FU?
BEGGING THE PARDON OF THE *BEEPING* FIGURE, BUT THIS IS THE FINAL INGREDIENT OF THE PERFECT SANDWICH . . . AND MY LUNCH!
BEEP YOU WOULDN'T TAKE PEANUT BUTTER FROM A LITTLE OLD LADY, WOULD YOU? PREPARE TO SUFFER THE CONSEQUENCES! *BEEP*

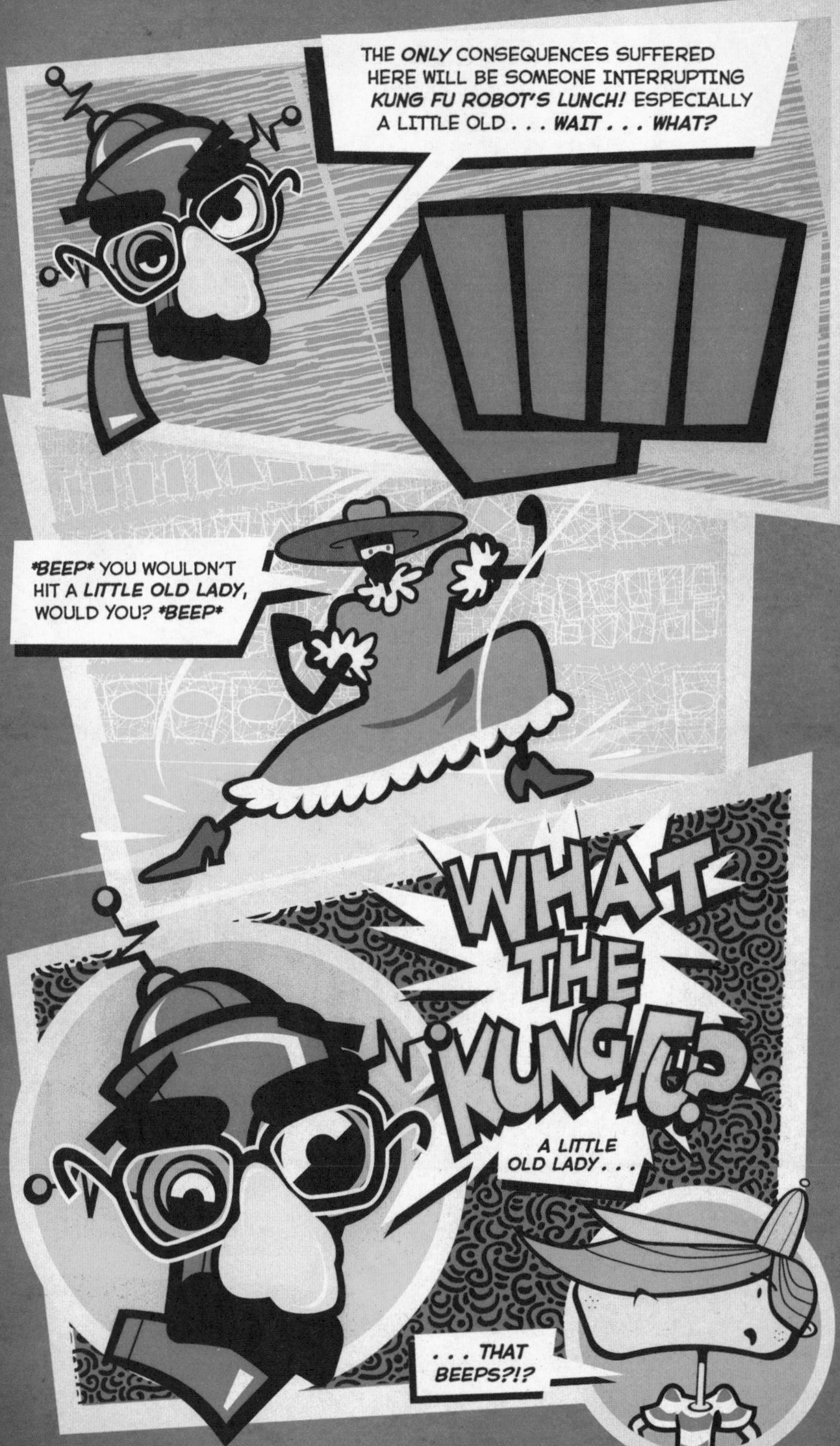
THE ONLY CONSEQUENCES SUFFERED HERE WILL BE SOMEONE INTERRUPTING KUNG FU ROBOT'S LUNCH! ESPECIALLY A LITTLE OLD . . . WAIT . . . WHAT?
BEEP YOU WOULDN'T HIT A LITTLE OLD LADY, WOULD YOU? *BEEP*
WHAT THE KUNG FU?
A LITTLE OLD LADY . . .
. . . THAT BEEPS?!?

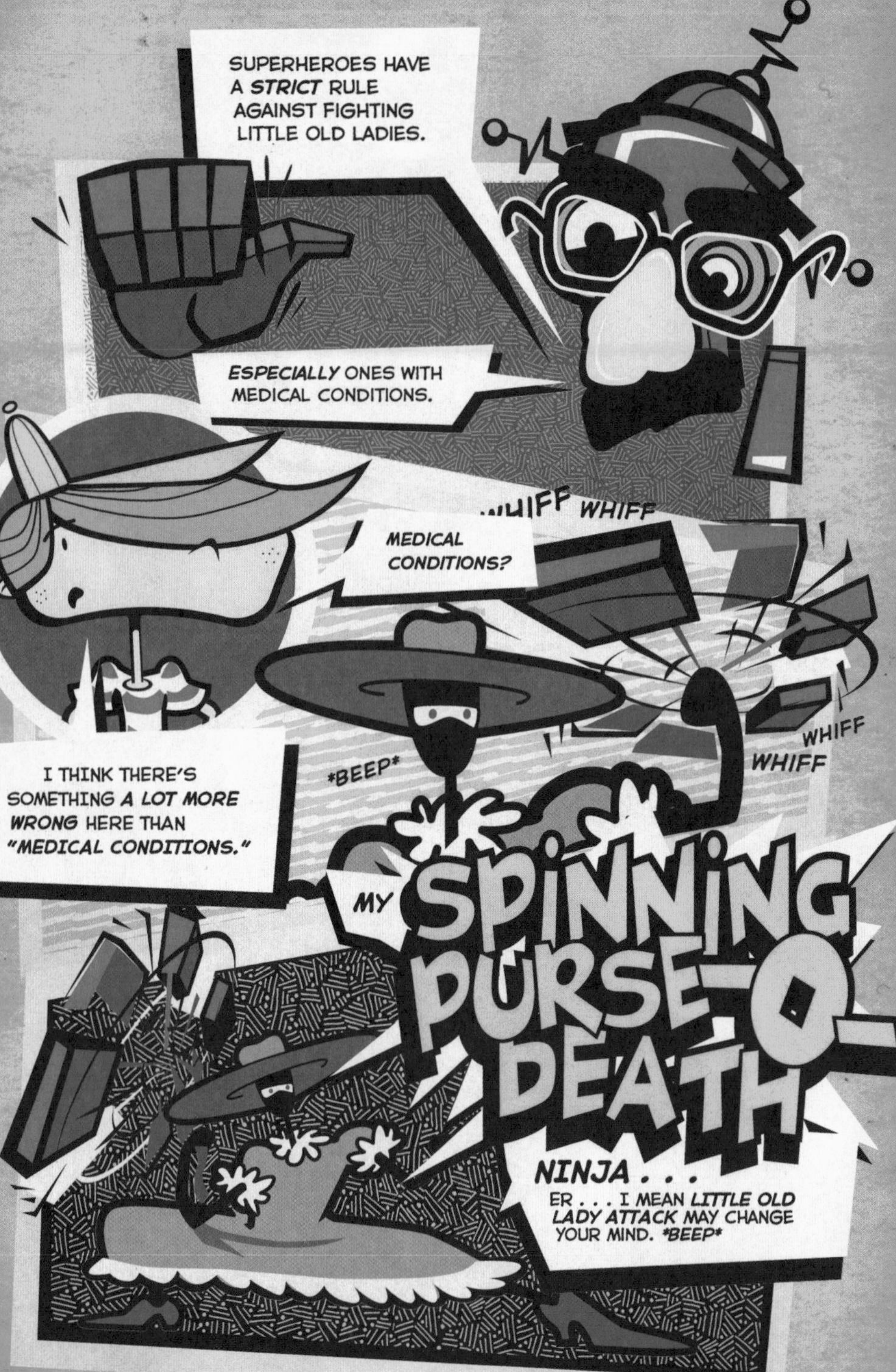
SUPERHEROES HAVE A STRICT RULE AGAINST FIGHTING LITTLE OLD LADIES.
ESPECIALLY ONES WITH MEDICAL CONDITIONS.
WHIFF WHIFF
MEDICAL CONDITIONS?
WHIFF
WHIFF
BEEP
I THINK THERE'S SOMETHING A LOT MORE WRONG HERE THAN "MEDICAL CONDITIONS."
MY SPINNING PURSE-O-DEATH
NINJA . . .
ER . . . I MEAN LITTLE OLD LADY ATTACK MAY CHANGE YOUR MIND. *BEEP*

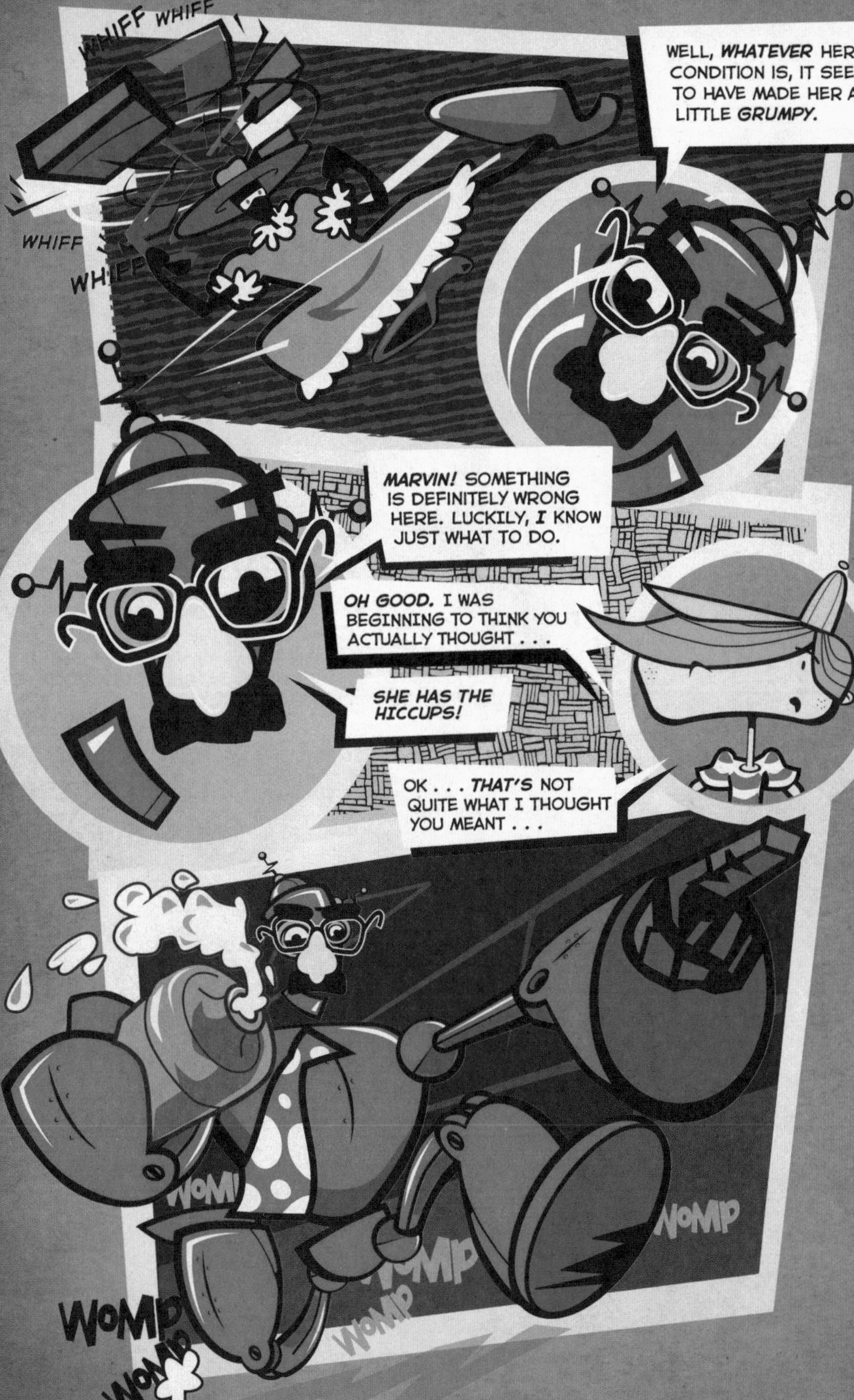
WHIFF WHIFF
WHIFF
WHIFF
WELL, WHATEVER HER CONDITION IS, IT SEEMS TO HAVE MADE HER A LITTLE GRUMPY.
MARVIN! SOMETHING IS DEFINITELY WRONG HERE. LUCKILY, I KNOW JUST WHAT TO DO.
OH GOOD. I WAS BEGINNING TO THINK YOU ACTUALLY THOUGHT . . .
SHE HAS THE HICCUPS!
OK . . . THAT'S NOT QUITE WHAT I THOUGHT YOU MEANT . . .
WOMP
WOMP
WOMP
WOMP
WOMP
WOMP

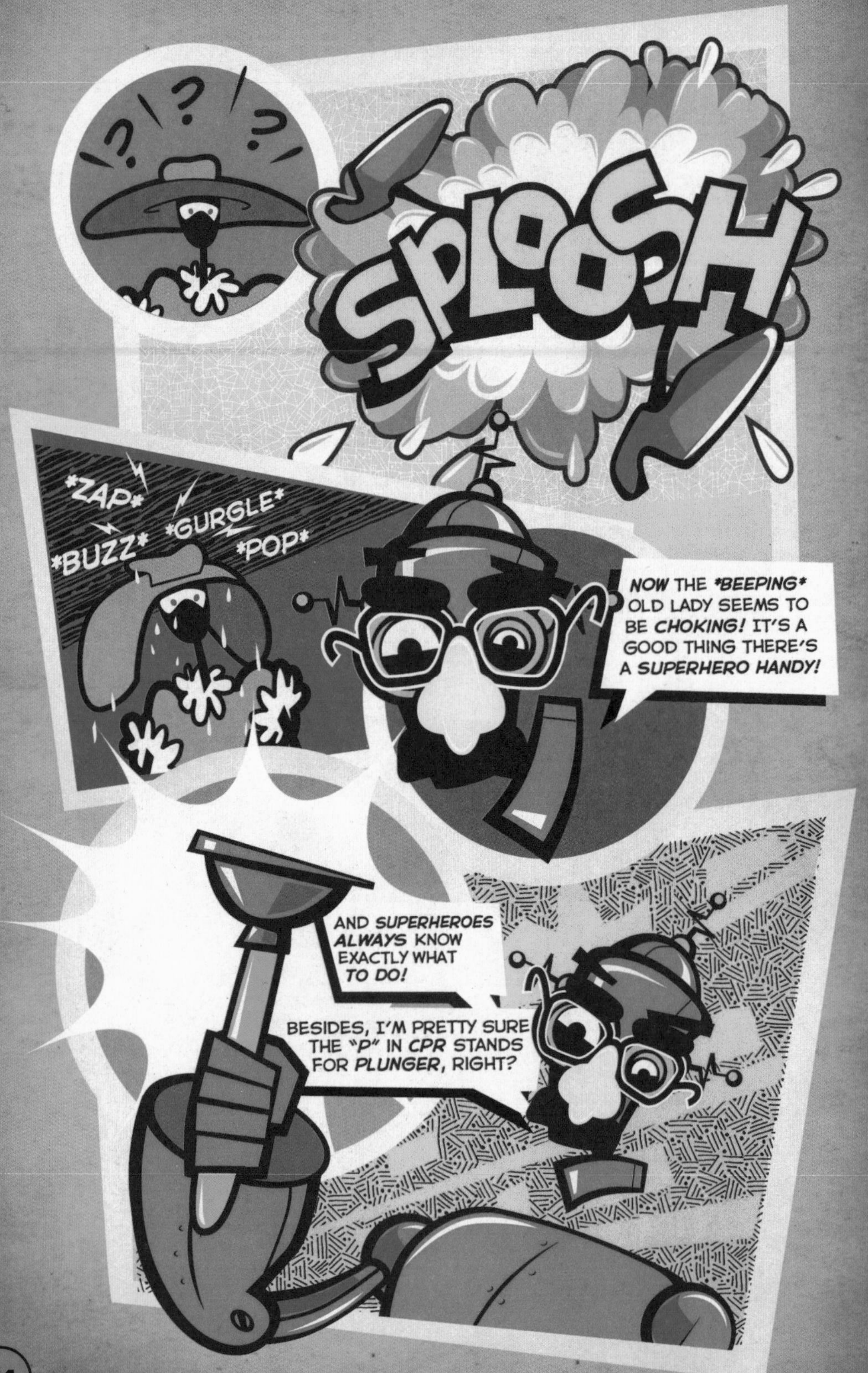
?!?!?!
SPLOOSH
ZAP
GURGLE
BUZZ
POP
NOW THE *BEEPING* OLD LADY SEEMS TO BE CHOKING! IT'S A GOOD THING THERE'S A SUPERHERO HANDY!
AND SUPERHEROES ALWAYS KNOW EXACTLY WHAT TO DO!
BESIDES, I'M PRETTY SURE THE "P" IN CPR STANDS FOR PLUNGER, RIGHT?

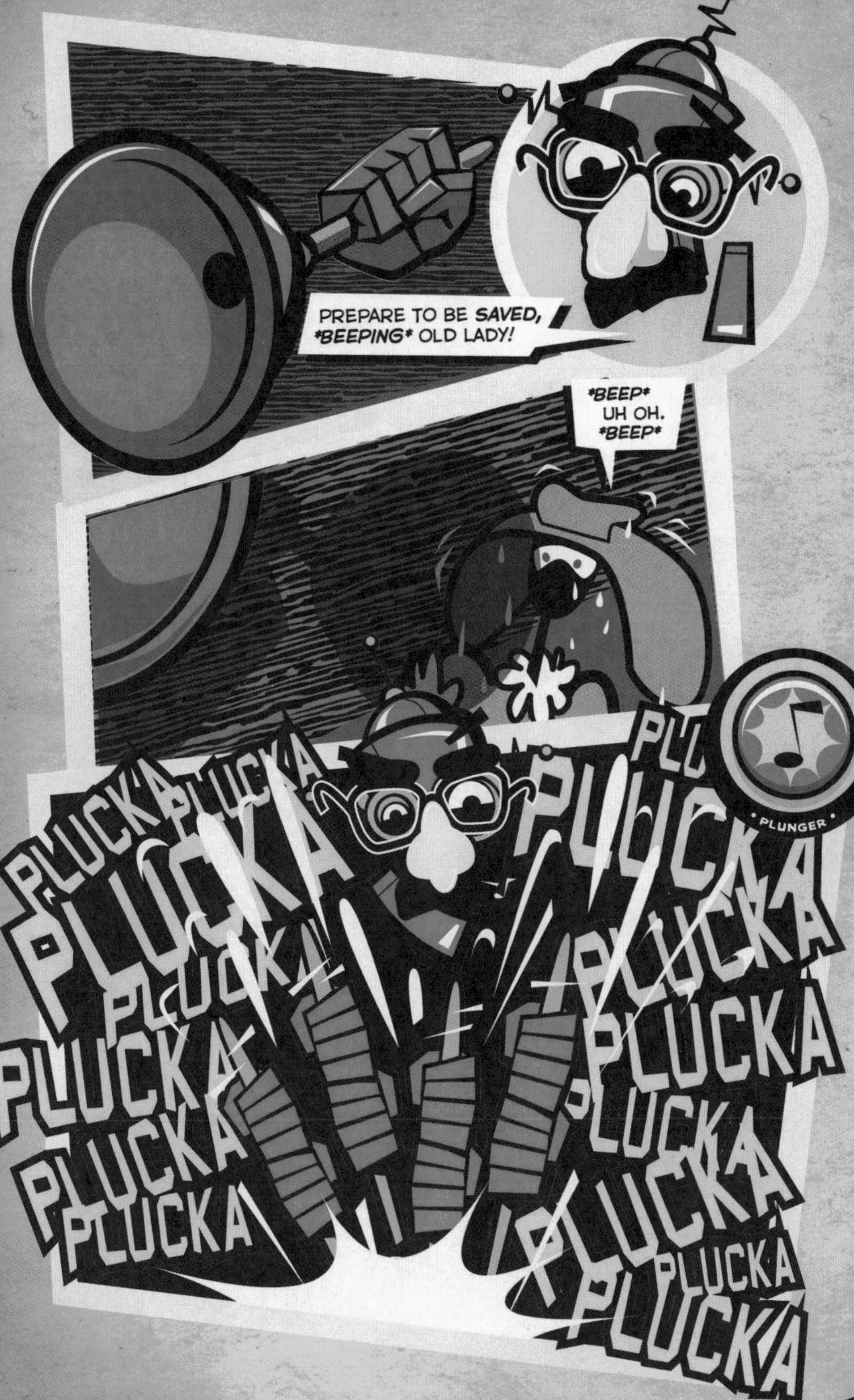

PREPARE TO BE SAVED, *BEEPING* OLD LADY!
BEEP UH OH. *BEEP*
PLUNGER
PLUCKA PLUCKA PLUCKA PLUCKA PLUCKA PLUCKA PLUCKA PLUCKA
PLUCKA PLUCKA PLUCKA PLUCKA PLUCKA PLUCKA PLUCKA PLUCKA

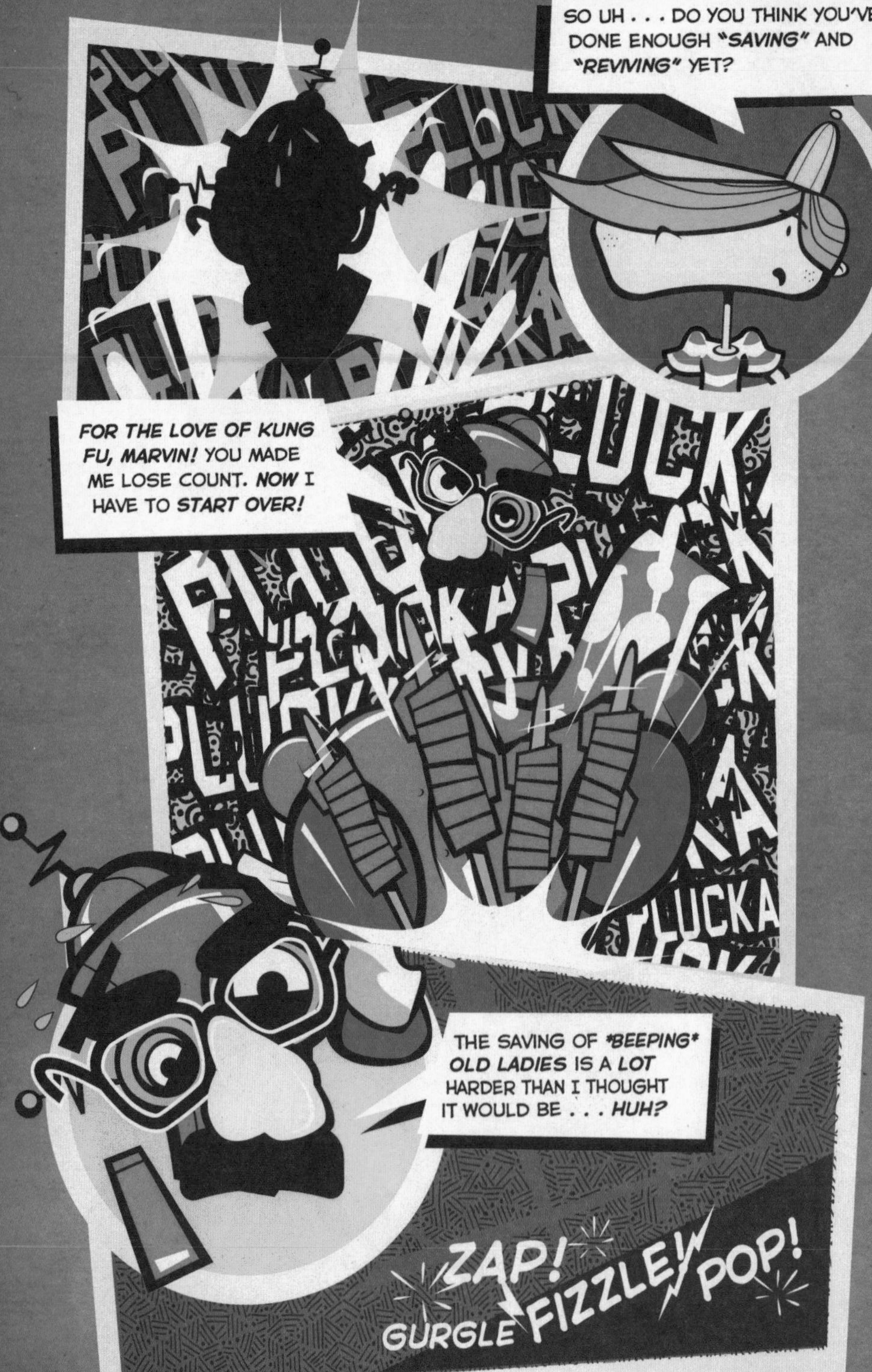
SO UH . . . DO YOU THINK YOU'VE DONE ENOUGH "SAVING" AND "REVIVING" YET?
FOR THE LOVE OF KUNG FU, MARVIN! YOU MADE ME LOSE COUNT. NOW I HAVE TO START OVER!
THE SAVING OF *BEEPING* OLD LADIES IS A LOT HARDER THAN I THOUGHT IT WOULD BE . . . HUH?
ZAP!
GURGLE
FIZZLE!
POP!

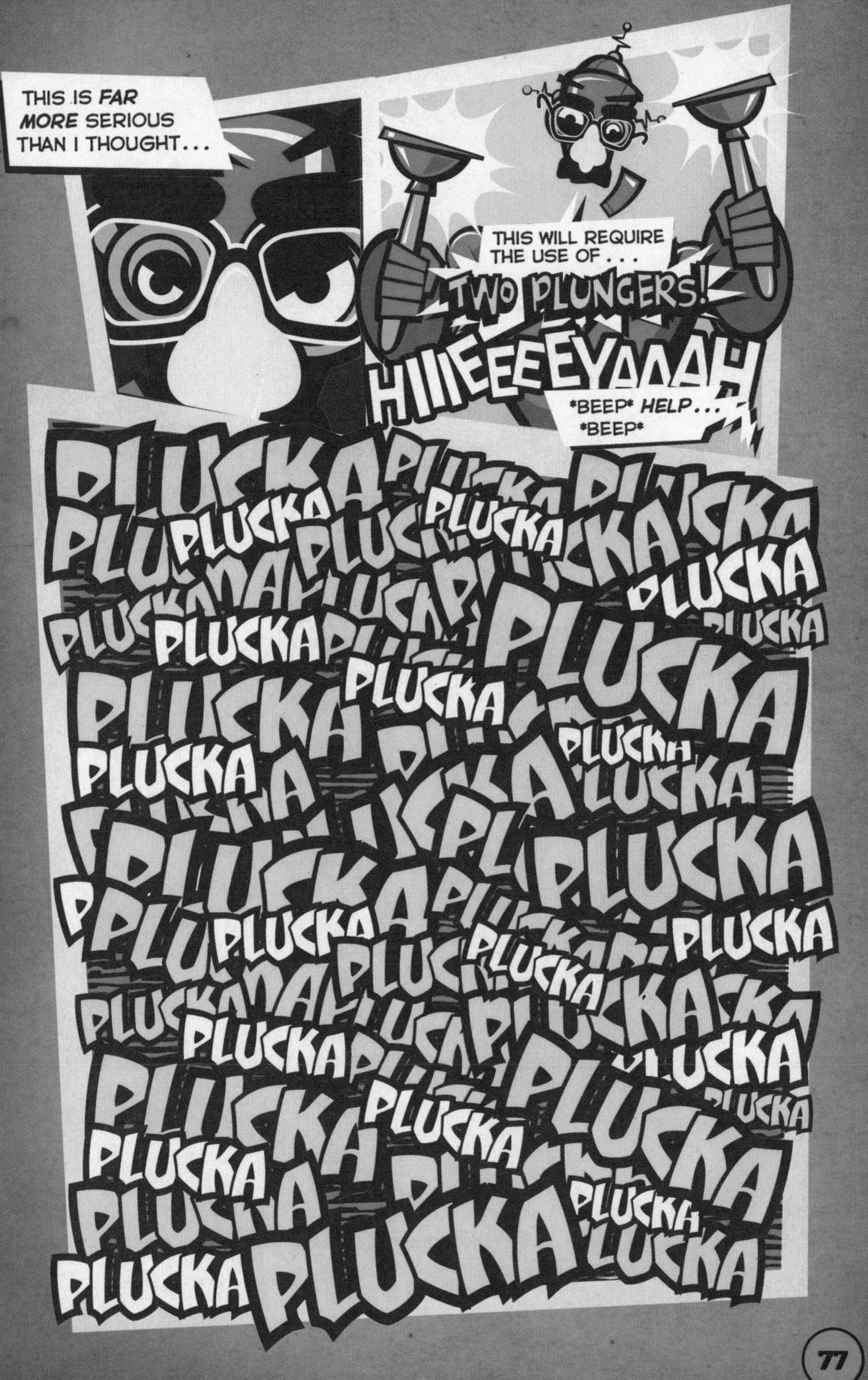
THIS IS *FAR MORE* SERIOUS THAN I THOUGHT . . .
THIS WILL REQUIRE THE USE OF . . .
TWO PLUNGERS!
HIIIEEEEYAAAH
BEEP *HELP . . .* *BEEP*
PLUCKA
PLUCKA
PLUCKA
PLUCKA
PLUCKA
PLUCKA
PLUCKA
PLUCKA

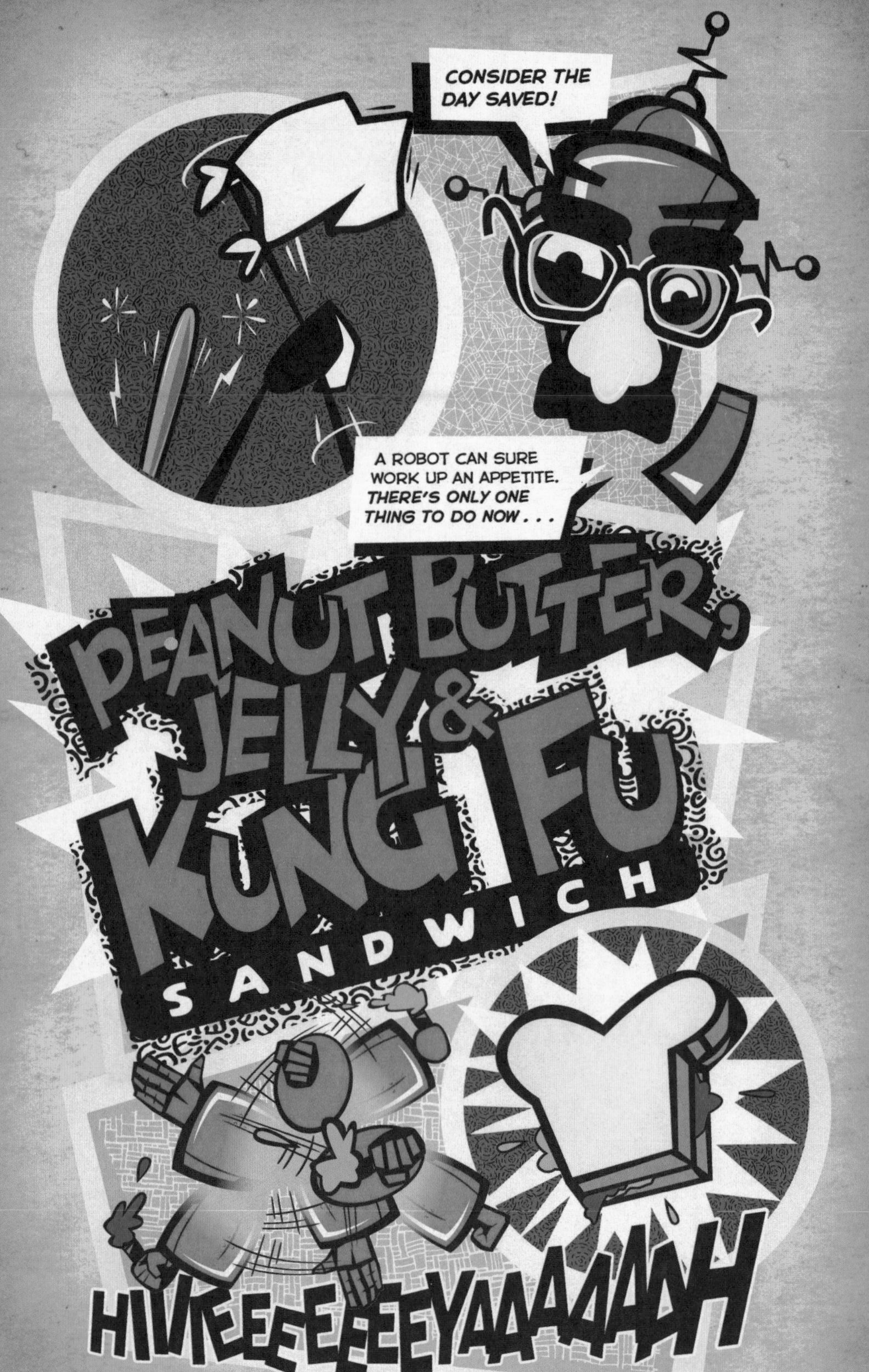
CONSIDER THE DAY SAVED!
A ROBOT CAN SURE WORK UP AN APPETITE. THERE'S ONLY ONE THING TO DO NOW . . .
PEANUT BUTTER, JELLY & KUNG FU SANDWICH
HIYEEEEEEEYAAAAAAH

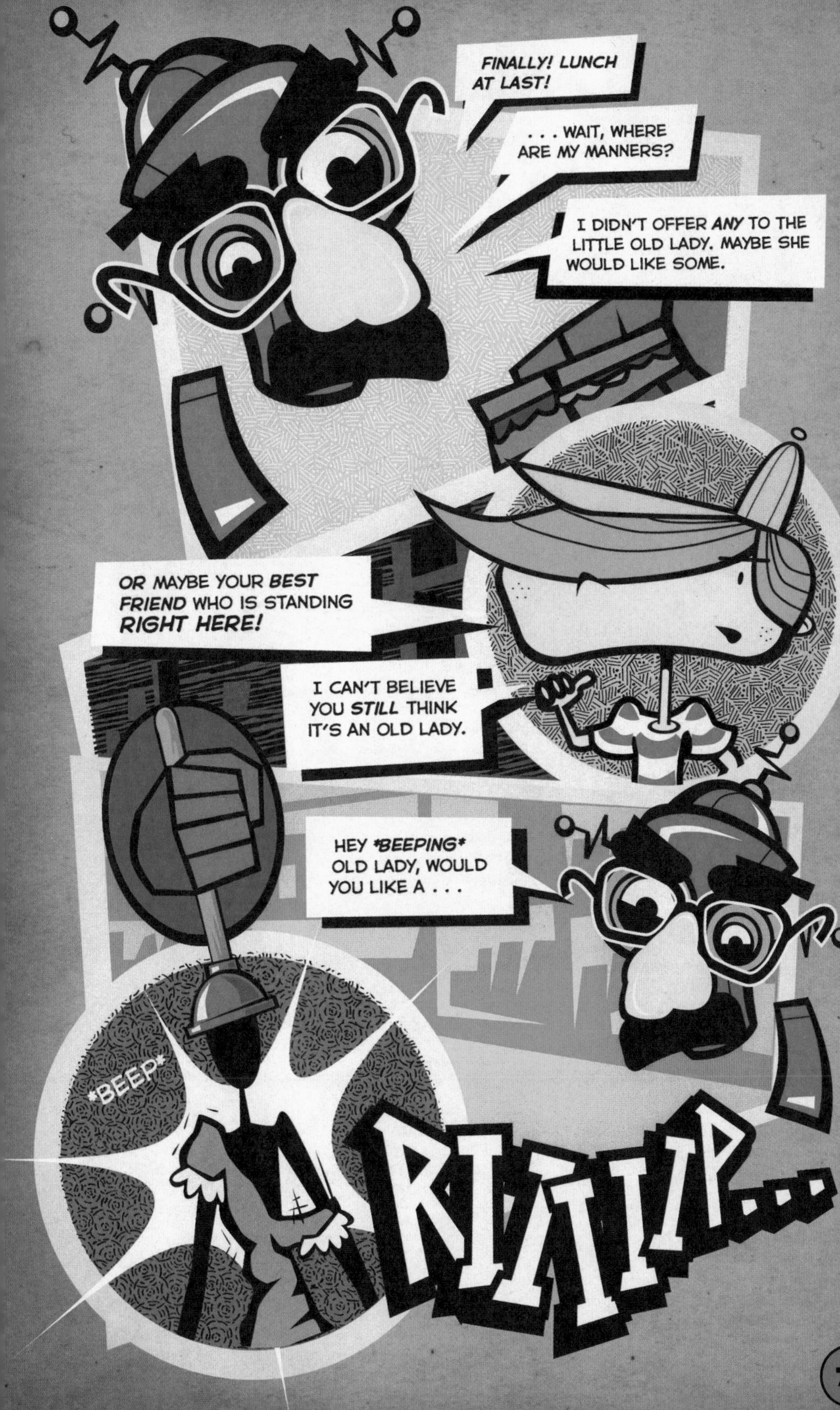
FINALLY! LUNCH AT LAST!
. . . WAIT, WHERE ARE MY MANNERS?
I DIDN'T OFFER ANY TO THE LITTLE OLD LADY. MAYBE SHE WOULD LIKE SOME.
OR MAYBE YOUR BEST FRIEND WHO IS STANDING RIGHT HERE!
I CAN'T BELIEVE YOU STILL THINK IT'S AN OLD LADY.
HEY *BEEPING* OLD LADY, WOULD YOU LIKE A . . .
BEEP
RIIIIP...

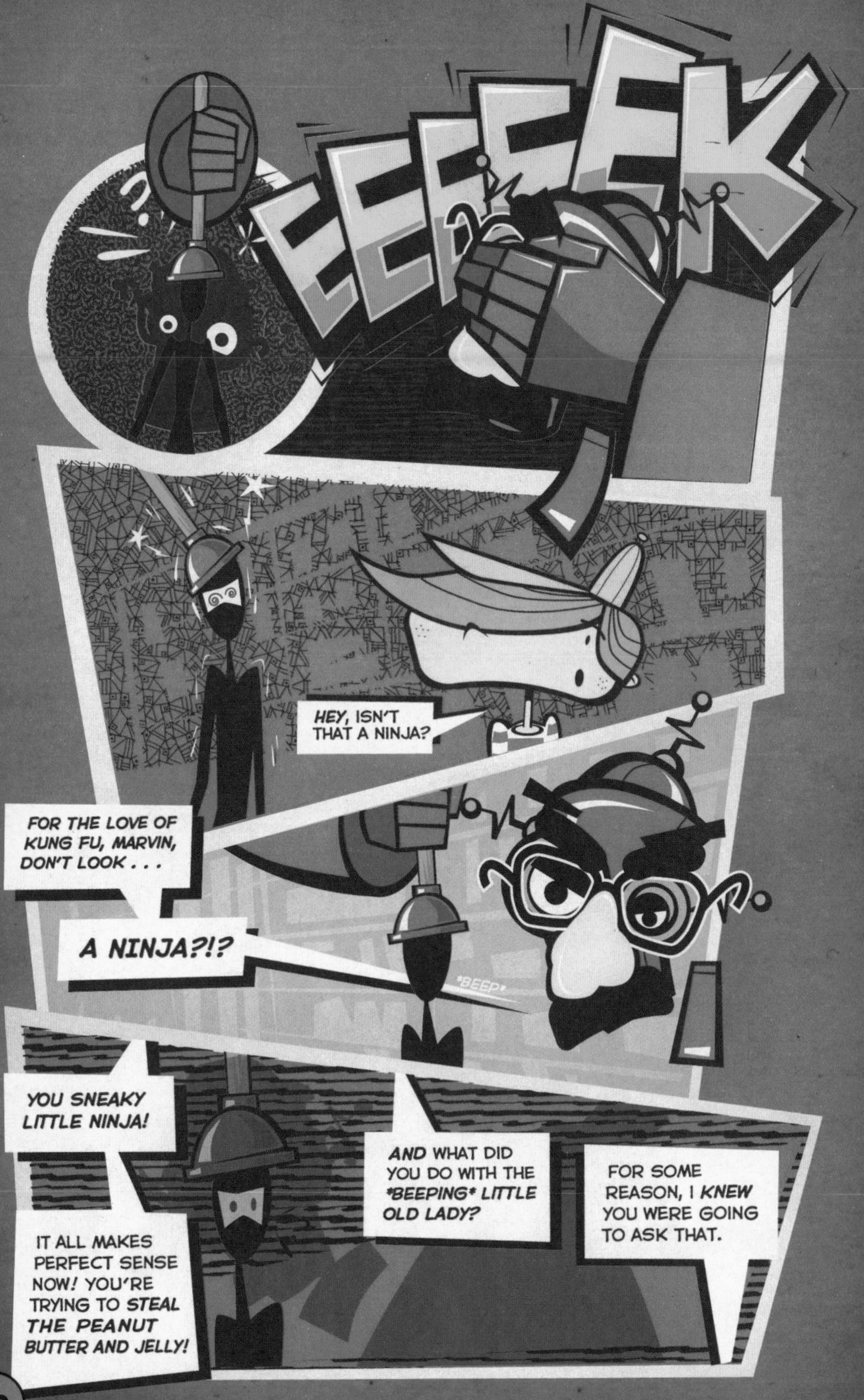
EEEEEK
HEY, ISN'T THAT A NINJA?
FOR THE LOVE OF KUNG FU, MARVIN, DON'T LOOK . . .
A NINJA?!?
BEEP
YOU SNEAKY LITTLE NINJA!
IT ALL MAKES PERFECT SENSE NOW! YOU'RE TRYING TO STEAL THE PEANUT BUTTER AND JELLY!
AND WHAT DID YOU DO WITH THE *BEEPING* LITTLE OLD LADY?
FOR SOME REASON, I KNEW YOU WERE GOING TO ASK THAT.

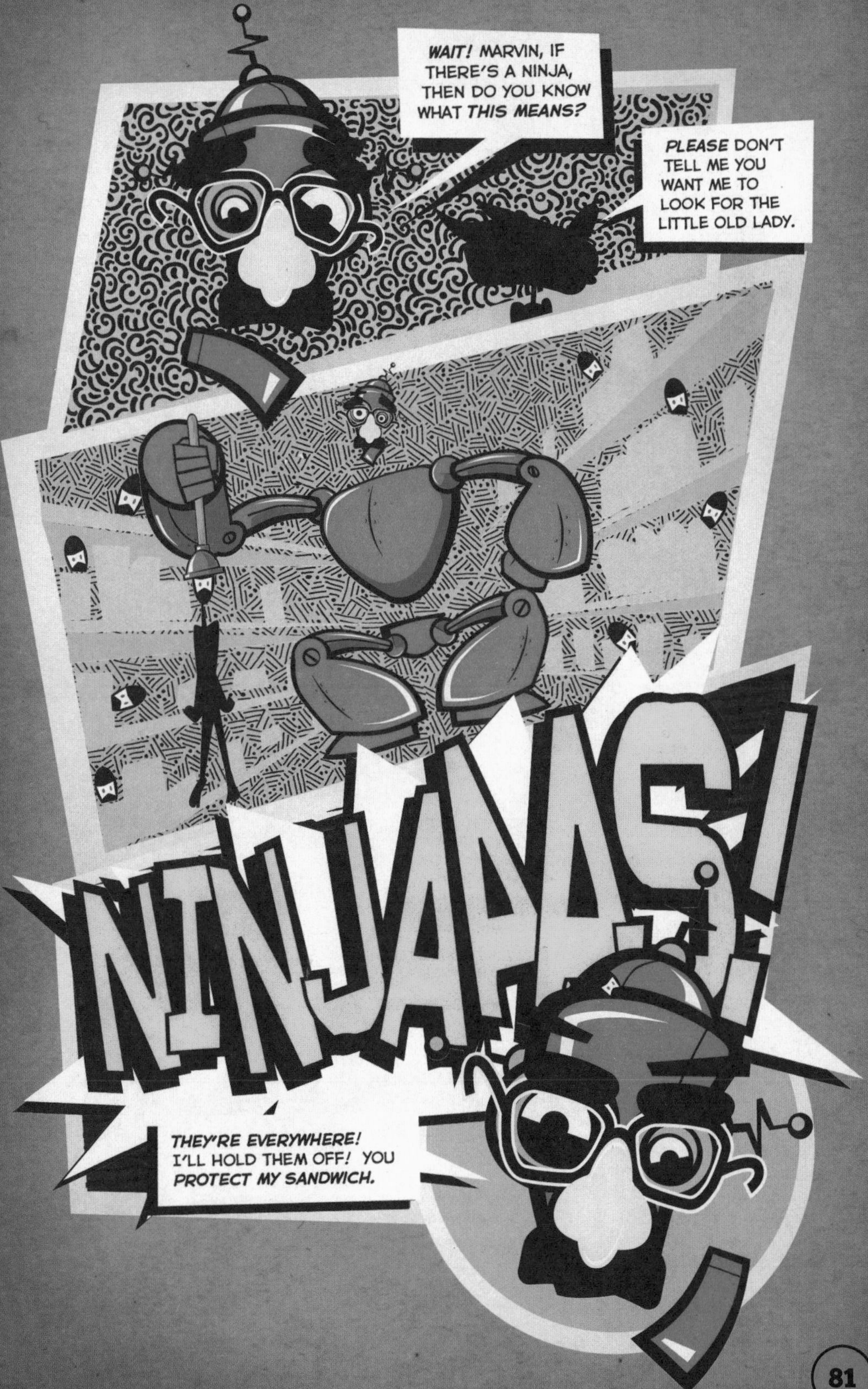
WAIT! MARVIN, IF THERE'S A NINJA, THEN DO YOU KNOW WHAT THIS MEANS?
PLEASE DON'T TELL ME YOU WANT ME TO LOOK FOR THE LITTLE OLD LADY.
NINJAPAS!
THEY'RE EVERYWHERE! I'LL HOLD THEM OFF! YOU PROTECT MY SANDWICH.

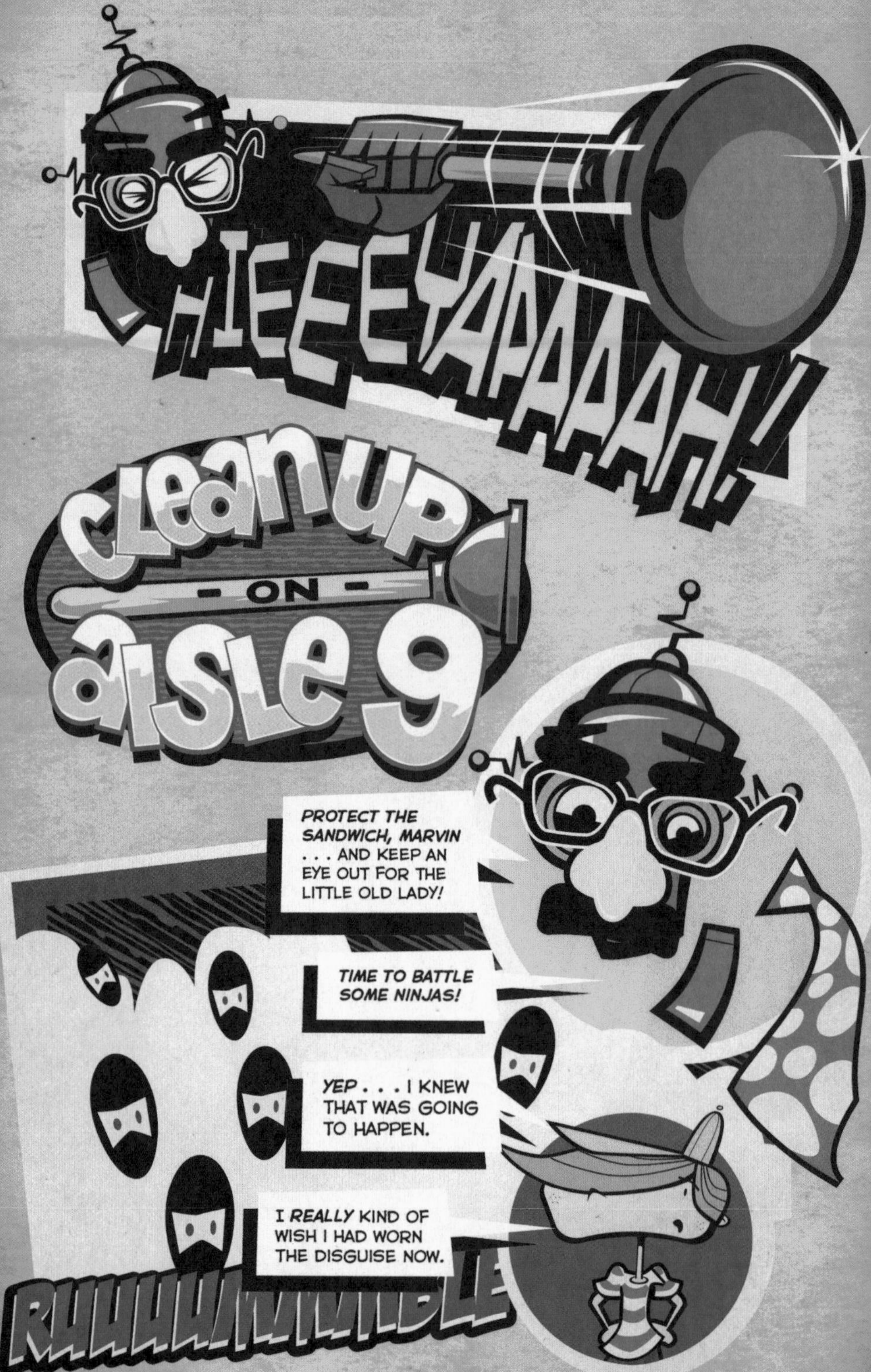
HIEEEYAPAAAH!
CLEAN UP ON AISLE 9
PROTECT THE SANDWICH, MARVIN . . . AND KEEP AN EYE OUT FOR THE LITTLE OLD LADY!
TIME TO BATTLE SOME NINJAS!
YEP . . . I KNEW THAT WAS GOING TO HAPPEN.
I REALLY KIND OF WISH I HAD WORN THE DISGUISE NOW.
RUUUMMMBLE

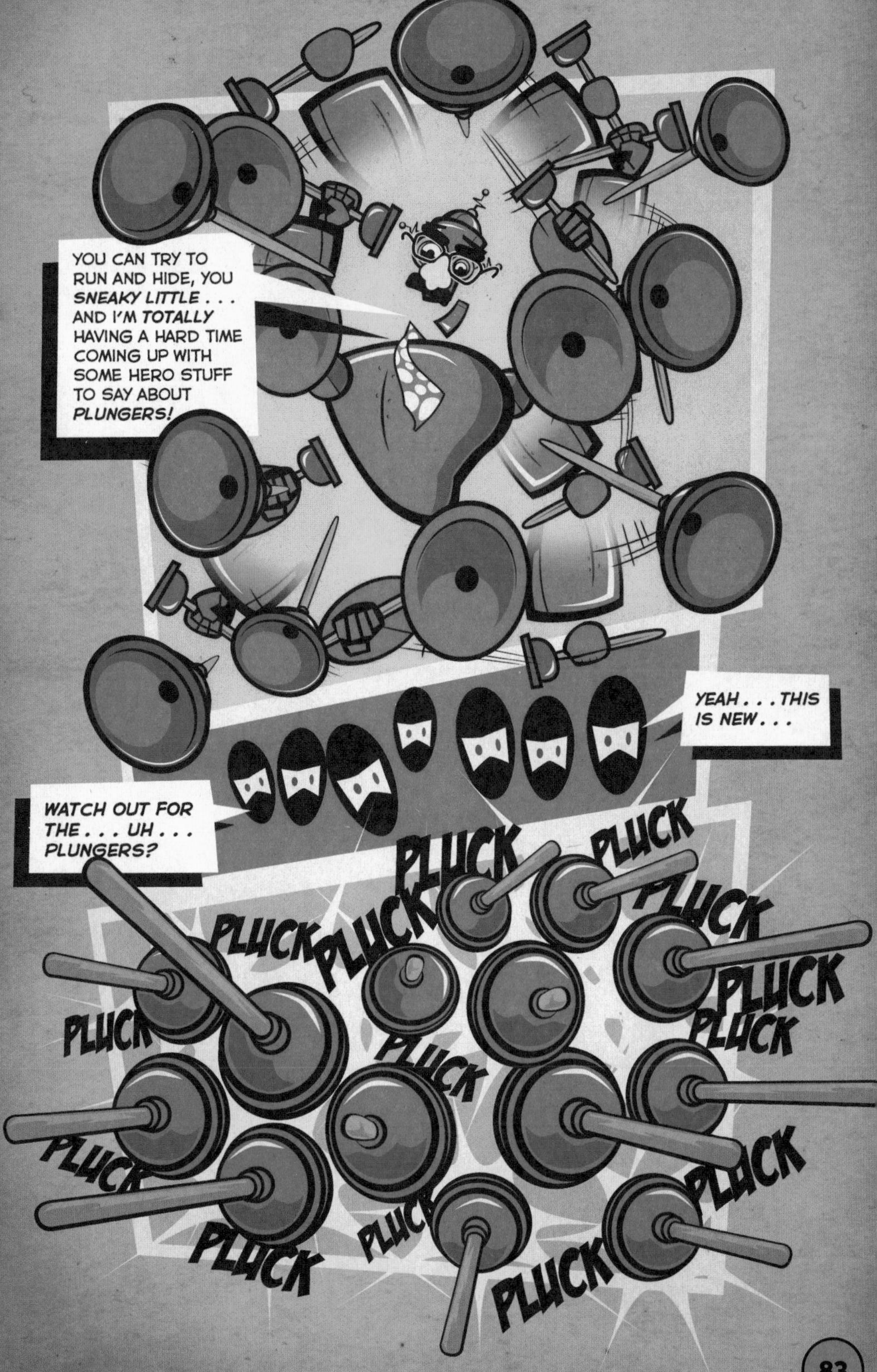
YOU CAN TRY TO RUN AND HIDE, YOU SNEAKY LITTLE . . . AND I'M TOTALLY HAVING A HARD TIME COMING UP WITH SOME HERO STUFF TO SAY ABOUT PLUNGERS!
YEAH . . . THIS IS NEW . . .
WATCH OUT FOR THE . . . UH . . . PLUNGERS?
PLUCK PLUCK PLUCK PLUCK PLUCK PLUCK PLUCK PLUCK PLUCK PLUCK PLUCK PLUCK PLUCK PLUCK PLUCK

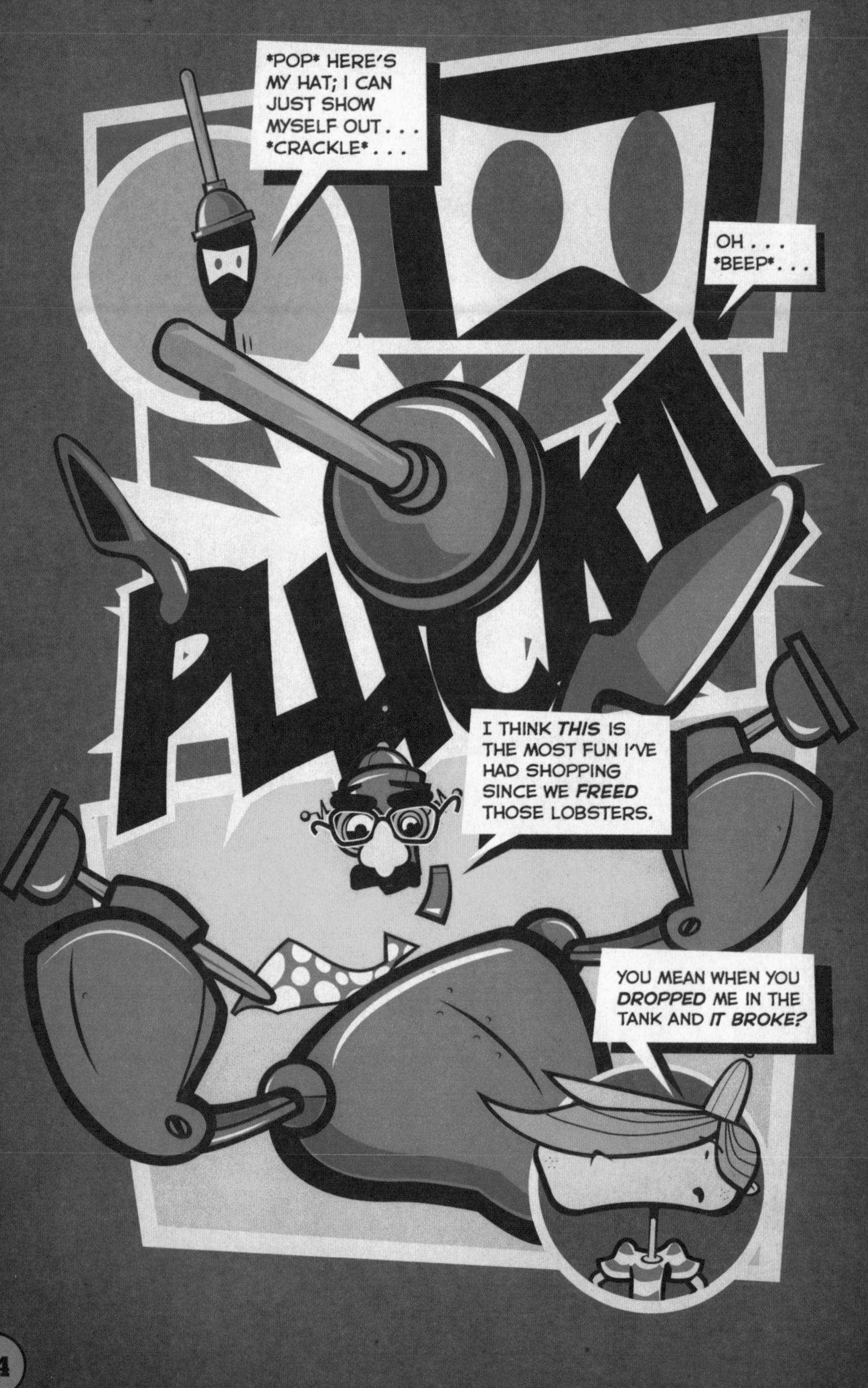
POP HERE'S MY HAT; I CAN JUST SHOW MYSELF OUT . . . *CRACKLE* . . .
OH . . . *BEEP* . . .
I THINK *THIS* IS THE MOST FUN I'VE HAD SHOPPING SINCE WE *FREED* THOSE LOBSTERS.
YOU MEAN WHEN YOU *DROPPED* ME IN THE TANK AND *IT BROKE?*

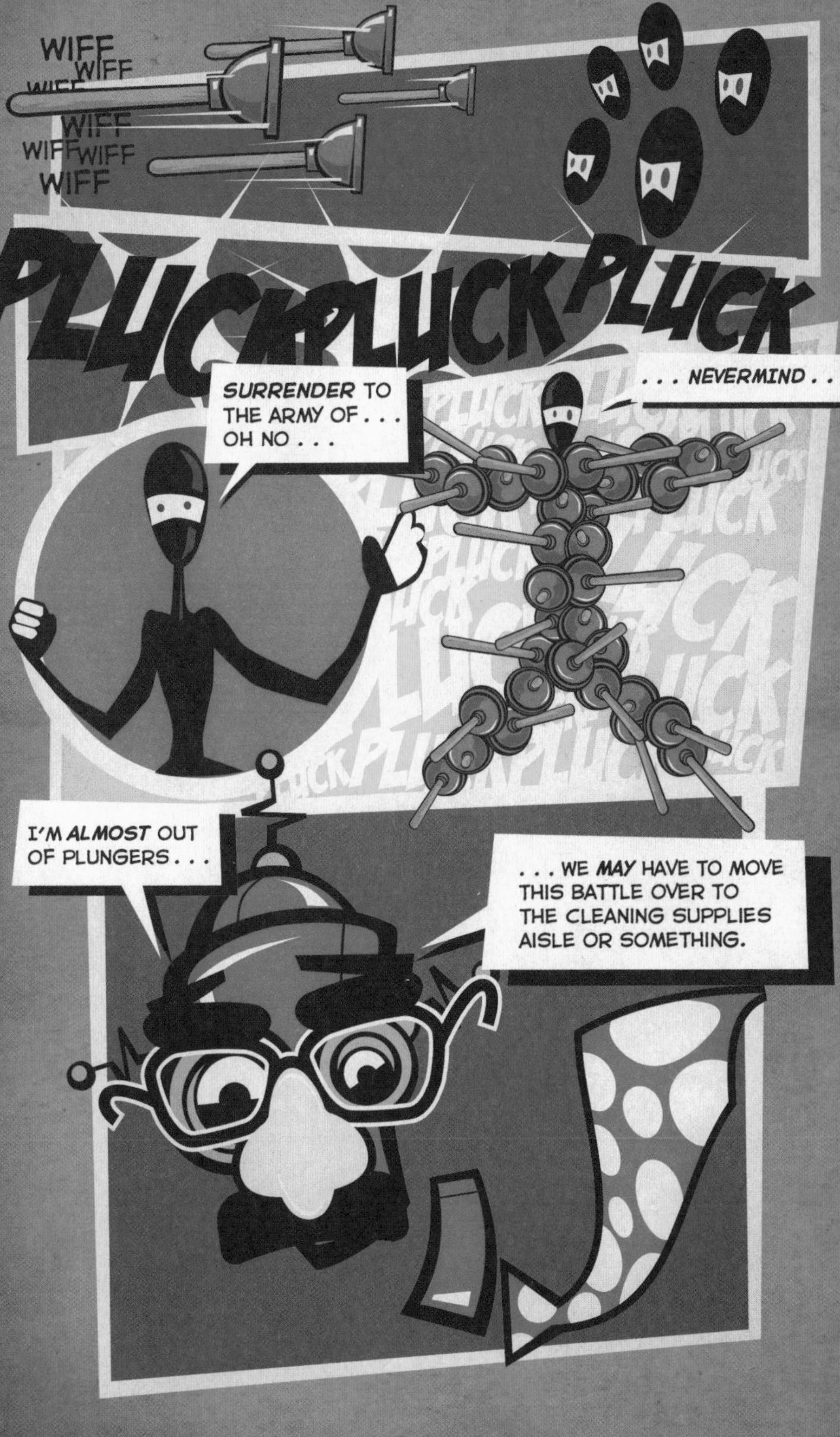
WIFF
WIFF
WIFF
WIFF
WIFF WIFF
WIFF
PLUCK PLUCK PLUCK
SURRENDER TO THE ARMY OF . . . OH NO . . .
. . . NEVERMIND . . .
PLUCK
I'M ALMOST OUT OF PLUNGERS . . .
. . . WE MAY HAVE TO MOVE THIS BATTLE OVER TO THE CLEANING SUPPLIES AISLE OR SOMETHING.

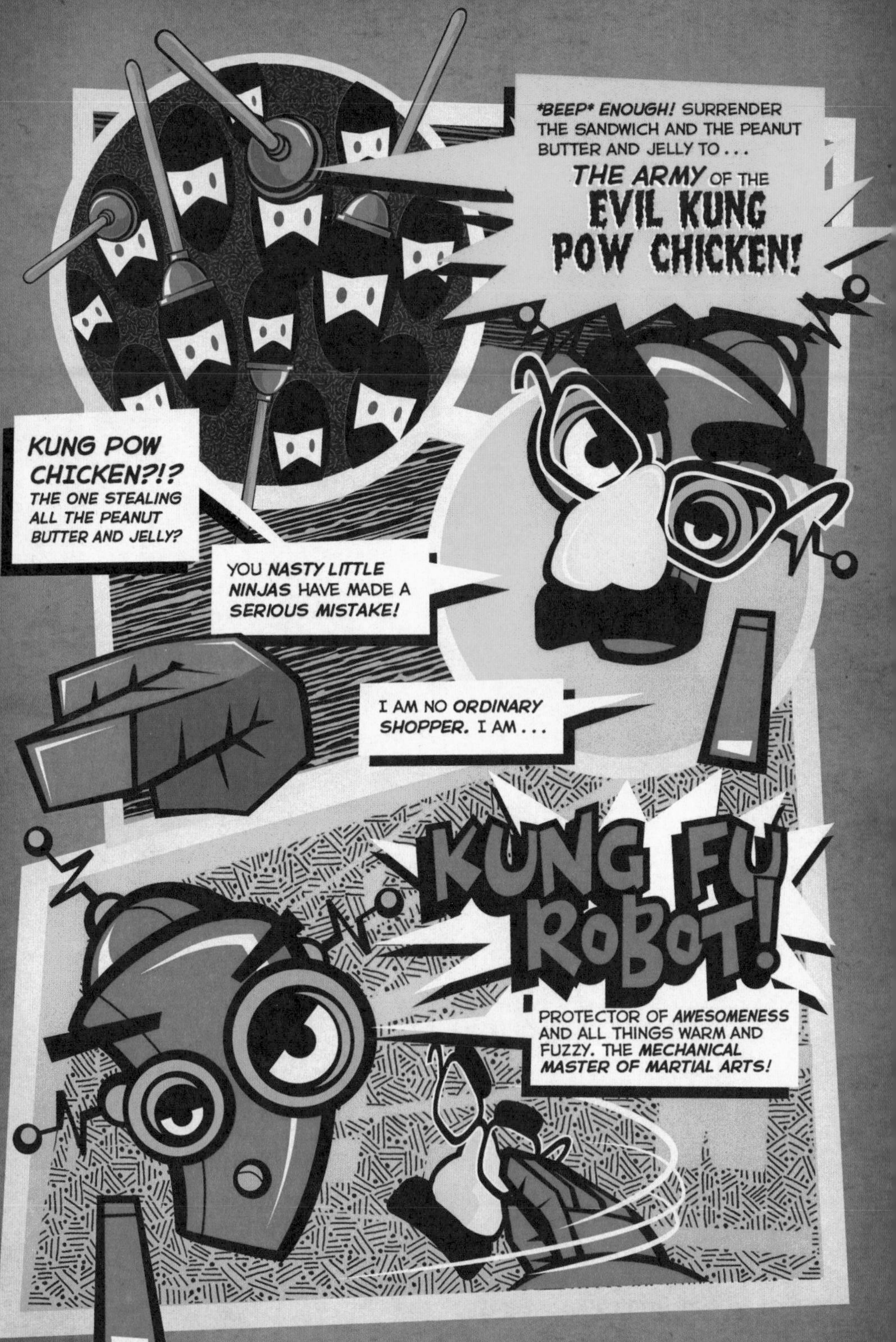
BEEP ENOUGH! SURRENDER THE SANDWICH AND THE PEANUT BUTTER AND JELLY TO . . .
THE ARMY OF THE
EVIL KUNG POW CHICKEN!
KUNG POW CHICKEN?!? THE ONE STEALING ALL THE PEANUT BUTTER AND JELLY?
YOU NASTY LITTLE NINJAS HAVE MADE A SERIOUS MISTAKE!
I AM NO ORDINARY SHOPPER. I AM . . .
KUNG FU ROBOT!
PROTECTOR OF AWESOMENESS AND ALL THINGS WARM AND FUZZY. THE MECHANICAL MASTER OF MARTIAL ARTS!

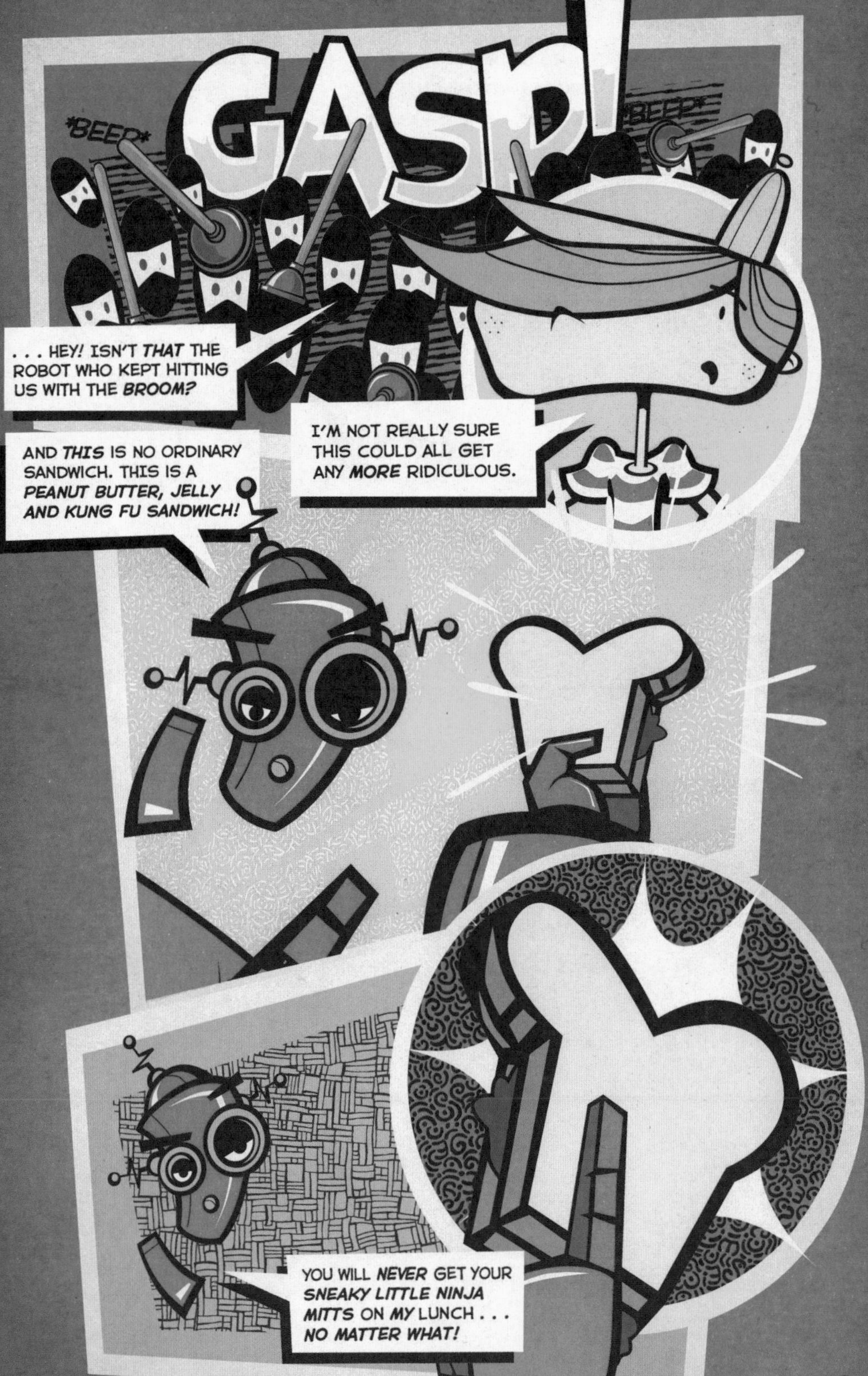
BEEP
GASP!
BEEP
. . . HEY! ISN'T *THAT* THE ROBOT WHO KEPT HITTING US WITH THE *BROOM?*
I'M NOT REALLY SURE THIS COULD ALL GET ANY *MORE* RIDICULOUS.
AND *THIS* IS NO ORDINARY SANDWICH. THIS IS A *PEANUT BUTTER, JELLY AND KUNG FU SANDWICH!*
YOU WILL *NEVER* GET YOUR *SNEAKY LITTLE NINJA MITTS* ON *MY* LUNCH . . . *NO MATTER WHAT!*

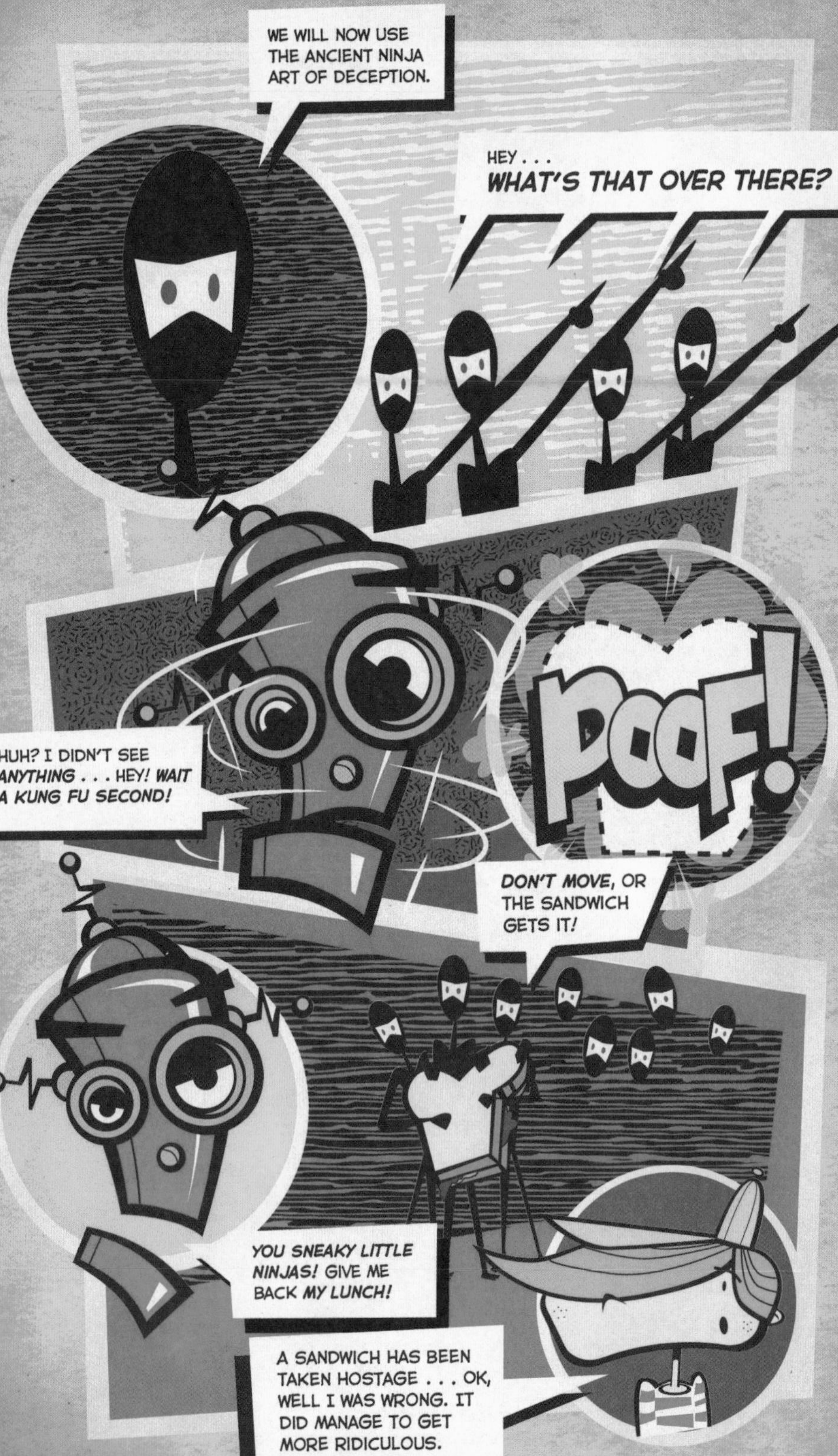
WE WILL NOW USE THE ANCIENT NINJA ART OF DECEPTION.
HEY . . . WHAT'S THAT OVER THERE?
POOF!
HUH? I DIDN'T SEE ANYTHING . . . HEY! WAIT A KUNG FU SECOND!
DON'T MOVE, OR THE SANDWICH GETS IT!
YOU SNEAKY LITTLE NINJAS! GIVE ME BACK MY LUNCH!
A SANDWICH HAS BEEN TAKEN HOSTAGE . . . OK, WELL I WAS WRONG. IT DID MANAGE TO GET MORE RIDICULOUS.

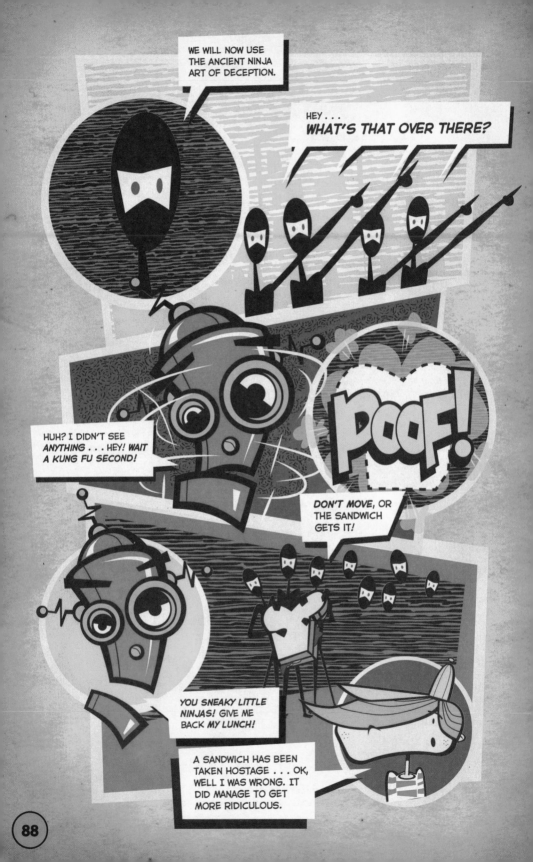

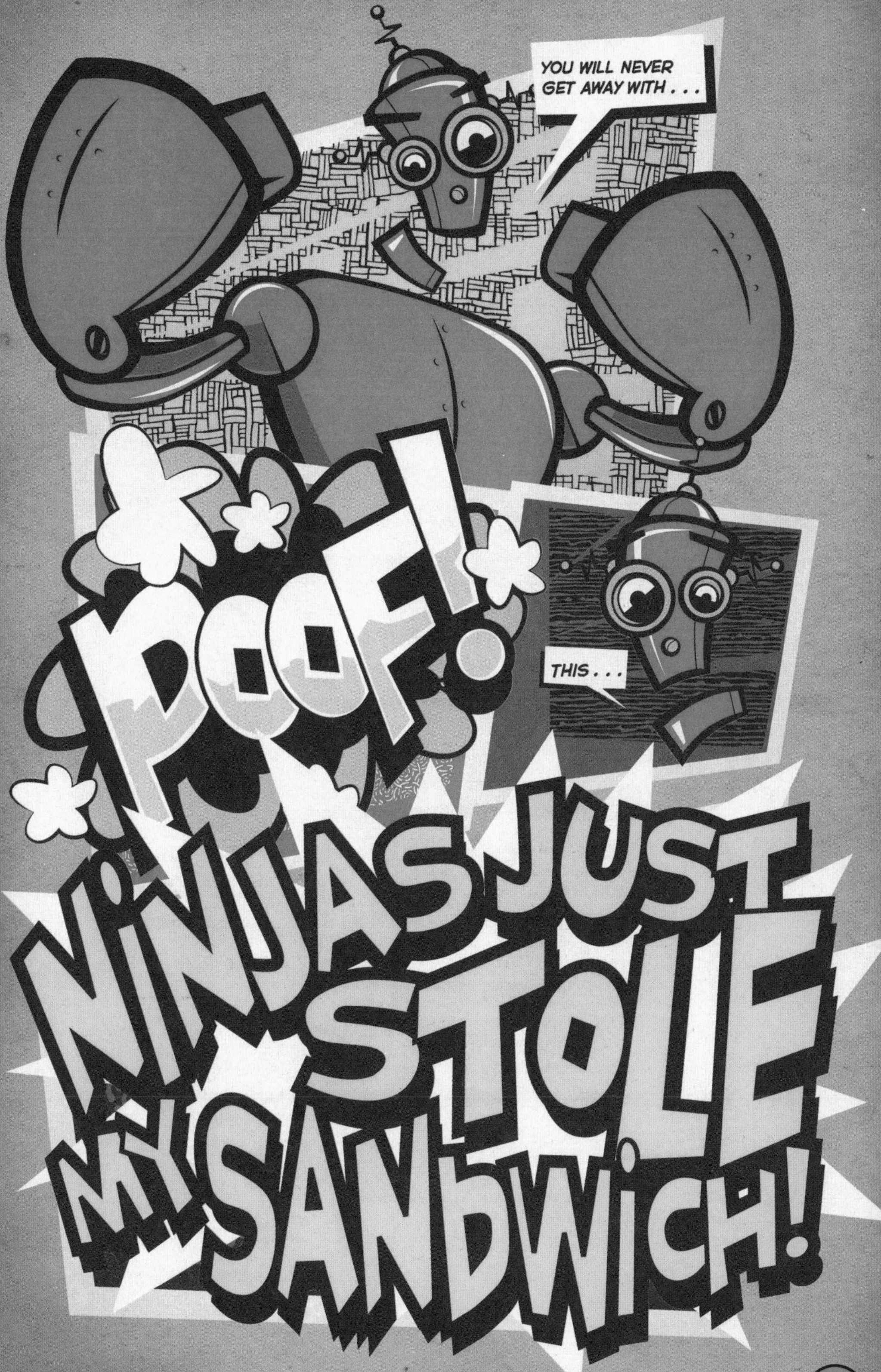

YOU WILL NEVER GET AWAY WITH . . .
POOF!
THIS . . .
NINJAS JUST STOLE MY SANDWICH!

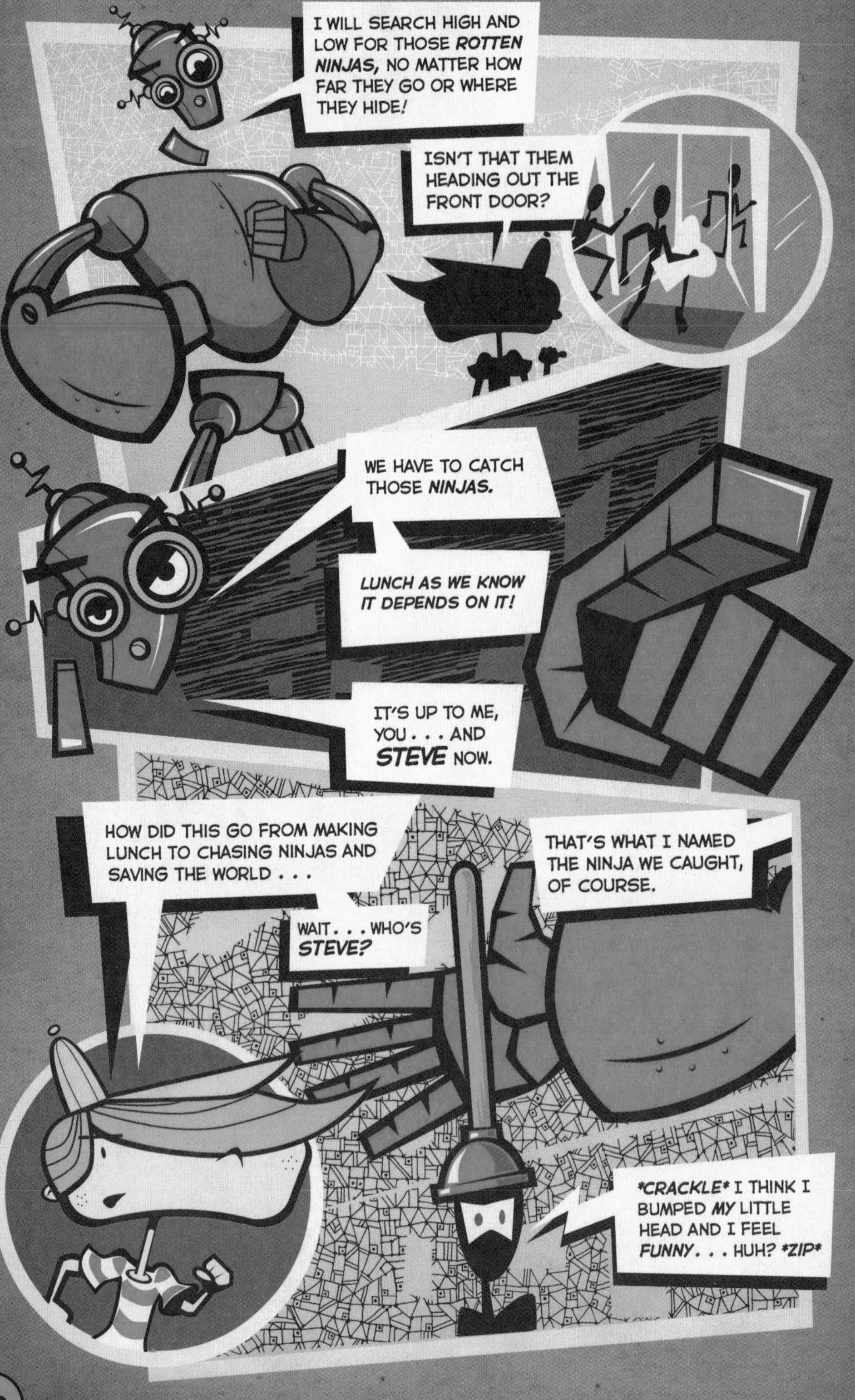
I WILL SEARCH HIGH AND LOW FOR THOSE *ROTTEN NINJAS,* NO MATTER HOW FAR THEY GO OR WHERE THEY HIDE!
ISN'T THAT THEM HEADING OUT THE FRONT DOOR?
WE HAVE TO CATCH THOSE *NINJAS.*
LUNCH AS WE KNOW IT DEPENDS ON IT!
IT'S UP TO ME, YOU . . . AND **STEVE** NOW.
HOW DID THIS GO FROM MAKING LUNCH TO CHASING NINJAS AND SAVING THE WORLD . . .
WAIT. . . WHO'S ***STEVE?***
THAT'S WHAT I NAMED THE NINJA WE CAUGHT, OF COURSE.
CRACKLE I THINK I BUMPED *MY* LITTLE HEAD AND I FEEL *FUNNY*. . . HUH? **ZIP**

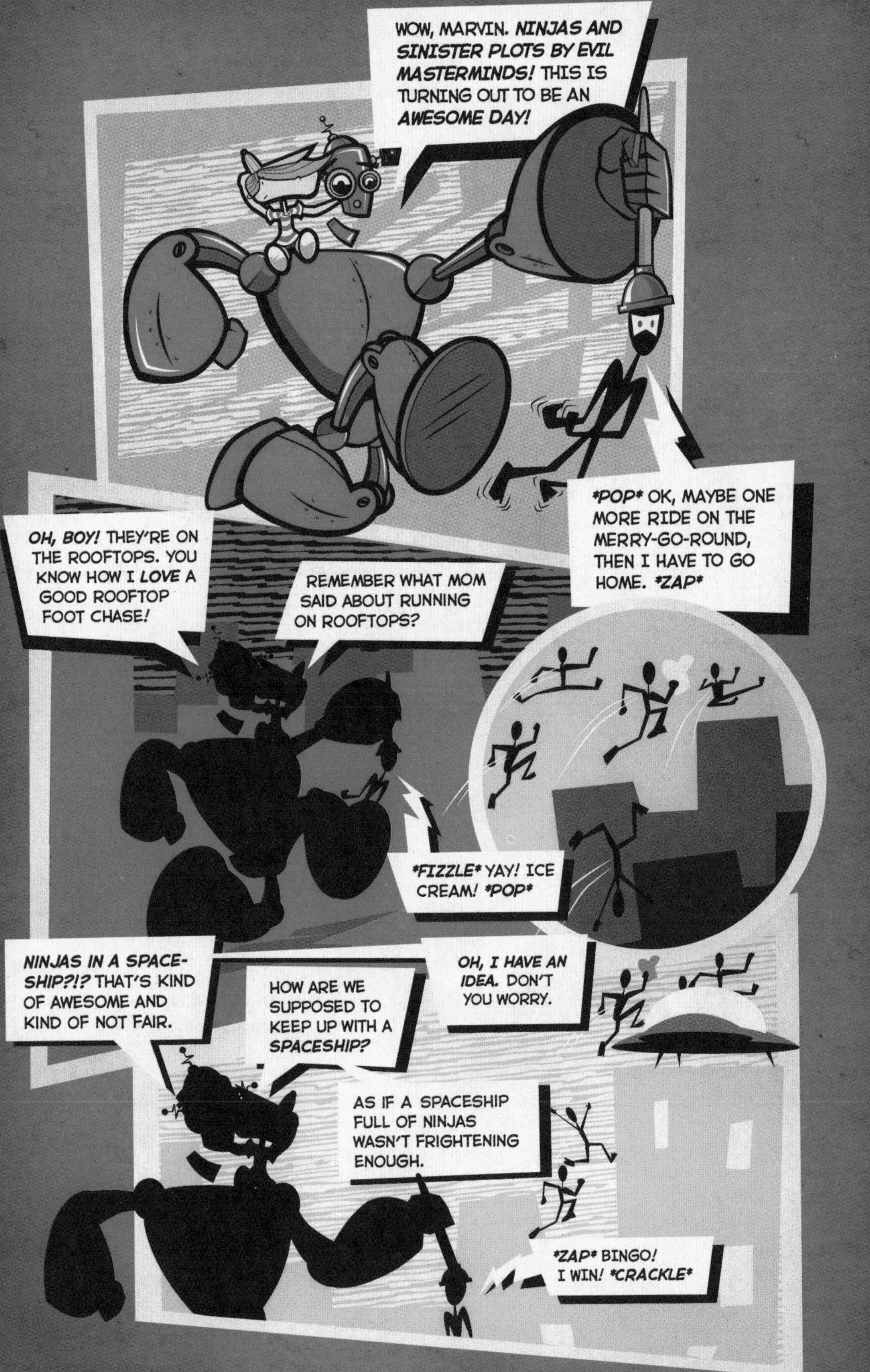
WOW, MARVIN. NINJAS AND SINISTER PLOTS BY EVIL MASTERMINDS! THIS IS TURNING OUT TO BE AN AWESOME DAY!
POP OK, MAYBE ONE MORE RIDE ON THE MERRY-GO-ROUND, THEN I HAVE TO GO HOME. *ZAP*
OH, BOY! THEY'RE ON THE ROOFTOPS. YOU KNOW HOW I LOVE A GOOD ROOFTOP FOOT CHASE!
REMEMBER WHAT MOM SAID ABOUT RUNNING ON ROOFTOPS?
FIZZLE YAY! ICE CREAM! *POP*
NINJAS IN A SPACE-SHIP?!? THAT'S KIND OF AWESOME AND KIND OF NOT FAIR.
HOW ARE WE SUPPOSED TO KEEP UP WITH A SPACESHIP?
OH, I HAVE AN IDEA. DON'T YOU WORRY.
AS IF A SPACESHIP FULL OF NINJAS WASN'T FRIGHTENING ENOUGH.
ZAP BINGO! I WIN! *CRACKLE*

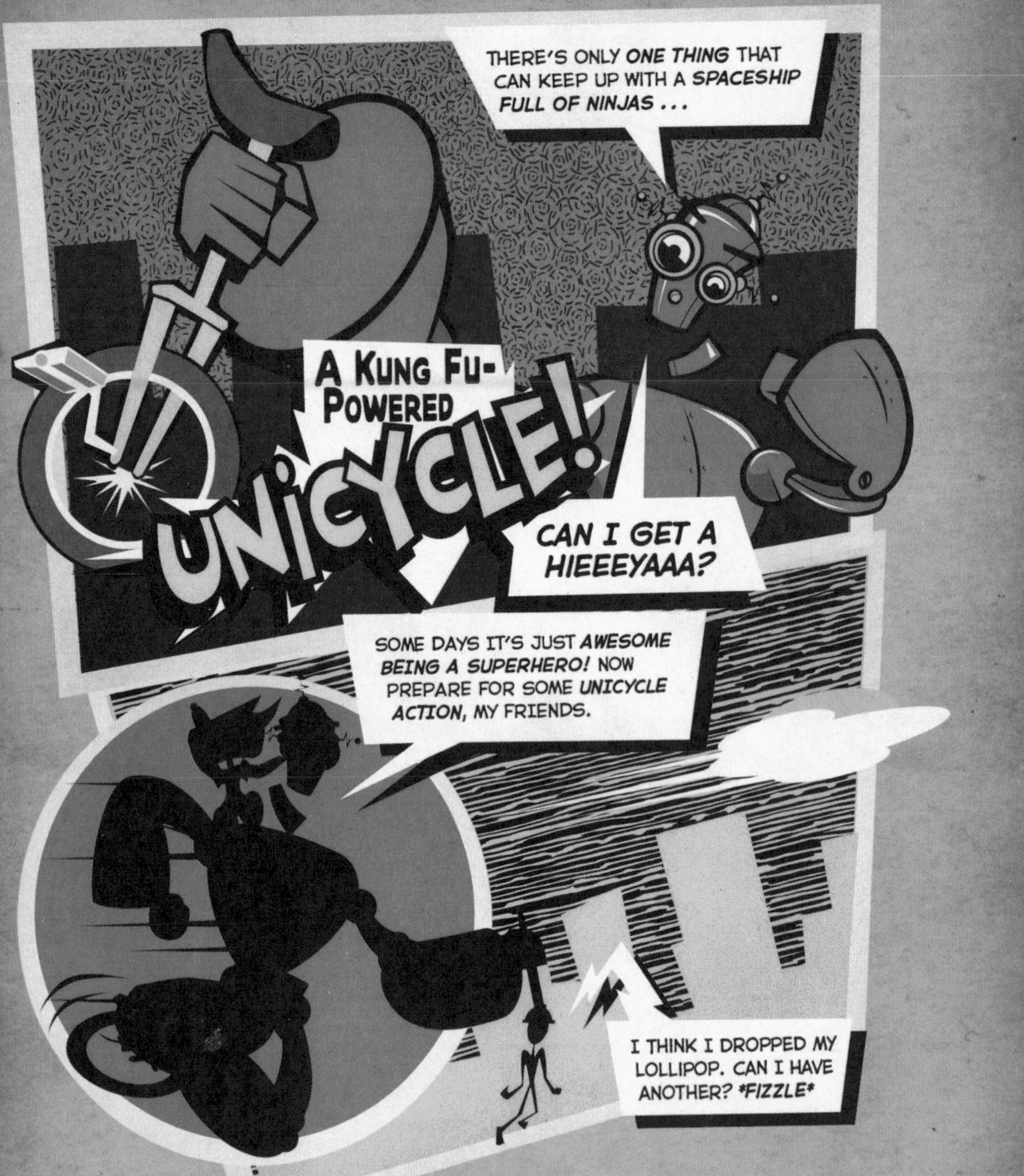

THERE'S ONLY ONE THING THAT CAN KEEP UP WITH A SPACESHIP FULL OF NINJAS . . .
A KUNG FU-POWERED
UNICYCLE!
CAN I GET A HIEEEYAAA?
SOME DAYS IT'S JUST AWESOME BEING A SUPERHERO! NOW PREPARE FOR SOME UNICYCLE ACTION, MY FRIENDS.
I THINK I DROPPED MY LOLLIPOP. CAN I HAVE ANOTHER? *FIZZLE*

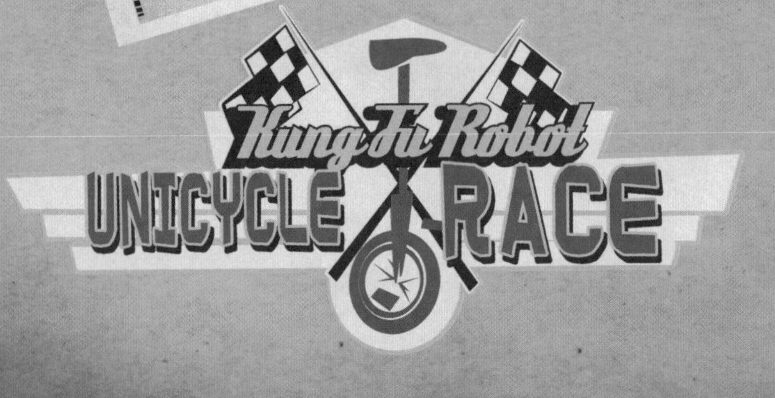

Kung Fu Robot
UNICYCLE RACE

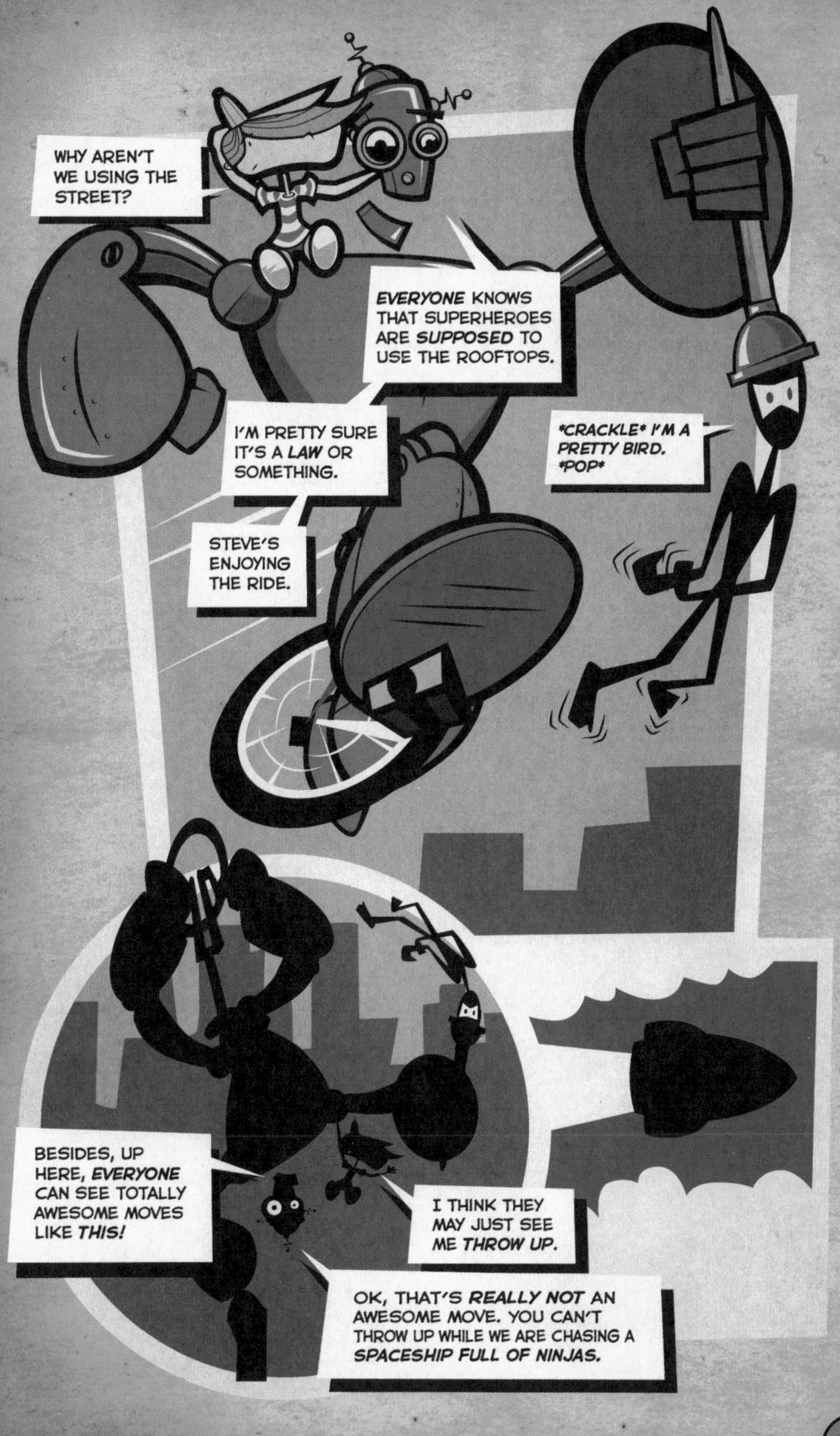
WHY AREN'T WE USING THE STREET?
EVERYONE KNOWS THAT SUPERHEROES ARE *SUPPOSED* TO USE THE ROOFTOPS.
I'M PRETTY SURE IT'S A *LAW* OR SOMETHING.
STEVE'S ENJOYING THE RIDE.
CRACKLE I'M A PRETTY BIRD. *POP*
BESIDES, UP HERE, *EVERYONE* CAN SEE TOTALLY AWESOME MOVES LIKE *THIS!*
I THINK THEY MAY JUST SEE ME *THROW UP*.
OK, THAT'S *REALLY NOT* AN AWESOME MOVE. YOU CAN'T THROW UP WHILE WE ARE CHASING A *SPACESHIP FULL OF NINJAS*.

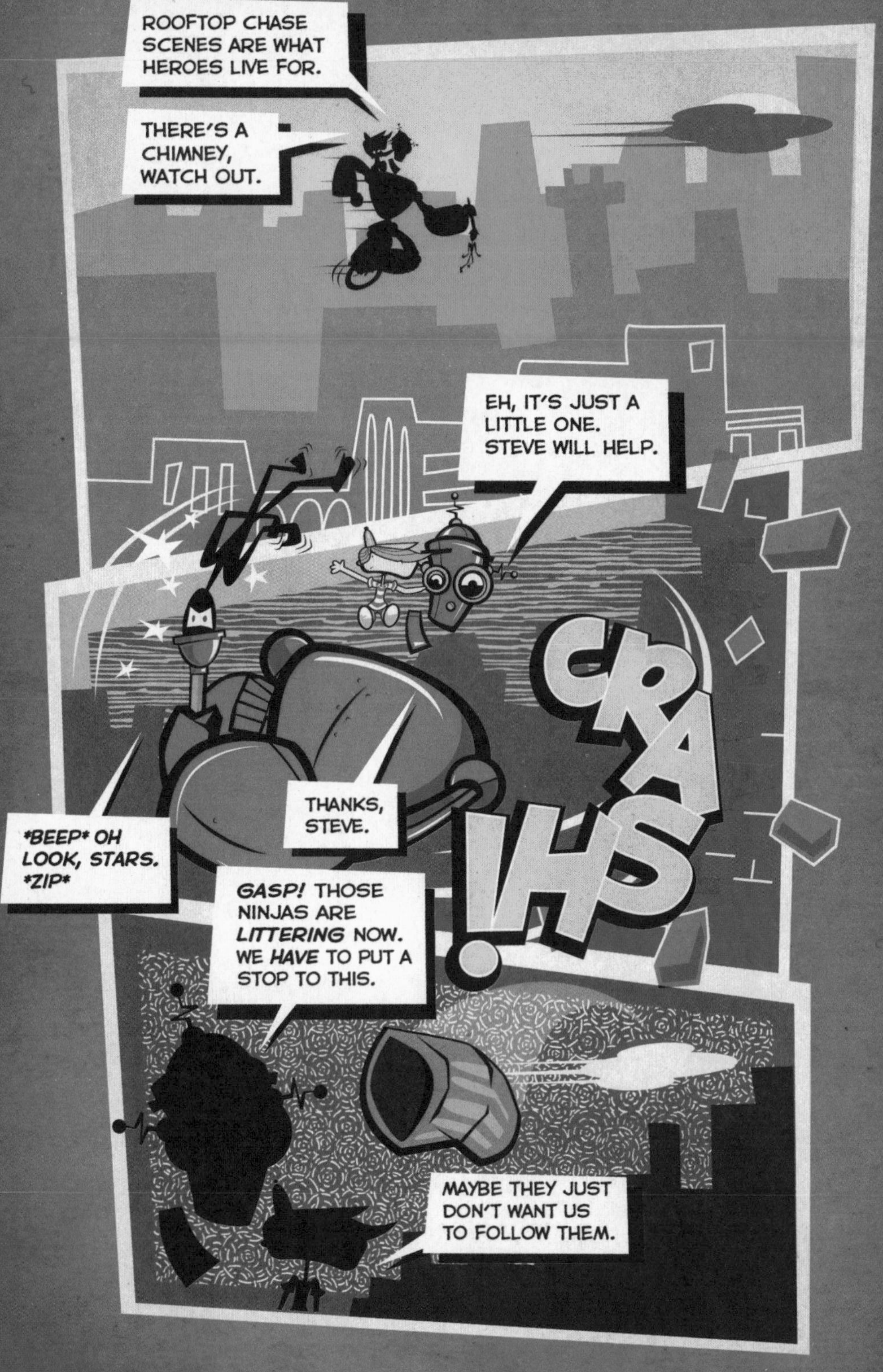
ROOFTOP CHASE SCENES ARE WHAT HEROES LIVE FOR.
THERE'S A CHIMNEY, WATCH OUT.
EH, IT'S JUST A LITTLE ONE. STEVE WILL HELP.
CRASH!
THANKS, STEVE.
BEEP OH LOOK, STARS. *ZIP*
GASP! THOSE NINJAS ARE LITTERING NOW. WE HAVE TO PUT A STOP TO THIS.
MAYBE THEY JUST DON'T WANT US TO FOLLOW THEM.

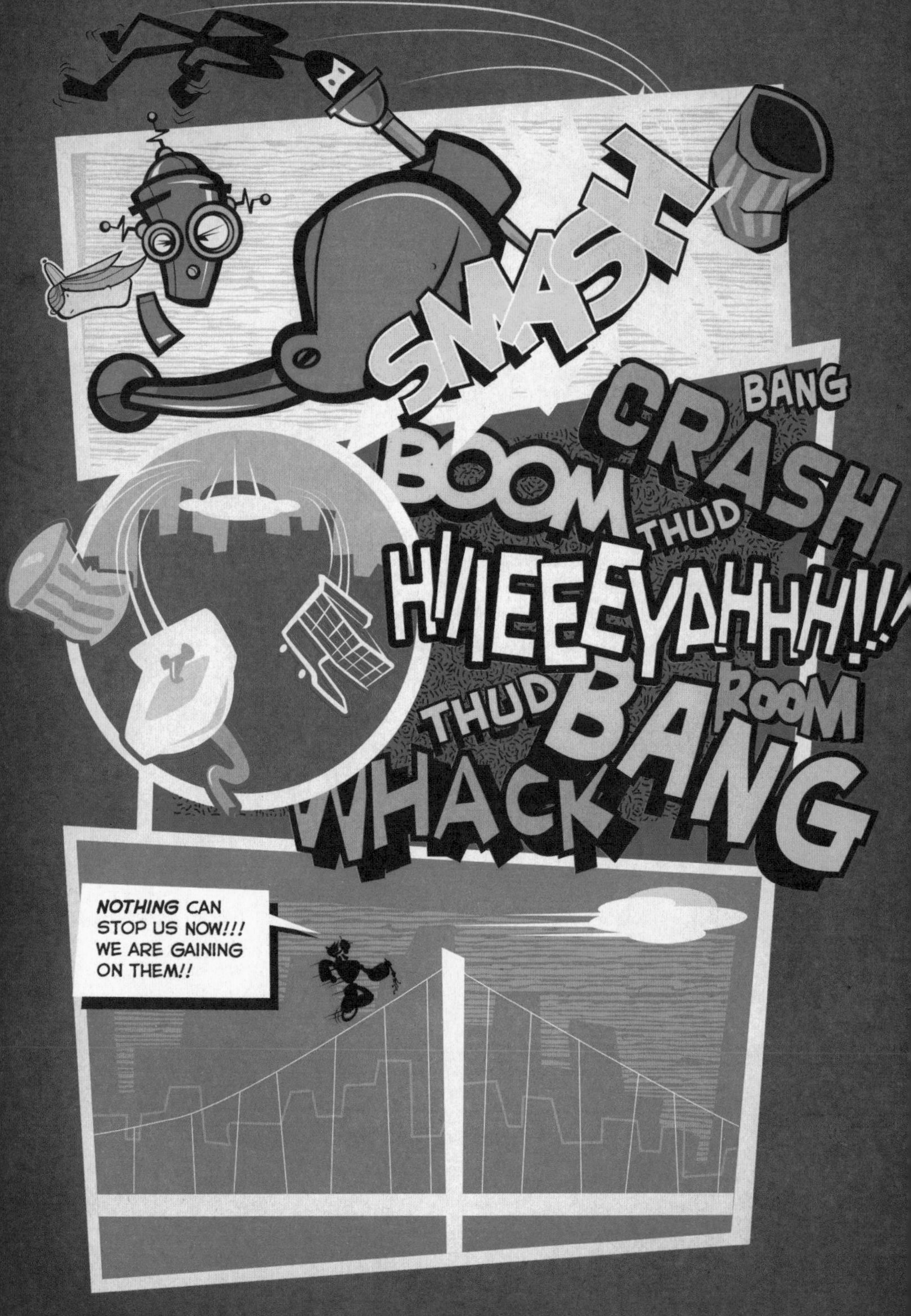
SMASH
BANG
CRASH
BOOM
THUD
HIIEEEYAHHH!!!
THUD
ROOM
BANG
WHACK
BANG
NOTHING CAN STOP US NOW!!! WE ARE GAINING ON THEM!!

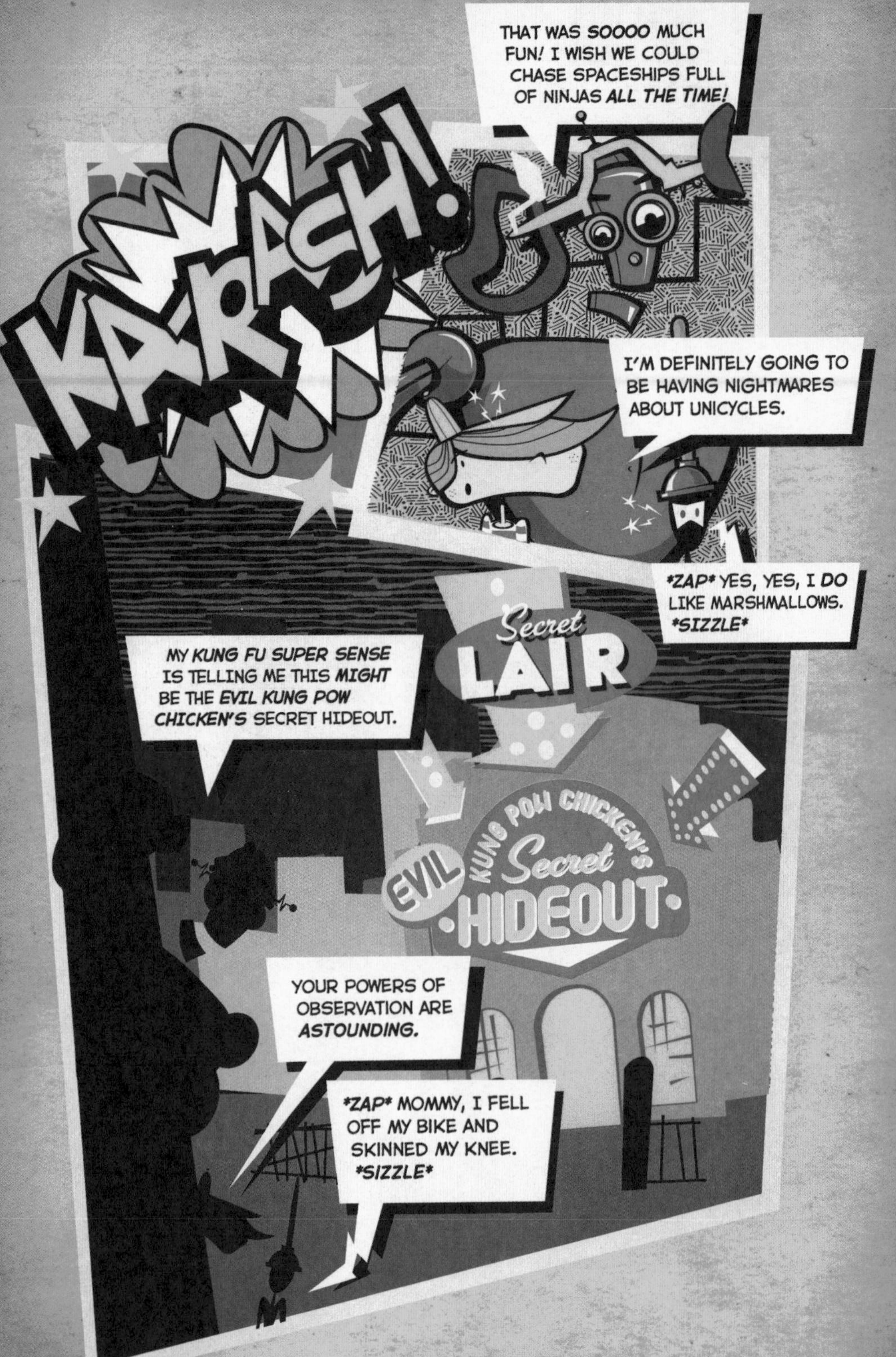
THAT WAS SOOOO MUCH FUN! I WISH WE COULD CHASE SPACESHIPS FULL OF NINJAS ALL THE TIME!
KA-RASH!
I'M DEFINITELY GOING TO BE HAVING NIGHTMARES ABOUT UNICYCLES.
ZAP YES, YES, I DO LIKE MARSHMALLOWS. *SIZZLE*
Secret LAIR
MY KUNG FU SUPER SENSE IS TELLING ME THIS MIGHT BE THE EVIL KUNG POW CHICKEN'S SECRET HIDEOUT.
EVIL KUNG POW CHICKEN'S Secret HIDEOUT
YOUR POWERS OF OBSERVATION ARE ASTOUNDING.
ZAP MOMMY, I FELL OFF MY BIKE AND SKINNED MY KNEE. *SIZZLE*

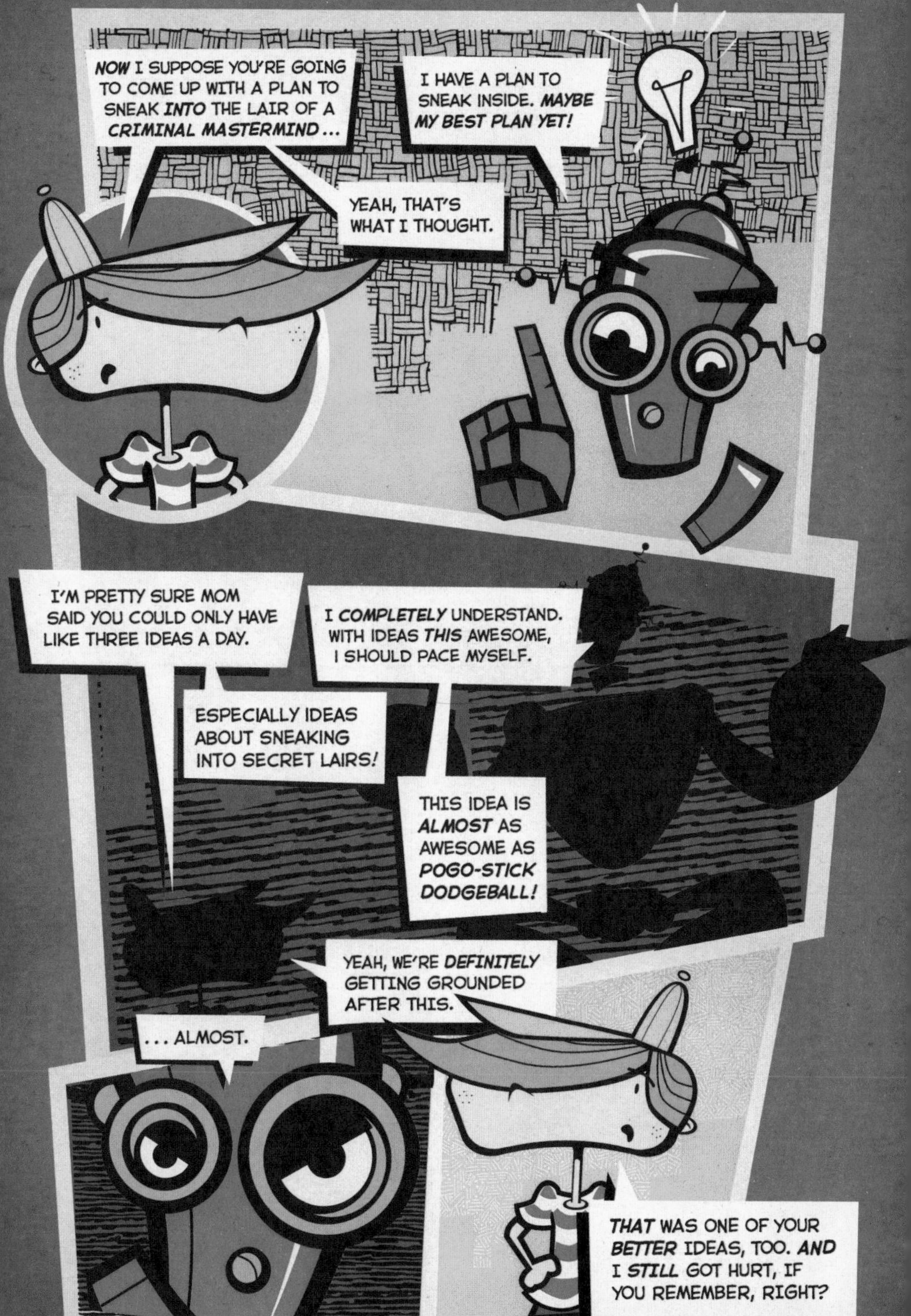
NOW I SUPPOSE YOU'RE GOING TO COME UP WITH A PLAN TO SNEAK INTO THE LAIR OF A CRIMINAL MASTERMIND ...
I HAVE A PLAN TO SNEAK INSIDE. MAYBE MY BEST PLAN YET!
YEAH, THAT'S WHAT I THOUGHT.
I'M PRETTY SURE MOM SAID YOU COULD ONLY HAVE LIKE THREE IDEAS A DAY.
I COMPLETELY UNDERSTAND. WITH IDEAS THIS AWESOME, I SHOULD PACE MYSELF.
ESPECIALLY IDEAS ABOUT SNEAKING INTO SECRET LAIRS!
THIS IDEA IS ALMOST AS AWESOME AS POGO-STICK DODGEBALL!
YEAH, WE'RE DEFINITELY GETTING GROUNDED AFTER THIS.
... ALMOST.
THAT WAS ONE OF YOUR BETTER IDEAS, TOO. AND I STILL GOT HURT, IF YOU REMEMBER, RIGHT?

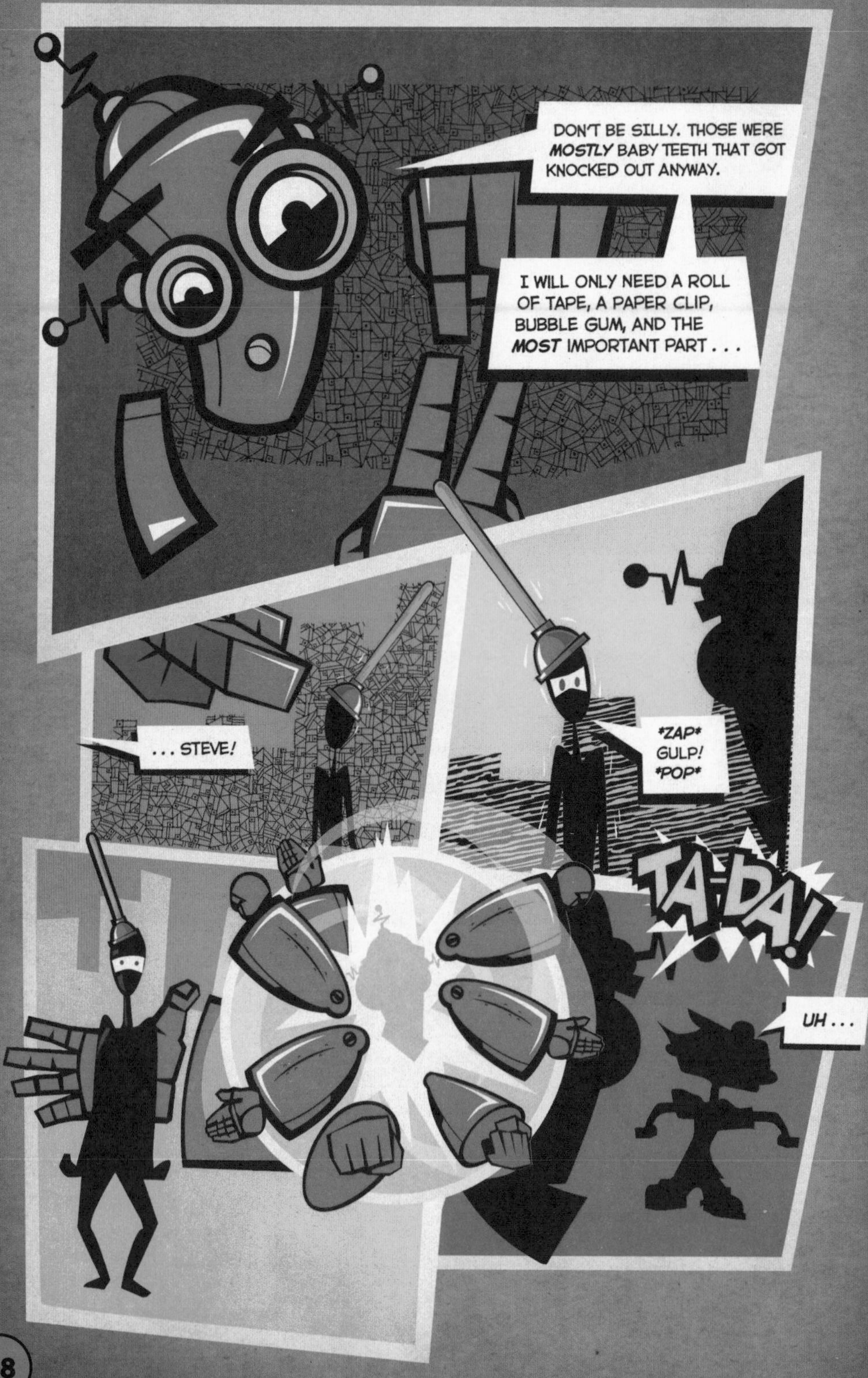
DON'T BE SILLY. THOSE WERE *MOSTLY* BABY TEETH THAT GOT KNOCKED OUT ANYWAY.
I WILL ONLY NEED A ROLL OF TAPE, A PAPER CLIP, BUBBLE GUM, AND THE *MOST* IMPORTANT PART . . .
. . . STEVE!
ZAP GULP! *POP*
TA-DA!
UH . . .

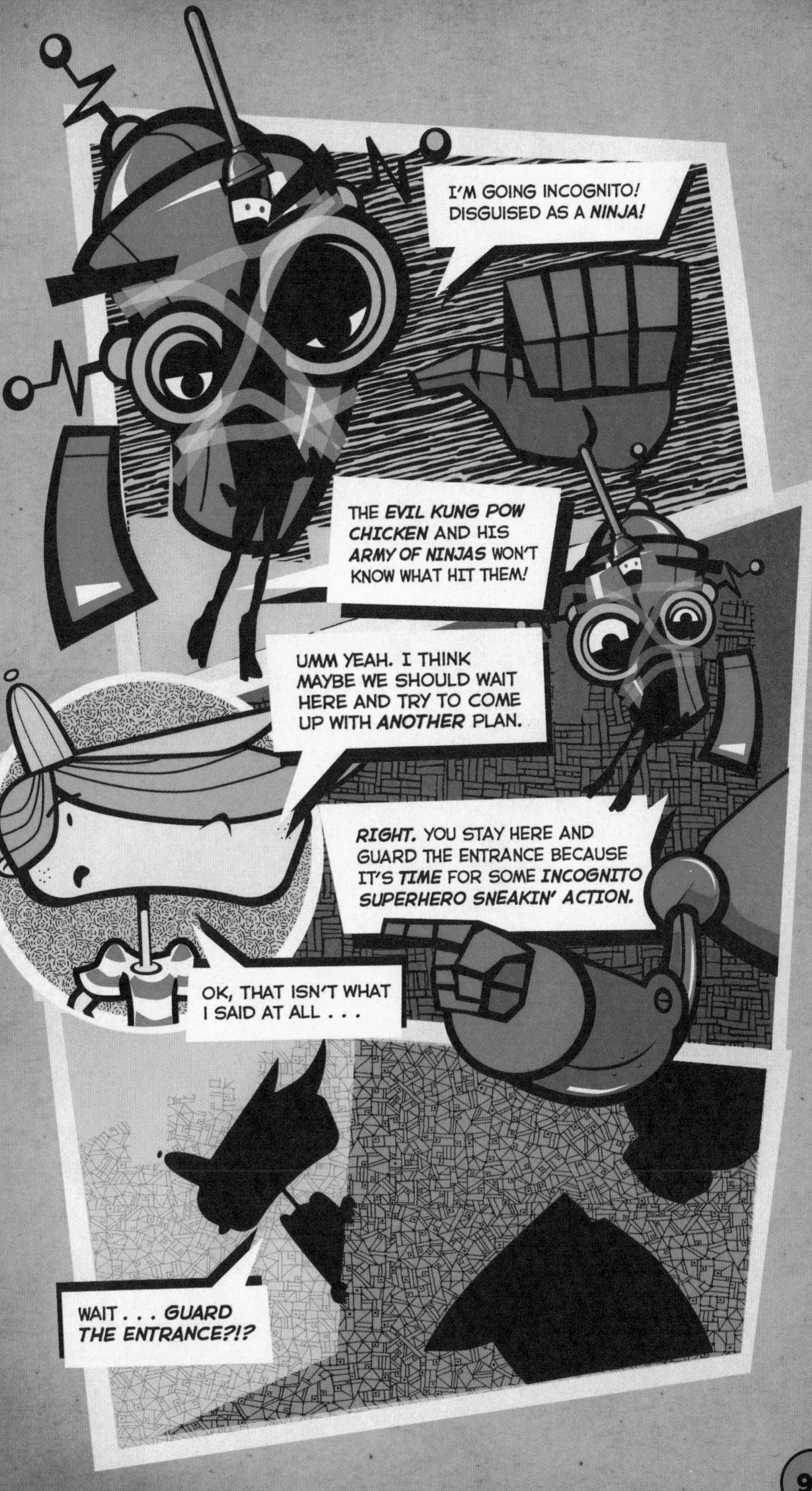
I'M GOING INCOGNITO! DISGUISED AS A NINJA!
THE EVIL KUNG POW CHICKEN AND HIS ARMY OF NINJAS WON'T KNOW WHAT HIT THEM!
UMM YEAH. I THINK MAYBE WE SHOULD WAIT HERE AND TRY TO COME UP WITH ANOTHER PLAN.
RIGHT. YOU STAY HERE AND GUARD THE ENTRANCE BECAUSE IT'S TIME FOR SOME INCOGNITO SUPERHERO SNEAKIN' ACTION.
OK, THAT ISN'T WHAT I SAID AT ALL . . .
WAIT . . . GUARD THE ENTRANCE?!?

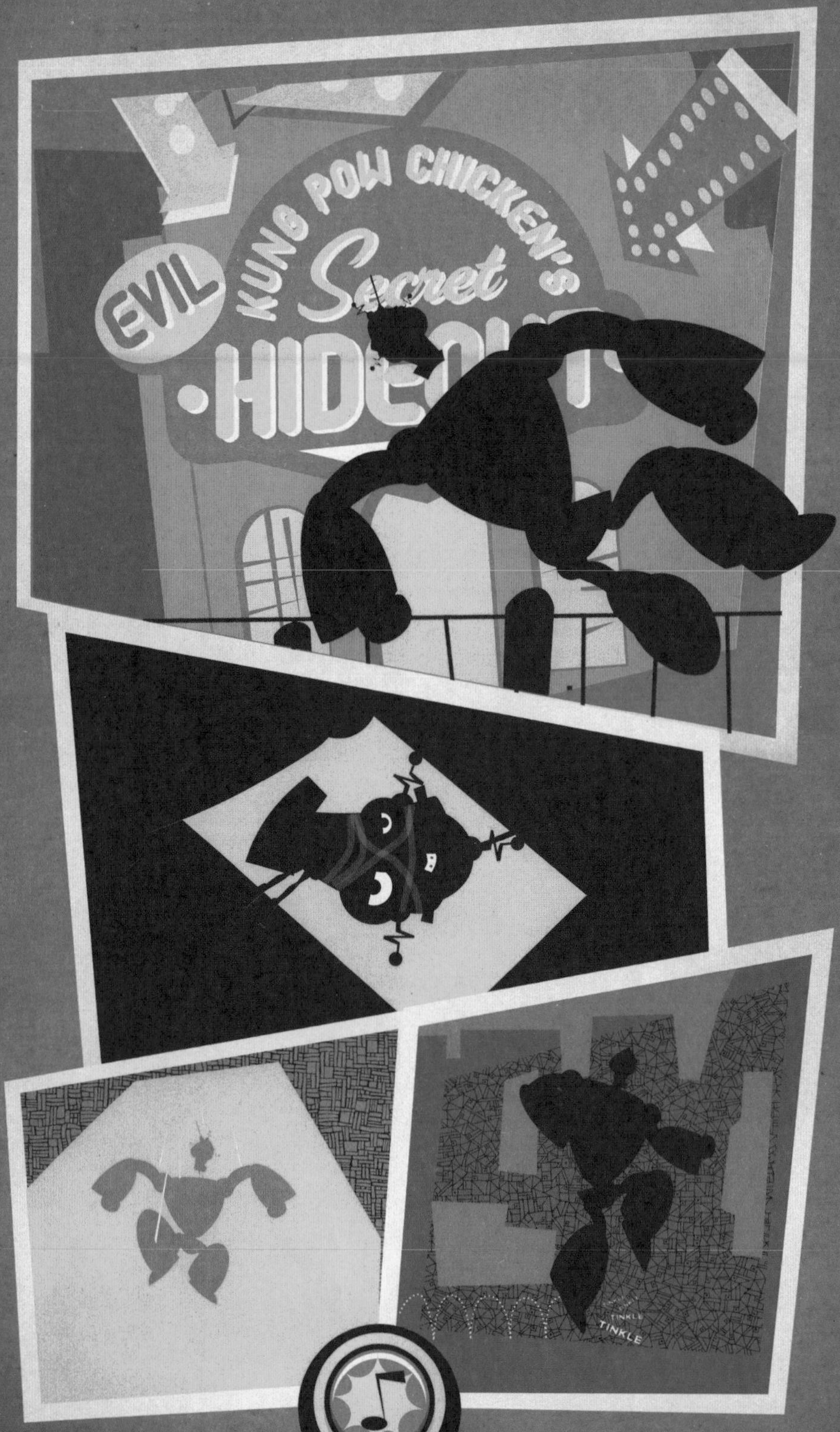
EVIL
KUNG POW CHICKEN'S
Secret
HIDE
TINKLE
TINKLE
SNEAKY TINKLE

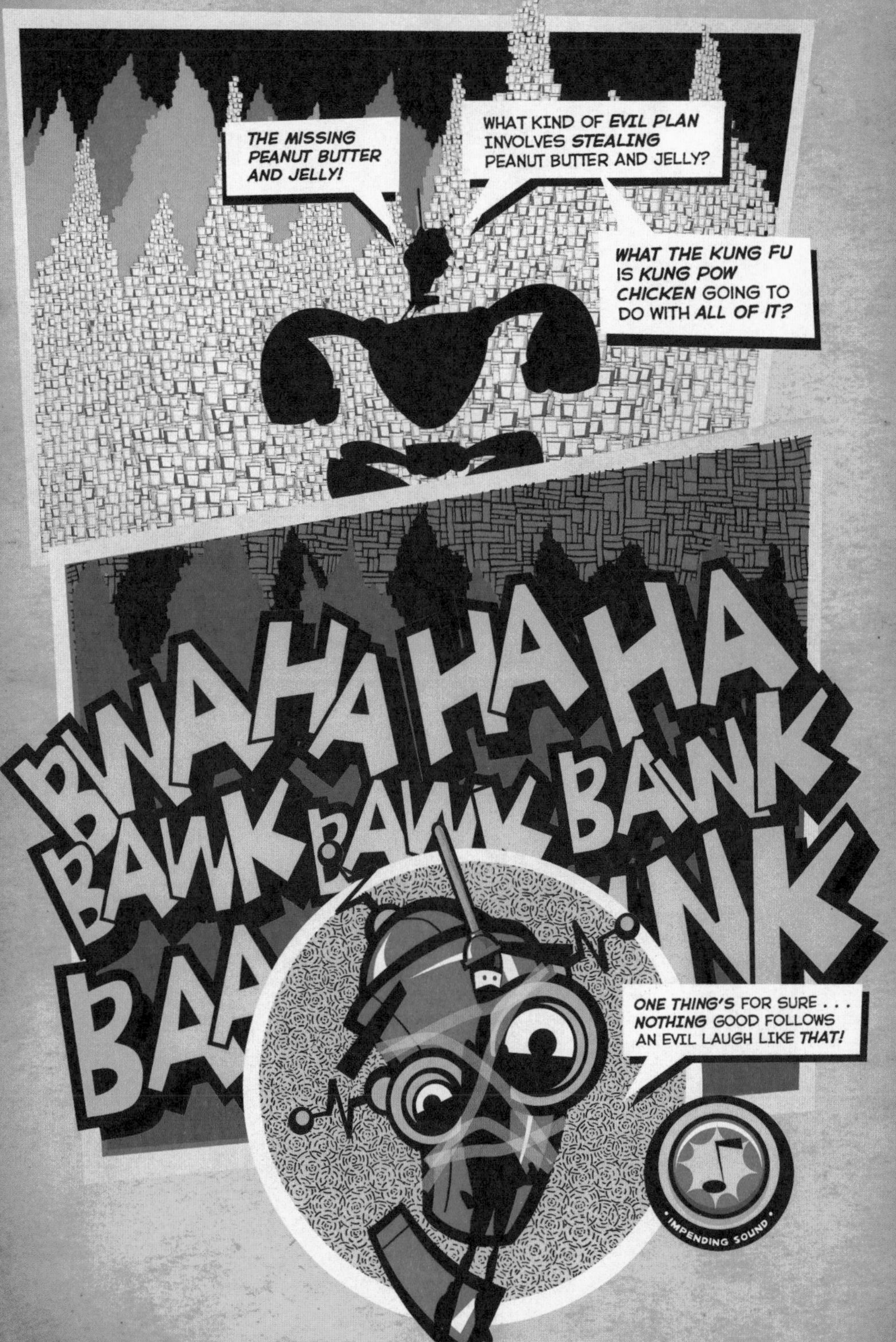
THE MISSING PEANUT BUTTER AND JELLY!
WHAT KIND OF EVIL PLAN INVOLVES STEALING PEANUT BUTTER AND JELLY?
WHAT THE KUNG FU IS KUNG POW CHICKEN GOING TO DO WITH ALL OF IT?
BWAHAHAHAHA
BAWK BAWK BAWK
ONE THING'S FOR SURE . . . NOTHING GOOD FOLLOWS AN EVIL LAUGH LIKE THAT!
IMPENDING SOUND

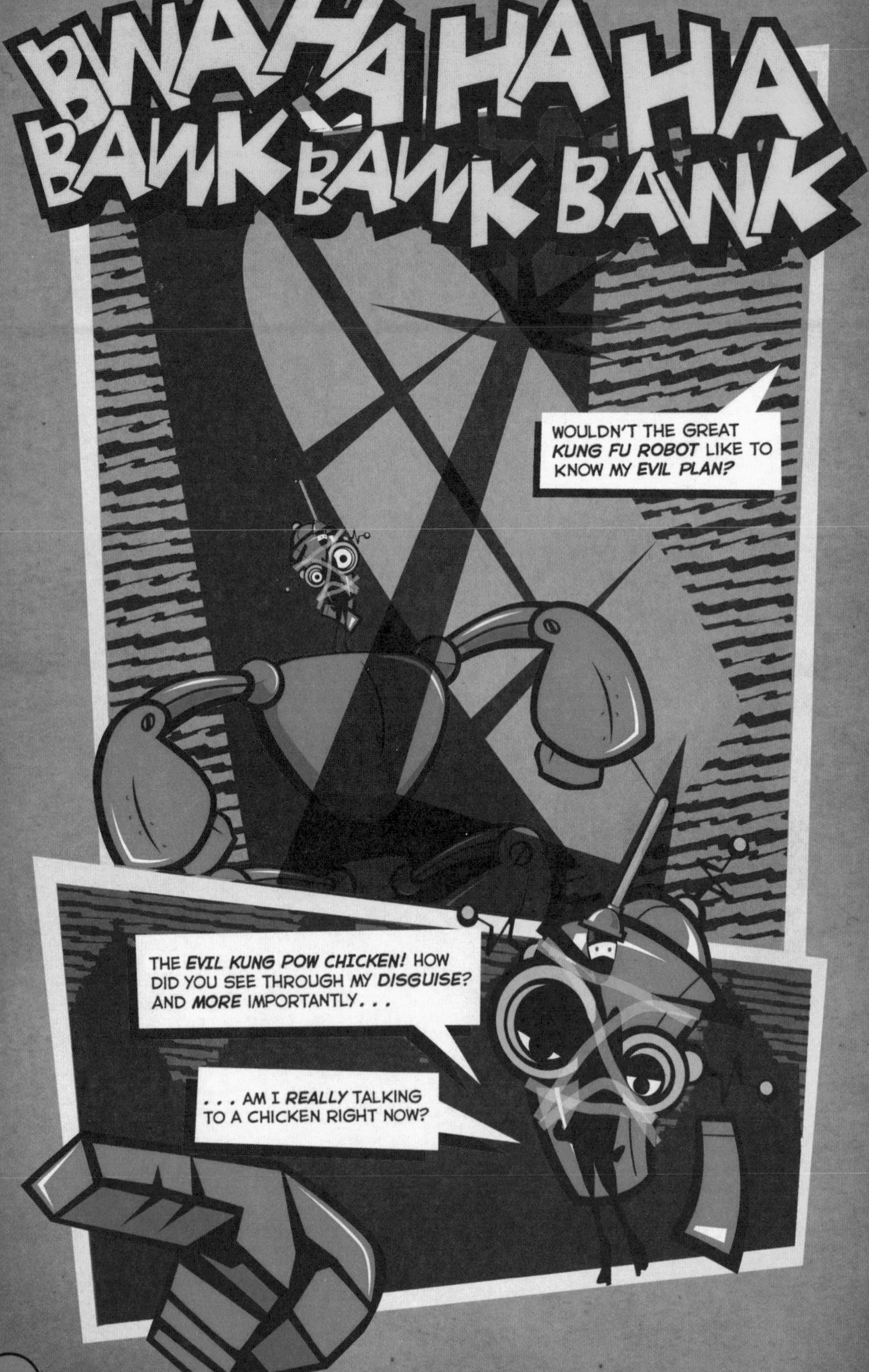
BWAHAHAHAHA
BAWK BAWK BAWK
WOULDN'T THE GREAT KUNG FU ROBOT LIKE TO KNOW MY EVIL PLAN?
THE EVIL KUNG POW CHICKEN! HOW DID YOU SEE THROUGH MY DISGUISE? AND MORE IMPORTANTLY . . .
. . . AM I REALLY TALKING TO A CHICKEN RIGHT NOW?

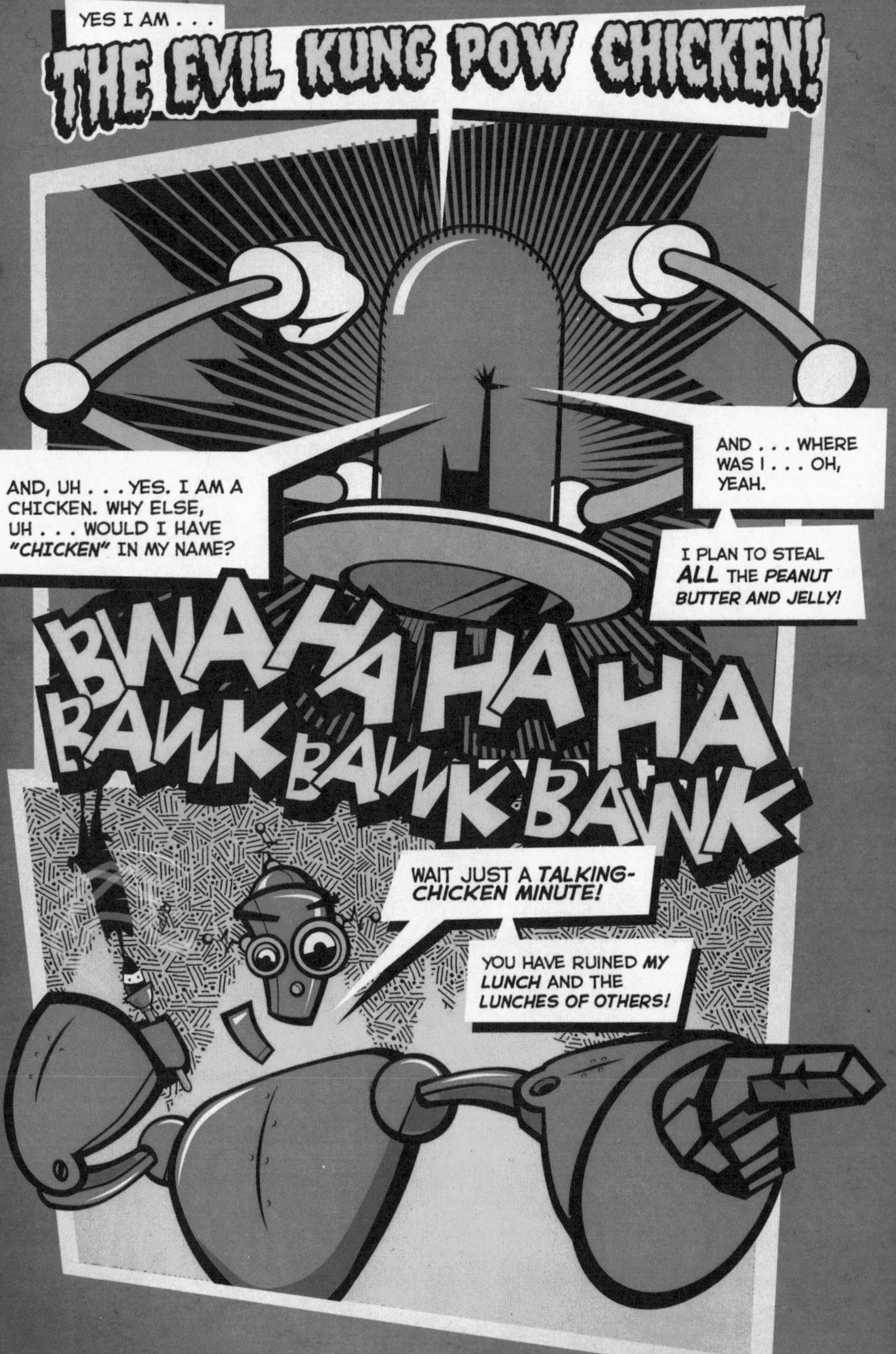
YES I AM . . .
THE EVIL KUNG POW CHICKEN!
AND, UH . . . YES. I AM A CHICKEN. WHY ELSE, UH . . . WOULD I HAVE "CHICKEN" IN MY NAME?
AND . . . WHERE WAS I . . . OH, YEAH.
I PLAN TO STEAL ALL THE PEANUT BUTTER AND JELLY!
BWAHAHAHAHA
BAWK BAWK BAWK
WAIT JUST A TALKING-CHICKEN MINUTE!
YOU HAVE RUINED MY LUNCH AND THE LUNCHES OF OTHERS!

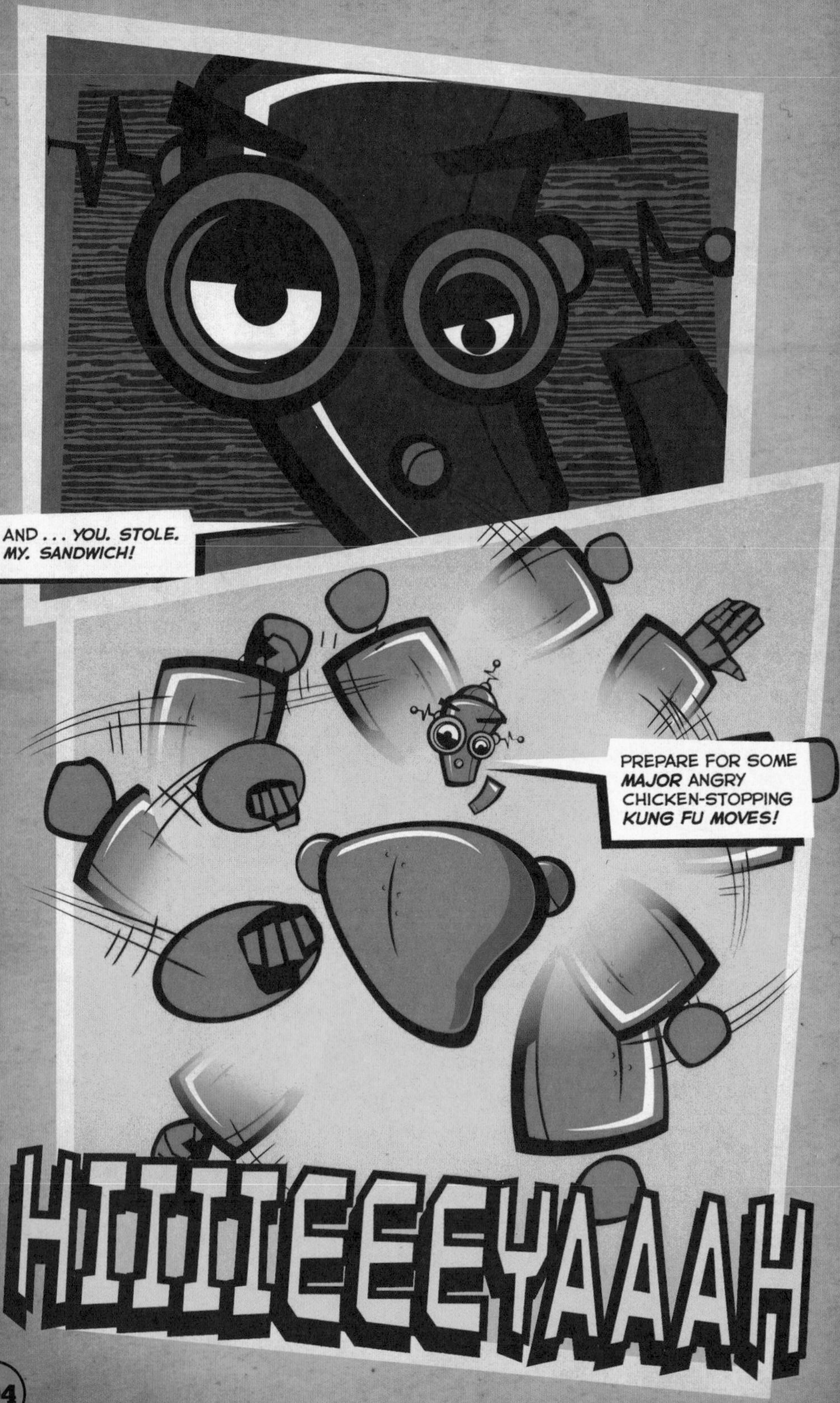
AND . . . YOU. STOLE. MY. SANDWICH!
PREPARE FOR SOME MAJOR ANGRY CHICKEN-STOPPING KUNG FU MOVES!
HIIIIEEEYAAAH

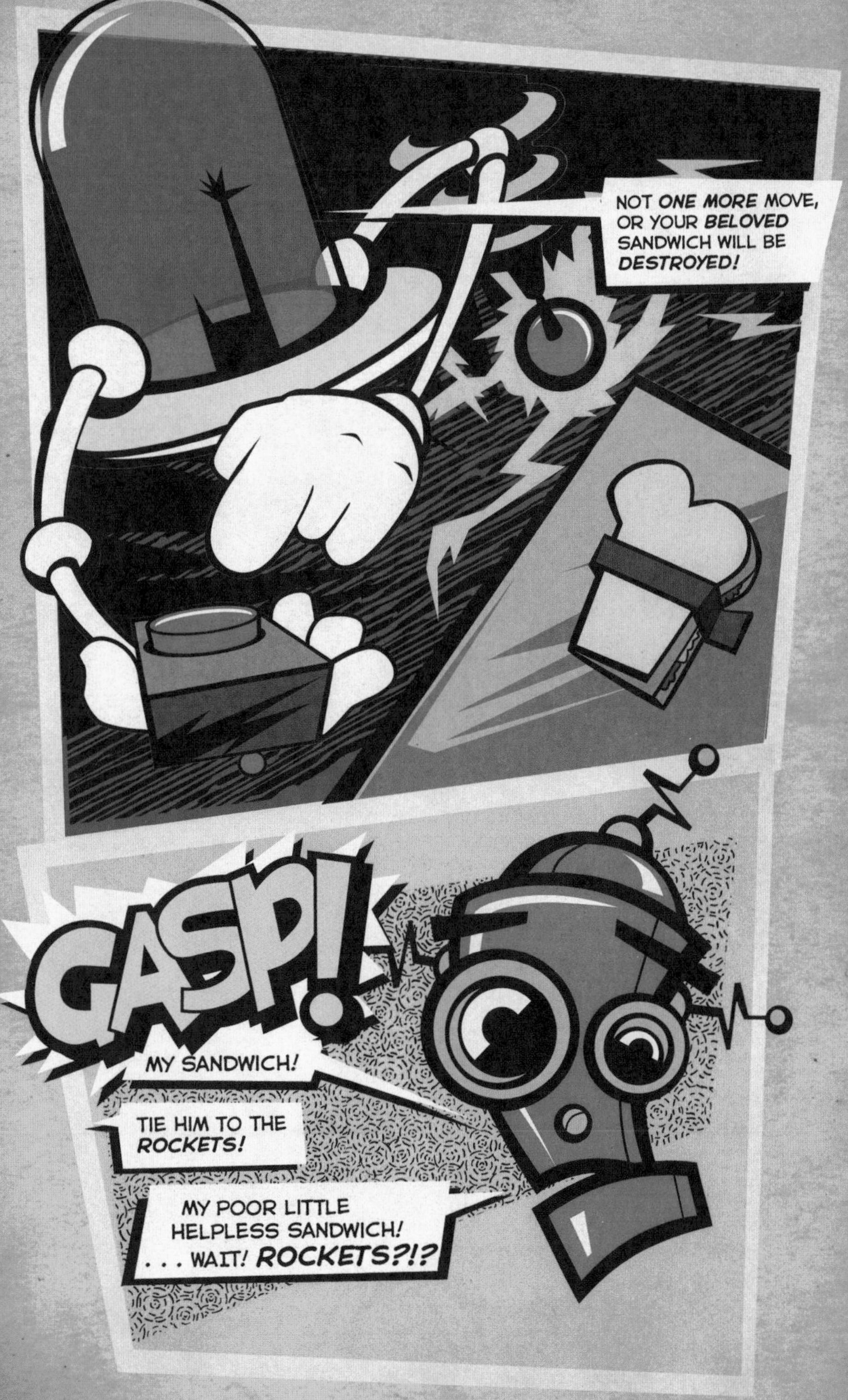
NOT ONE MORE MOVE, OR YOUR BELOVED SANDWICH WILL BE DESTROYED!
GASP!
MY SANDWICH!
TIE HIM TO THE ROCKETS!
MY POOR LITTLE HELPLESS SANDWICH! . . . WAIT! ROCKETS?!?

CHAPTER 3

BWAHHAHA BANK BANK BANG

AND *YES, KUNG POW CHICKEN* HAS BEEN LAUGHING THIS *WHOLE* TIME.

AHEM! CAN WE GET BACK TO THE PART WHERE THE HERO OF THE STORY CONFRONTS THE VILLAIN, PLEASE?

WHAT KIND OF EVIL FIEND WOULD STEAL THE WORLD'S PEANUT BUTTER AND JELLY? AND WHAT KIND OF VILLAIN HOLDS A HELPLESS SANDWICH HOSTAGE?

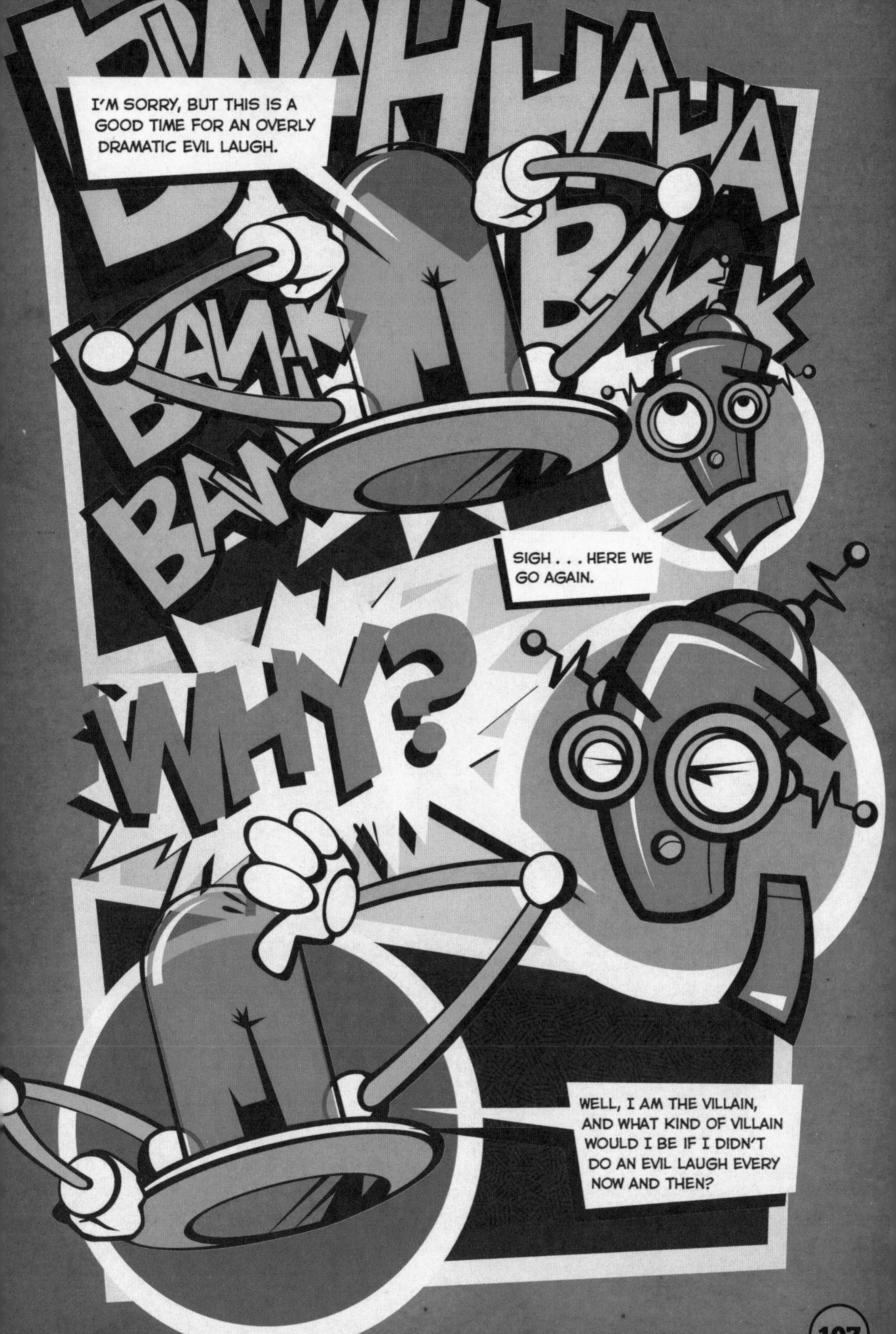
I'M SORRY, BUT THIS IS A GOOD TIME FOR AN OVERLY DRAMATIC EVIL LAUGH.
SIGH . . . HERE WE GO AGAIN.
WHY?
WELL, I AM THE VILLAIN, AND WHAT KIND OF VILLAIN WOULD I BE IF I DIDN'T DO AN EVIL LAUGH EVERY NOW AND THEN?

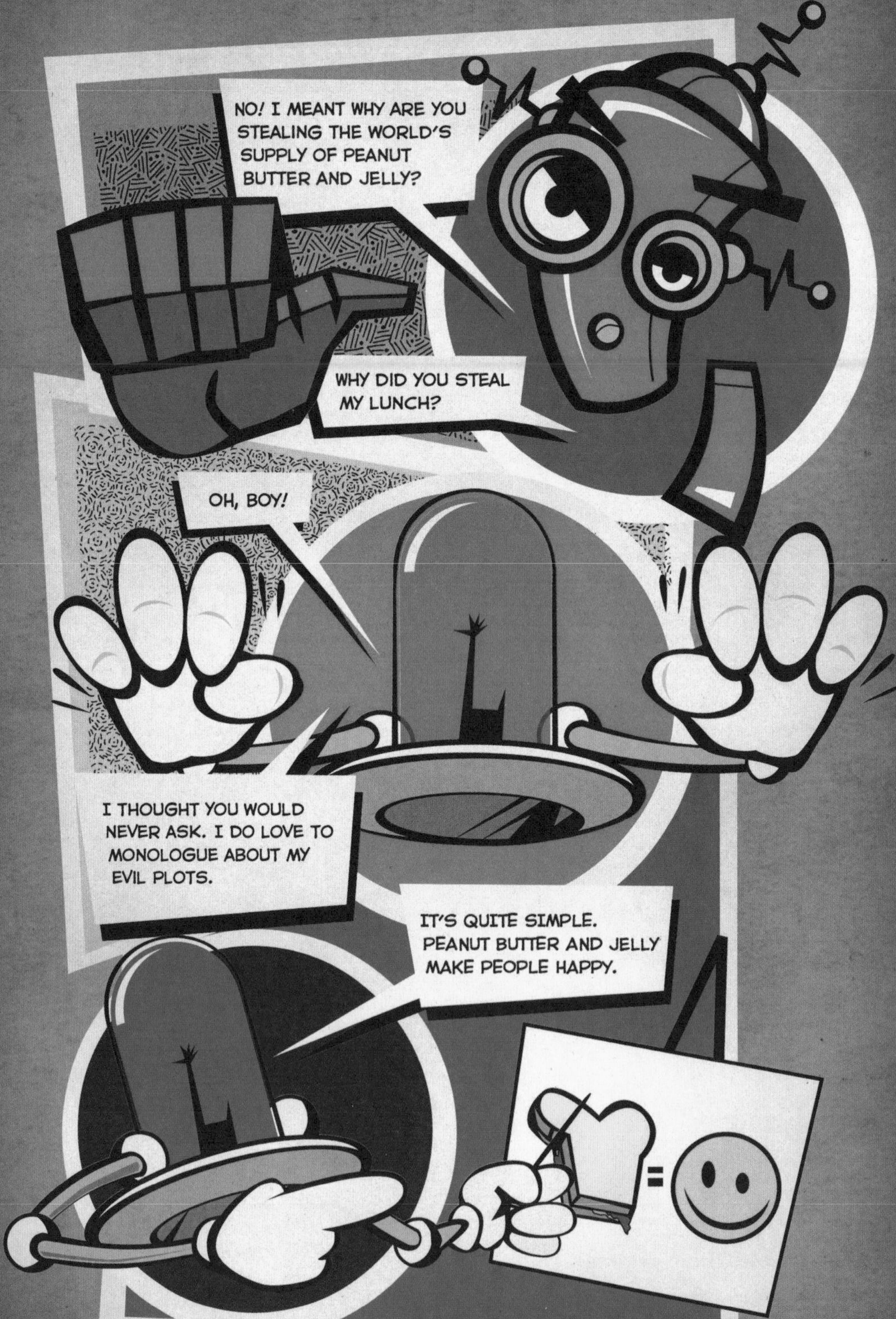
NO! I MEANT WHY ARE YOU STEALING THE WORLD'S SUPPLY OF PEANUT BUTTER AND JELLY?
WHY DID YOU STEAL MY LUNCH?
OH, BOY!
I THOUGHT YOU WOULD NEVER ASK. I DO LOVE TO MONOLOGUE ABOUT MY EVIL PLOTS.
IT'S QUITE SIMPLE. PEANUT BUTTER AND JELLY MAKE PEOPLE HAPPY.
=

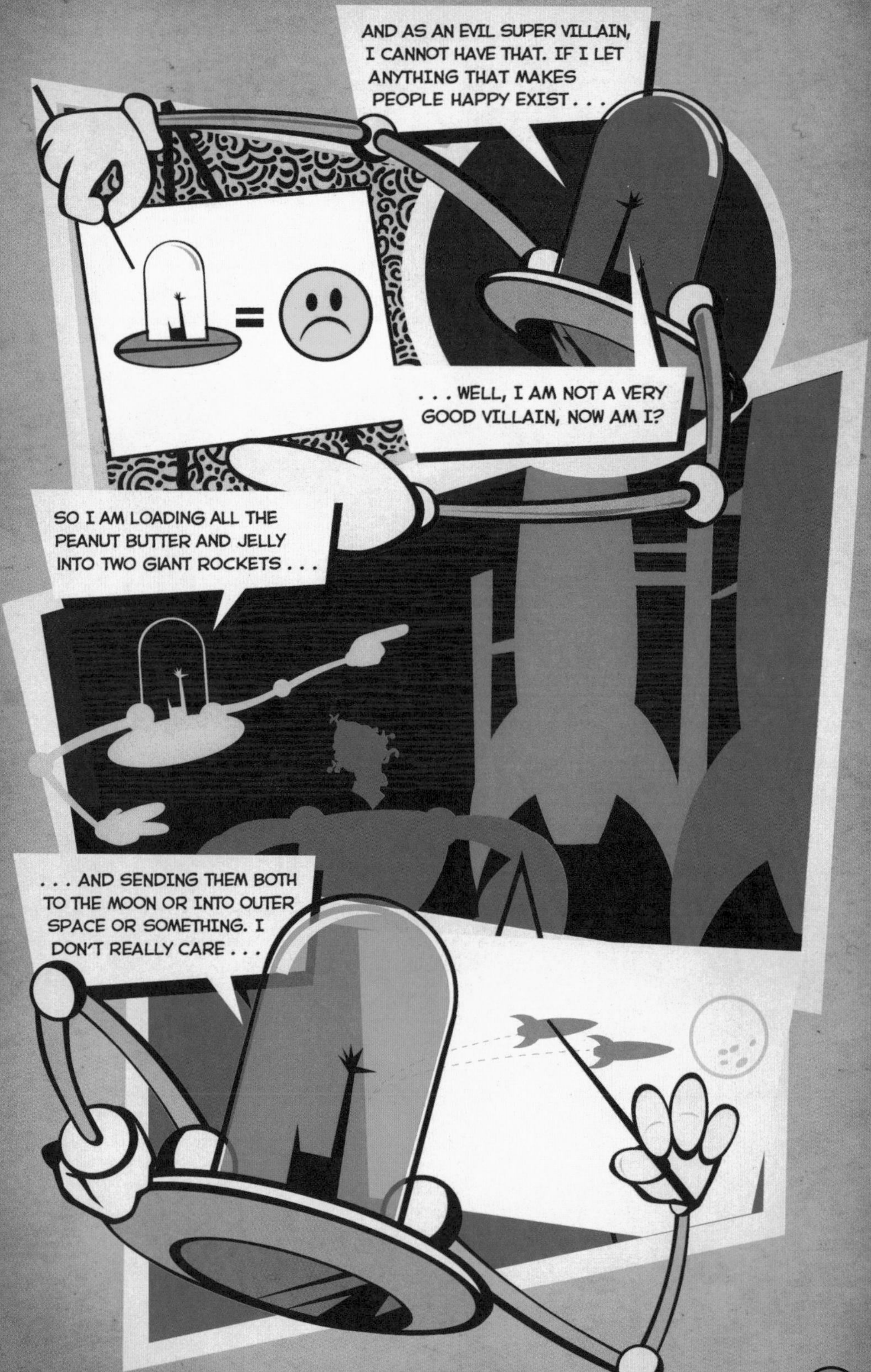
AND AS AN EVIL SUPER VILLAIN, I CANNOT HAVE THAT. IF I LET ANYTHING THAT MAKES PEOPLE HAPPY EXIST . . .
. . . WELL, I AM NOT A VERY GOOD VILLAIN, NOW AM I?
SO I AM LOADING ALL THE PEANUT BUTTER AND JELLY INTO TWO GIANT ROCKETS . . .
. . . AND SENDING THEM BOTH TO THE MOON OR INTO OUTER SPACE OR SOMETHING. I DON'T REALLY CARE . . .

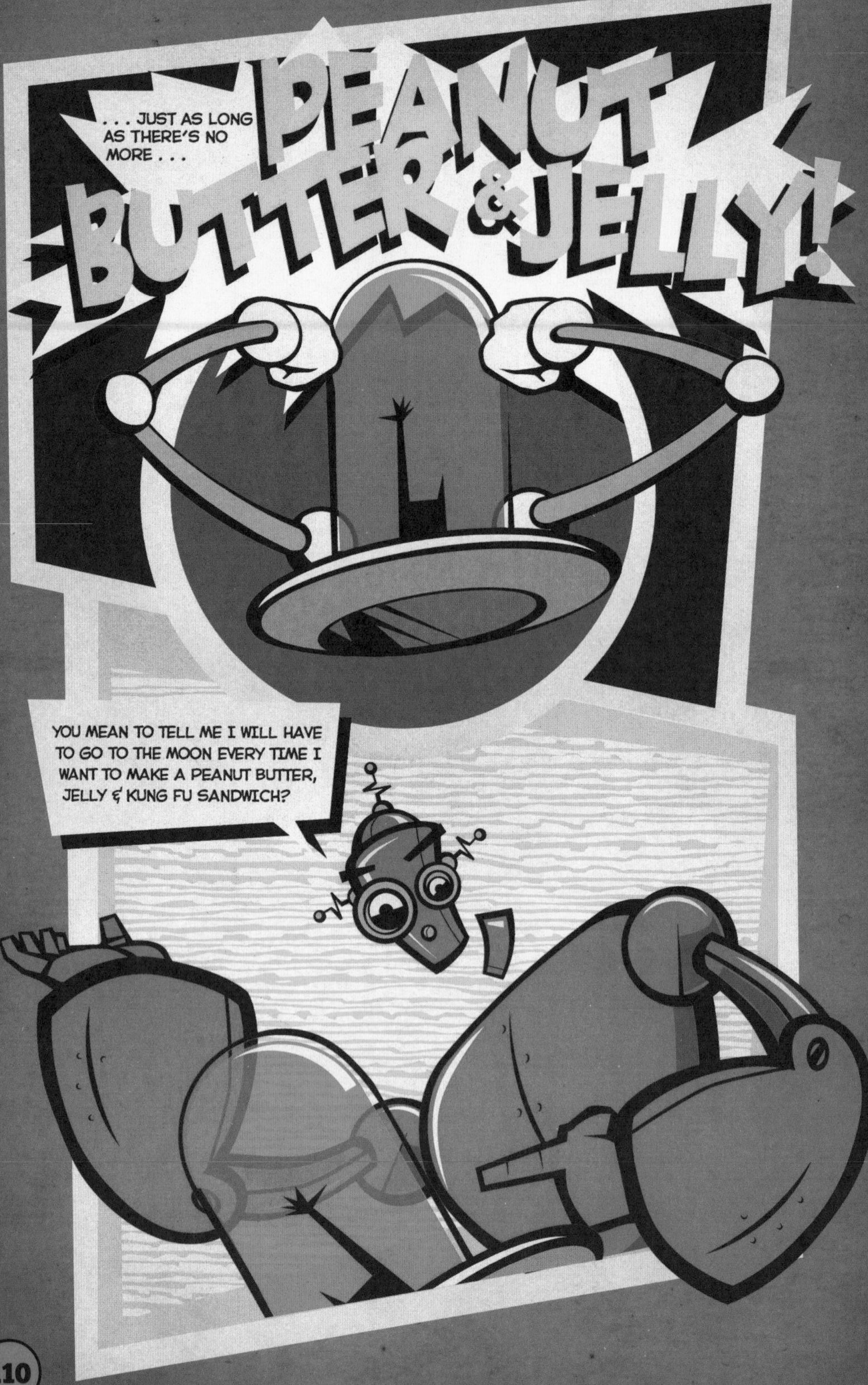
. . . JUST AS LONG AS THERE'S NO MORE . . .
PEANUT BUTTER & JELLY!
YOU MEAN TO TELL ME I WILL HAVE TO GO TO THE MOON EVERY TIME I WANT TO MAKE A PEANUT BUTTER, JELLY & KUNG FU SANDWICH?

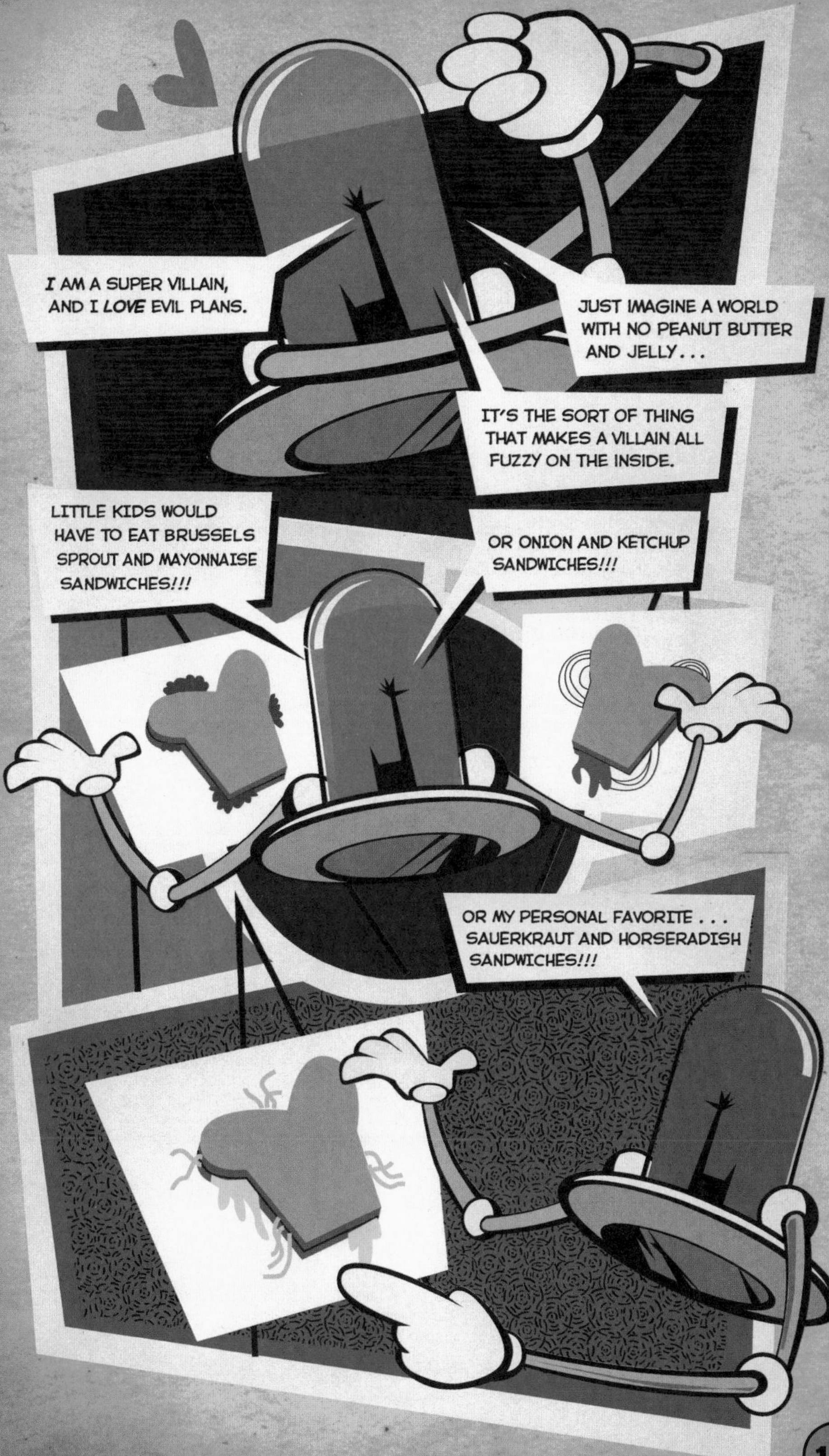
I AM A SUPER VILLAIN, AND I LOVE EVIL PLANS.
JUST IMAGINE A WORLD WITH NO PEANUT BUTTER AND JELLY . . .
IT'S THE SORT OF THING THAT MAKES A VILLAIN ALL FUZZY ON THE INSIDE.
LITTLE KIDS WOULD HAVE TO EAT BRUSSELS SPROUT AND MAYONNAISE SANDWICHES!!!
OR ONION AND KETCHUP SANDWICHES!!!
OR MY PERSONAL FAVORITE . . . SAUERKRAUT AND HORSERADISH SANDWICHES!!!

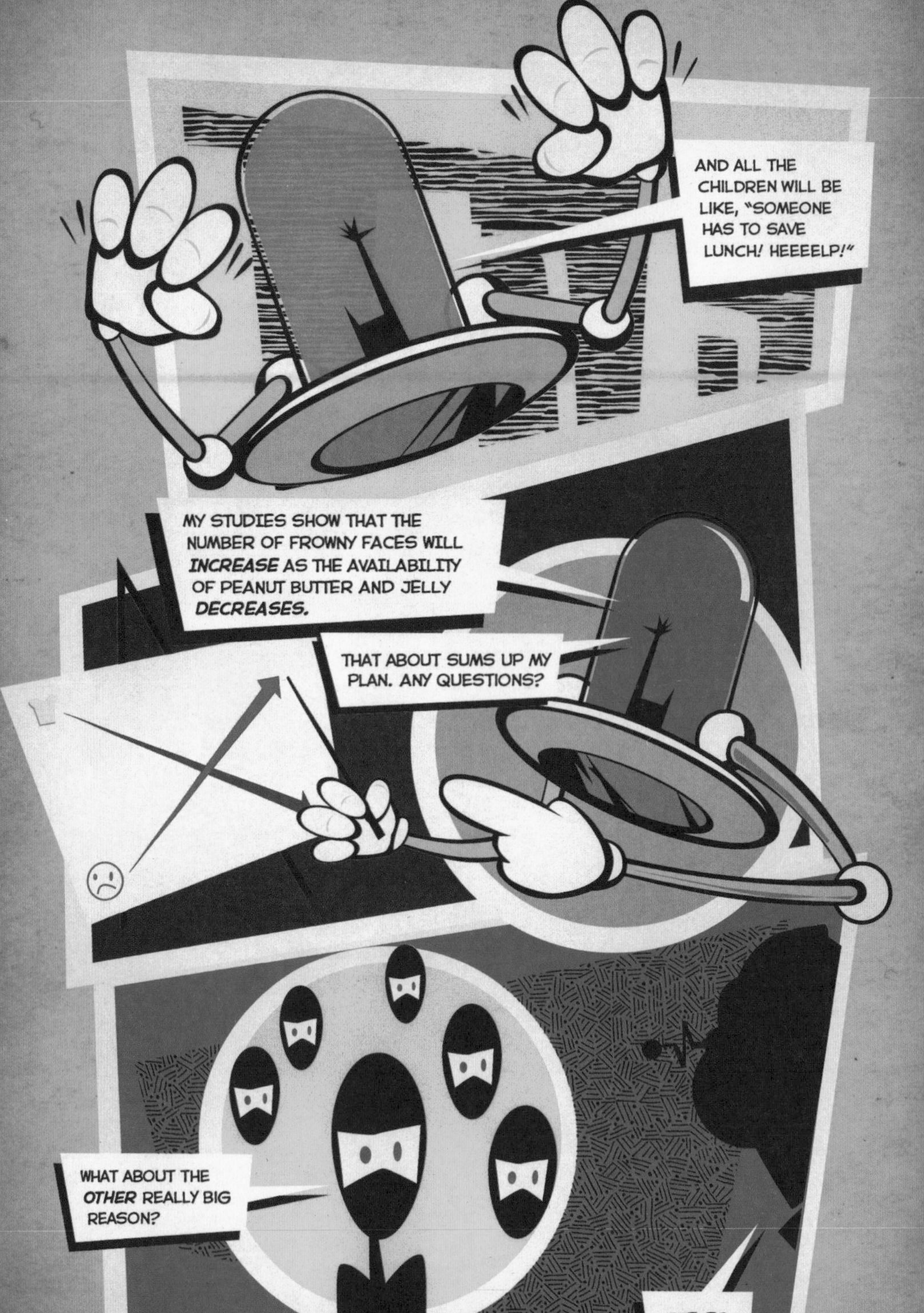
AND ALL THE CHILDREN WILL BE LIKE, "SOMEONE HAS TO SAVE LUNCH! HEEEELP!"
MY STUDIES SHOW THAT THE NUMBER OF FROWNY FACES WILL *INCREASE* AS THE AVAILABILITY OF PEANUT BUTTER AND JELLY *DECREASES.*
THAT ABOUT SUMS UP MY PLAN. ANY QUESTIONS?
WHAT ABOUT THE *OTHER* REALLY BIG REASON?
STEVE?

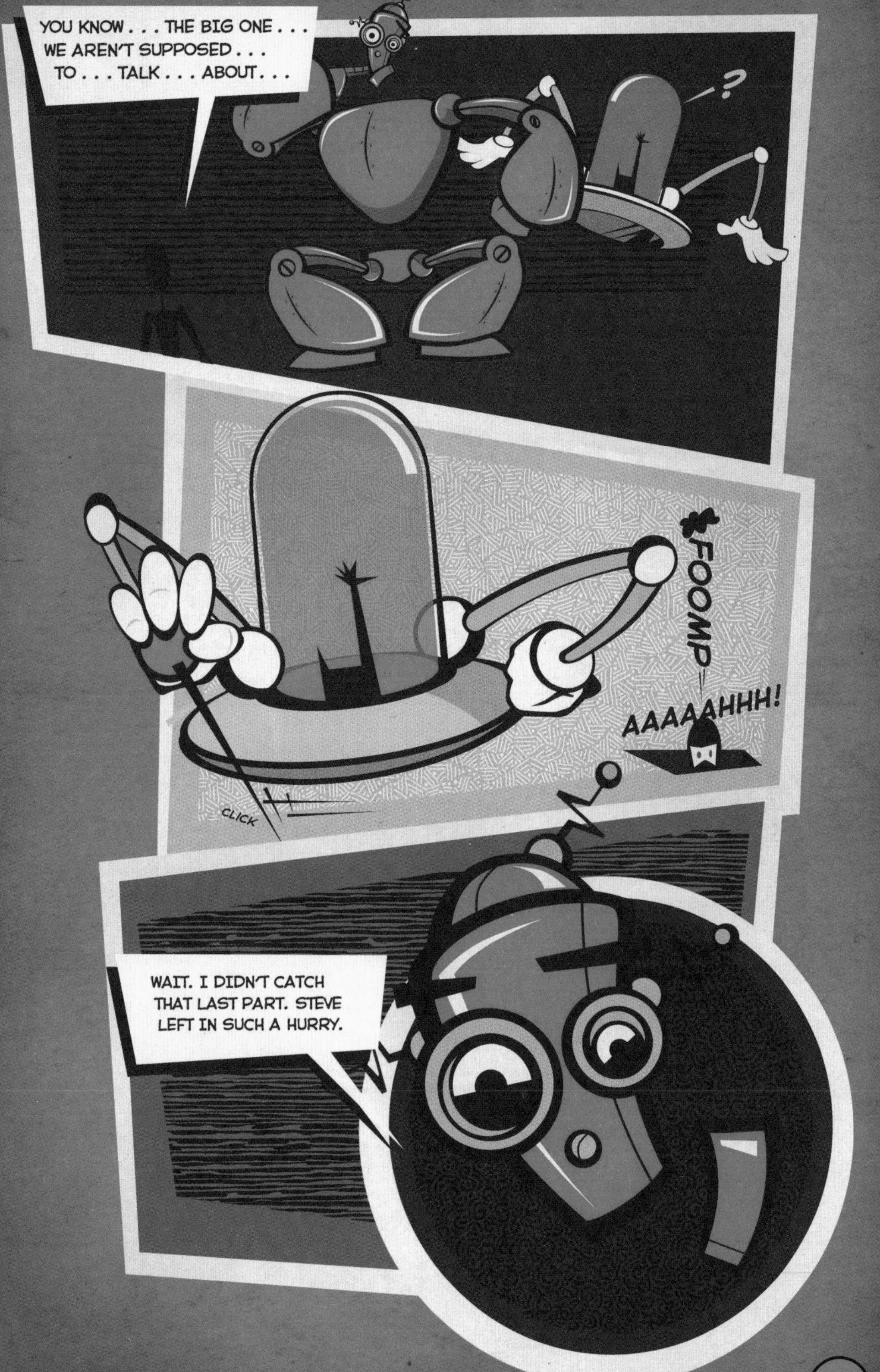
YOU KNOW . . . THE BIG ONE . . . WE AREN'T SUPPOSED . . . TO . . . TALK . . . ABOUT . . .
?
FOOMP
AAAAAHHH!
CLICK
WAIT. I DIDN'T CATCH THAT LAST PART. STEVE LEFT IN SUCH A HURRY.

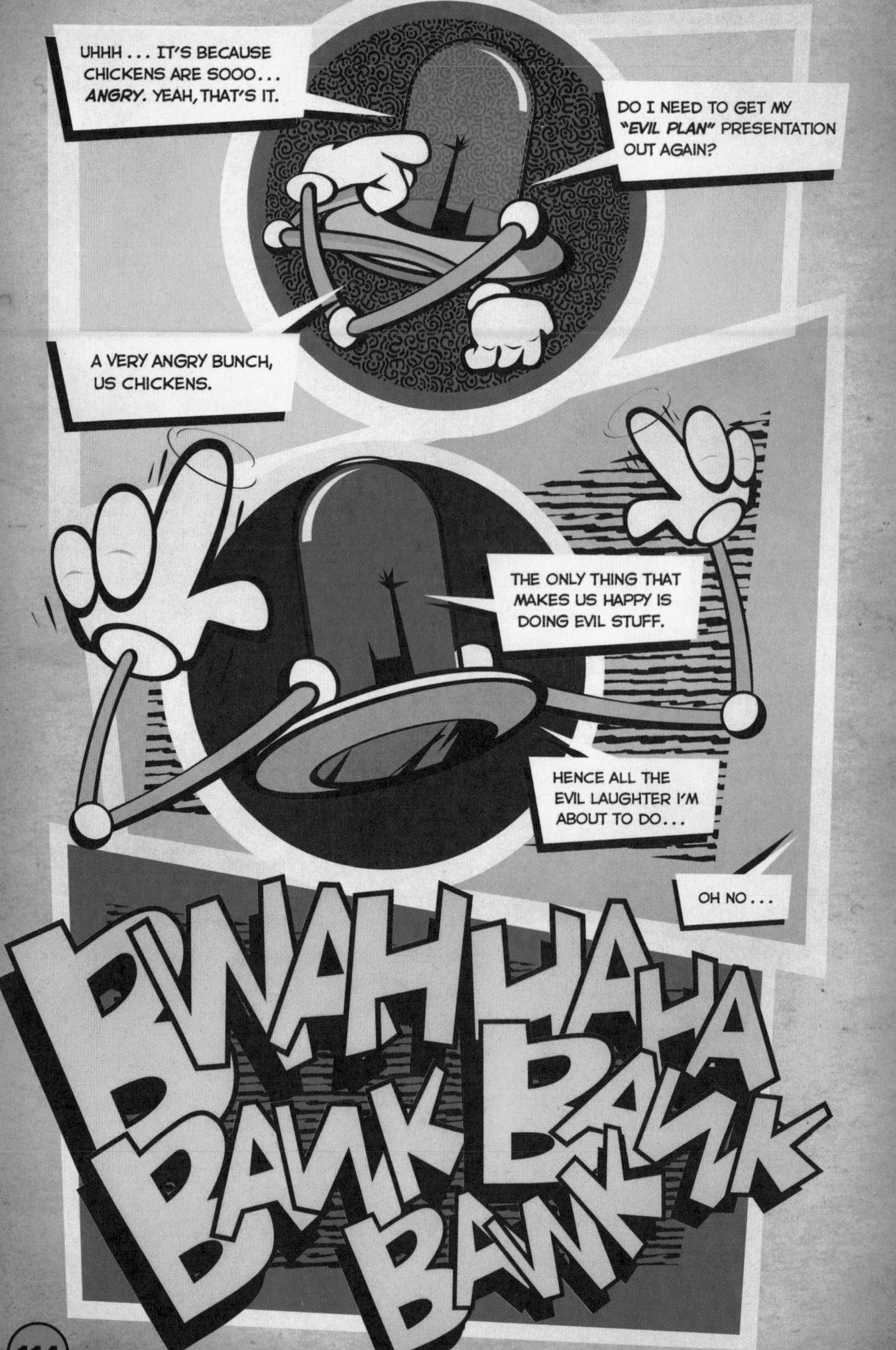
UHHH . . . IT'S BECAUSE CHICKENS ARE SOOO . . . *ANGRY.* YEAH, THAT'S IT.
DO I NEED TO GET MY *"EVIL PLAN"* PRESENTATION OUT AGAIN?
A VERY ANGRY BUNCH, US CHICKENS.
THE ONLY THING THAT MAKES US HAPPY IS DOING EVIL STUFF.
HENCE ALL THE EVIL LAUGHTER I'M ABOUT TO DO . . .
OH NO . . .
BWAHAHA
BAWK BAWK
BAWK

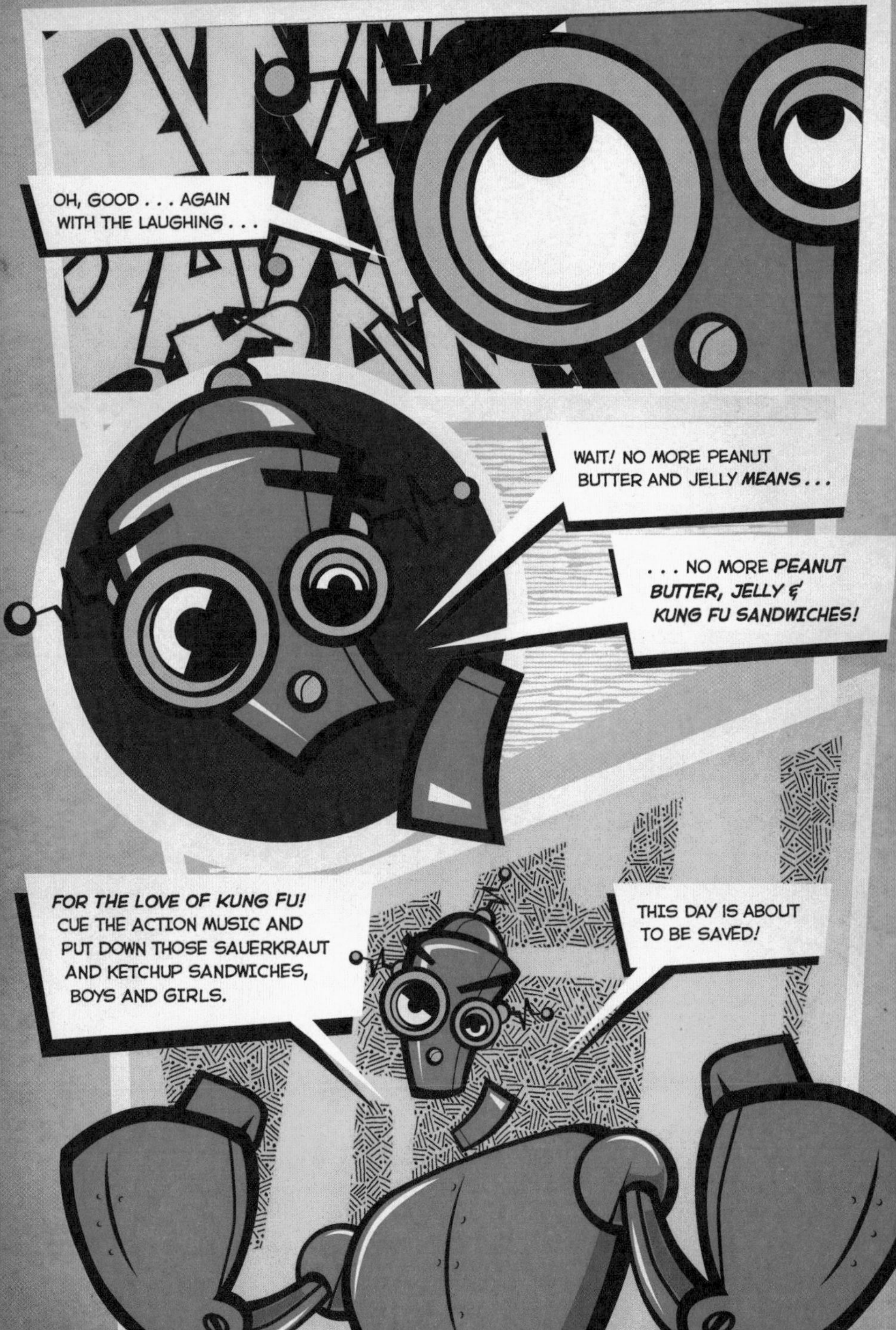
OH, GOOD . . . AGAIN WITH THE LAUGHING . . .
WAIT! NO MORE PEANUT BUTTER AND JELLY MEANS . . .
. . . NO MORE PEANUT BUTTER, JELLY & KUNG FU SANDWICHES!
FOR THE LOVE OF KUNG FU! CUE THE ACTION MUSIC AND PUT DOWN THOSE SAUERKRAUT AND KETCHUP SANDWICHES, BOYS AND GIRLS.
THIS DAY IS ABOUT TO BE SAVED!

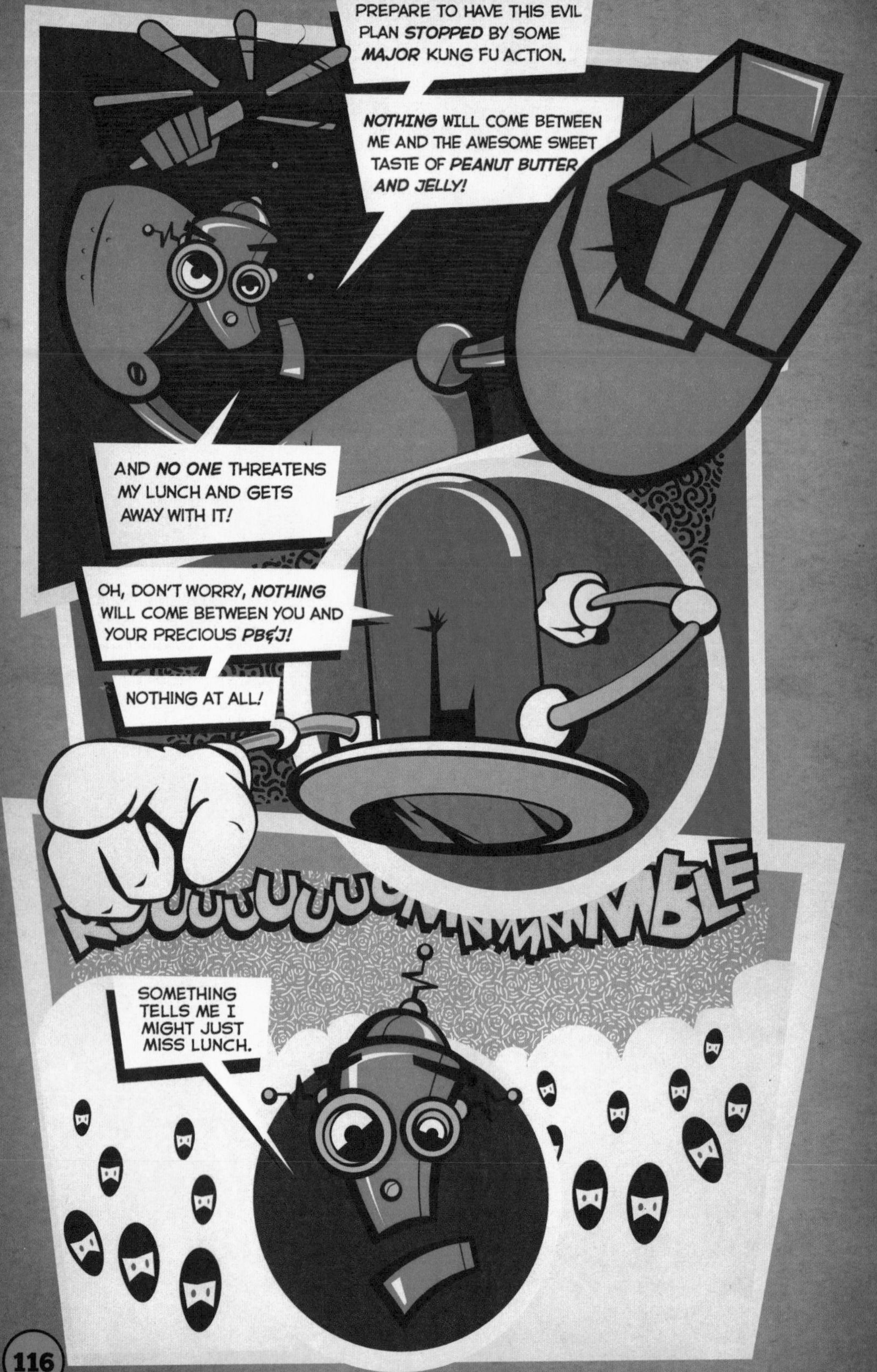

PREPARE TO HAVE THIS EVIL PLAN STOPPED BY SOME MAJOR KUNG FU ACTION.
NOTHING WILL COME BETWEEN ME AND THE AWESOME SWEET TASTE OF PEANUT BUTTER AND JELLY!
AND NO ONE THREATENS MY LUNCH AND GETS AWAY WITH IT!
OH, DON'T WORRY, NOTHING WILL COME BETWEEN YOU AND YOUR PRECIOUS PB&J!
NOTHING AT ALL!
SOMETHING TELLS ME I MIGHT JUST MISS LUNCH.

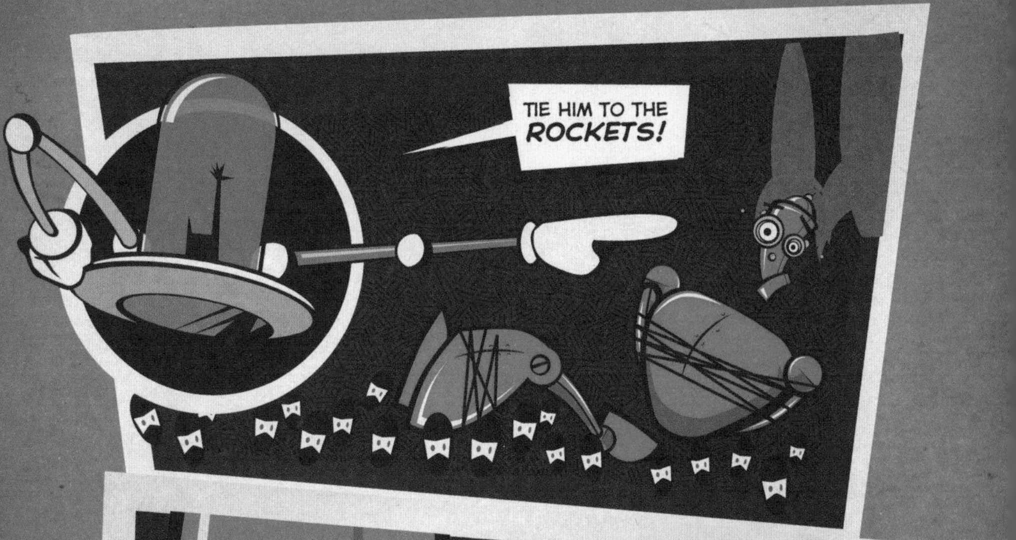
TIE HIM TO THE *ROCKETS!*

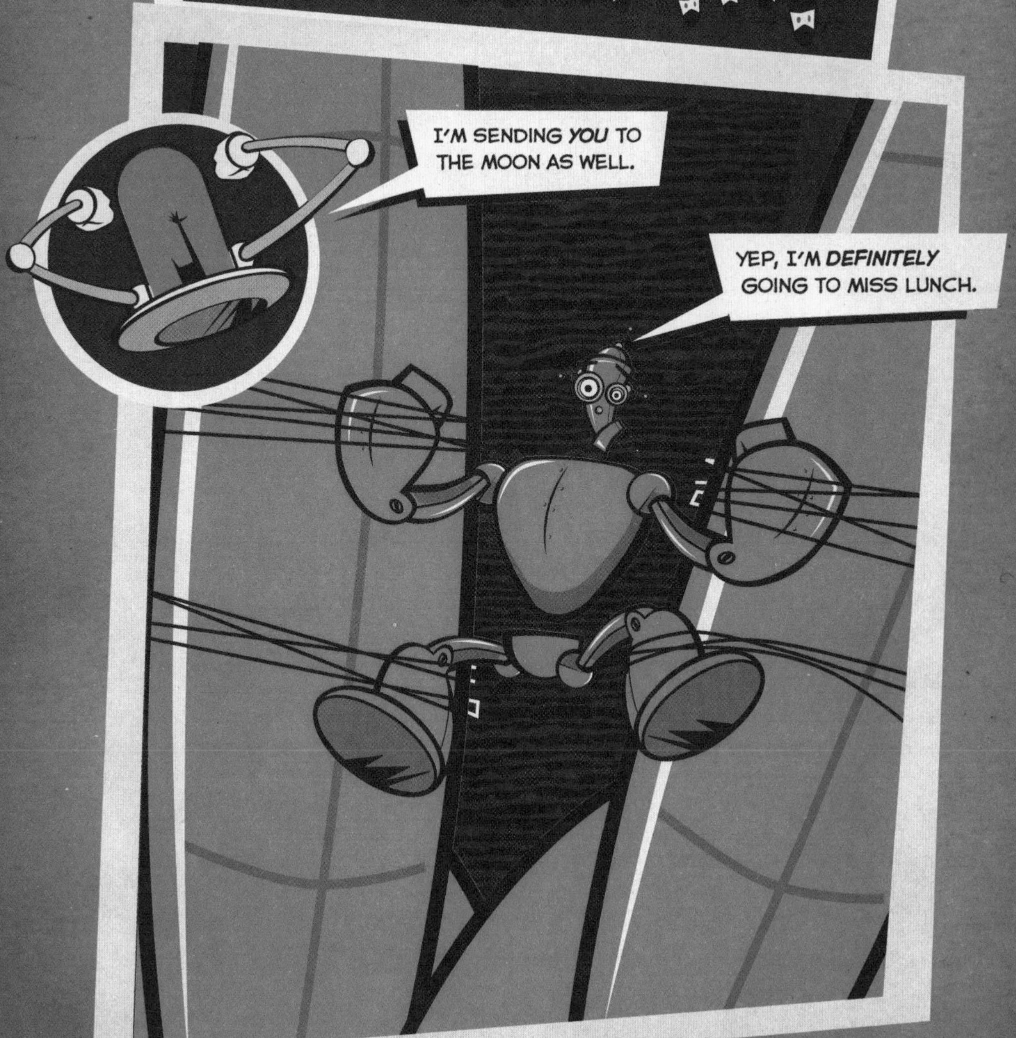
I'M SENDING *YOU* TO THE MOON AS WELL.
YEP, I'M *DEFINITELY* GOING TO MISS LUNCH.

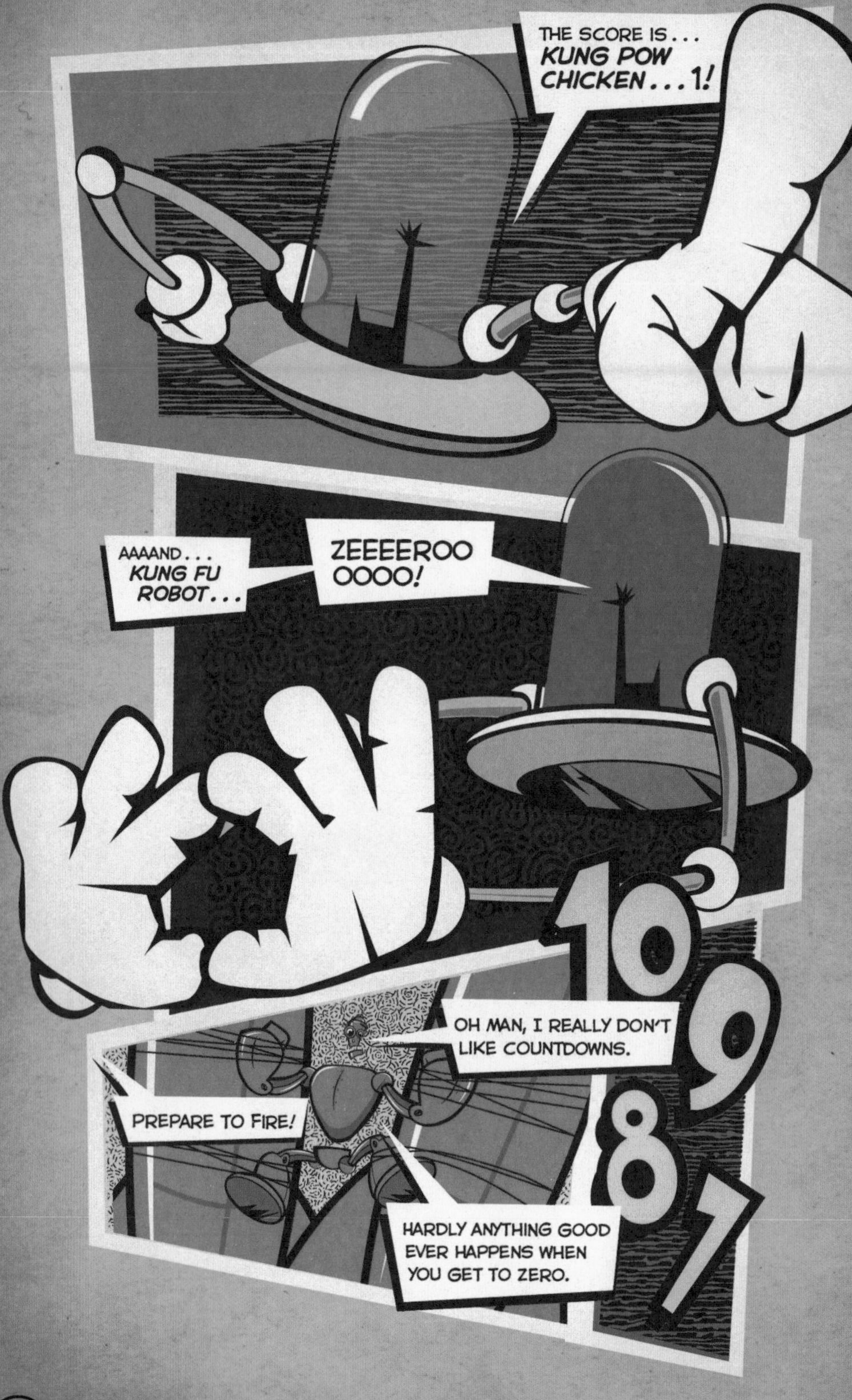
THE SCORE IS . . . KUNG POW CHICKEN . . . 1!
AAAAND . . . KUNG FU ROBOT . . .
ZEEEEROO OOOO!
10
9
8
7
OH MAN, I REALLY DON'T LIKE COUNTDOWNS.
PREPARE TO FIRE!
HARDLY ANYTHING GOOD EVER HAPPENS WHEN YOU GET TO ZERO.

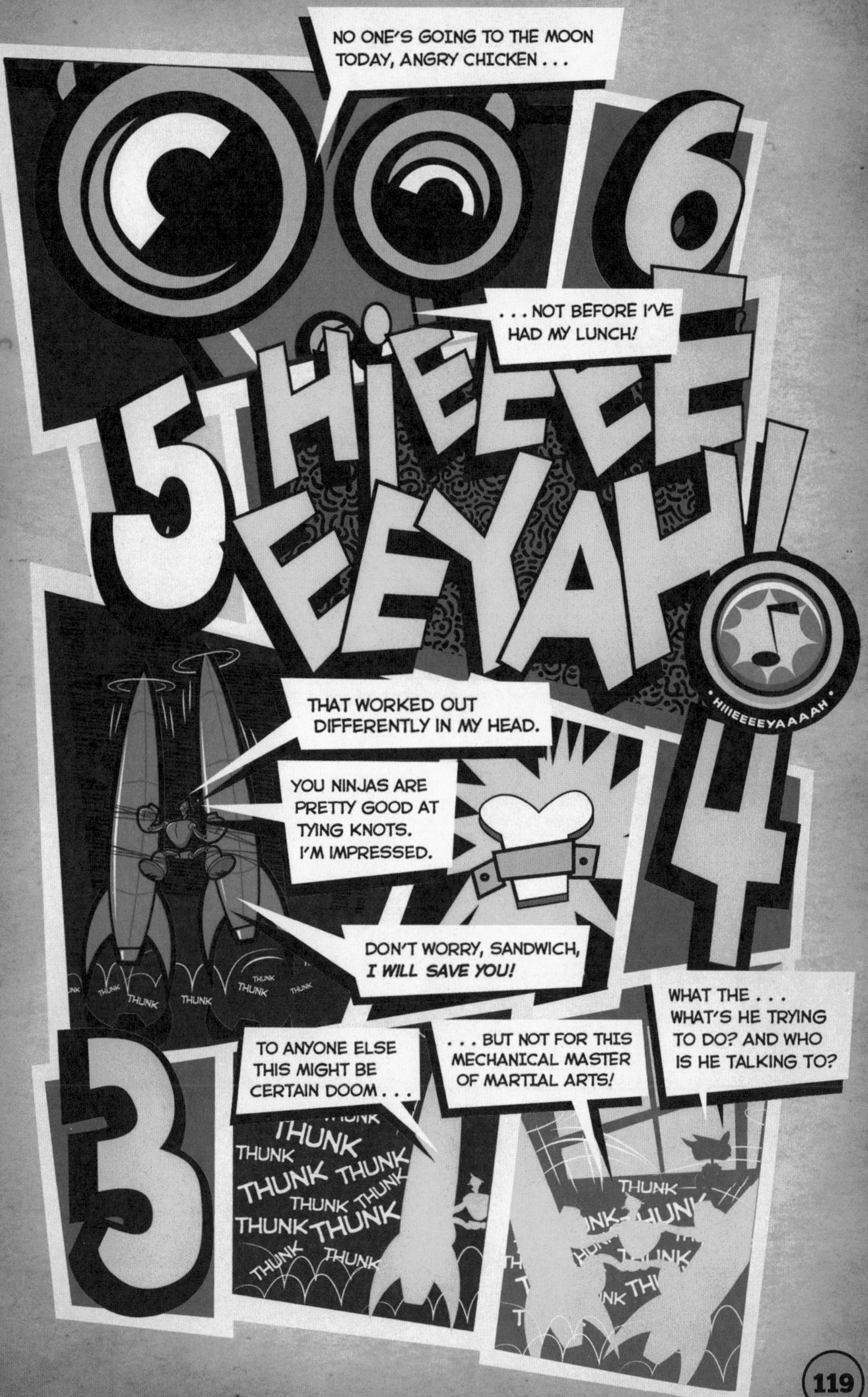

NO ONE'S GOING TO THE MOON TODAY, ANGRY CHICKEN . . .
6
. . . NOT BEFORE I'VE HAD MY LUNCH!
5
HIEEEE EEYAH!
HIIIEEEEYAAAAH
THAT WORKED OUT DIFFERENTLY IN MY HEAD.
YOU NINJAS ARE PRETTY GOOD AT TYING KNOTS. I'M IMPRESSED.
4
DON'T WORRY, SANDWICH, *I WILL SAVE YOU!*
THUNK THUNK THUNK THUNK THUNK
WHAT THE . . . WHAT'S HE TRYING TO DO? AND WHO IS HE TALKING TO?
3
TO ANYONE ELSE THIS MIGHT BE CERTAIN DOOM . . .
. . . BUT NOT FOR THIS MECHANICAL MASTER OF MARTIAL ARTS!
THUNK THUNK THUNK THUNK THUNK THUNK THUNK THUNK THUNK THUNK
THUNK

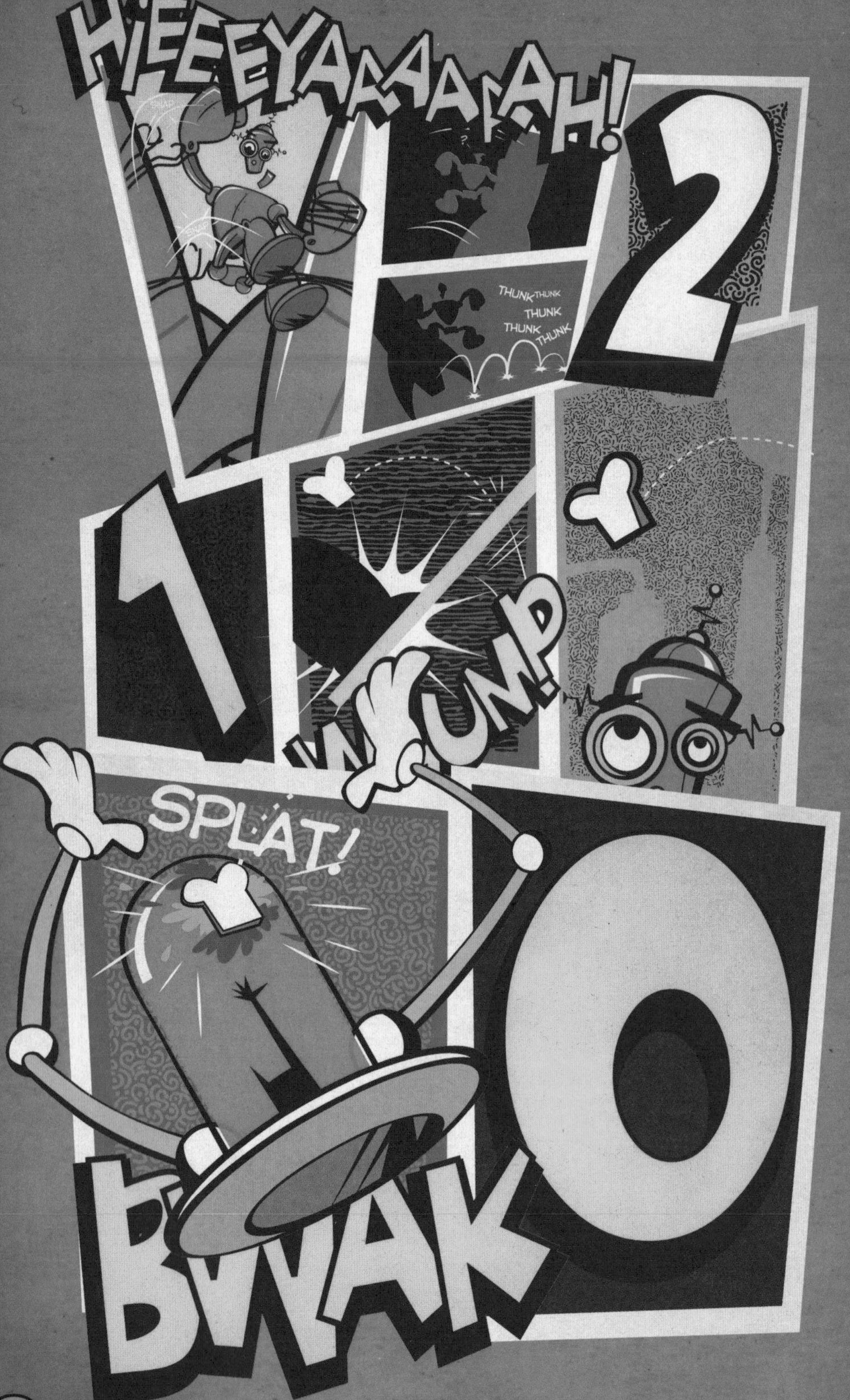
HiEEEYAAAAAAH!
SNAP
SNAP
THUNK THUNK
THUNK
THUNK THUNK
2
1
WUMP!
SPLAT!
BWAK
0

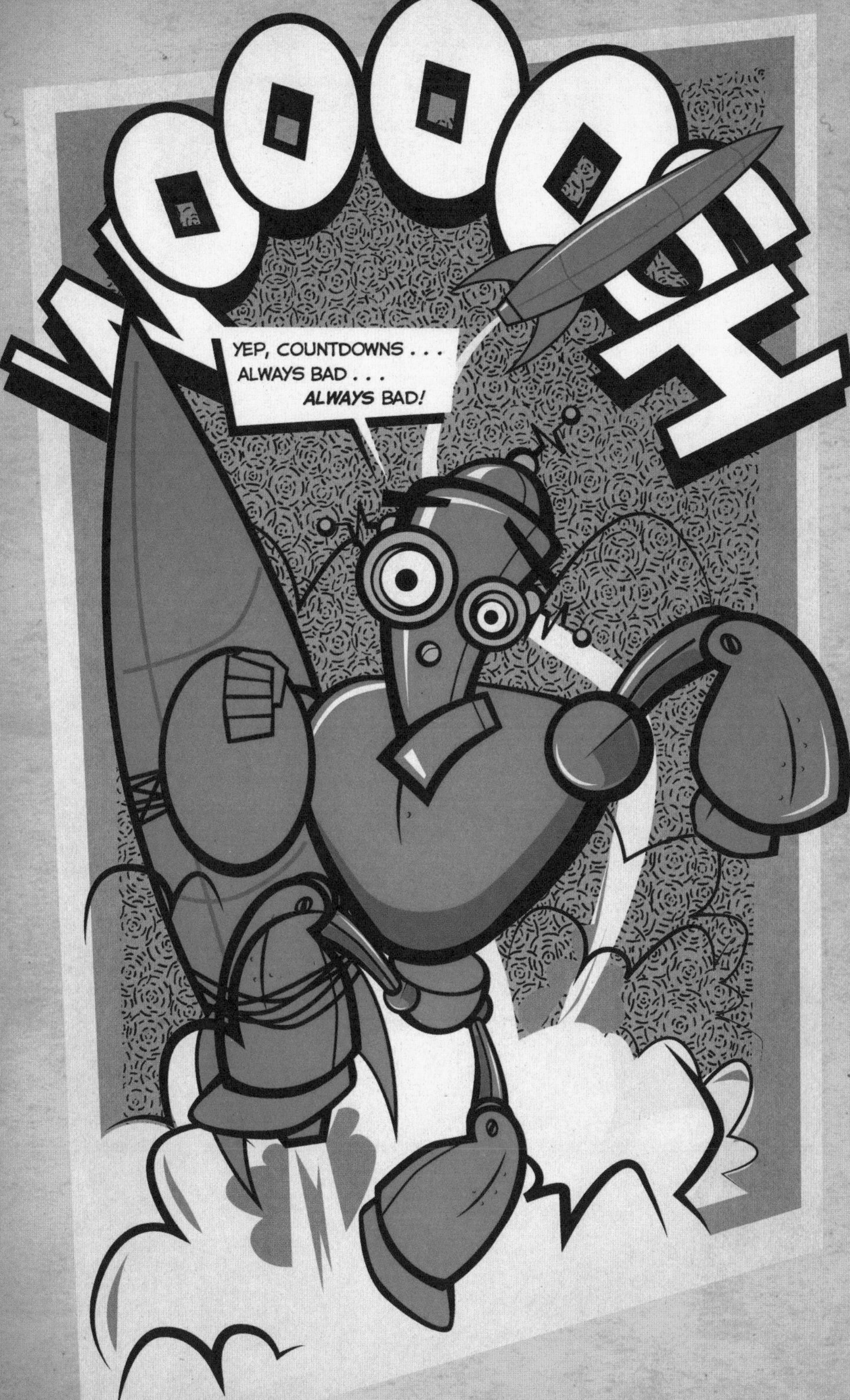
WOOOOSH
YEP, COUNTDOWNS . . .
ALWAYS BAD . . .
ALWAYS BAD!

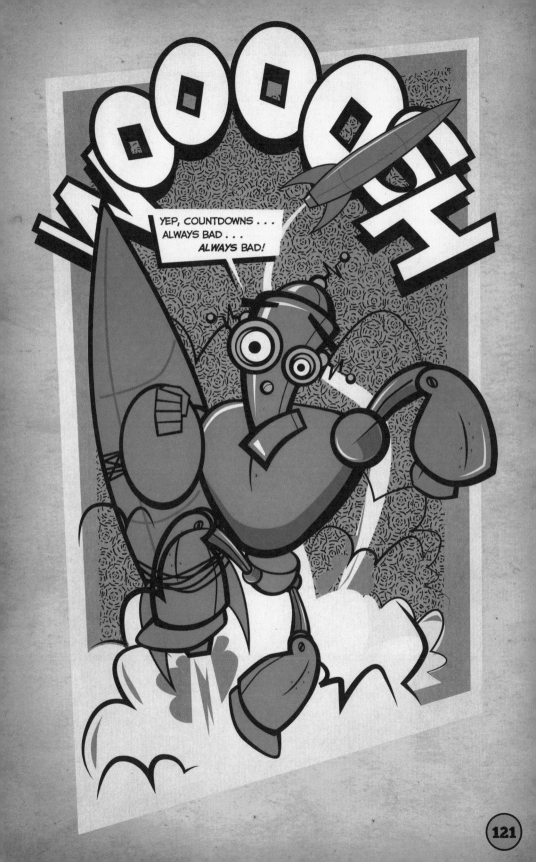

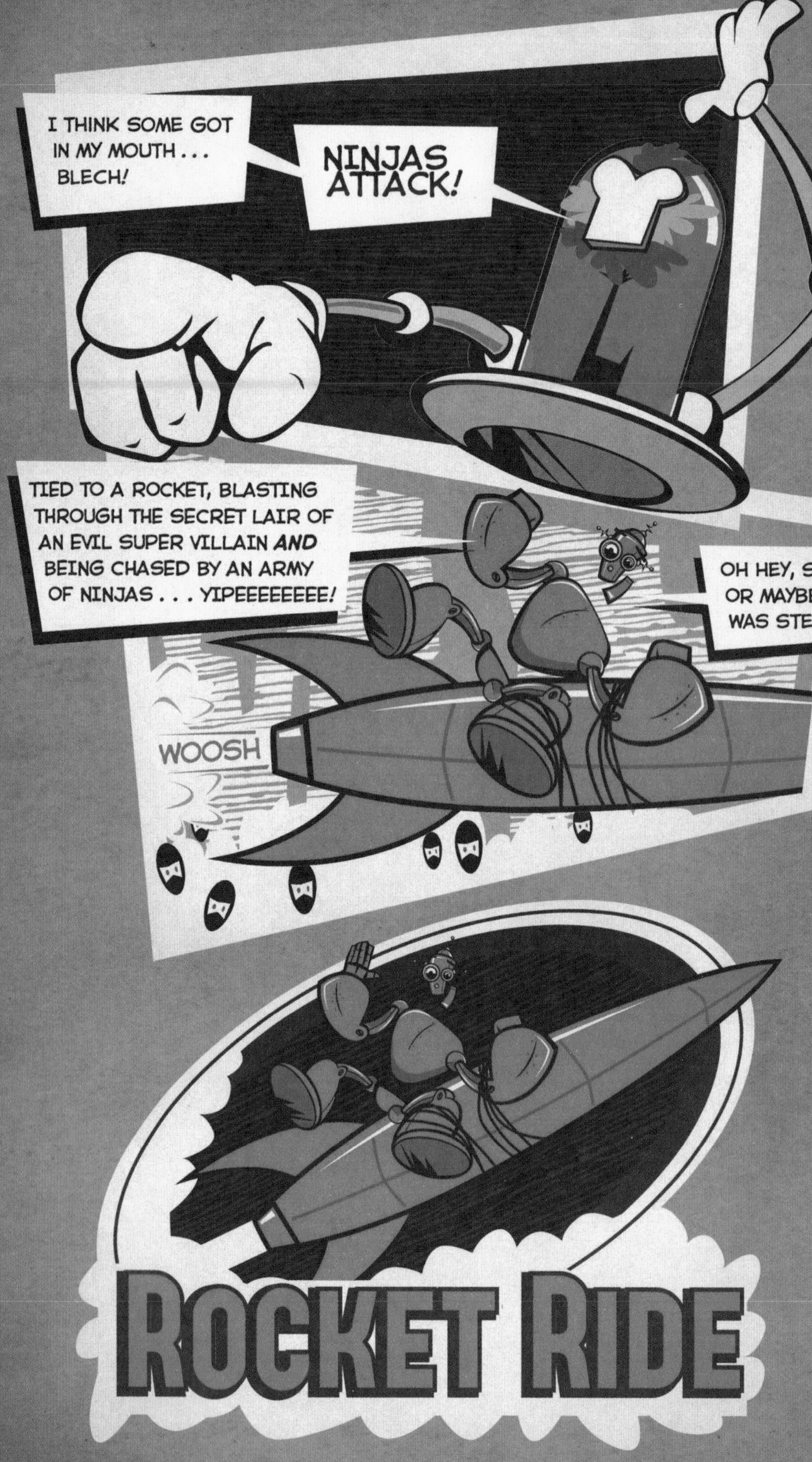
I THINK SOME GOT IN MY MOUTH . . . BLECH!
NINJAS ATTACK!
TIED TO A ROCKET, BLASTING THROUGH THE SECRET LAIR OF AN EVIL SUPER VILLAIN *AND* BEING CHASED BY AN ARMY OF NINJAS . . . YIPEEEEEEEEE!
OH HEY, STEVE. OR MAYBE THAT WAS STEVE . . .
WOOSH
ROCKET RIDE

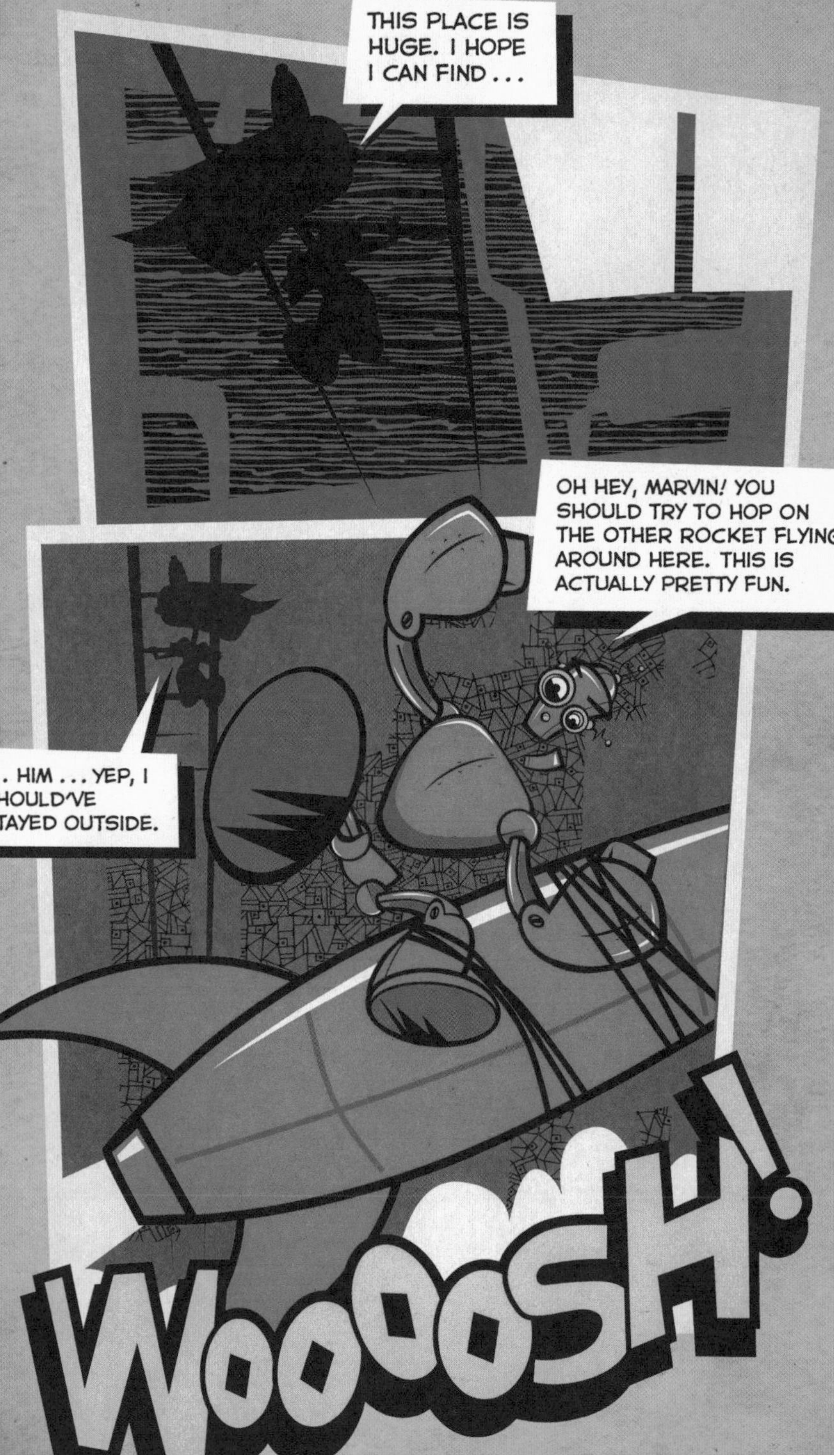
THIS PLACE IS HUGE. I HOPE I CAN FIND . . .
OH HEY, MARVIN! YOU SHOULD TRY TO HOP ON THE OTHER ROCKET FLYING AROUND HERE. THIS IS ACTUALLY PRETTY FUN.
. . . HIM . . . YEP, I SHOULD'VE STAYED OUTSIDE.
WOOOOSH!

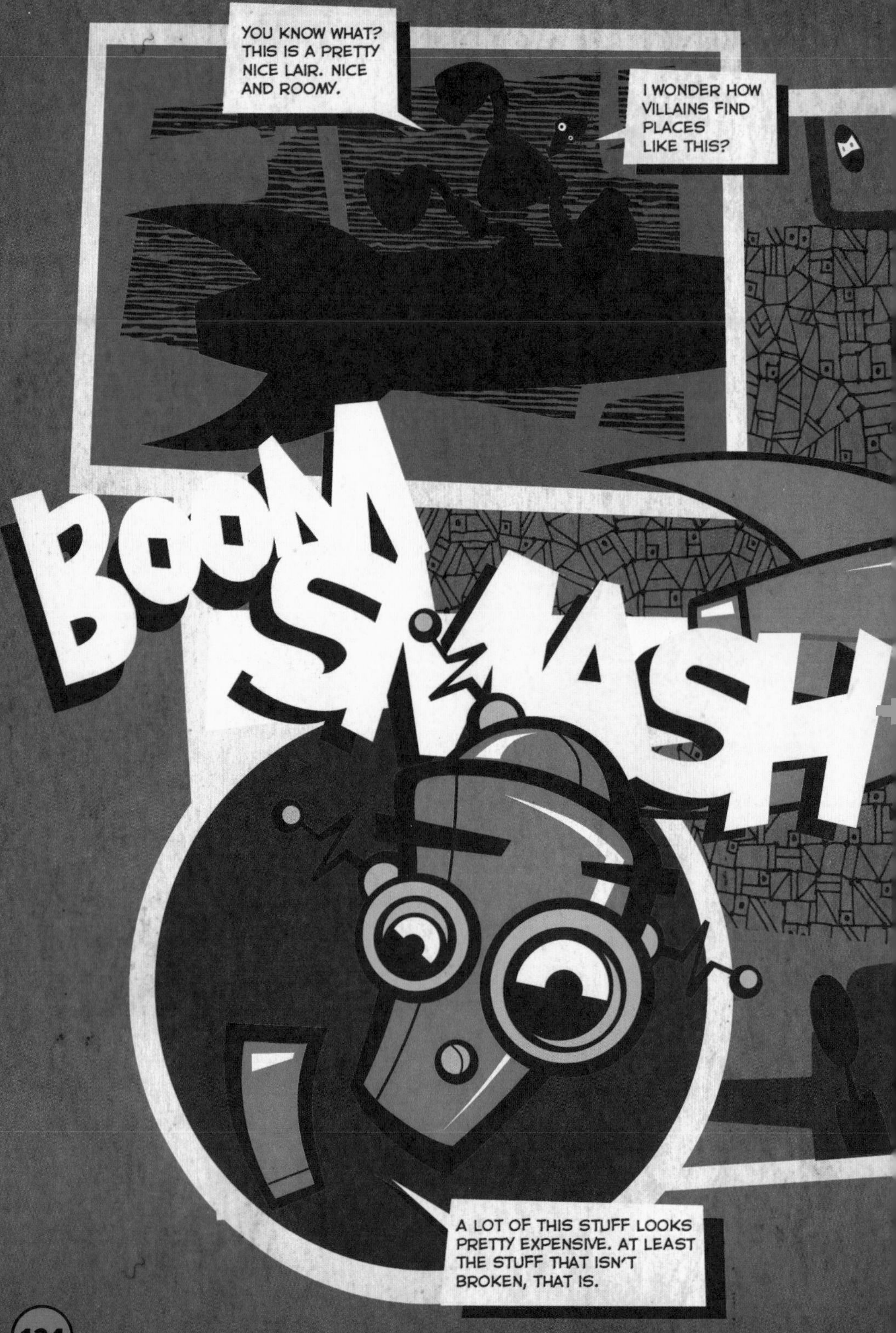
YOU KNOW WHAT? THIS IS A PRETTY NICE LAIR. NICE AND ROOMY.
I WONDER HOW VILLAINS FIND PLACES LIKE THIS?
BOOM
SMASH
A LOT OF THIS STUFF LOOKS PRETTY EXPENSIVE. AT LEAST THE STUFF THAT ISN'T BROKEN, THAT IS.

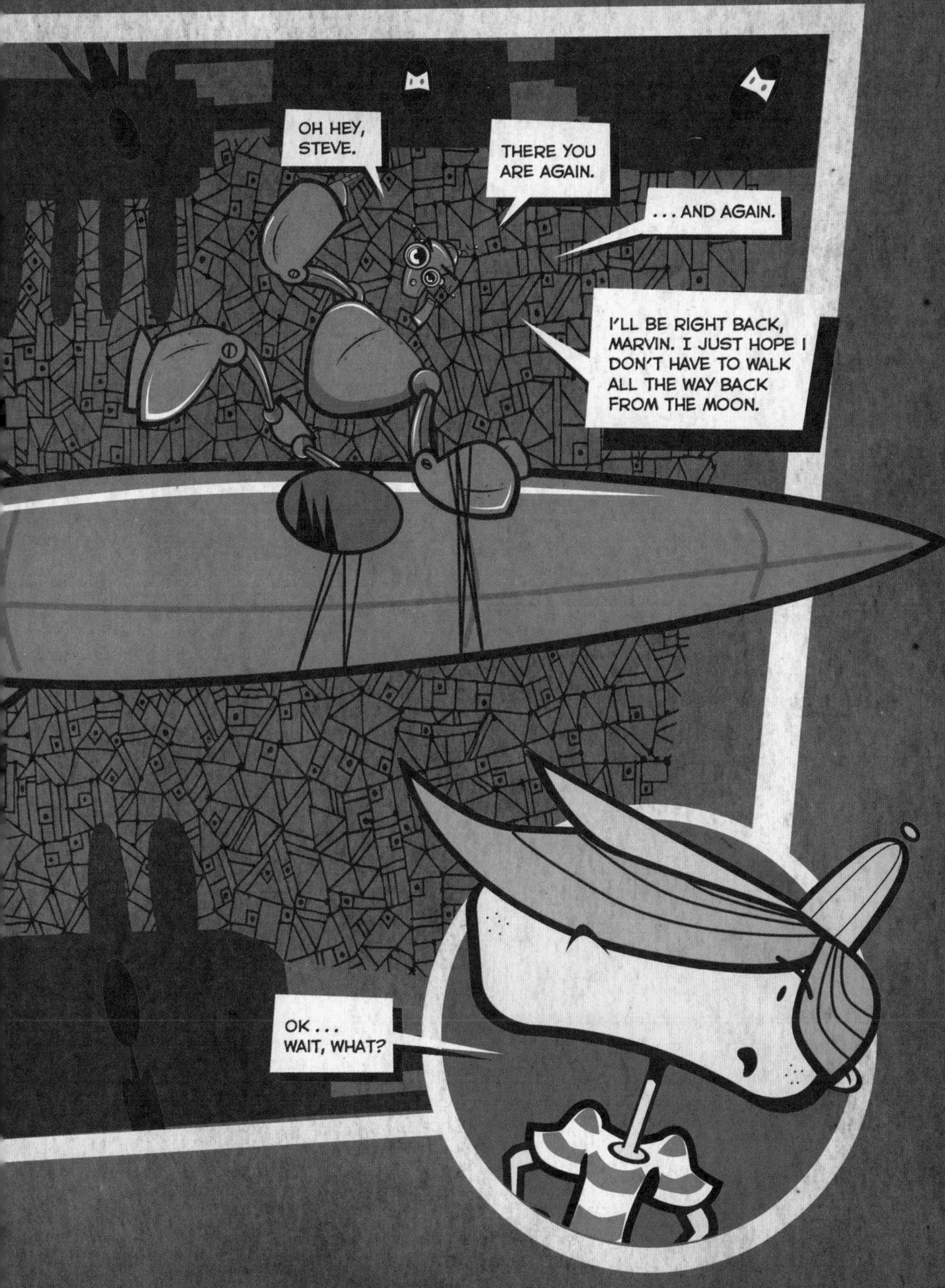
OH HEY,
STEVE.
THERE YOU
ARE AGAIN.
. . . AND AGAIN.
I'LL BE RIGHT BACK,
MARVIN. I JUST HOPE I
DON'T HAVE TO WALK
ALL THE WAY BACK
FROM THE MOON.
OK . . .
WAIT, WHAT?

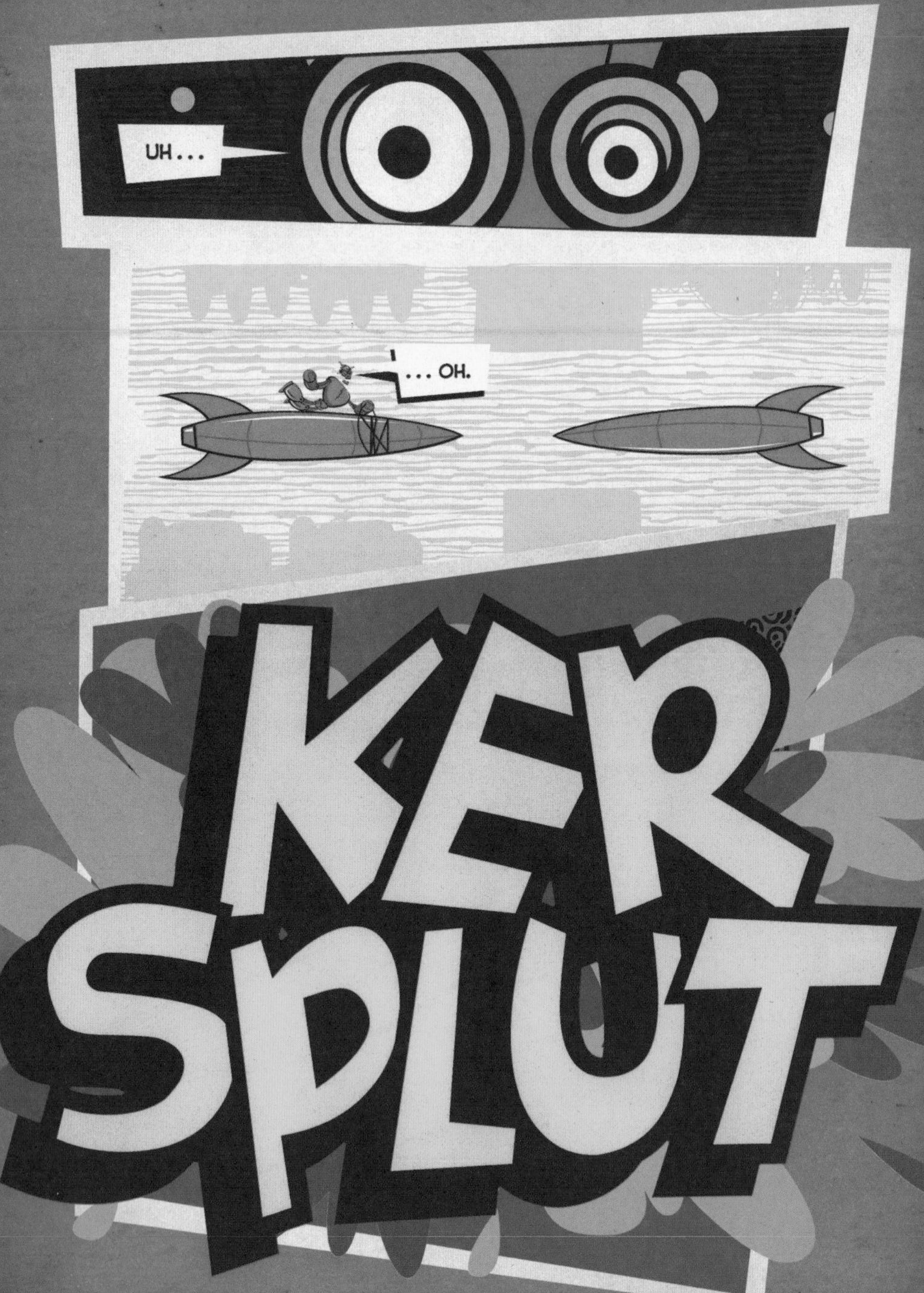
UH...
...OH.
KER SPLUT

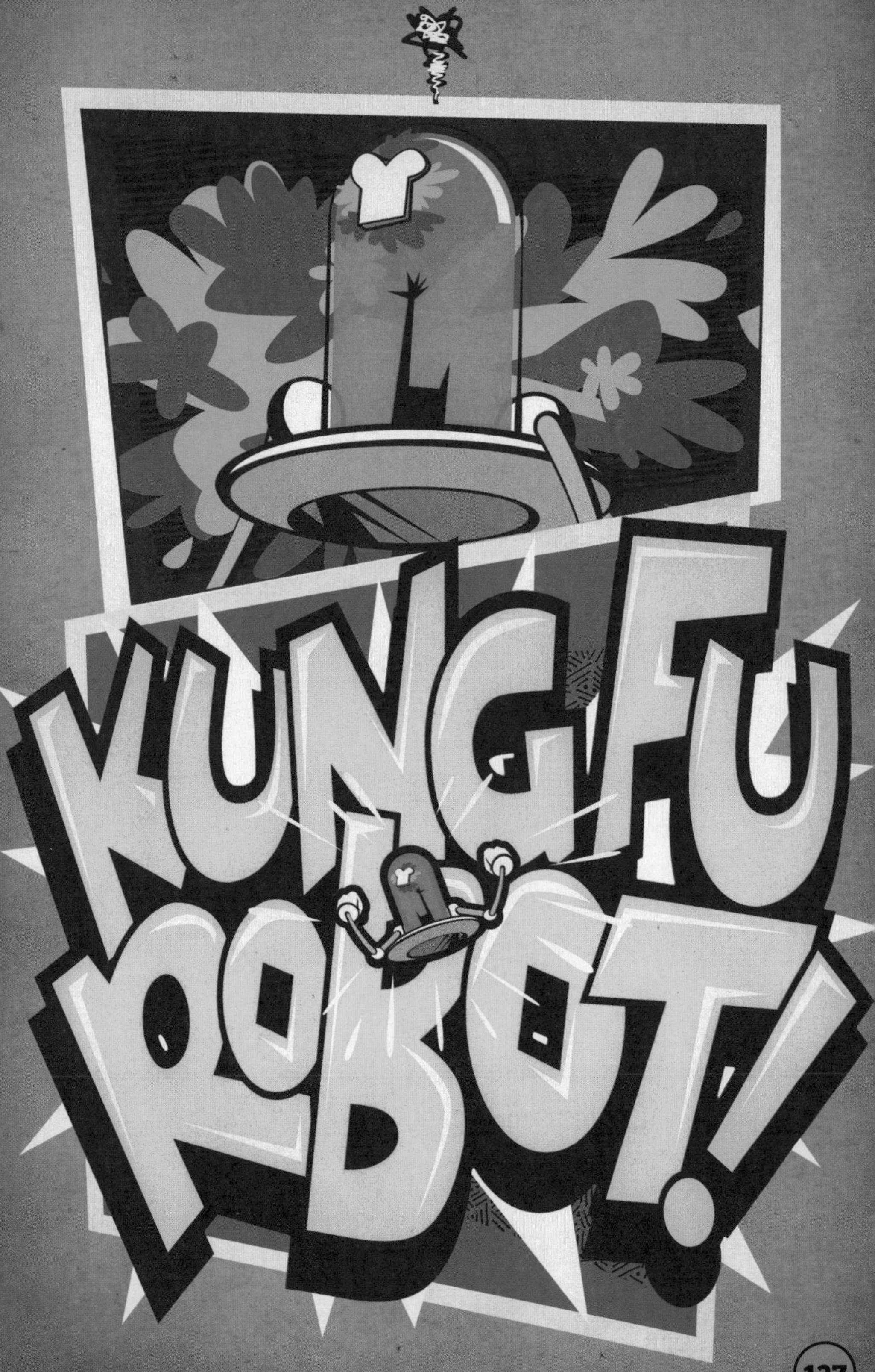
KUNG-FU ROBOT!

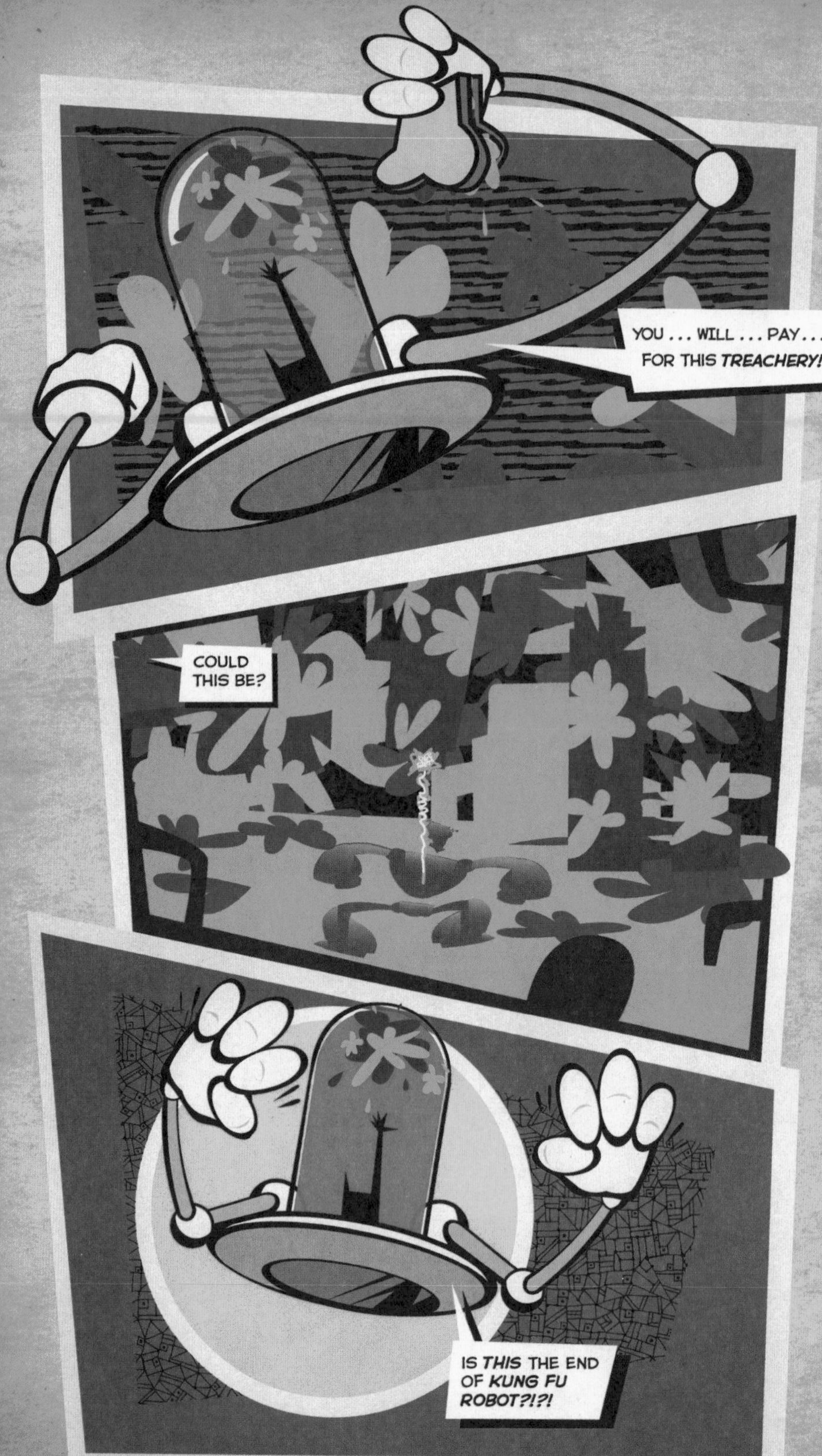
YOU . . . WILL . . . PAY . . . FOR THIS TREACHERY!
COULD THIS BE?
IS THIS THE END OF KUNG FU ROBOT?!?!

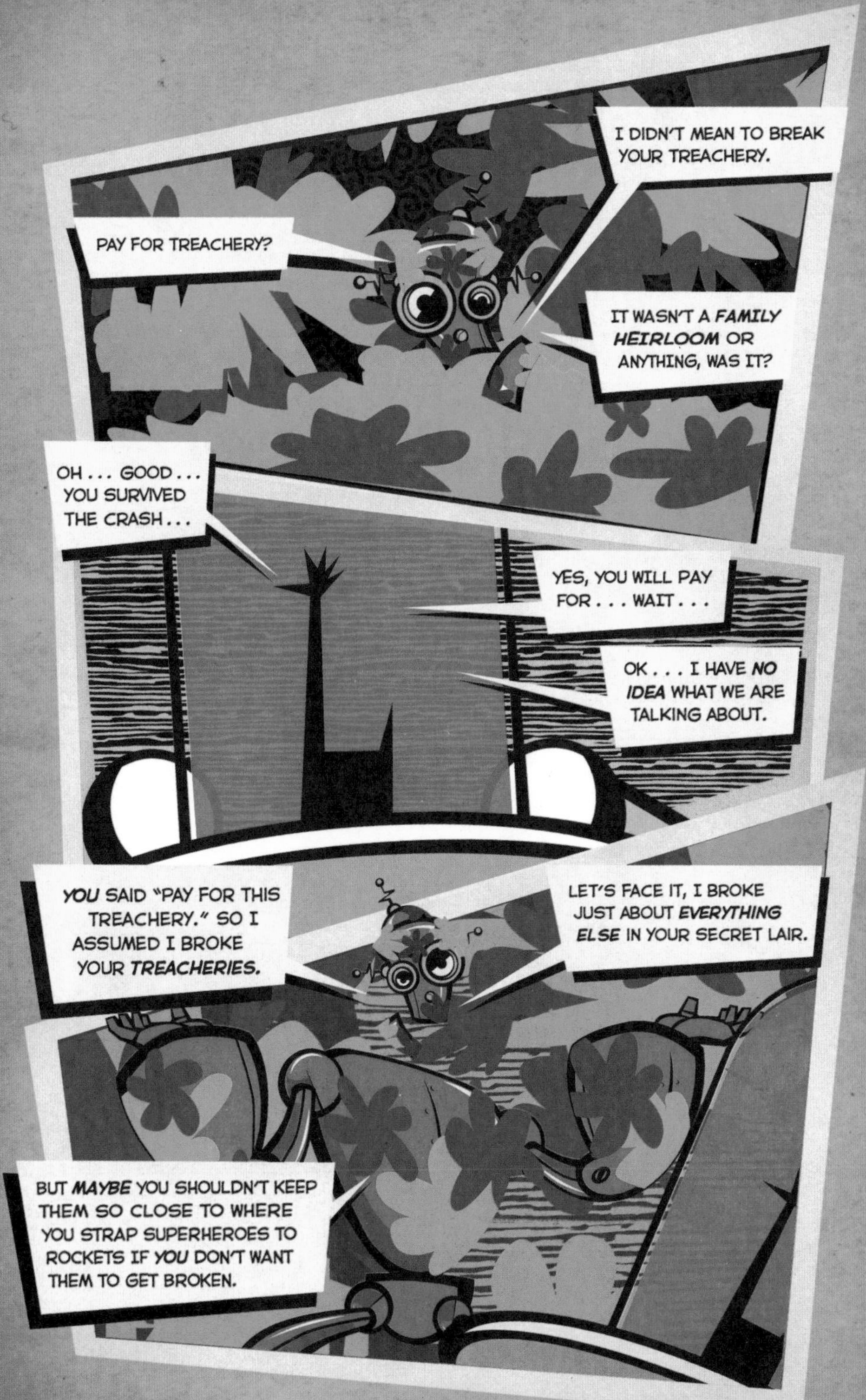
PAY FOR TREACHERY?
I DIDN'T MEAN TO BREAK YOUR TREACHERY.
IT WASN'T A *FAMILY HEIRLOOM* OR ANYTHING, WAS IT?
OH . . . GOOD . . . YOU SURVIVED THE CRASH . . .
YES, YOU WILL PAY FOR . . . WAIT . . .
OK . . . I HAVE *NO IDEA* WHAT WE ARE TALKING ABOUT.
YOU SAID "PAY FOR THIS TREACHERY." SO I ASSUMED I BROKE YOUR *TREACHERIES.*
LET'S FACE IT, I BROKE JUST ABOUT *EVERYTHING ELSE* IN YOUR SECRET LAIR.
BUT *MAYBE* YOU SHOULDN'T KEEP THEM SO CLOSE TO WHERE YOU STRAP SUPERHEROES TO ROCKETS IF *YOU* DON'T WANT THEM TO GET BROKEN.

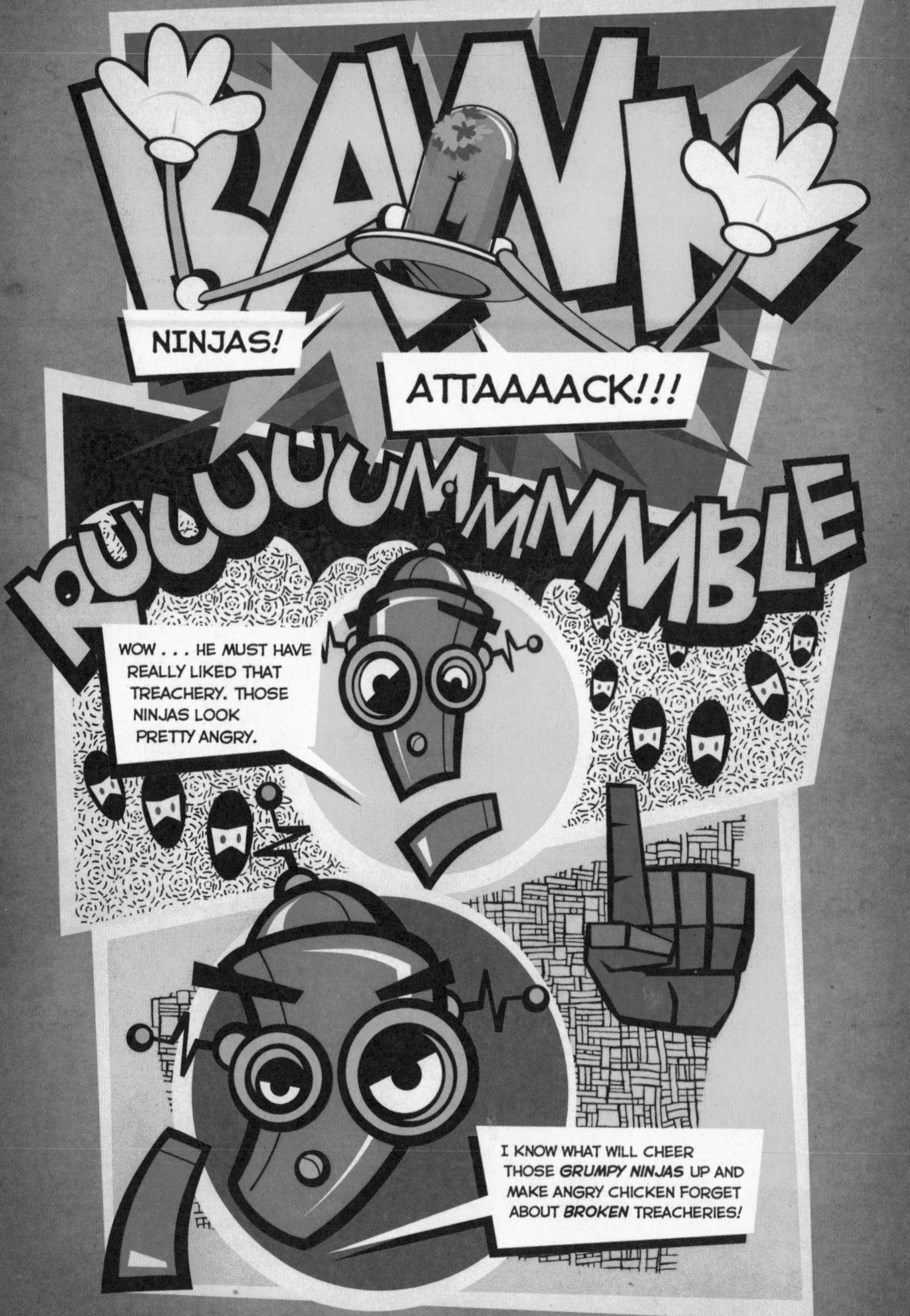
BAM!
NINJAS!
ATTAAAACK!!!
RUUUUUMMMMMBLE
WOW . . . HE MUST HAVE REALLY LIKED THAT TREACHERY. THOSE NINJAS LOOK PRETTY ANGRY.
I KNOW WHAT WILL CHEER THOSE GRUMPY NINJAS UP AND MAKE ANGRY CHICKEN FORGET ABOUT BROKEN TREACHERIES!

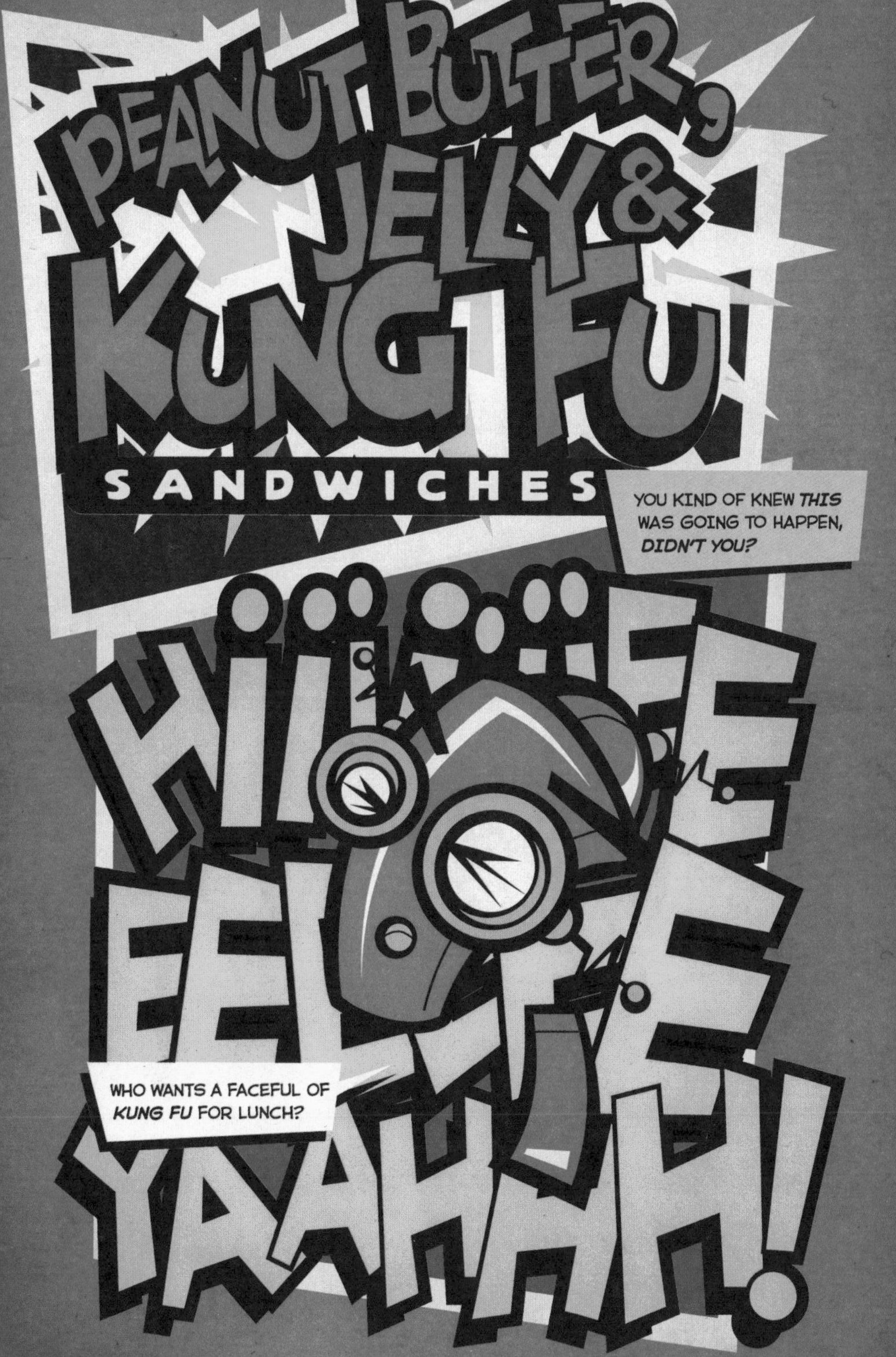
PEANUT BUTTER, JELLY & KUNG FU SANDWICHES
YOU KIND OF KNEW THIS WAS GOING TO HAPPEN, DIDN'T YOU?
WHO WANTS A FACEFUL OF KUNG FU FOR LUNCH?
YAAHHH!

GET YOUR FACES READY, BECAUSE THERE'S ONE *HEAPING HELPING OF KUNG FU* COMING RIGHT UP!

HIIIIEEEEYAAAAH!

RUUUUUMMBLE!

SPLAT SPLAT SPLATSPLA SPLAT SPLAT SPLA SPLAT SPLAT

THESE NINJAS *MUST BE* HUNGRY, LOOK AT THEM RUNNING TO GET SANDWICHES!

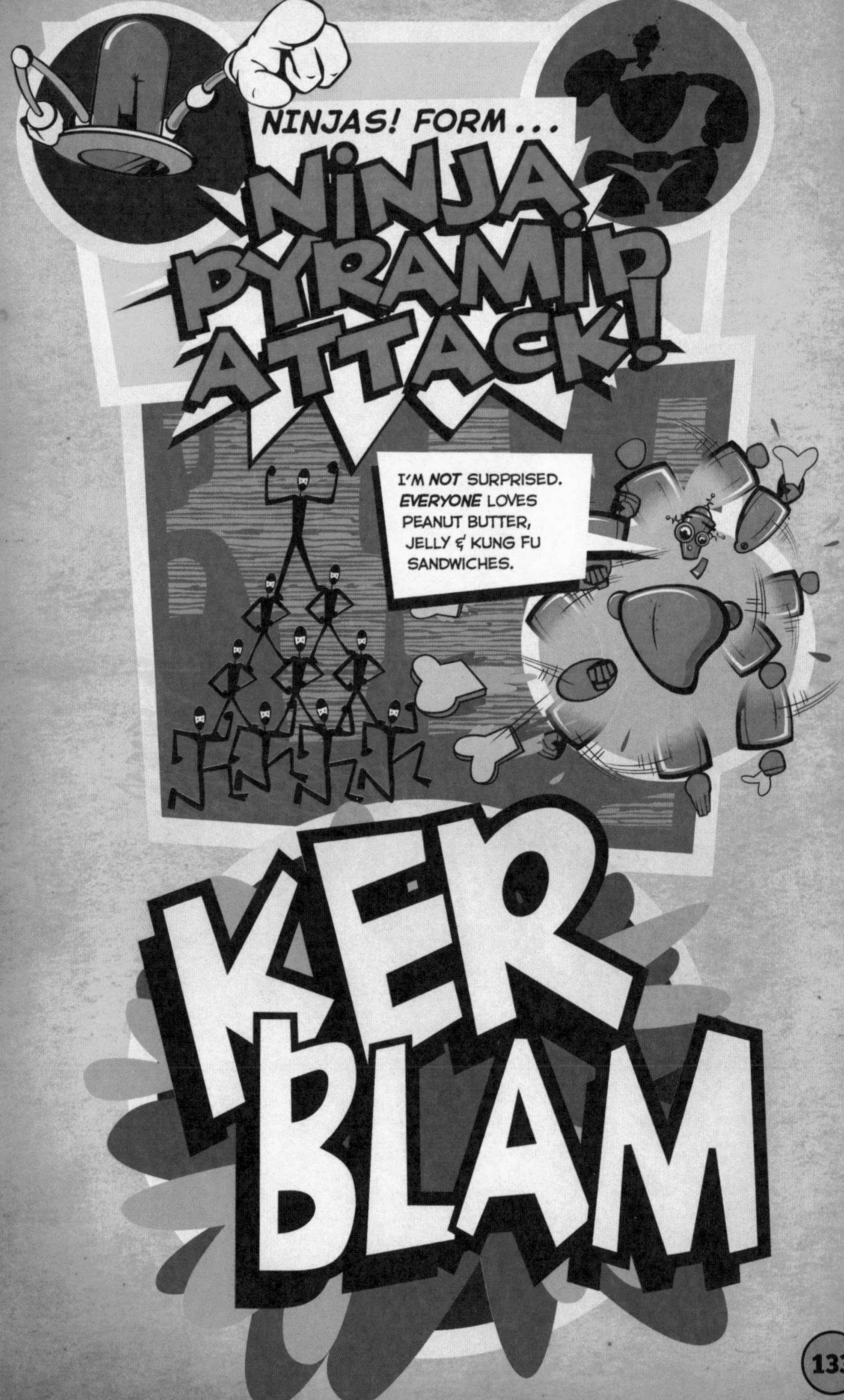
NINJAS! FORM . . .
NINJA PYRAMID ATTACK!
I'M NOT SURPRISED. EVERYONE LOVES PEANUT BUTTER, JELLY & KUNG FU SANDWICHES.
KER BLAM

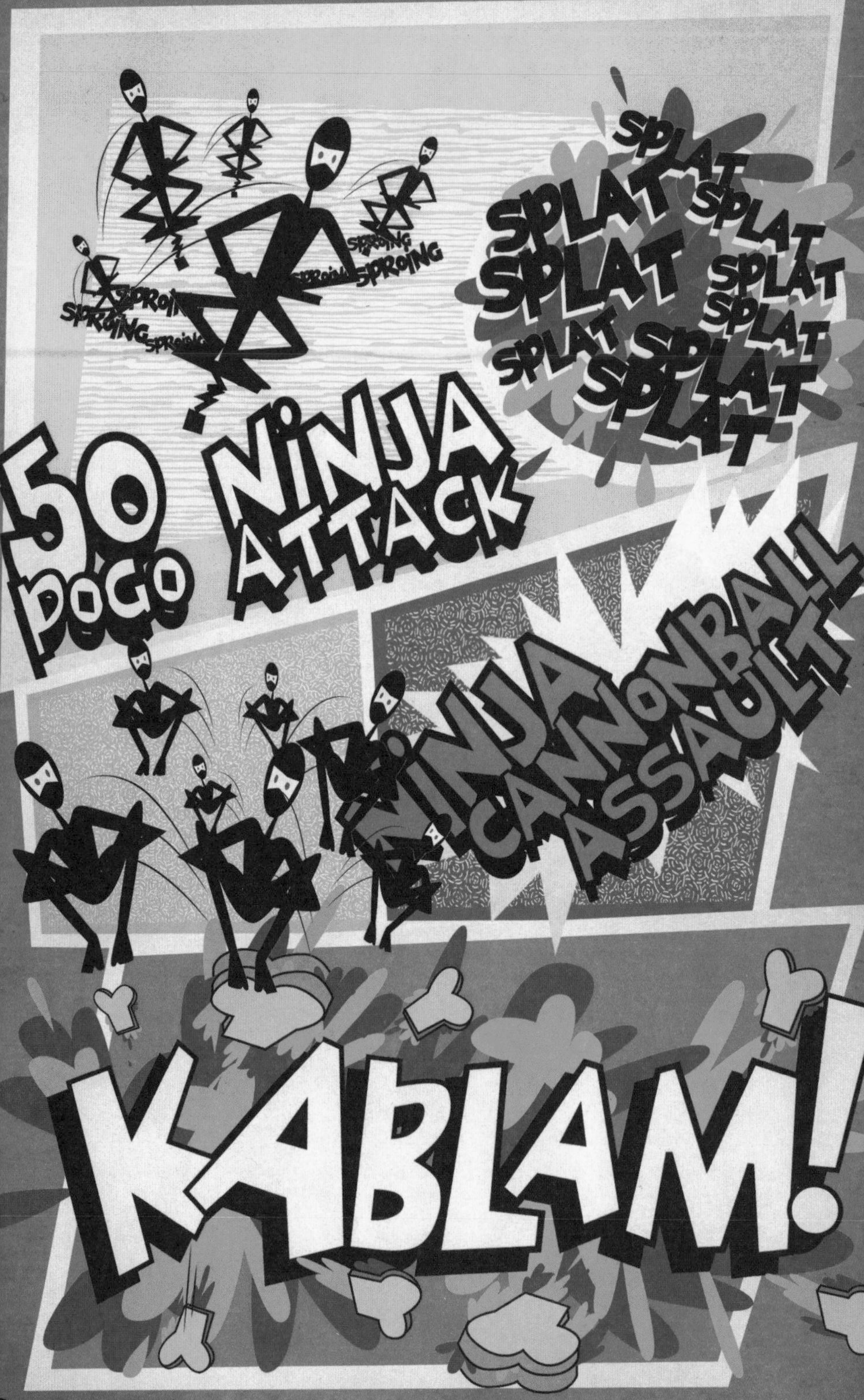
SPROING
SPROING
SPROING
SPROING
SPROING
SPROING
SPLAT
SPLAT
SPLAT
SPLAT
SPLAT
SPLAT
SPLAT
SPLAT
SPLAT
SPLAT
50 POGO NINJA ATTACK
NINJA CANNONBALL ASSAULT
KABLAM!

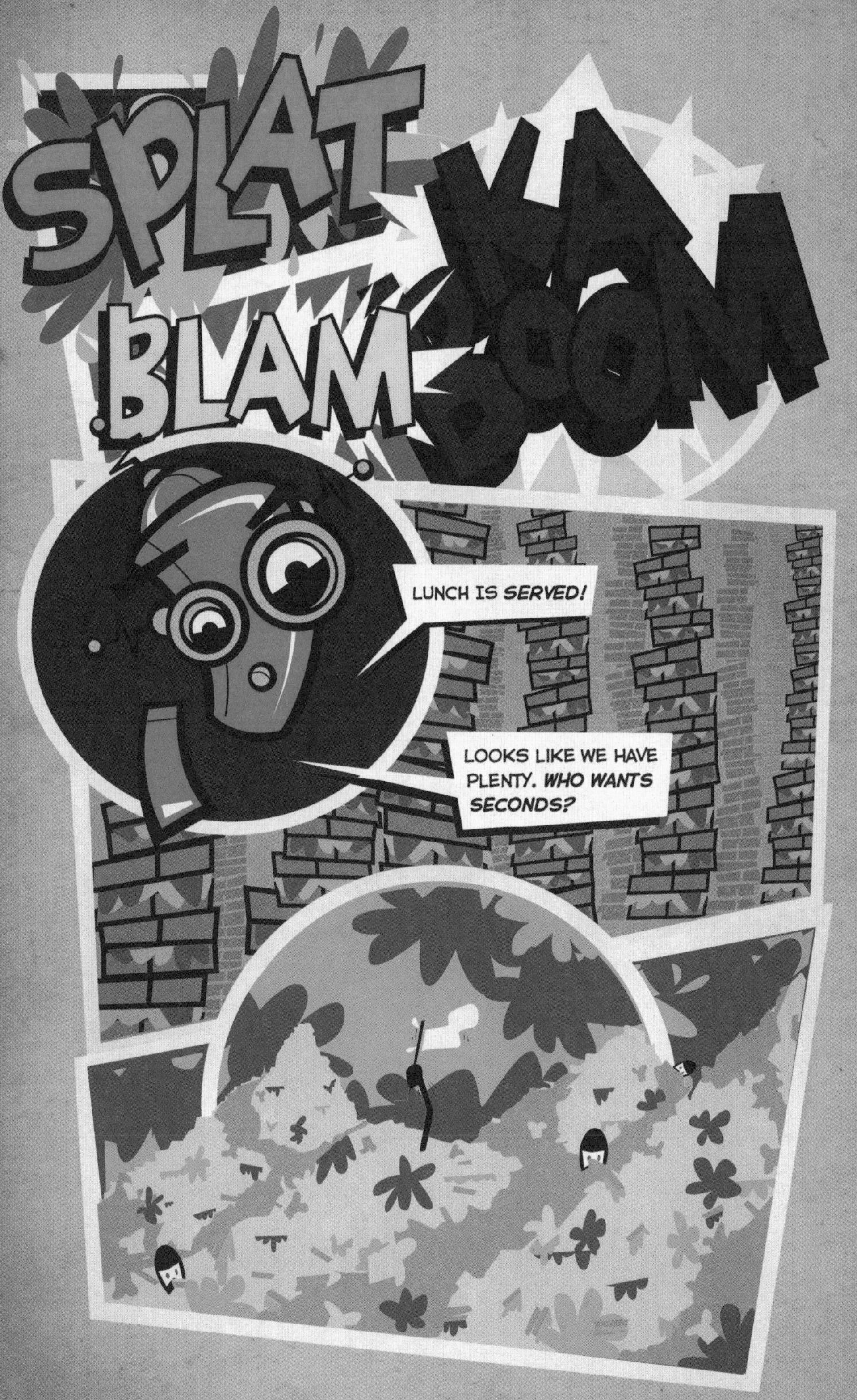
SPLAT
KA-BOOM
BLAM
LUNCH IS *SERVED!*
LOOKS LIKE WE HAVE PLENTY. *WHO WANTS SECONDS?*

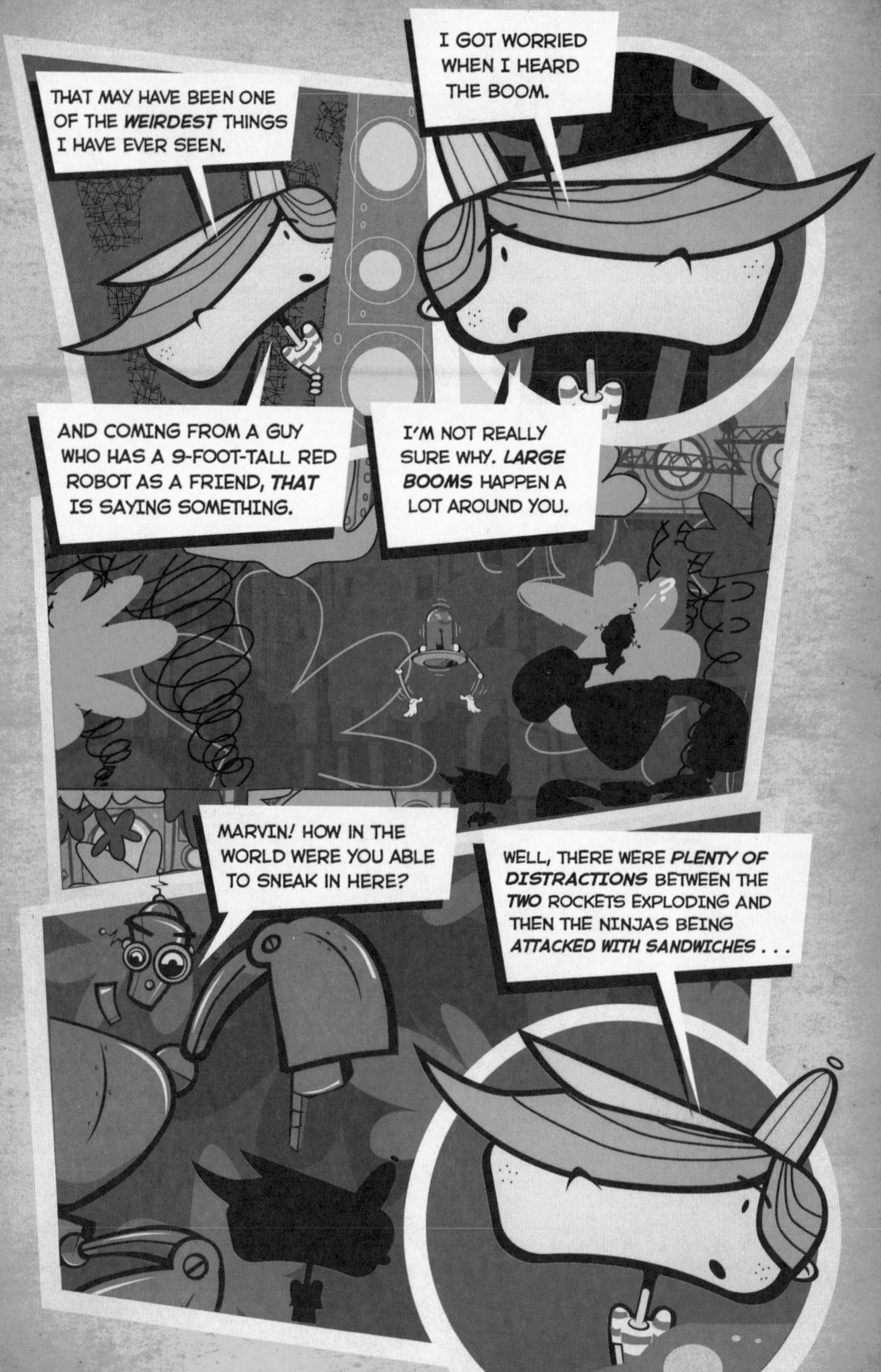
THAT MAY HAVE BEEN ONE OF THE WEIRDEST THINGS I HAVE EVER SEEN.
I GOT WORRIED WHEN I HEARD THE BOOM.
AND COMING FROM A GUY WHO HAS A 9-FOOT-TALL RED ROBOT AS A FRIEND, THAT IS SAYING SOMETHING.
I'M NOT REALLY SURE WHY. LARGE BOOMS HAPPEN A LOT AROUND YOU.
MARVIN! HOW IN THE WORLD WERE YOU ABLE TO SNEAK IN HERE?
WELL, THERE WERE PLENTY OF DISTRACTIONS BETWEEN THE TWO ROCKETS EXPLODING AND THEN THE NINJAS BEING ATTACKED WITH SANDWICHES . . .

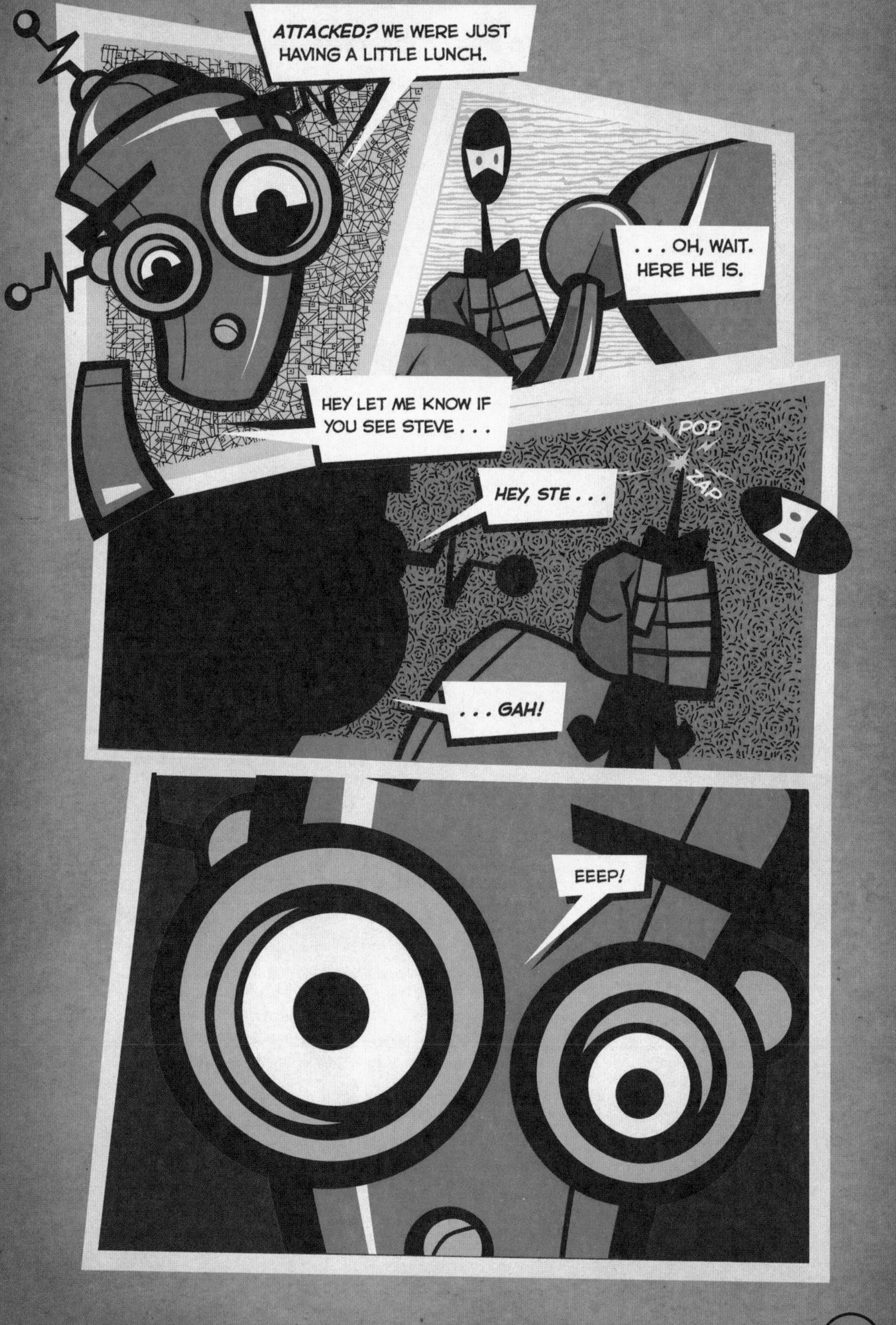
ATTACKED? WE WERE JUST HAVING A LITTLE LUNCH.
. . . OH, WAIT. HERE HE IS.
HEY LET ME KNOW IF YOU SEE STEVE . . .
POP
ZAP
HEY, STE . . .
. . . GAH!
EEEP!

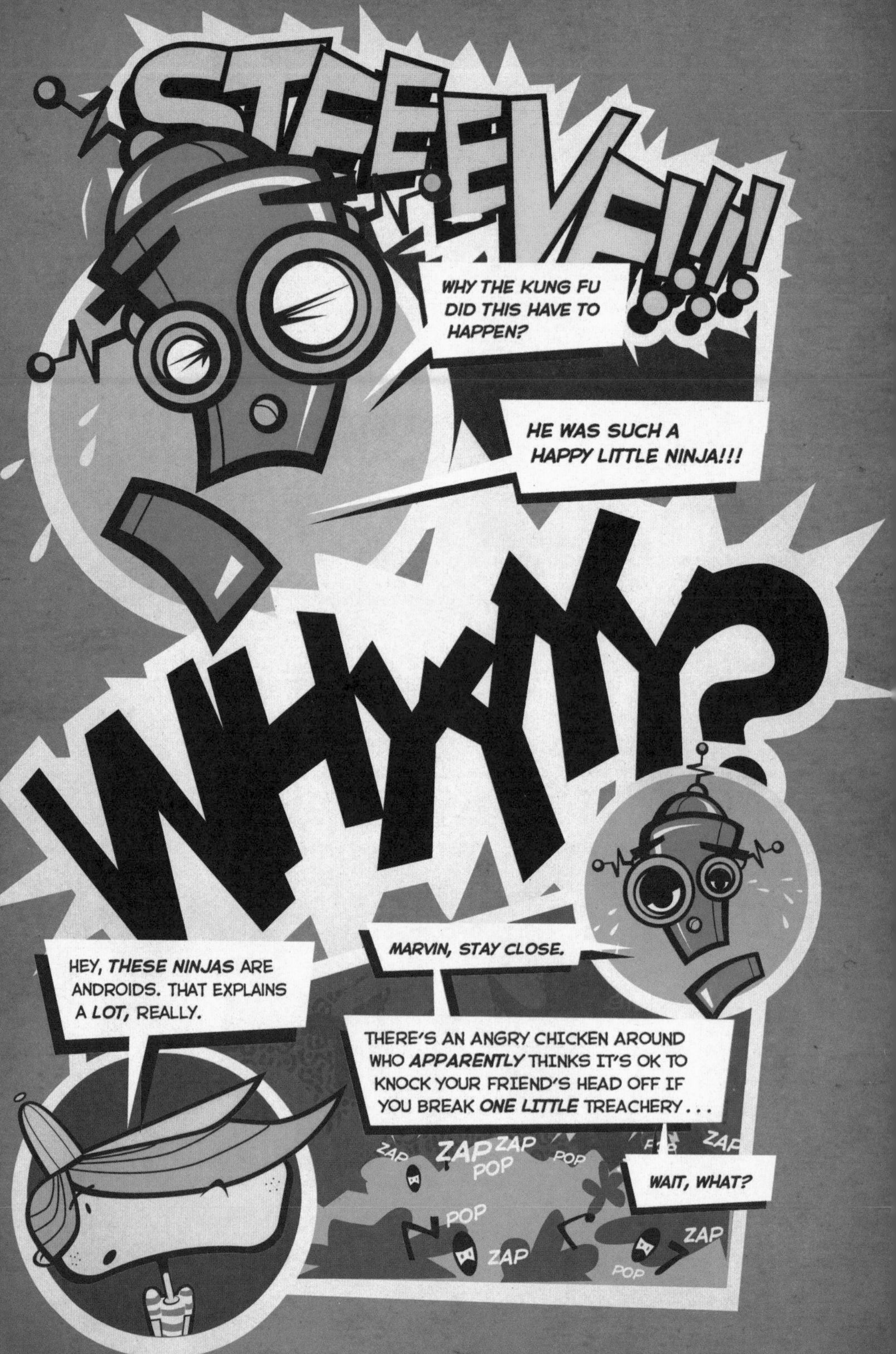
STEEEVE!!!
WHY THE KUNG FU DID THIS HAVE TO HAPPEN?
HE WAS SUCH A HAPPY LITTLE NINJA!!!
WHYYYY?
HEY, THESE NINJAS ARE ANDROIDS. THAT EXPLAINS A LOT, REALLY.
MARVIN, STAY CLOSE.
THERE'S AN ANGRY CHICKEN AROUND WHO APPARENTLY THINKS IT'S OK TO KNOCK YOUR FRIEND'S HEAD OFF IF YOU BREAK ONE LITTLE TREACHERY . . .
ZAP ZAP ZAP POP POP ZAP
WAIT, WHAT?
POP ZAP ZAP POP

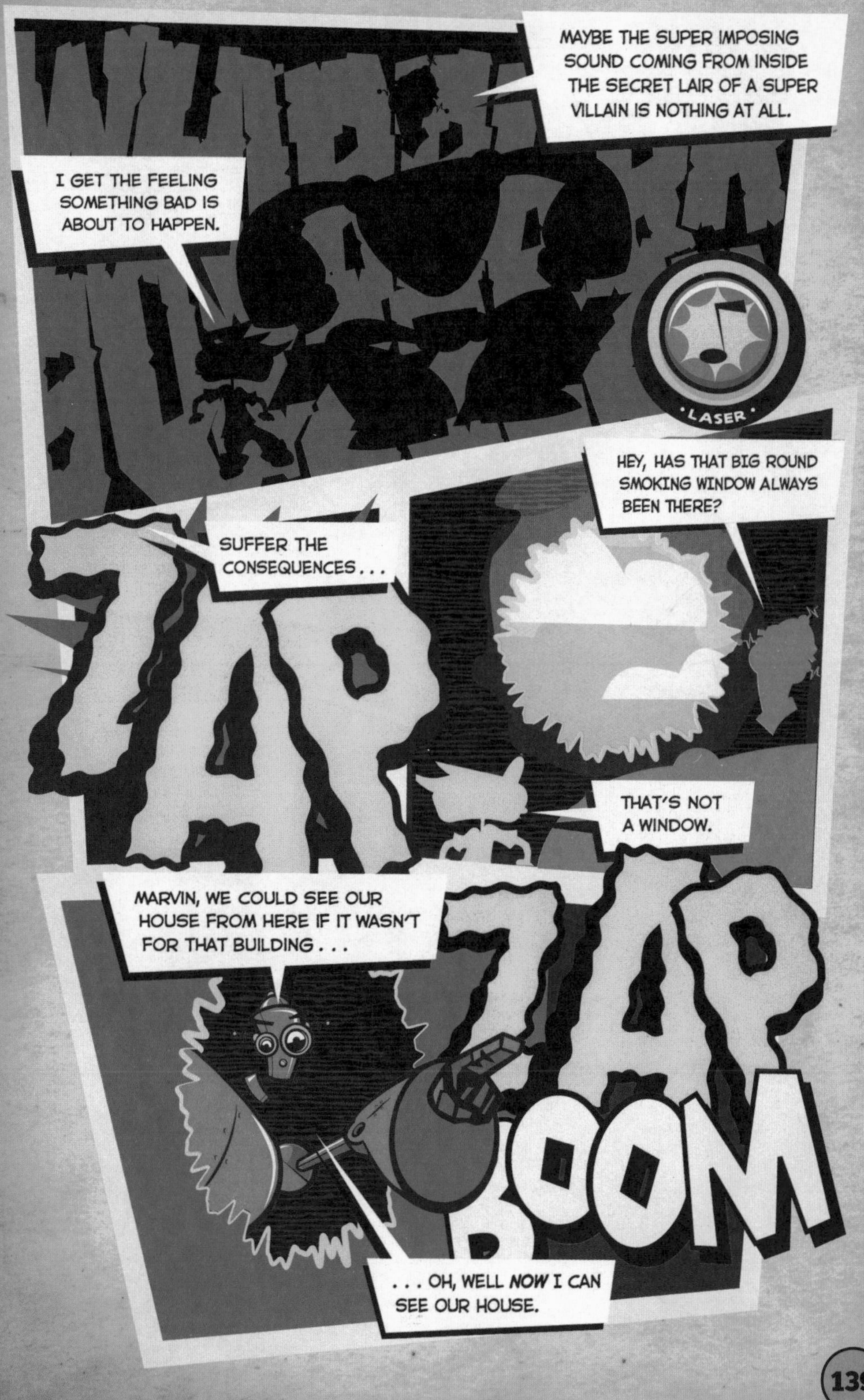
MAYBE THE SUPER IMPOSING SOUND COMING FROM INSIDE THE SECRET LAIR OF A SUPER VILLAIN IS NOTHING AT ALL.
I GET THE FEELING SOMETHING BAD IS ABOUT TO HAPPEN.
LASER
SUFFER THE CONSEQUENCES . . .
ZAP
HEY, HAS THAT BIG ROUND SMOKING WINDOW ALWAYS BEEN THERE?
THAT'S NOT A WINDOW.
MARVIN, WE COULD SEE OUR HOUSE FROM HERE IF IT WASN'T FOR THAT BUILDING . . .
ZAP
BOOM
. . . OH, WELL *NOW* I CAN SEE OUR HOUSE.

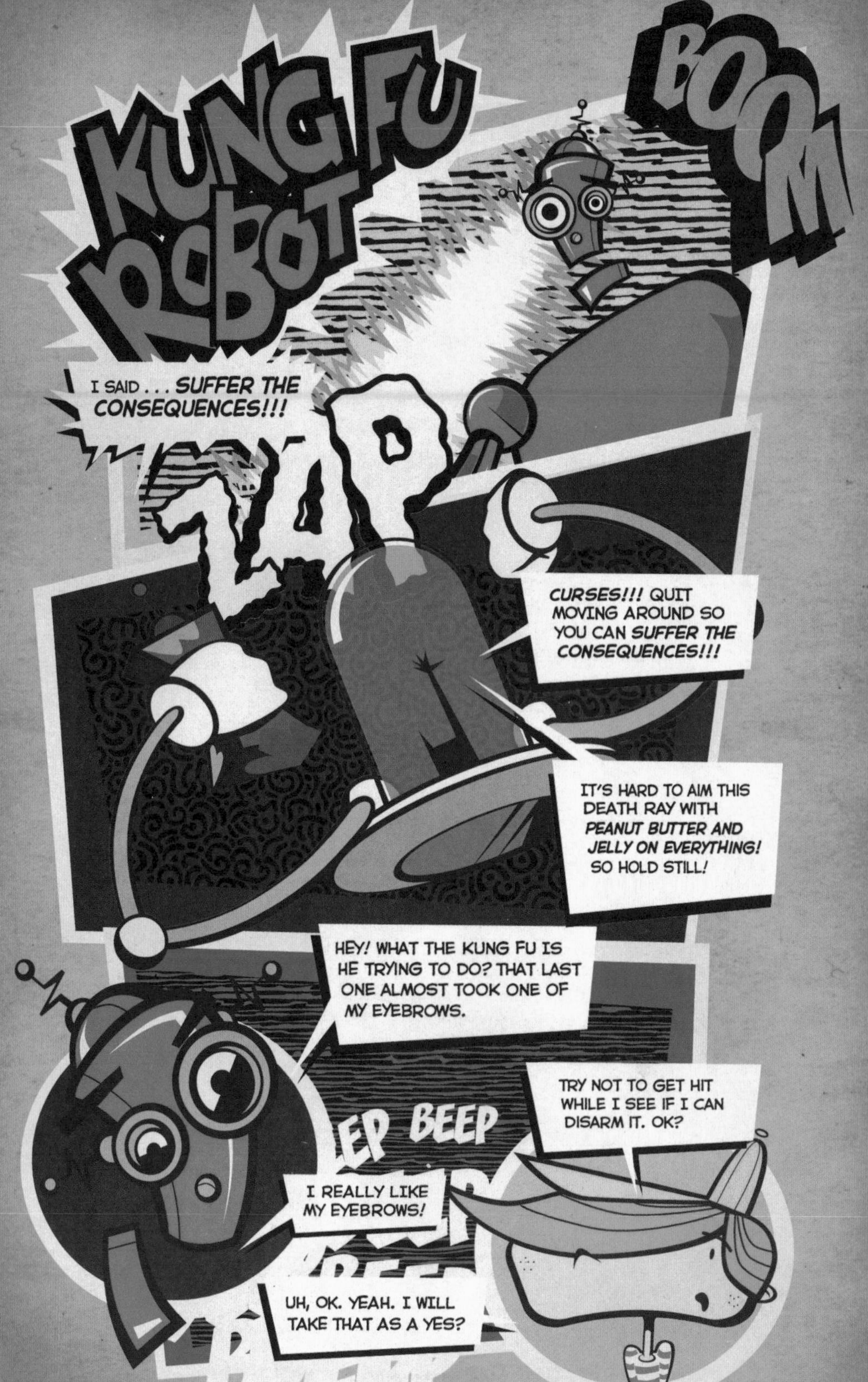
KUNG FU ROBOT
BOOM
I SAID . . . SUFFER THE CONSEQUENCES!!!
ZAP
CURSES!!! QUIT MOVING AROUND SO YOU CAN SUFFER THE CONSEQUENCES!!!
IT'S HARD TO AIM THIS DEATH RAY WITH PEANUT BUTTER AND JELLY ON EVERYTHING! SO HOLD STILL!
HEY! WHAT THE KUNG FU IS HE TRYING TO DO? THAT LAST ONE ALMOST TOOK ONE OF MY EYEBROWS.
TRY NOT TO GET HIT WHILE I SEE IF I CAN DISARM IT. OK?
EP BEEP
I REALLY LIKE MY EYEBROWS!
UH, OK. YEAH. I WILL TAKE THAT AS A YES?

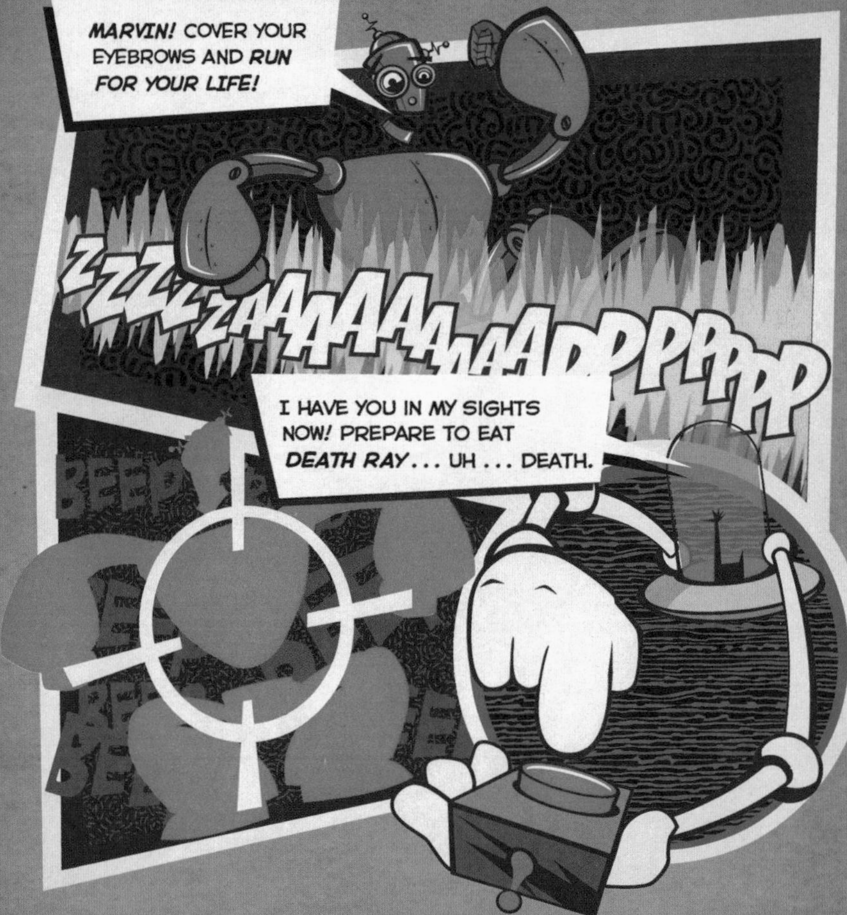

DISARM THE DEATH RAY

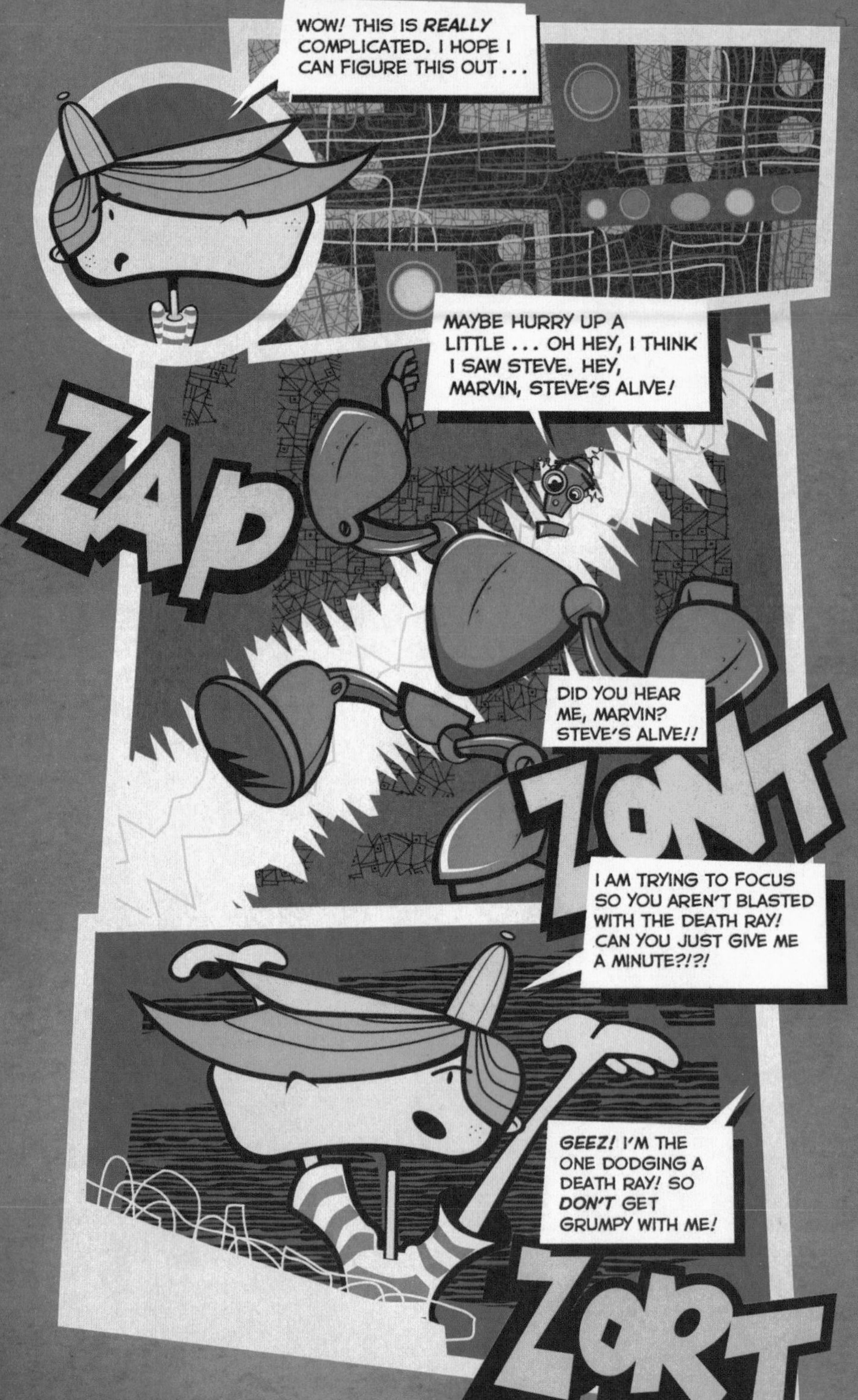
WOW! THIS IS *REALLY* COMPLICATED. I HOPE I CAN FIGURE THIS OUT . . .
MAYBE HURRY UP A LITTLE . . . OH HEY, I THINK I SAW STEVE. HEY, MARVIN, STEVE'S ALIVE!
ZAP
DID YOU HEAR ME, MARVIN? STEVE'S ALIVE!!
ZONT
I AM TRYING TO FOCUS SO YOU AREN'T BLASTED WITH THE DEATH RAY! CAN YOU JUST GIVE ME A MINUTE?!?!
GEEZ! I'M THE ONE DODGING A DEATH RAY! SO *DON'T* GET GRUMPY WITH ME!
ZORT

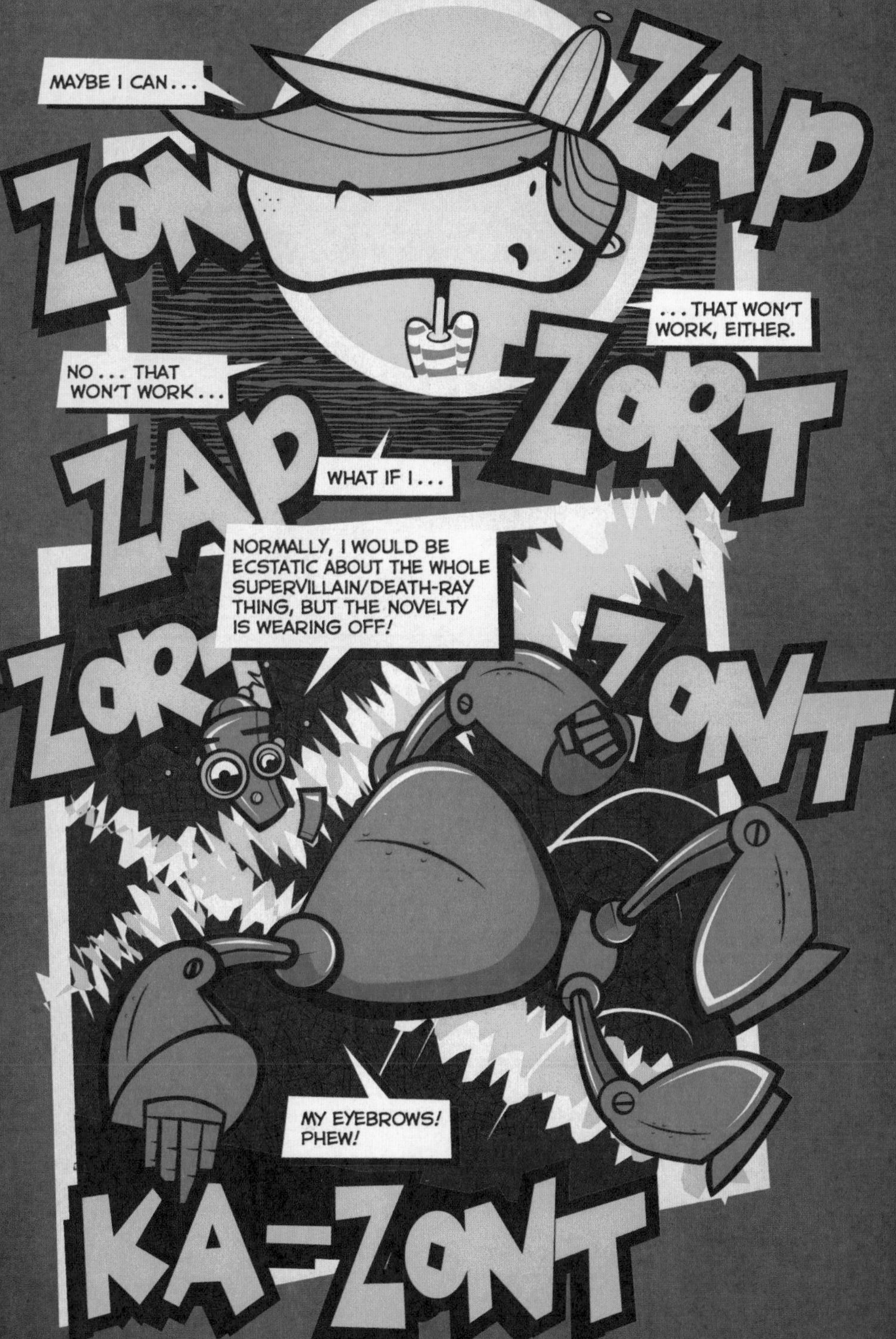
MAYBE I CAN . . .
ZON
ZAP
NO . . . THAT WON'T WORK . . .
. . . THAT WON'T WORK, EITHER.
ZAP
WHAT IF I . . .
ZORT
NORMALLY, I WOULD BE ECSTATIC ABOUT THE WHOLE SUPERVILLAIN/DEATH-RAY THING, BUT THE NOVELTY IS WEARING OFF!
ZONT
MY EYEBROWS! PHEW!
KA-ZONT

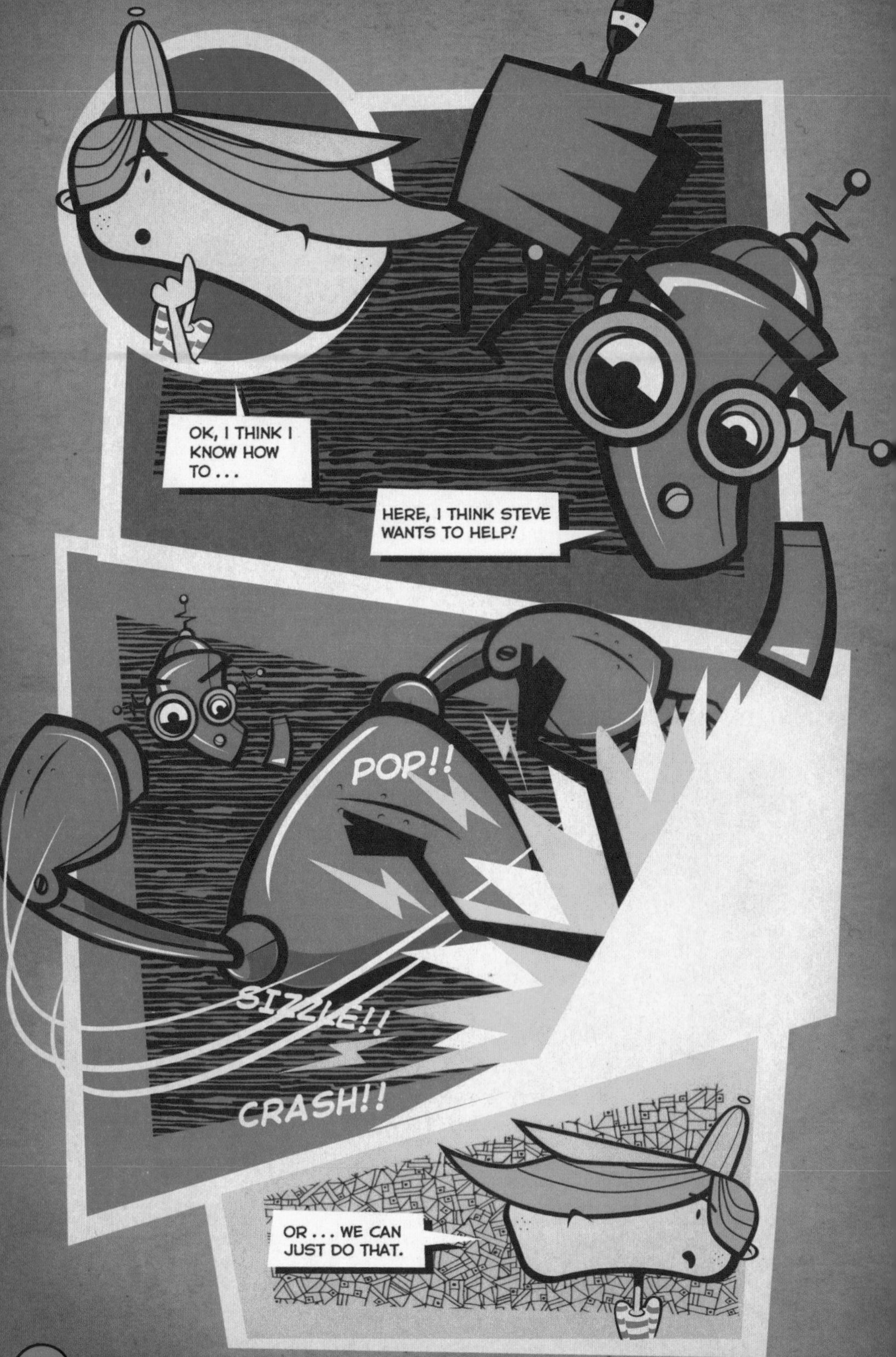

OK, I THINK I KNOW HOW TO . . .
HERE, I THINK STEVE WANTS TO HELP!
POP!!
SIZZLE!!
CRASH!!
OR . . . WE CAN JUST DO THAT.

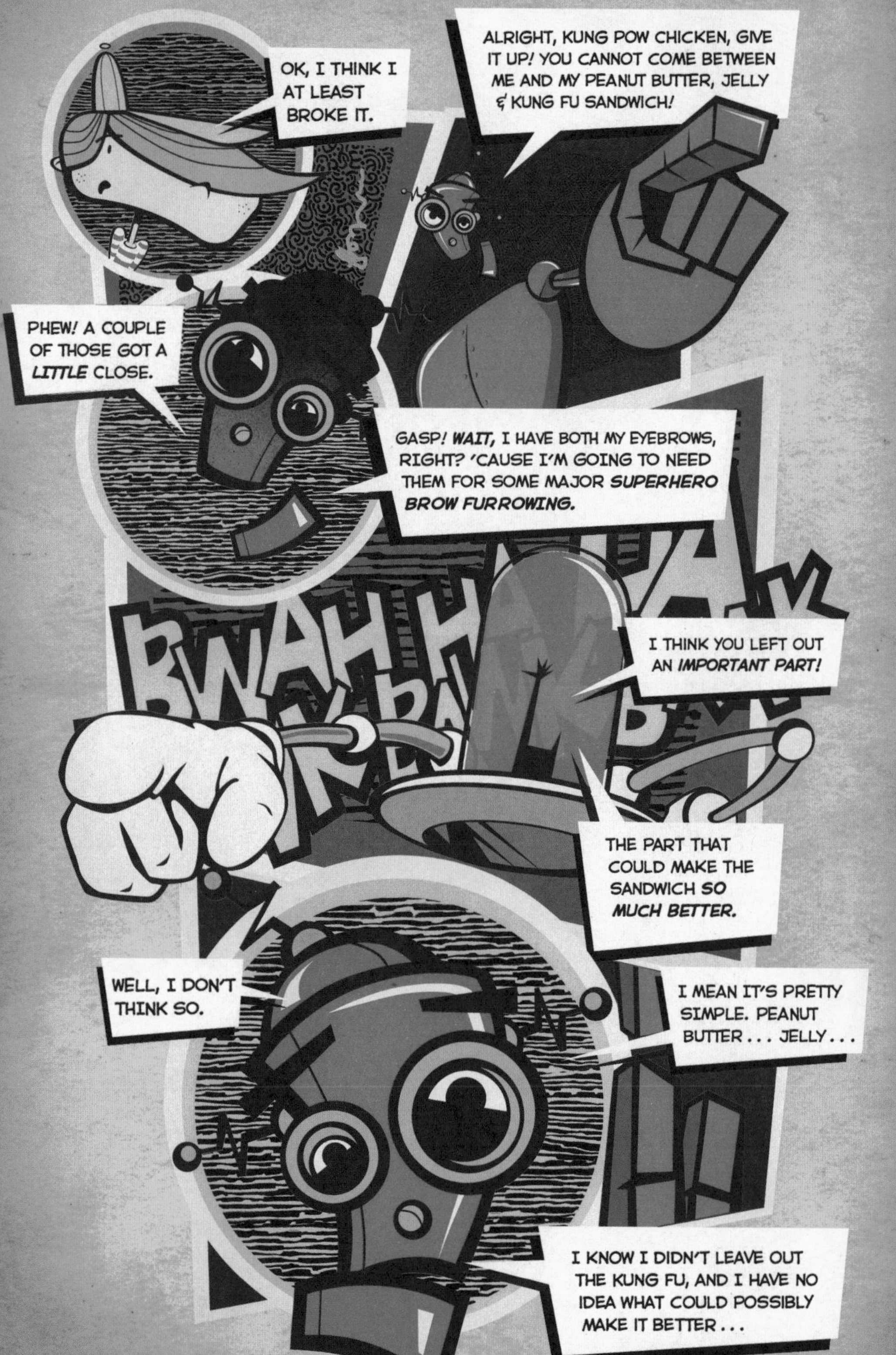
OK, I THINK I AT LEAST BROKE IT.
ALRIGHT, KUNG POW CHICKEN, GIVE IT UP! YOU CANNOT COME BETWEEN ME AND MY PEANUT BUTTER, JELLY & KUNG FU SANDWICH!
PHEW! A COUPLE OF THOSE GOT A *LITTLE* CLOSE.
GASP! ***WAIT,*** I HAVE BOTH MY EYEBROWS, RIGHT? 'CAUSE I'M GOING TO NEED THEM FOR SOME MAJOR ***SUPERHERO BROW FURROWING.***
BWAHH
I THINK YOU LEFT OUT AN *IMPORTANT PART!*
THE PART THAT COULD MAKE THE SANDWICH **SO *MUCH BETTER.***
WELL, I DON'T THINK SO.
I MEAN IT'S PRETTY SIMPLE. PEANUT BUTTER . . . JELLY . . .
I KNOW I DIDN'T LEAVE OUT THE KUNG FU, AND I HAVE NO IDEA WHAT COULD POSSIBLY MAKE IT BETTER . . .

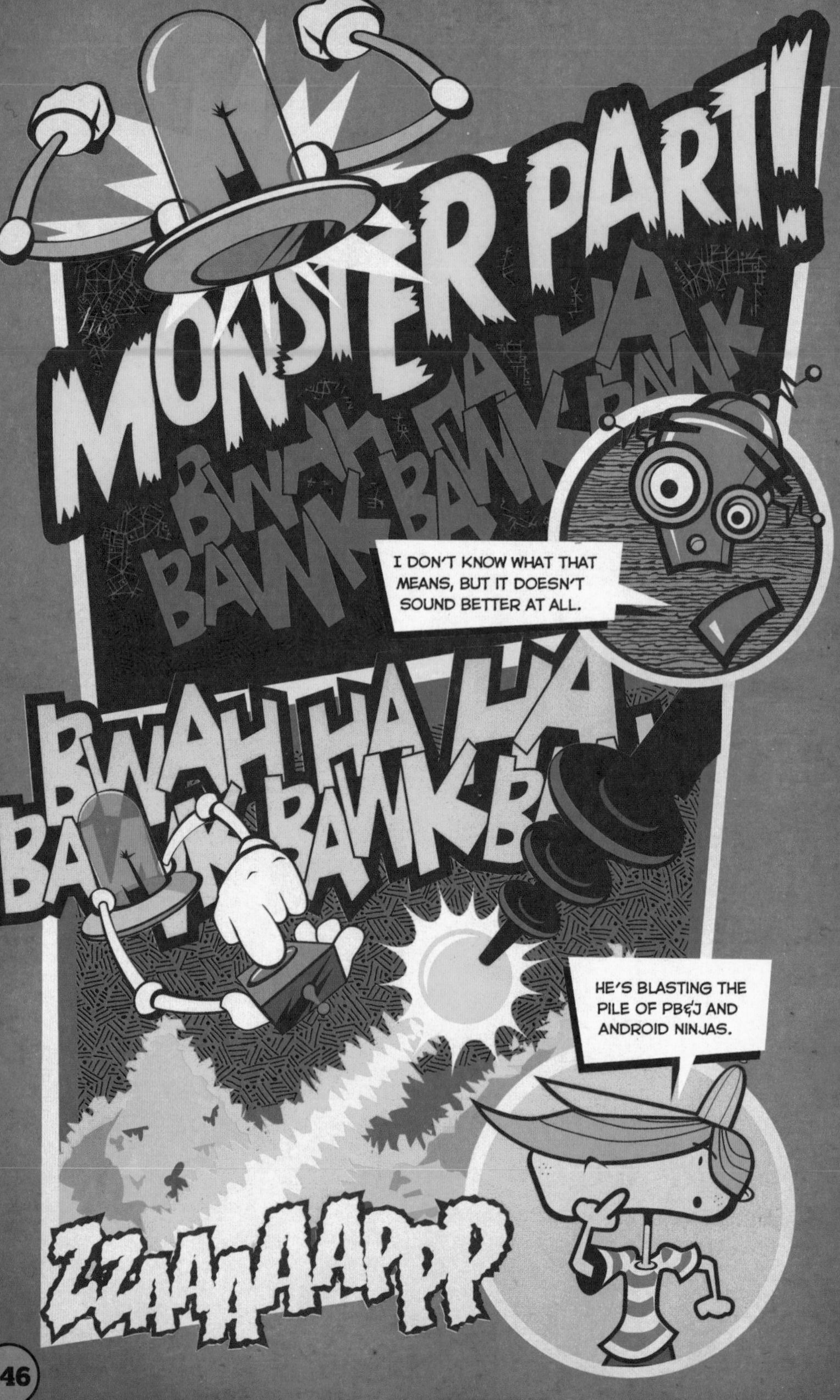
MONSTER PART!
BWAH HA HA
BAWK BAWK BAWK
I DON'T KNOW WHAT THAT MEANS, BUT IT DOESN'T SOUND BETTER AT ALL.
BWAH HA HA
BAWK BAWK
HE'S BLASTING THE PILE OF PB&J AND ANDROID NINJAS.
ZZAAAAAPPP

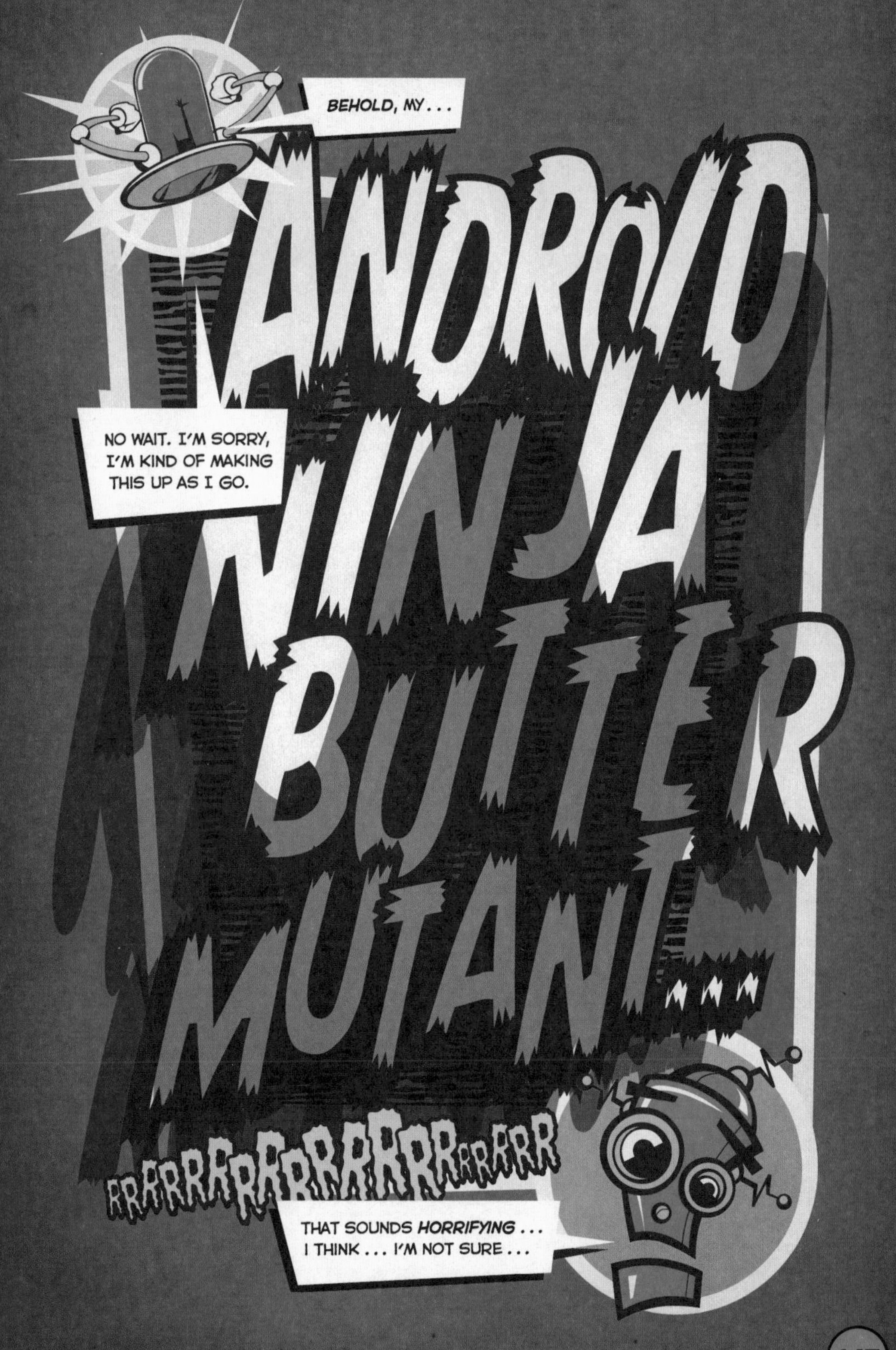
BEHOLD, MY . . .
ANDROID NINJA BUTTER MUTANT...
NO WAIT. I'M SORRY, I'M KIND OF MAKING THIS UP AS I GO.
RRARRRRRRRRRRRRRrrrrRR
THAT SOUNDS *HORRIFYING* . . . I THINK . . . I'M NOT SURE . . .

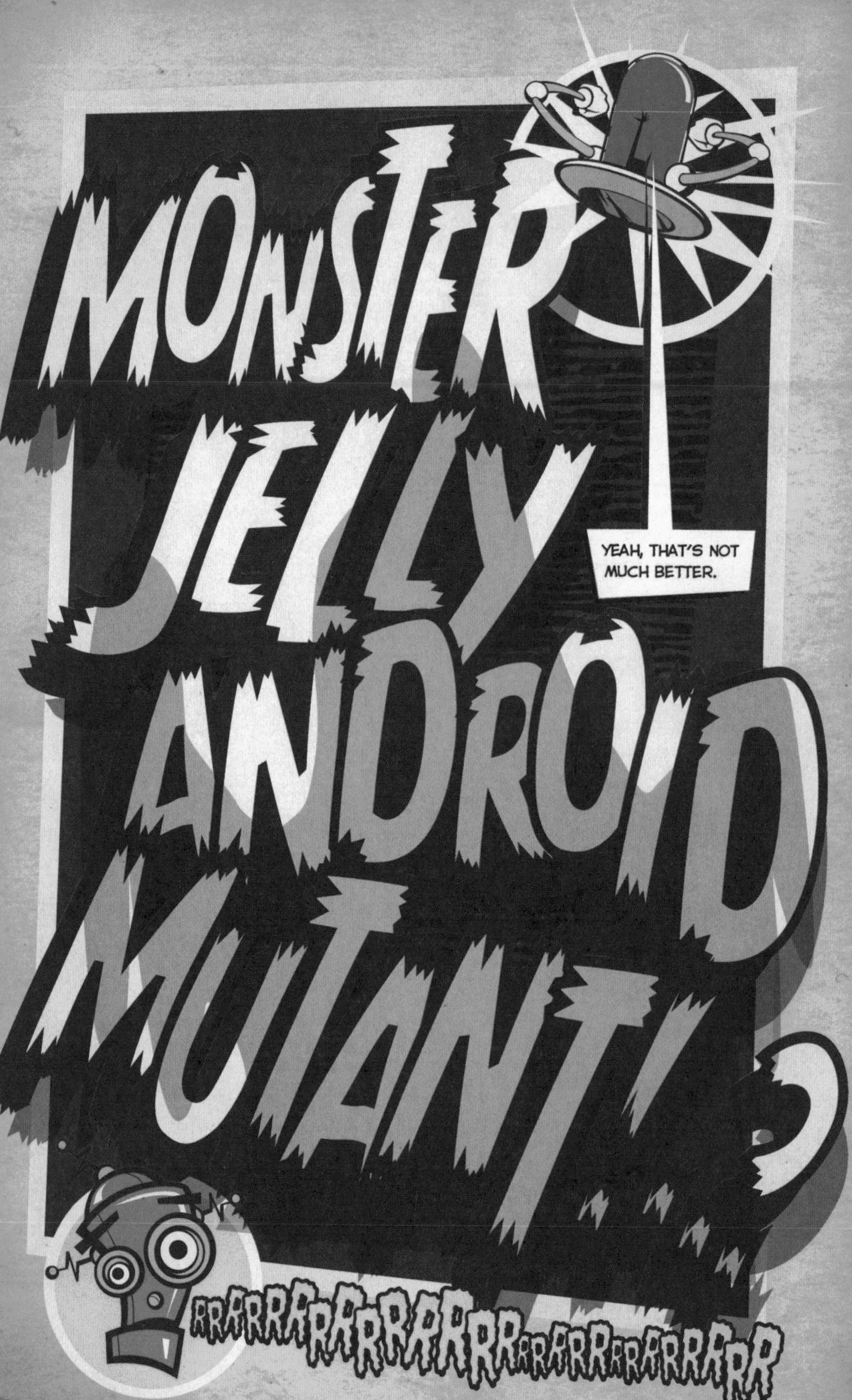

MONSTER JELLY ANDROID MUTANT?

YEAH, THAT'S NOT MUCH BETTER.

RRRRRRRRRRRRRRRRRRRRRRRRRRRRRRRR

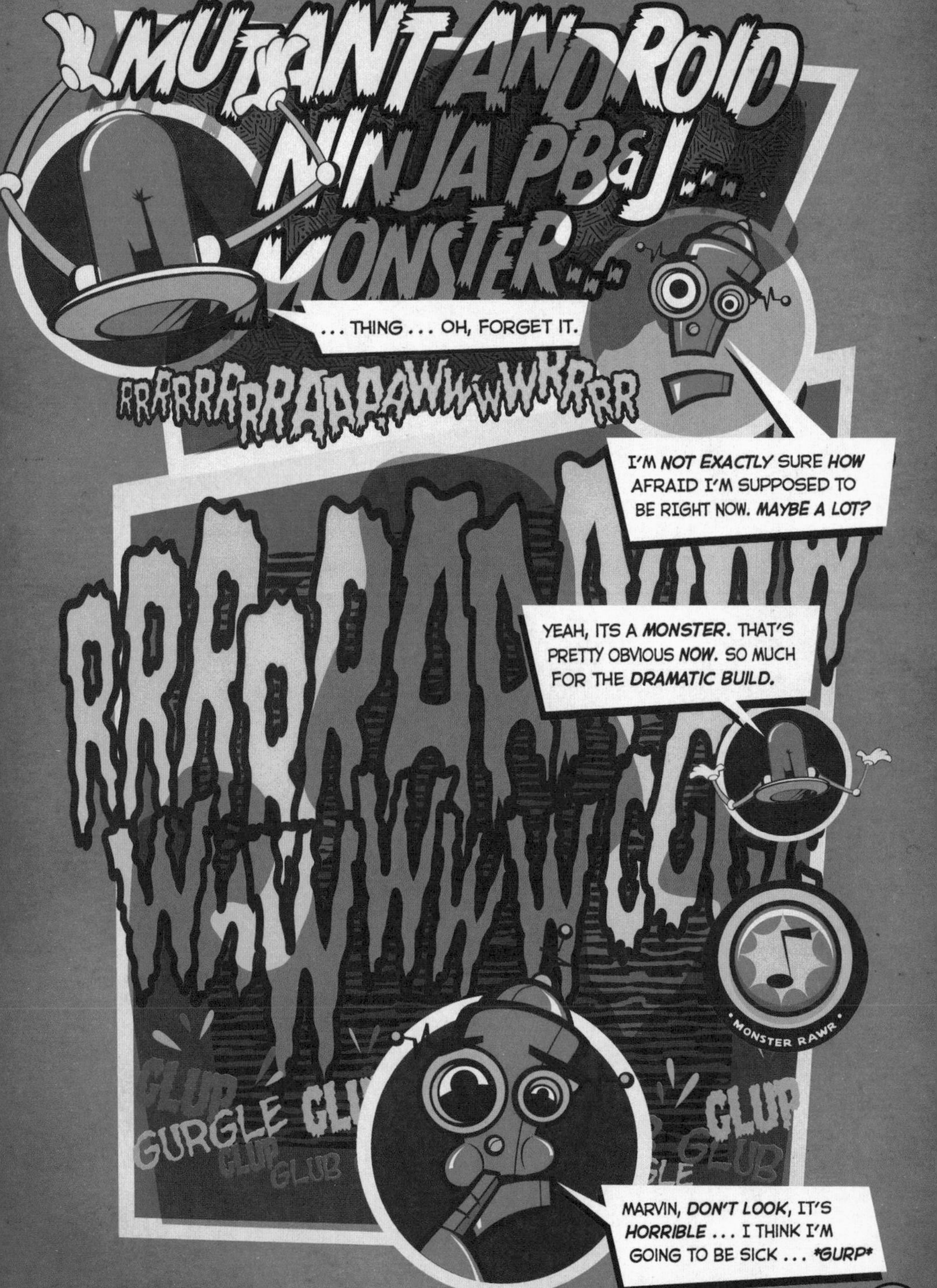
MUTANT ANDROID NINJA PB&J... MONSTER...
... THING ... OH, FORGET IT.
I'M NOT EXACTLY SURE HOW AFRAID I'M SUPPOSED TO BE RIGHT NOW. MAYBE A LOT?
YEAH, ITS A MONSTER. THAT'S PRETTY OBVIOUS NOW. SO MUCH FOR THE DRAMATIC BUILD.
MONSTER RAWR
GLUP GURGLE GLUP GLUP GLUB
GLUP GLUB
MARVIN, DON'T LOOK, IT'S HORRIBLE ... I THINK I'M GOING TO BE SICK ... *GURP*

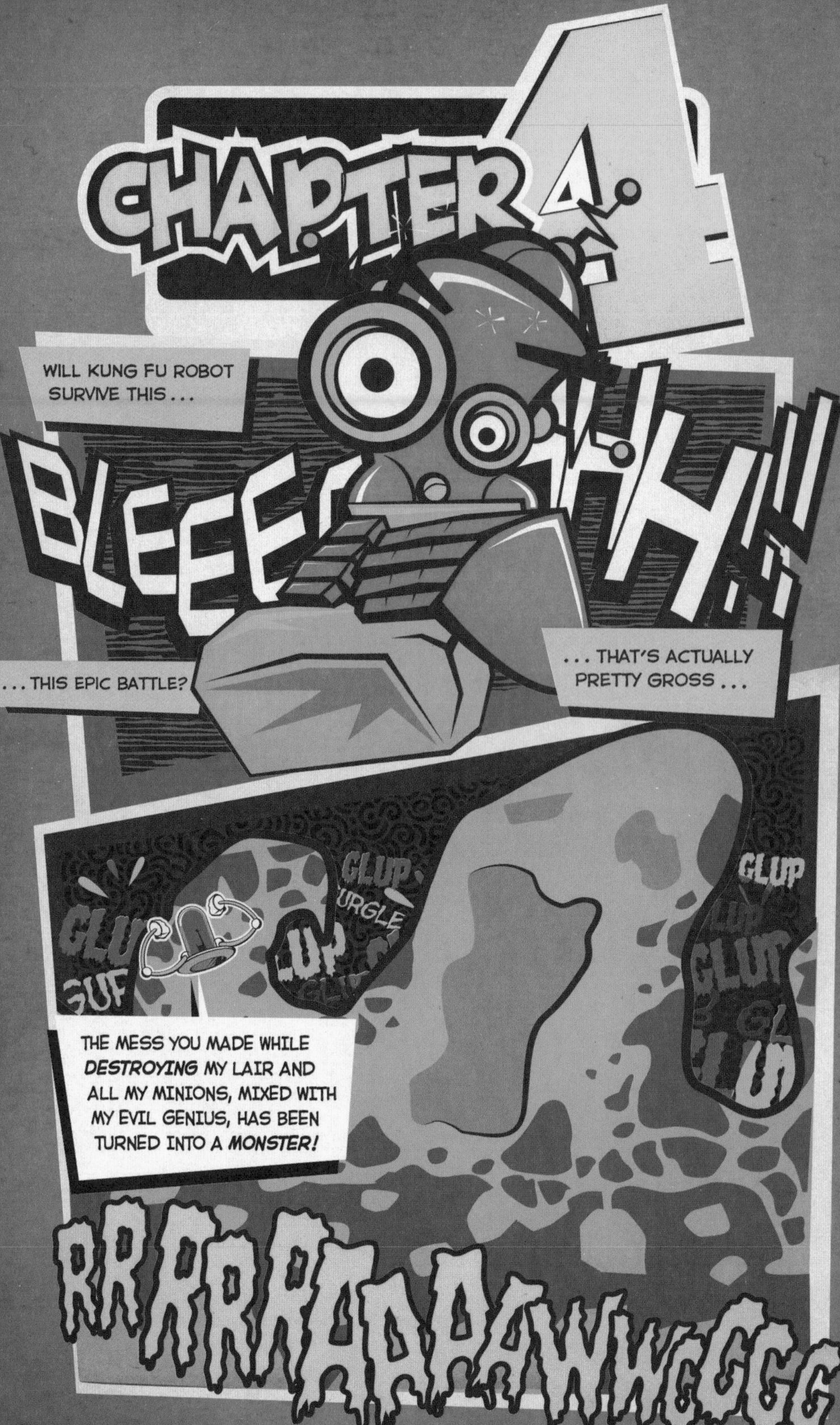
CHAPTER 4
WILL KUNG FU ROBOT SURVIVE THIS . . .
. . . THIS EPIC BATTLE?
. . . THAT'S ACTUALLY PRETTY GROSS . . .
GLUP
GLUP
THE MESS YOU MADE WHILE *DESTROYING* MY LAIR AND ALL MY MINIONS, MIXED WITH MY EVIL GENIUS, HAS BEEN TURNED INTO A *MONSTER!*
RRRRAAAAWWGGGG

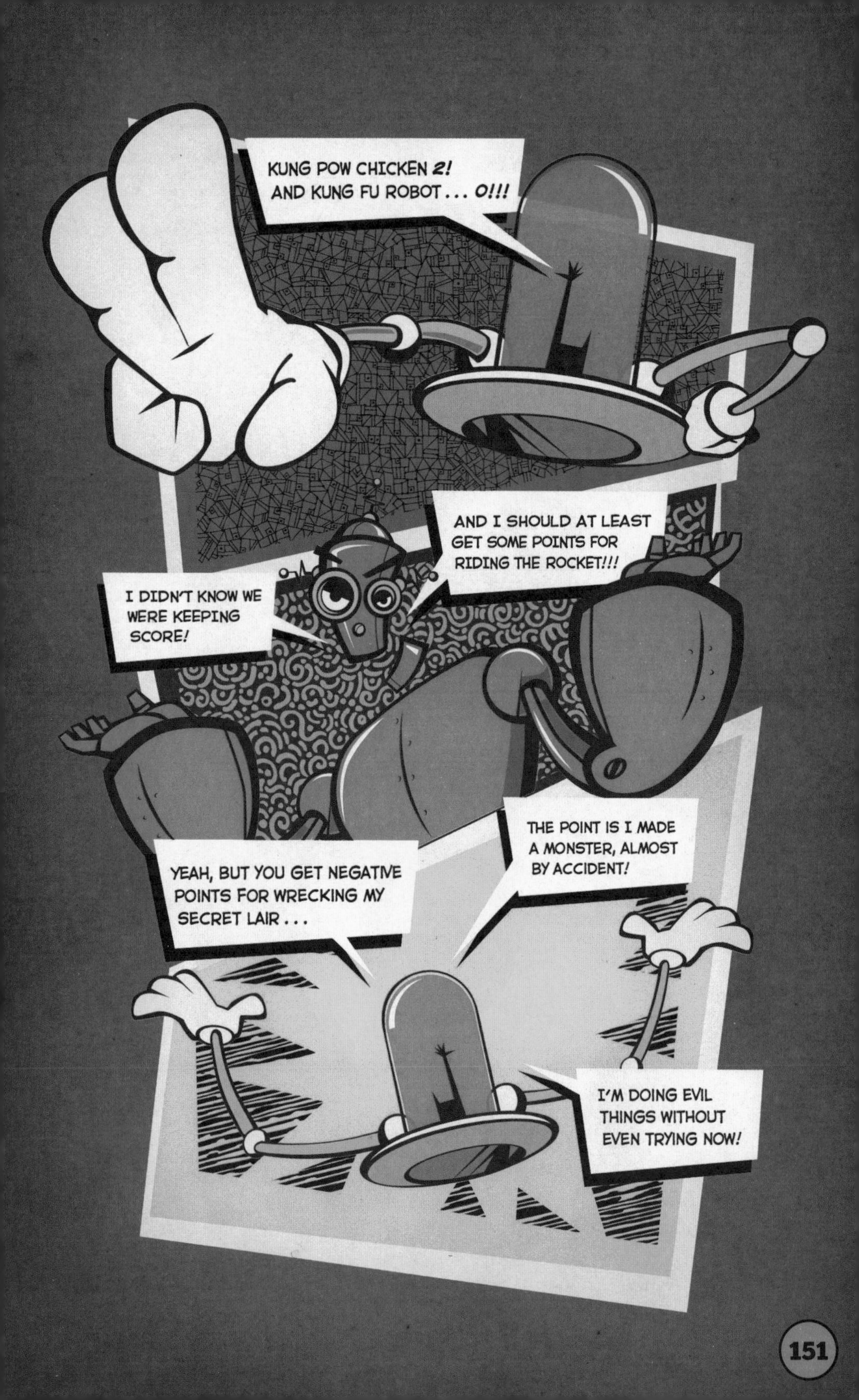
KUNG POW CHICKEN 2! AND KUNG FU ROBOT . . . 0!!!
AND I SHOULD AT LEAST GET SOME POINTS FOR RIDING THE ROCKET!!!
I DIDN'T KNOW WE WERE KEEPING SCORE!
YEAH, BUT YOU GET NEGATIVE POINTS FOR WRECKING MY SECRET LAIR . . .
THE POINT IS I MADE A MONSTER, ALMOST BY ACCIDENT!
I'M DOING EVIL THINGS WITHOUT EVEN TRYING NOW!

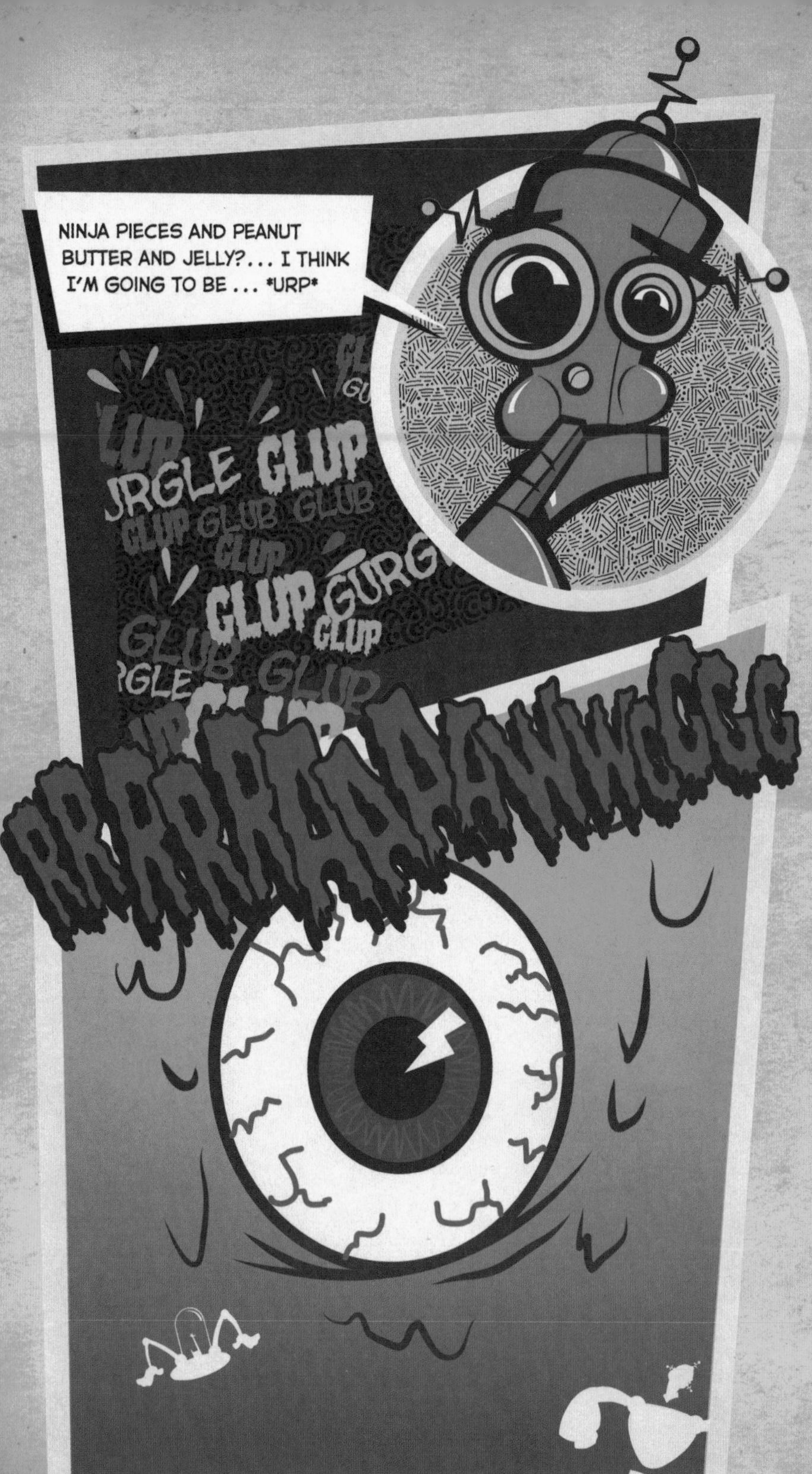
NINJA PIECES AND PEANUT BUTTER AND JELLY?... I THINK I'M GOING TO BE ... *URP*
GLUP
GURGLE GLUP
GLUP GLUB GLUB
GLUP
GLUP GURG
GLUP
GLUB
GLUB
RRRRAAAAWWGGG

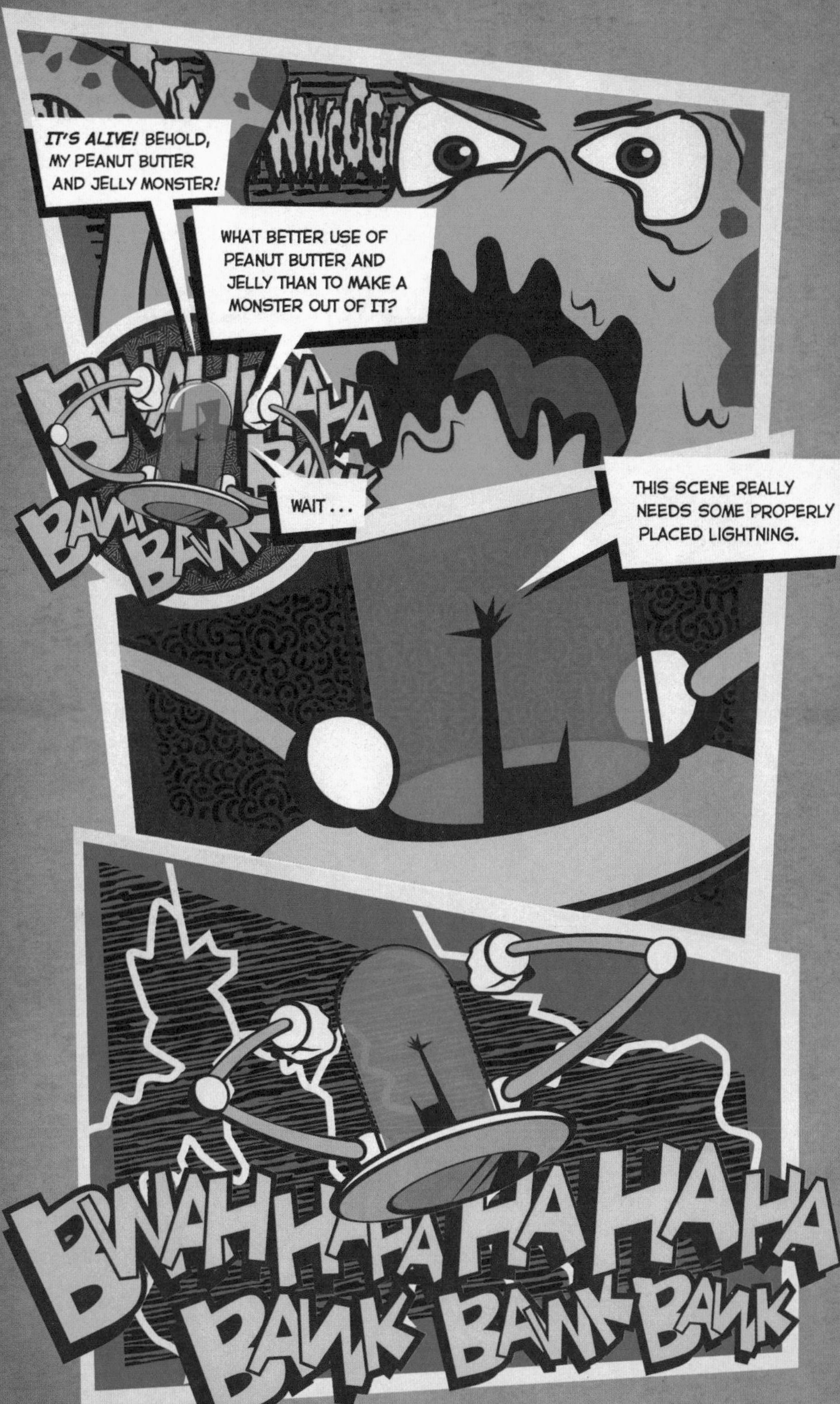
IT'S ALIVE! BEHOLD, MY PEANUT BUTTER AND JELLY MONSTER!
WHAT BETTER USE OF PEANUT BUTTER AND JELLY THAN TO MAKE A MONSTER OUT OF IT?
WAIT . . .
THIS SCENE REALLY NEEDS SOME PROPERLY PLACED LIGHTNING.
BANK BANK BANK

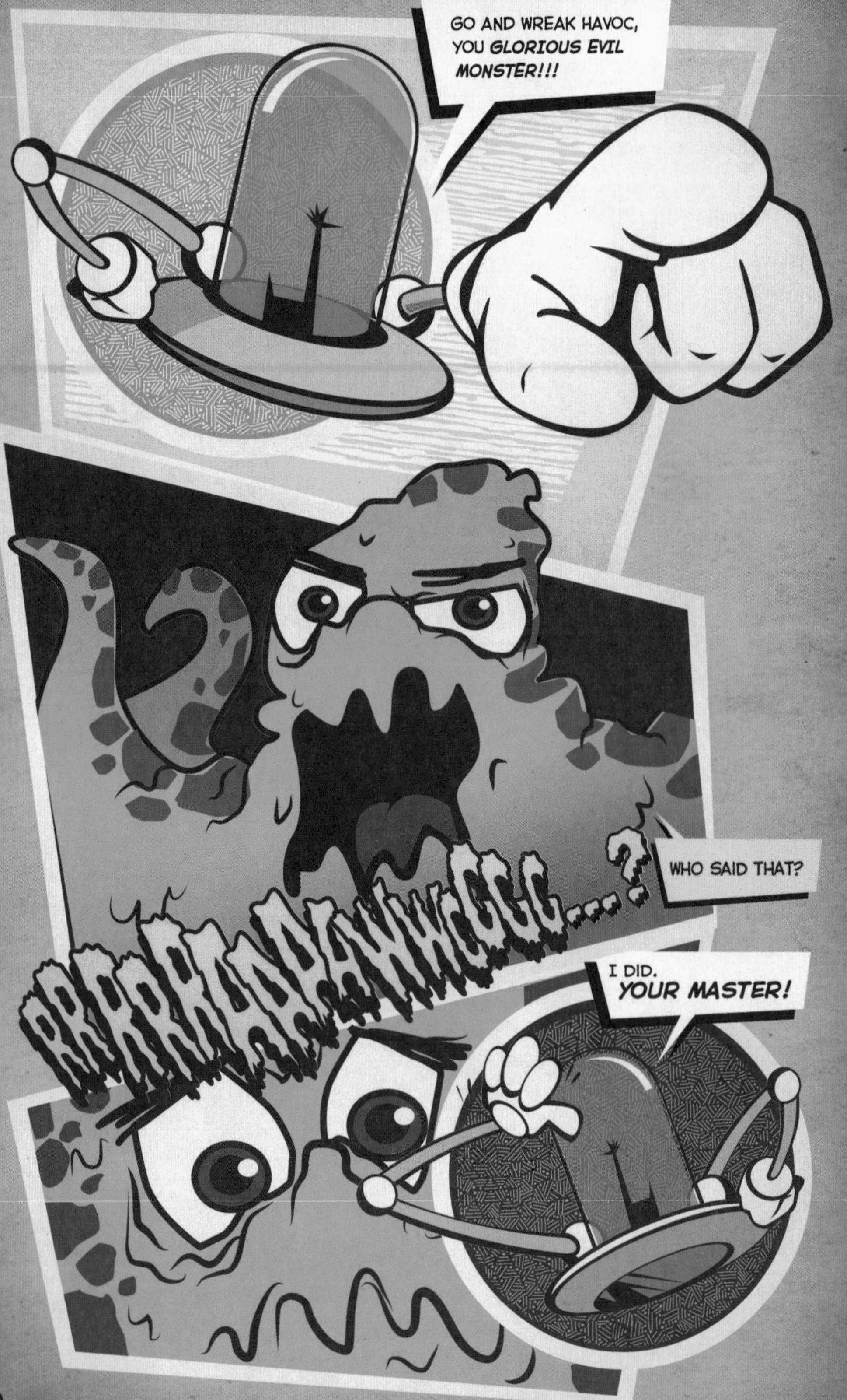
GO AND WREAK HAVOC, YOU GLORIOUS EVIL MONSTER!!!
BRRRAAAAWWGGG...?
WHO SAID THAT?
I DID. YOUR MASTER!

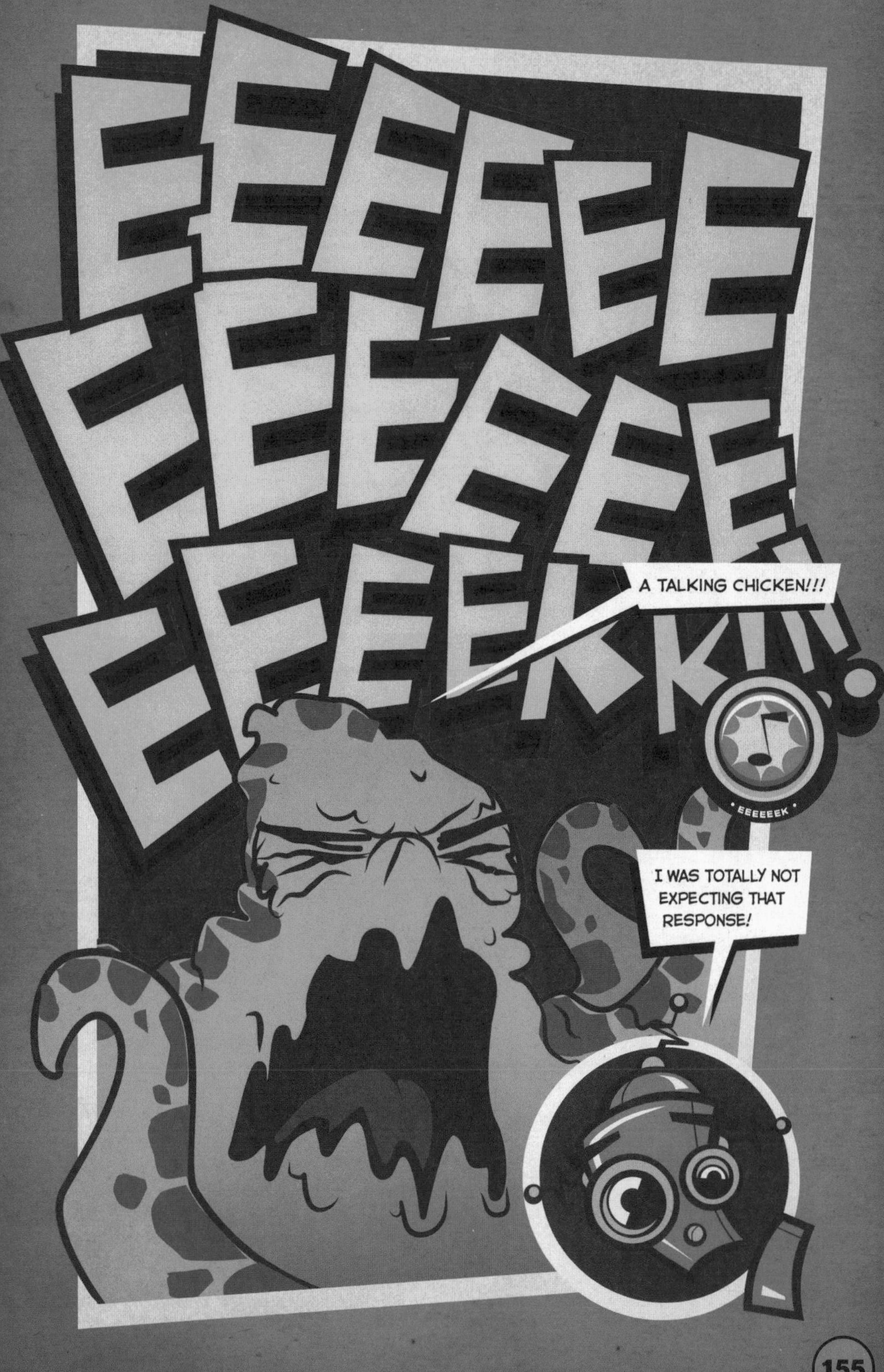
EEEEEEEEEEEEEEEEK!!!
A TALKING CHICKEN!!!
EEEEEEK
I WAS TOTALLY NOT EXPECTING THAT RESPONSE!

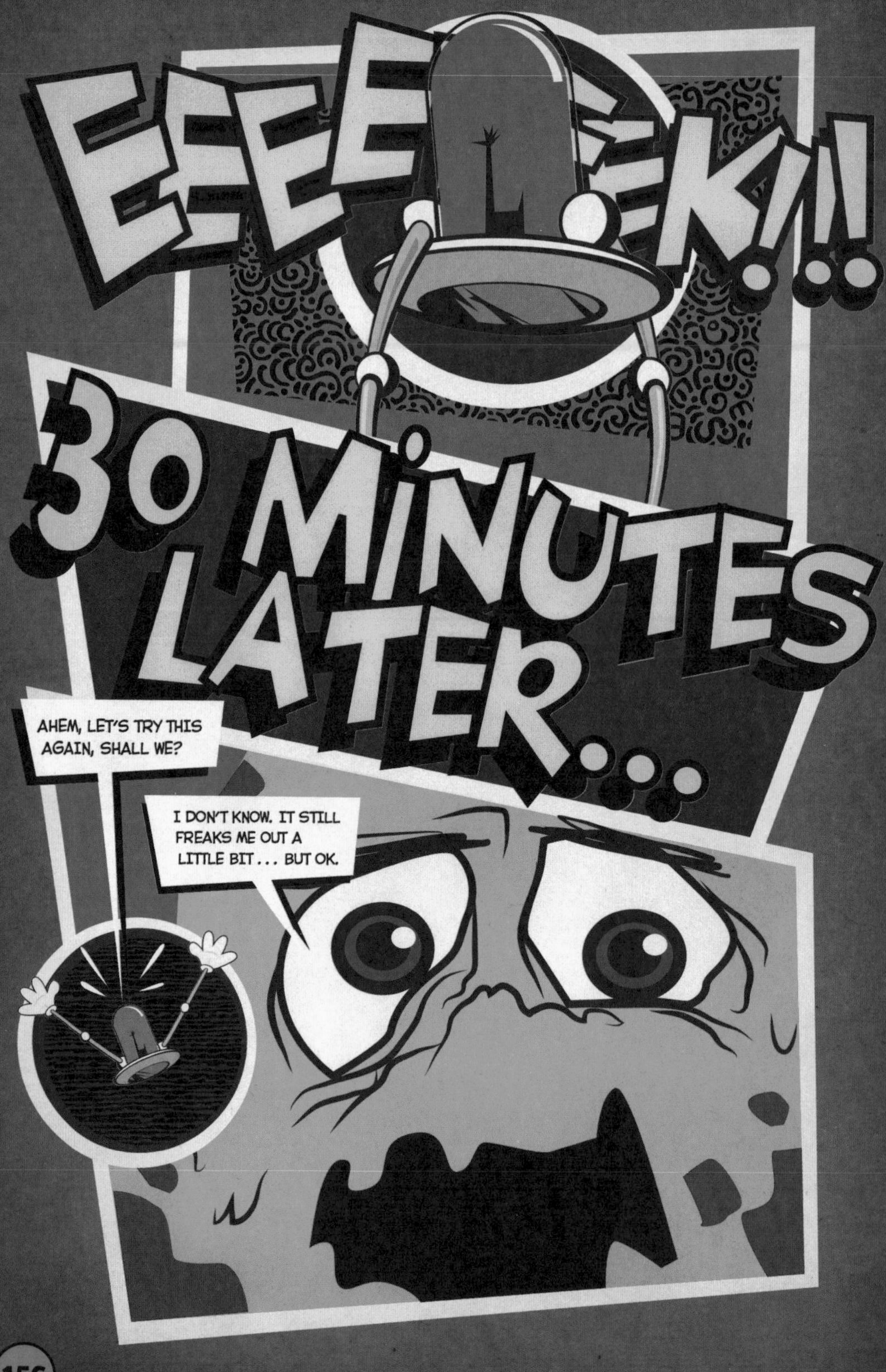
EEEEEEK!!!
30 MINUTES LATER...
AHEM, LET'S TRY THIS AGAIN, SHALL WE?
I DON'T KNOW. IT STILL FREAKS ME OUT A LITTLE BIT . . . BUT OK.

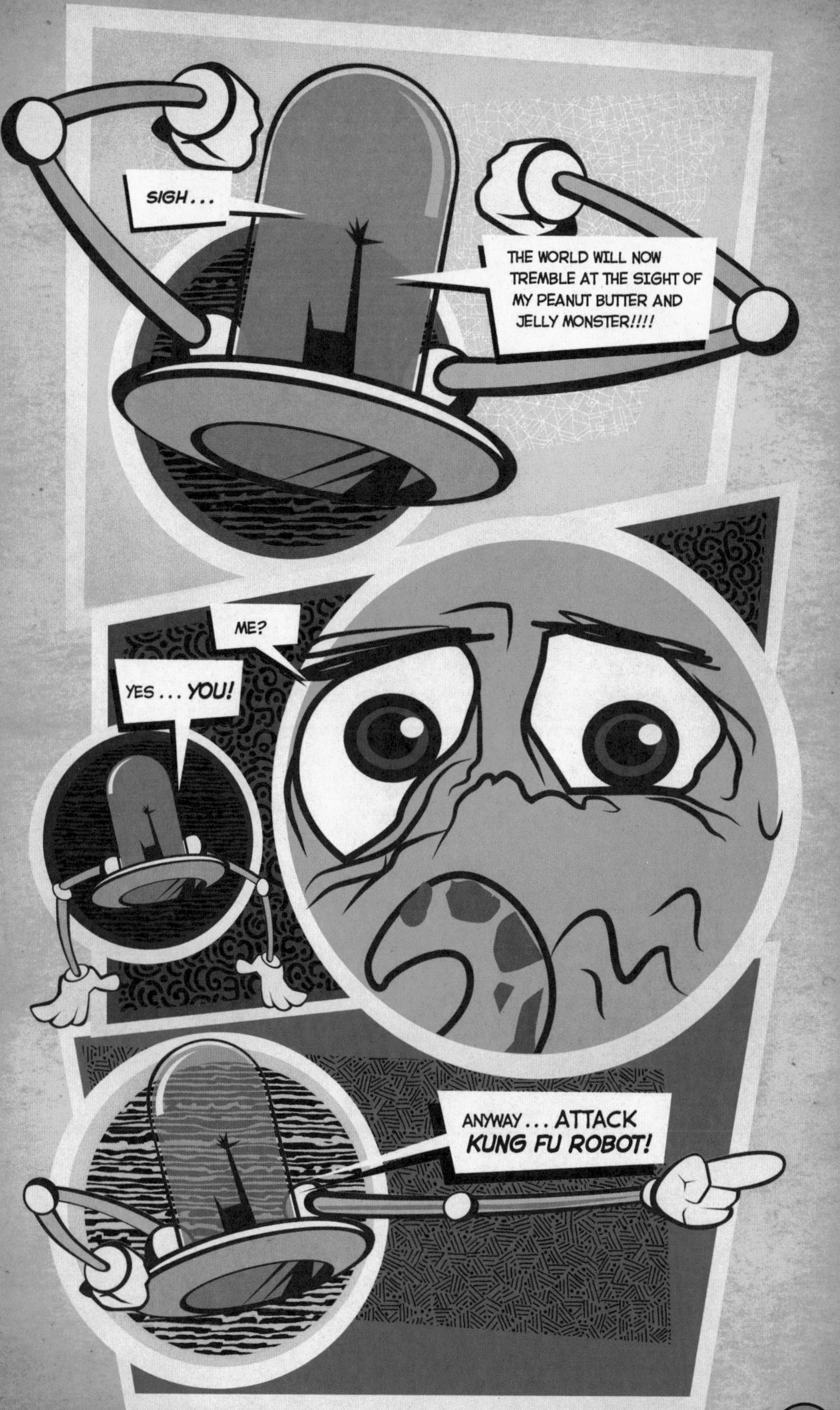
SIGH . . .
THE WORLD WILL NOW TREMBLE AT THE SIGHT OF MY PEANUT BUTTER AND JELLY MONSTER!!!!
ME?
YES . . . YOU!
ANYWAY . . . ATTACK KUNG FU ROBOT!

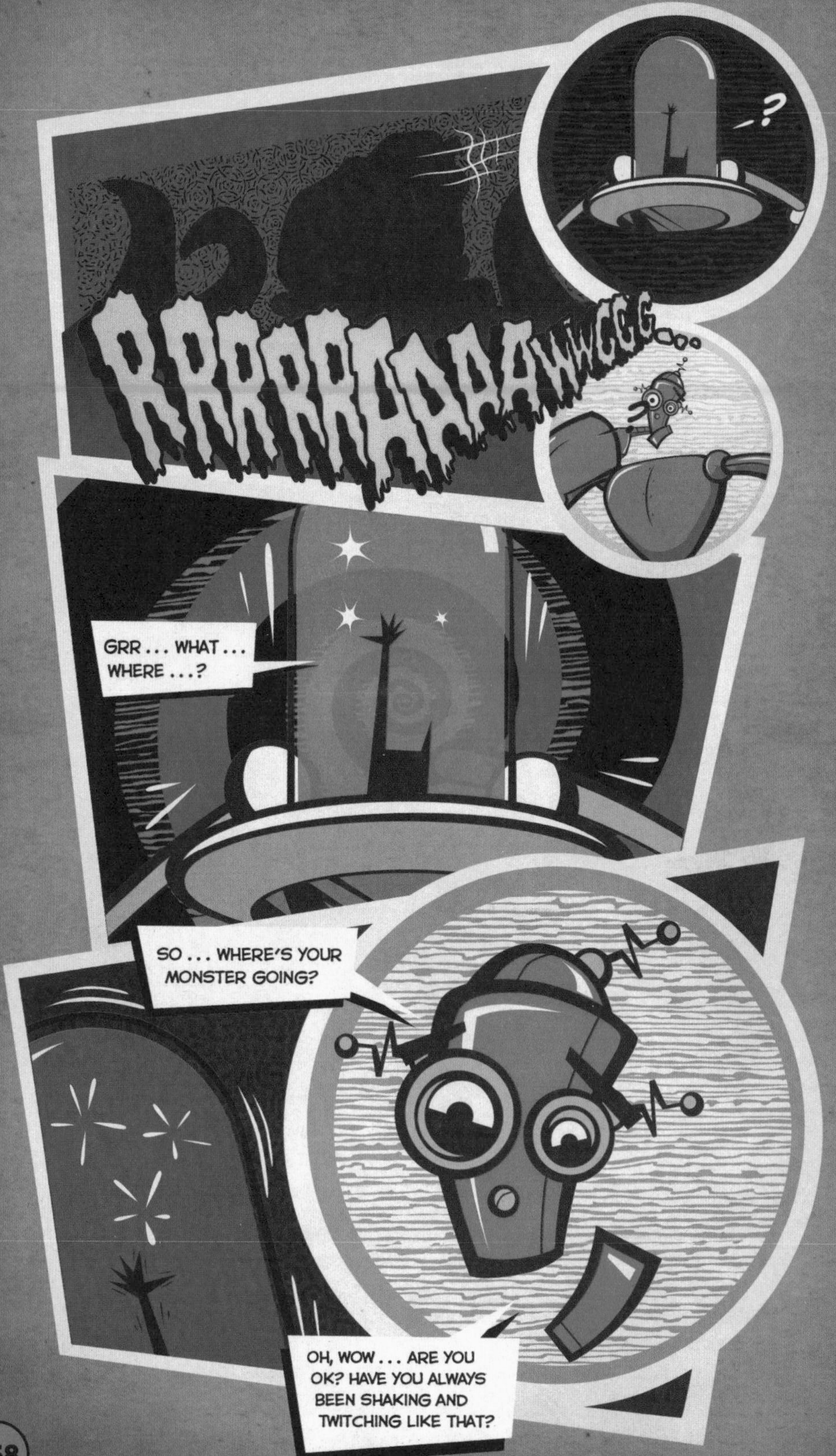

-?
RRRRRAAAAWGGG...
GRR ... WHAT ...
WHERE ...?
SO ... WHERE'S YOUR
MONSTER GOING?
OH, WOW ... ARE YOU
OK? HAVE YOU ALWAYS
BEEN SHAKING AND
TWITCHING LIKE THAT?

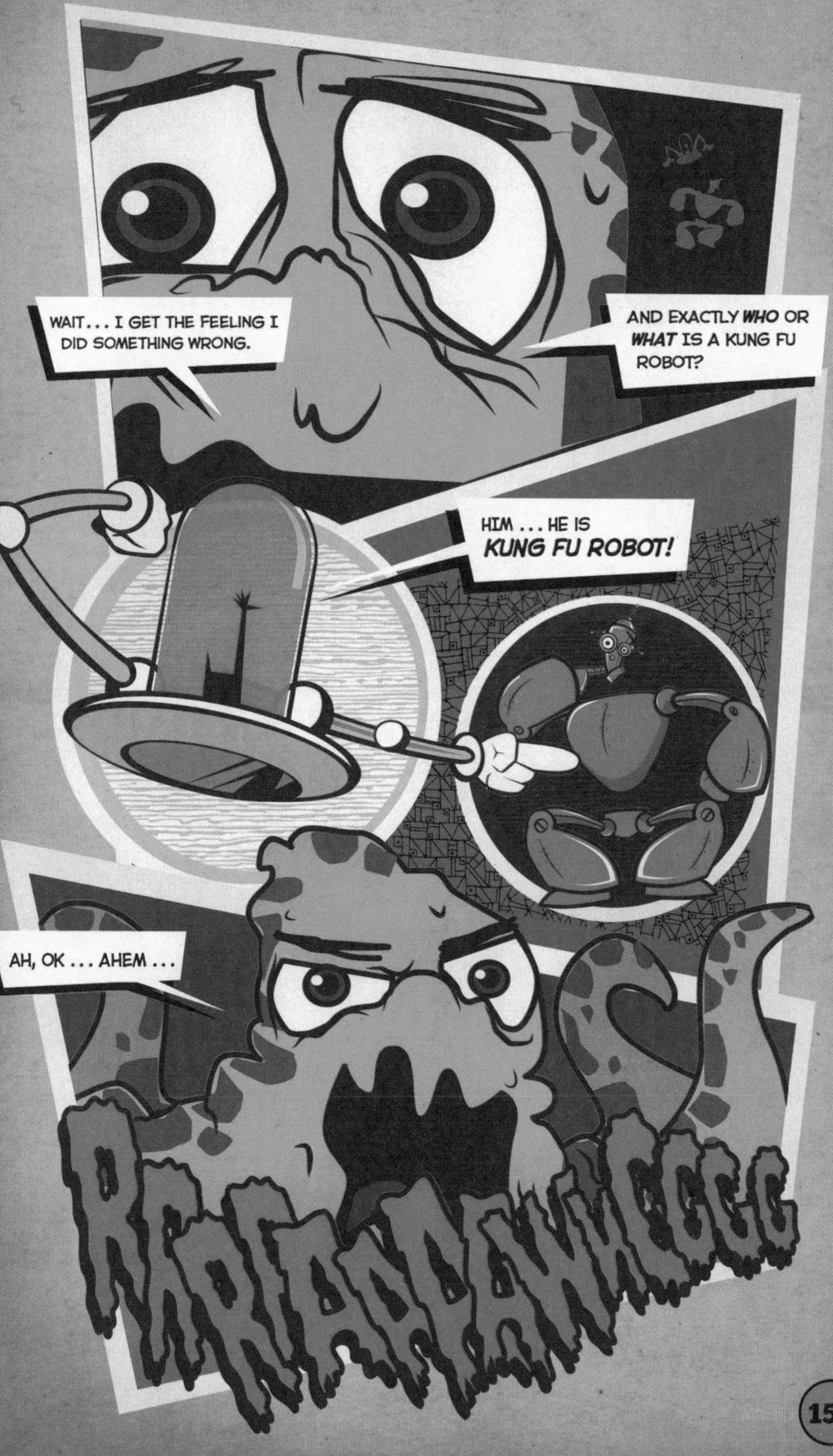
WAIT . . . I GET THE FEELING I DID SOMETHING WRONG.
AND EXACTLY WHO OR WHAT IS A KUNG FU ROBOT?
HIM . . . HE IS KUNG FU ROBOT!
AH, OK . . . AHEM . . .

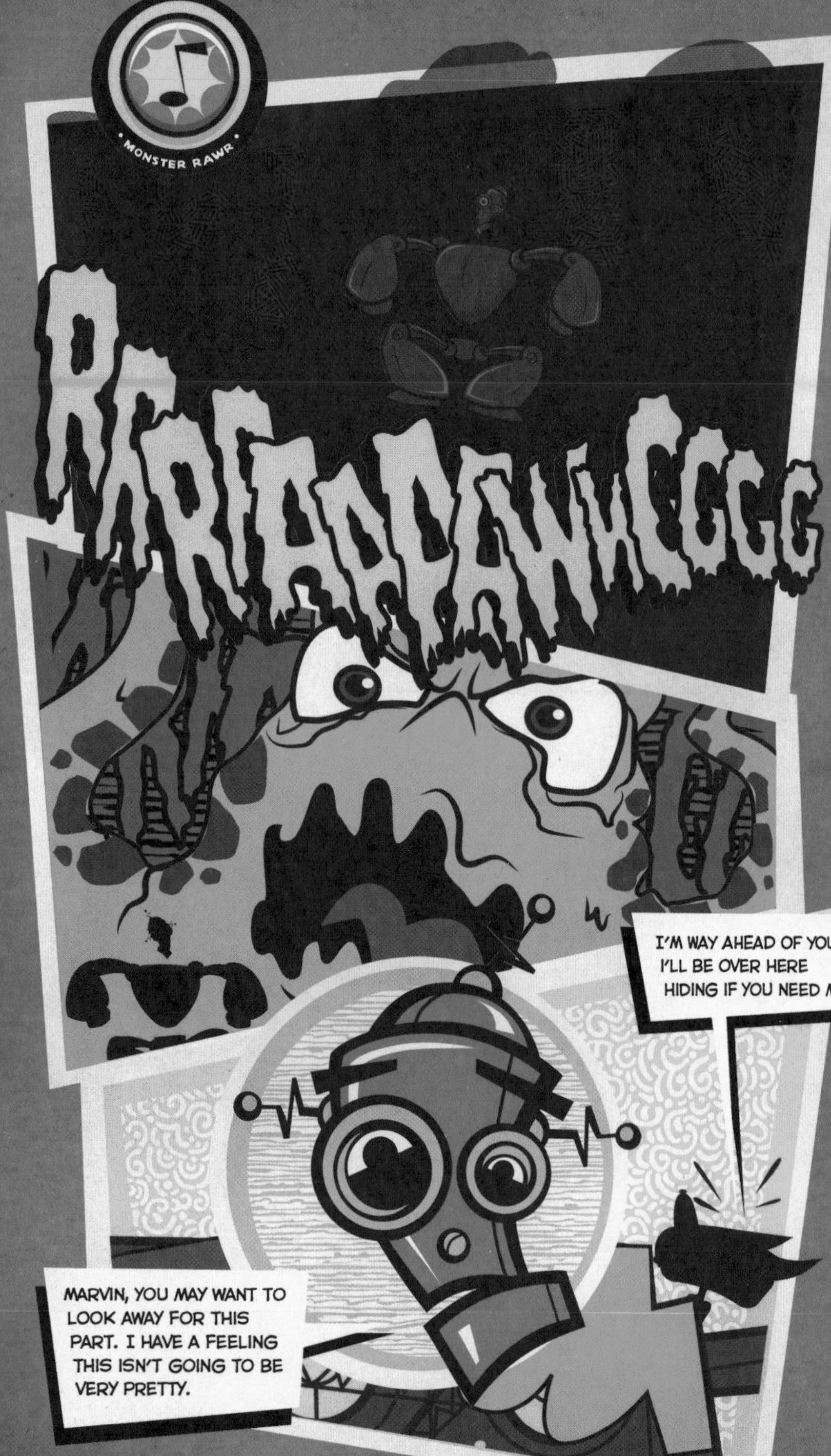
MONSTER RAWR
RARRAAAAWRGGG
I'M WAY AHEAD OF YOU. I'LL BE OVER HERE HIDING IF YOU NEED ME.
MARVIN, YOU MAY WANT TO LOOK AWAY FOR THIS PART. I HAVE A FEELING THIS ISN'T GOING TO BE VERY PRETTY.

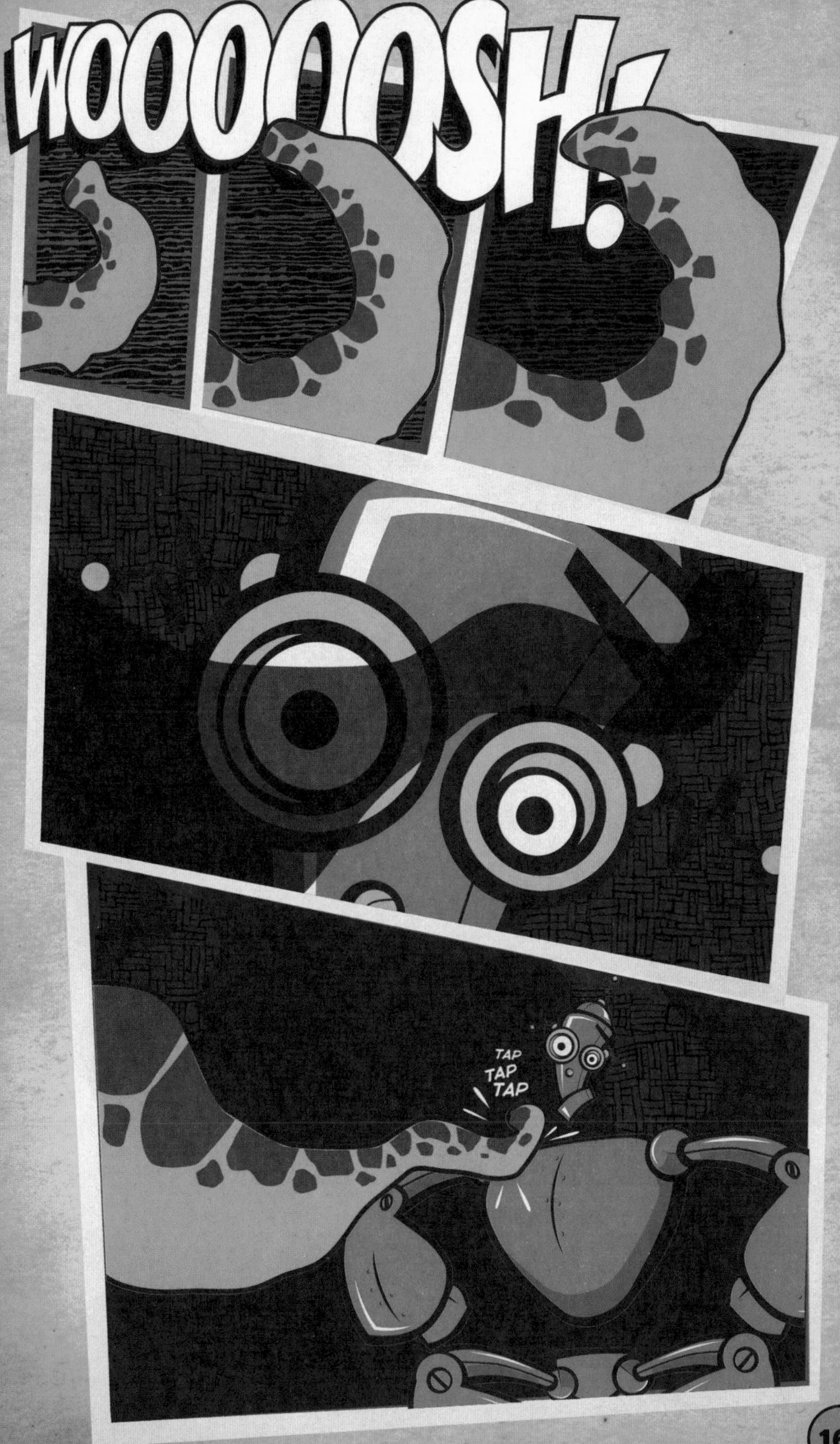
WOOOOOOSH!
TAP
TAP
TAP

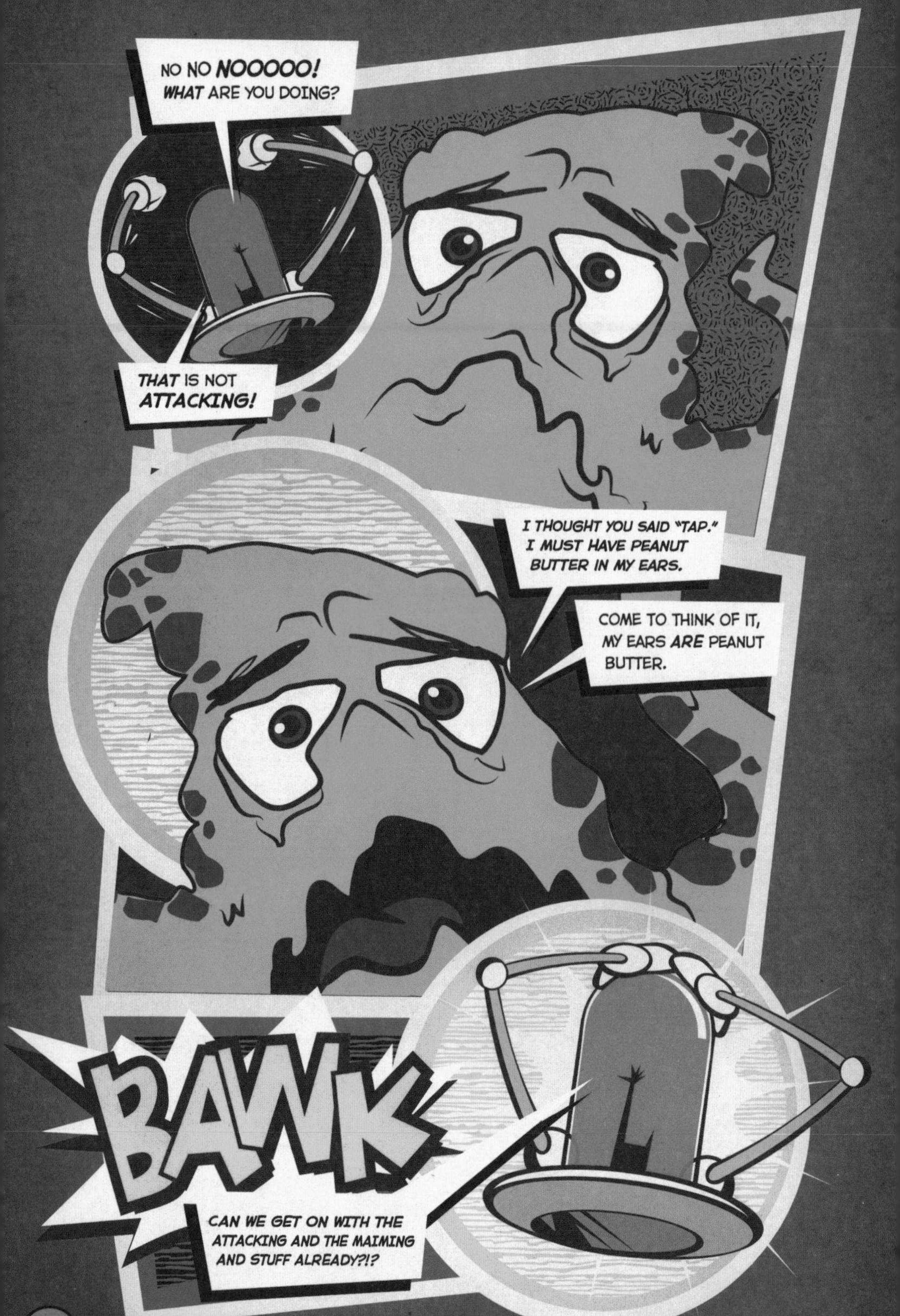
NO NO NOOOOO! WHAT ARE YOU DOING?
THAT IS NOT ATTACKING!
I THOUGHT YOU SAID "TAP." I MUST HAVE PEANUT BUTTER IN MY EARS.
COME TO THINK OF IT, MY EARS ARE PEANUT BUTTER.
BANK
CAN WE GET ON WITH THE ATTACKING AND THE MAIMING AND STUFF ALREADY?!?

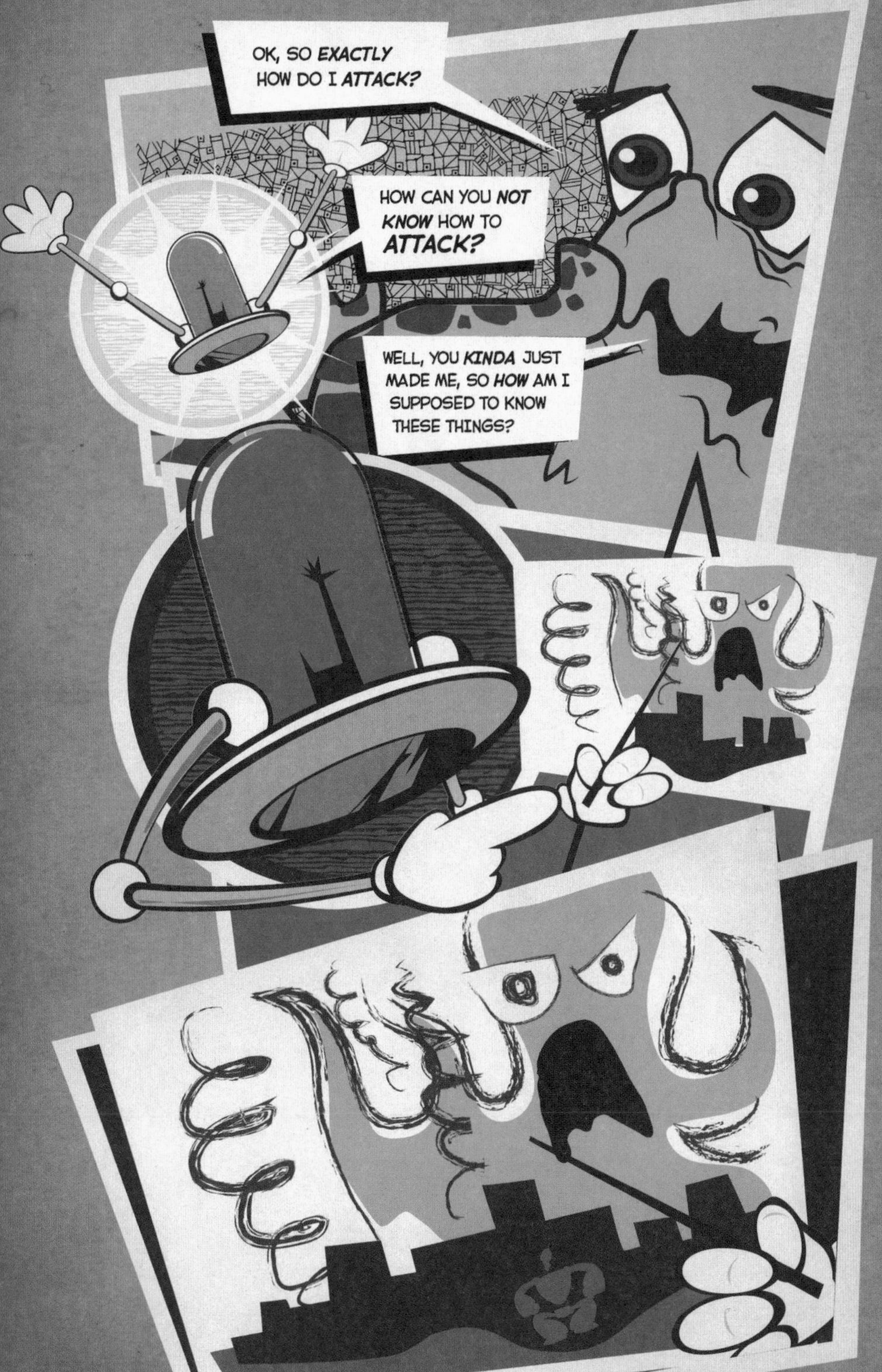
OK, SO EXACTLY HOW DO I ATTACK?
HOW CAN YOU NOT KNOW HOW TO ATTACK?
WELL, YOU KINDA JUST MADE ME, SO HOW AM I SUPPOSED TO KNOW THESE THINGS?

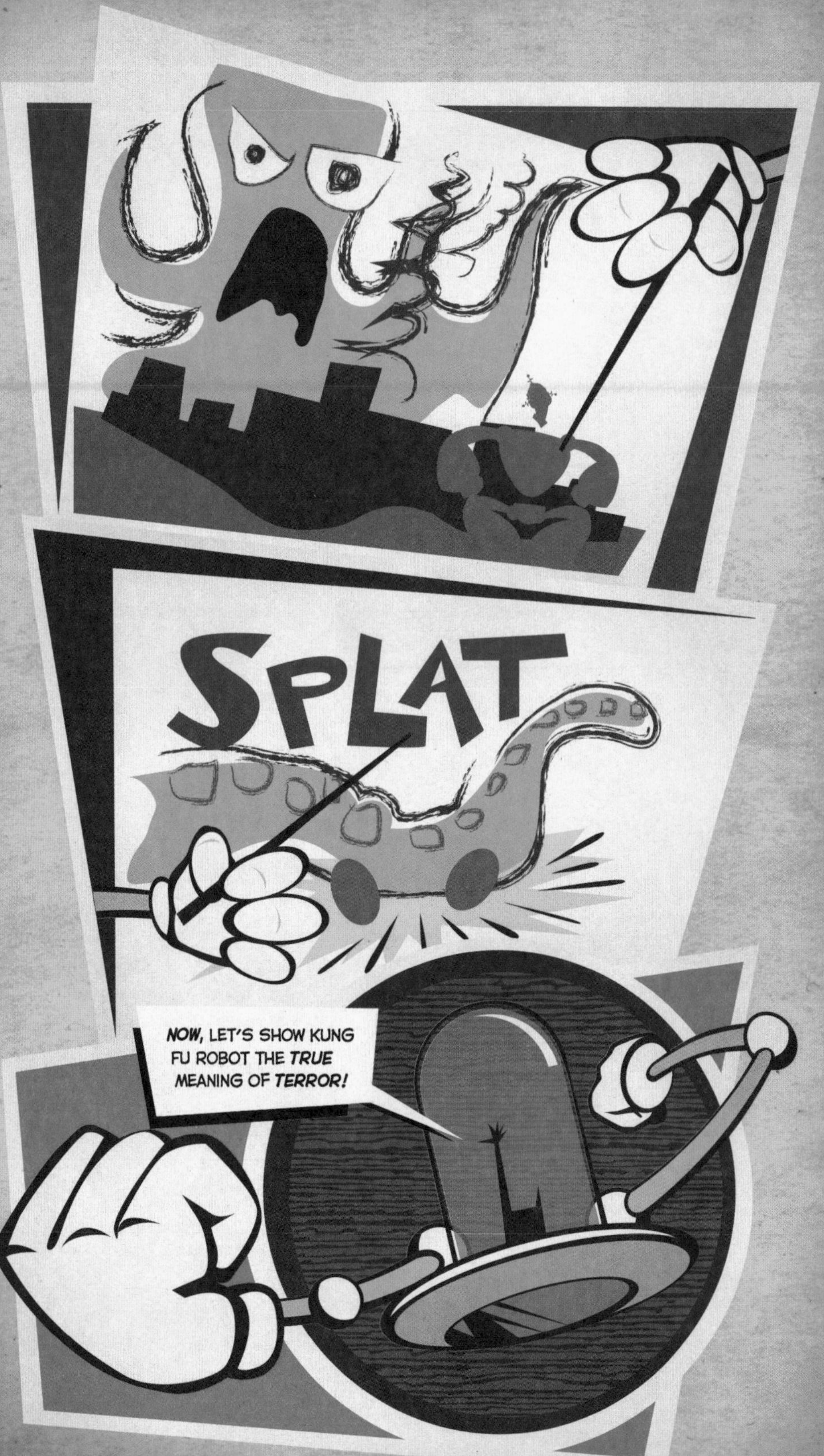
SPLAT
NOW, LET'S SHOW KUNG FU ROBOT THE TRUE MEANING OF TERROR!

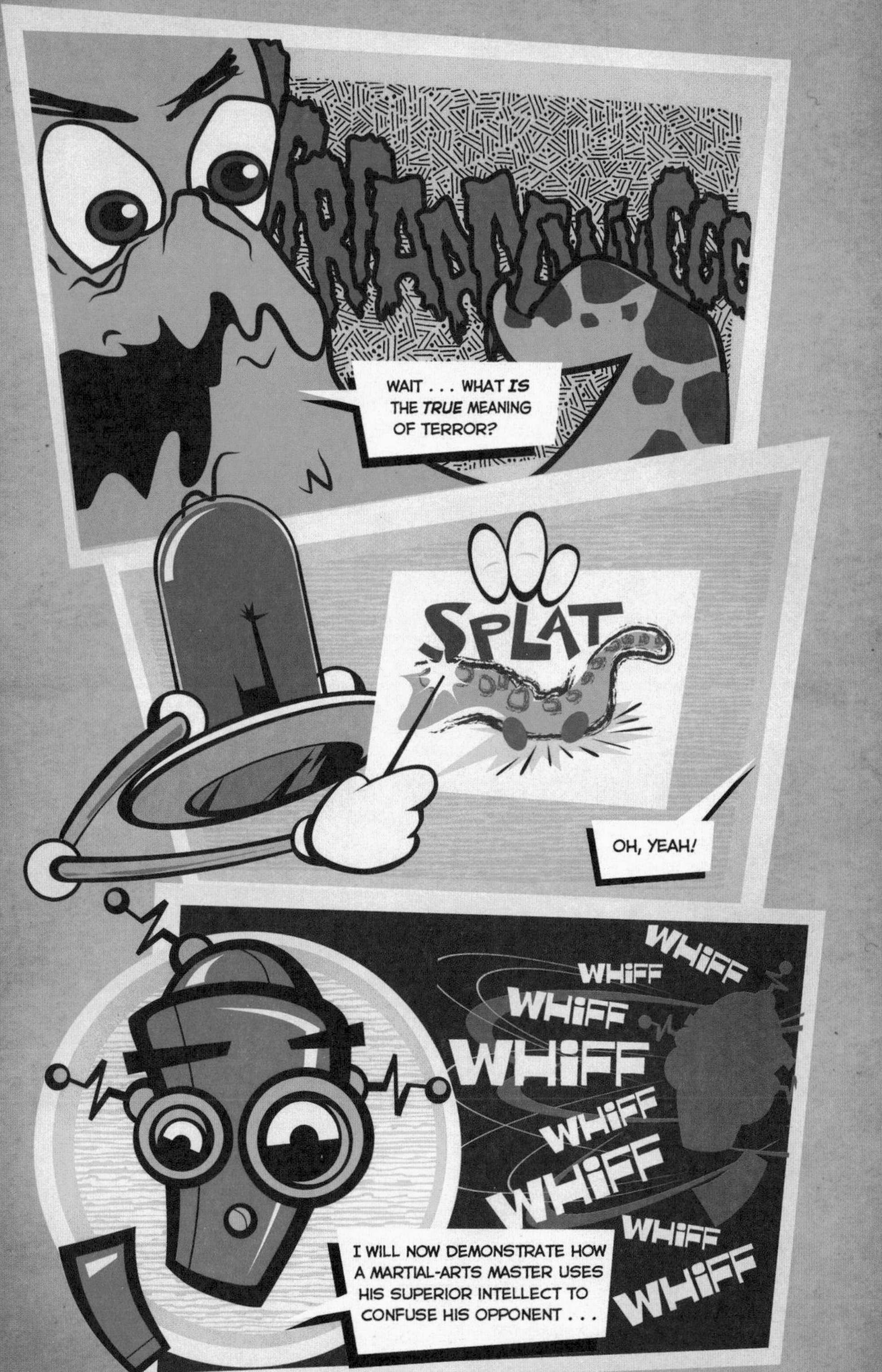

WAIT . . . WHAT *IS* THE *TRUE* MEANING OF TERROR?
SPLAT
OH, YEAH!
WHIFF
WHIFF
WHIFF
WHIFF
WHIFF
WHIFF
WHIFF
WHIFF
I WILL NOW DEMONSTRATE HOW A MARTIAL-ARTS MASTER USES HIS SUPERIOR INTELLECT TO CONFUSE HIS OPPONENT . . .

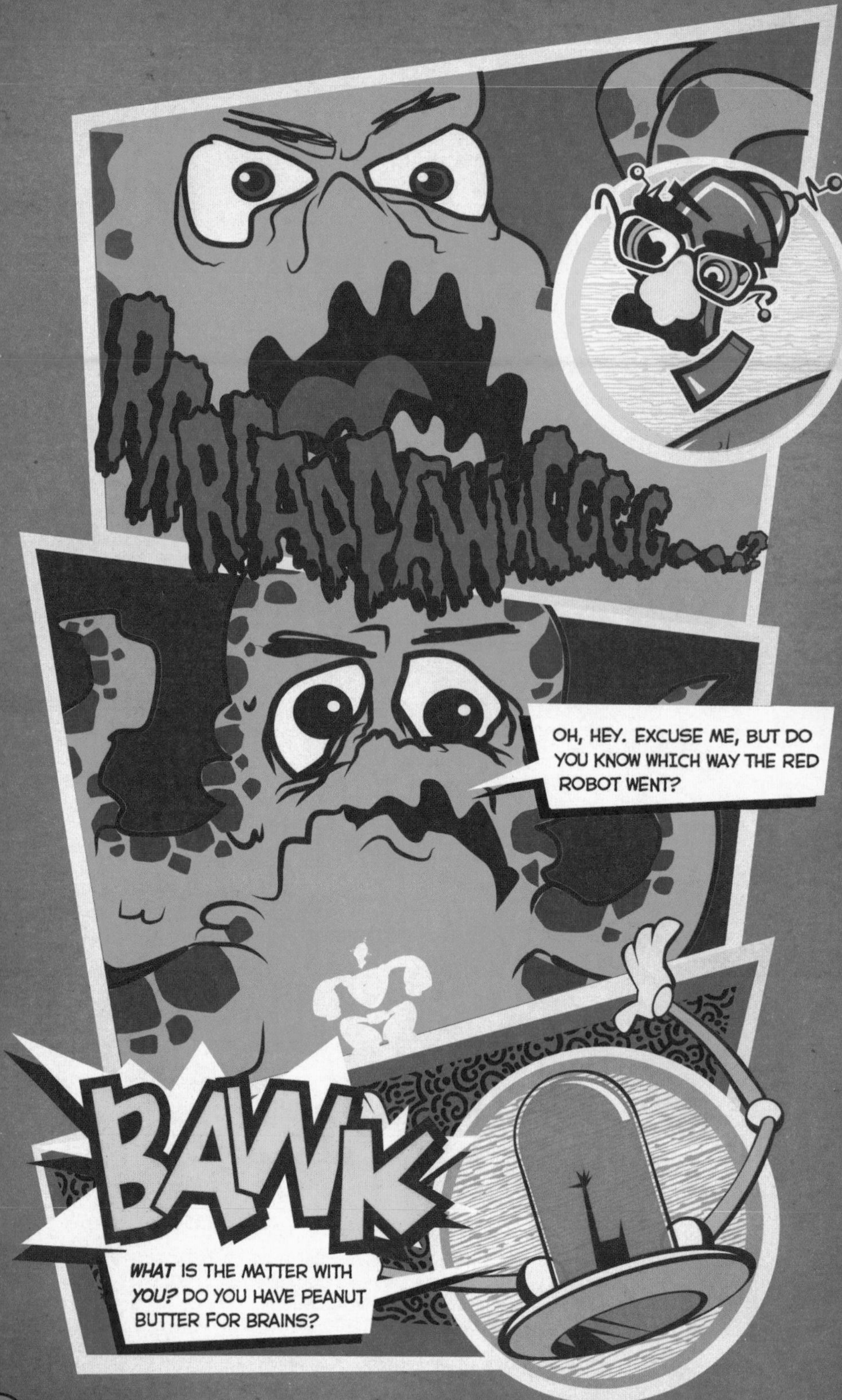
OH, HEY. EXCUSE ME, BUT DO YOU KNOW WHICH WAY THE RED ROBOT WENT?
BAWK
WHAT IS THE MATTER WITH *YOU?* DO YOU HAVE PEANUT BUTTER FOR BRAINS?

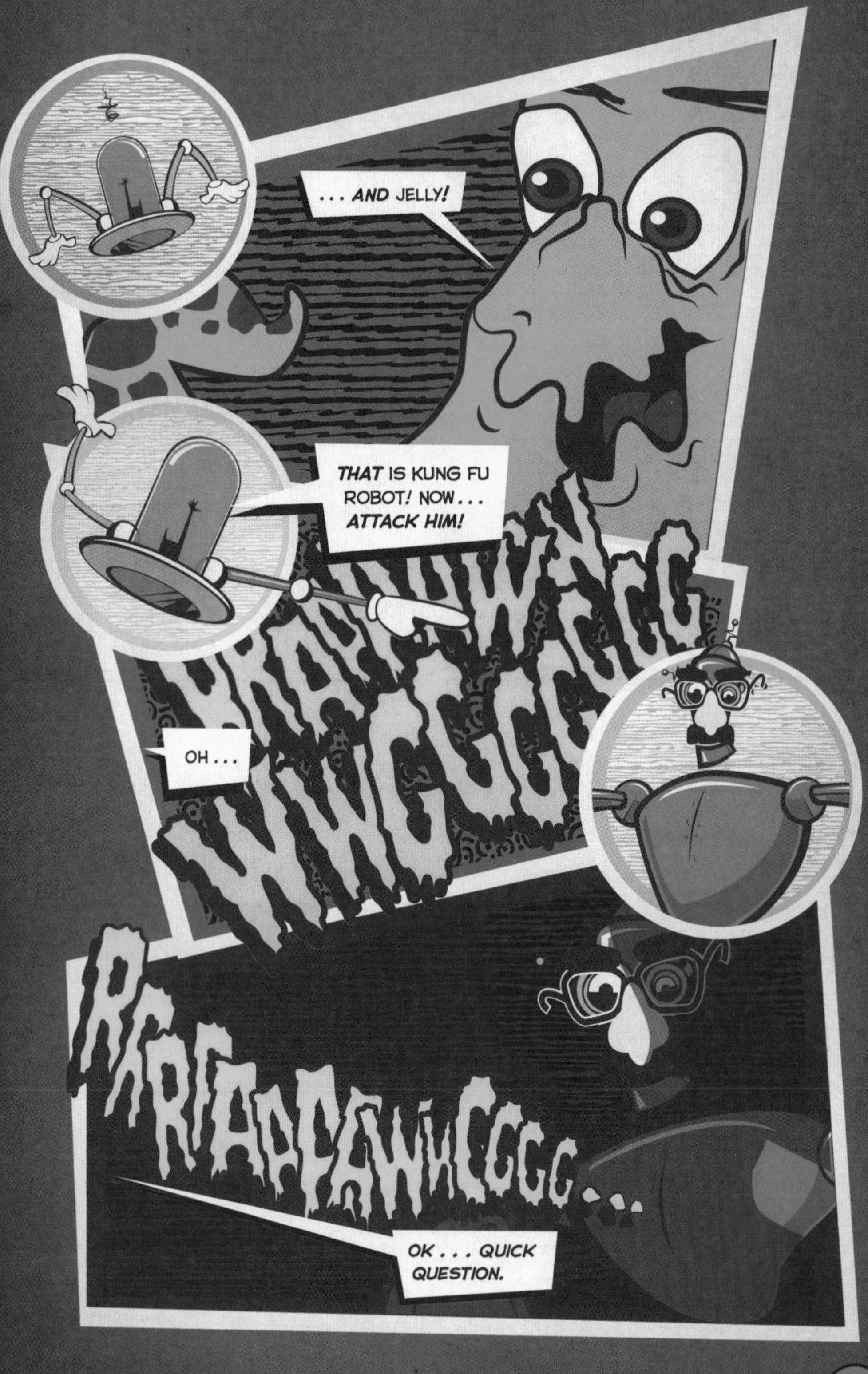

... *AND* JELLY!
THAT IS KUNG FU ROBOT! NOW... *ATTACK HIM!*
OH...
OK... QUICK QUESTION.

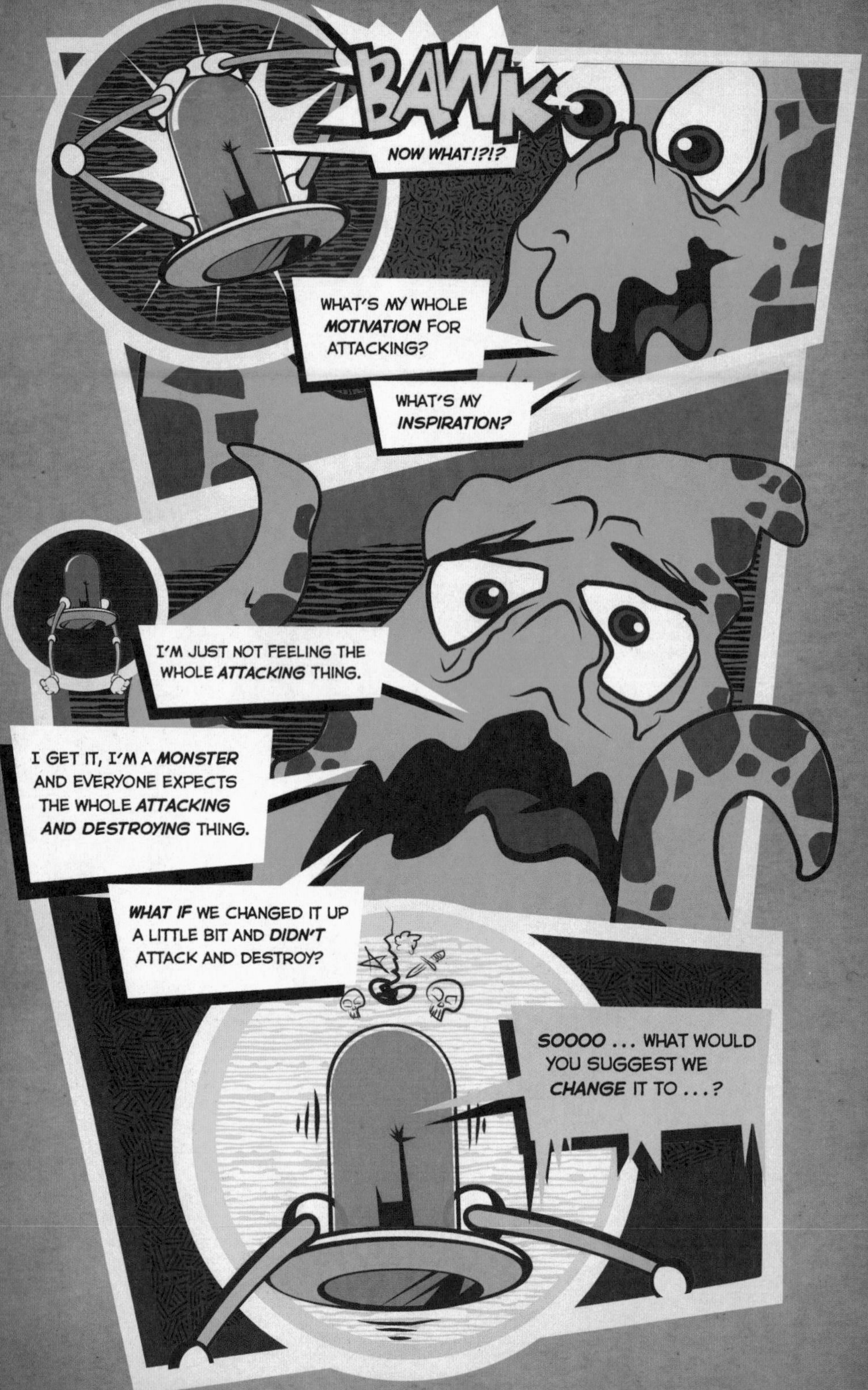
BAWK
NOW WHAT!?!?
WHAT'S MY WHOLE MOTIVATION FOR ATTACKING?
WHAT'S MY INSPIRATION?
I'M JUST NOT FEELING THE WHOLE ATTACKING THING.
I GET IT, I'M A MONSTER AND EVERYONE EXPECTS THE WHOLE ATTACKING AND DESTROYING THING.
WHAT IF WE CHANGED IT UP A LITTLE BIT AND DIDN'T ATTACK AND DESTROY?
SOOOO ... WHAT WOULD YOU SUGGEST WE CHANGE IT TO ...?

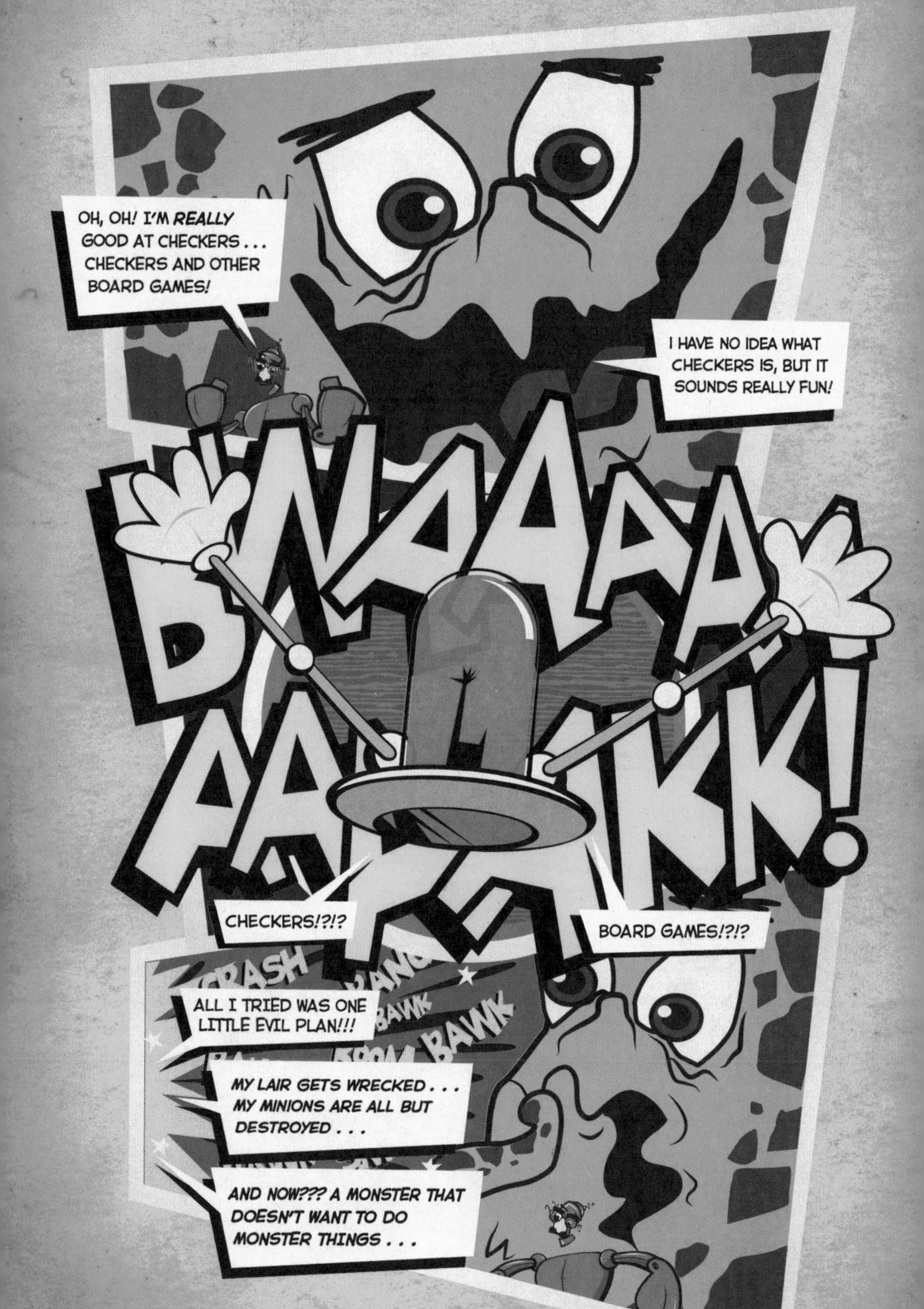
OH, OH! I'M *REALLY* GOOD AT CHECKERS . . . CHECKERS AND OTHER BOARD GAMES!
I HAVE NO IDEA WHAT CHECKERS IS, BUT IT SOUNDS REALLY FUN!
CHECKERS!?!?
BOARD GAMES!?!?
CRASH
BAWK
BAWK
ALL I TRIED WAS ONE LITTLE EVIL PLAN!!!
MY LAIR GETS WRECKED . . . MY MINIONS ARE ALL BUT DESTROYED . . .
AND NOW??? A MONSTER THAT DOESN'T WANT TO DO MONSTER THINGS . . .

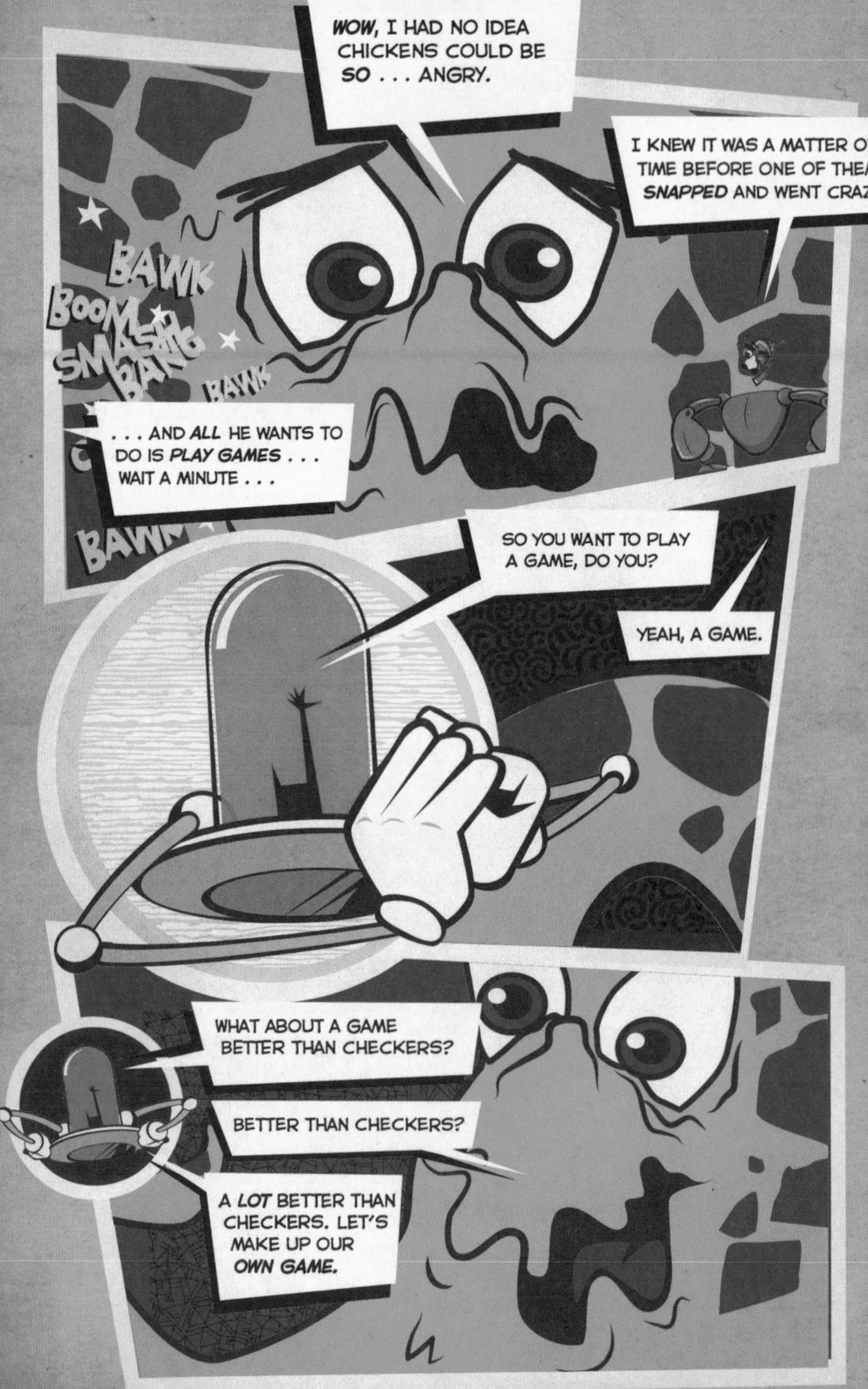
WOW, I HAD NO IDEA CHICKENS COULD BE SO . . . ANGRY.
I KNEW IT WAS A MATTER OF TIME BEFORE ONE OF THEM SNAPPED AND WENT CRAZY.
BAWK
BOOM
SMASH
BANG
BAWK
. . . AND ALL HE WANTS TO DO IS PLAY GAMES . . . WAIT A MINUTE . . .
SO YOU WANT TO PLAY A GAME, DO YOU?
YEAH, A GAME.
WHAT ABOUT A GAME BETTER THAN CHECKERS?
BETTER THAN CHECKERS?
A LOT BETTER THAN CHECKERS. LET'S MAKE UP OUR OWN GAME.

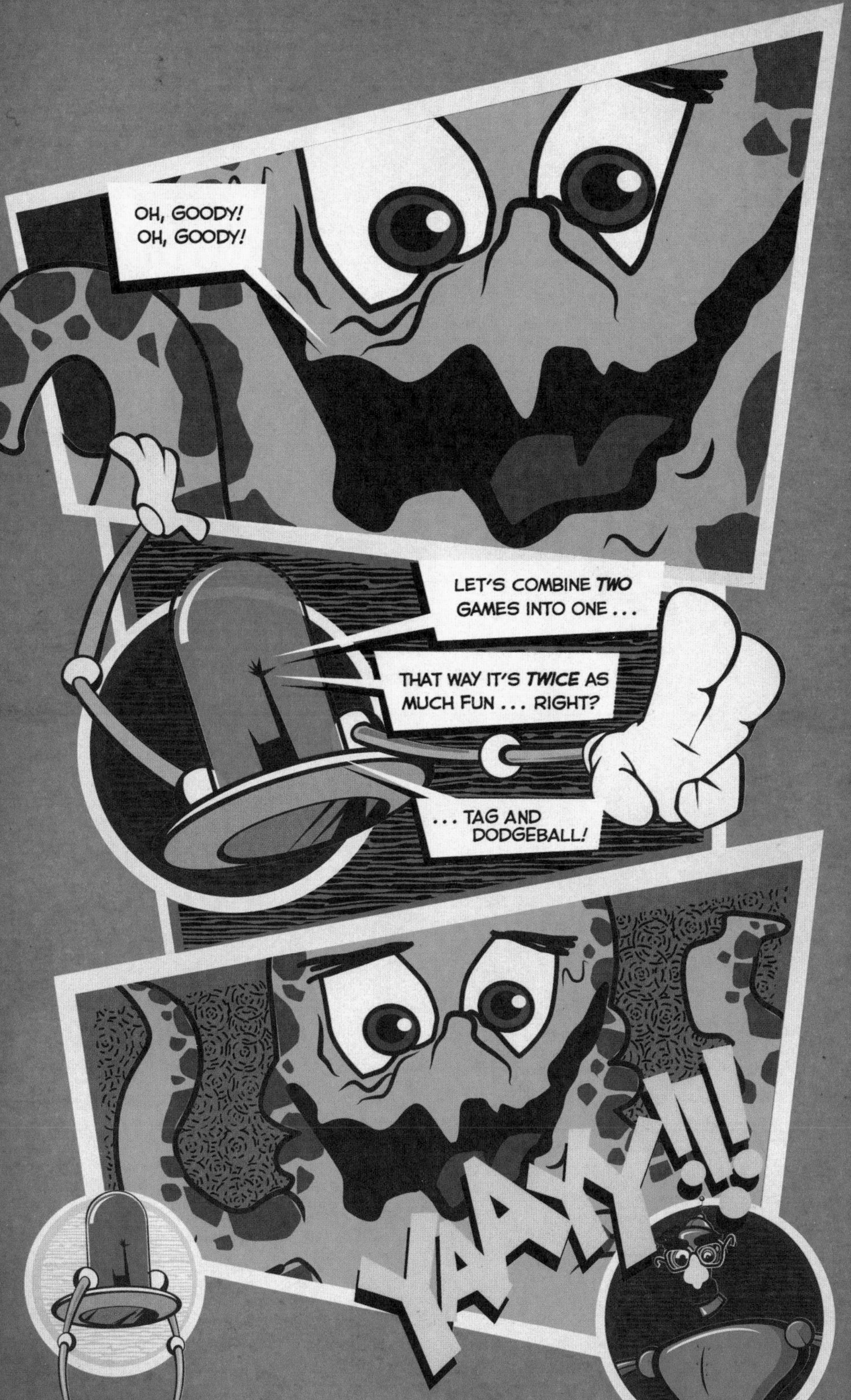
OH, GOODY!
OH, GOODY!
LET'S COMBINE *TWO* GAMES INTO ONE . . .
THAT WAY IT'S *TWICE* AS MUCH FUN . . . RIGHT?
. . . TAG AND DODGEBALL!
YAAAY!!!

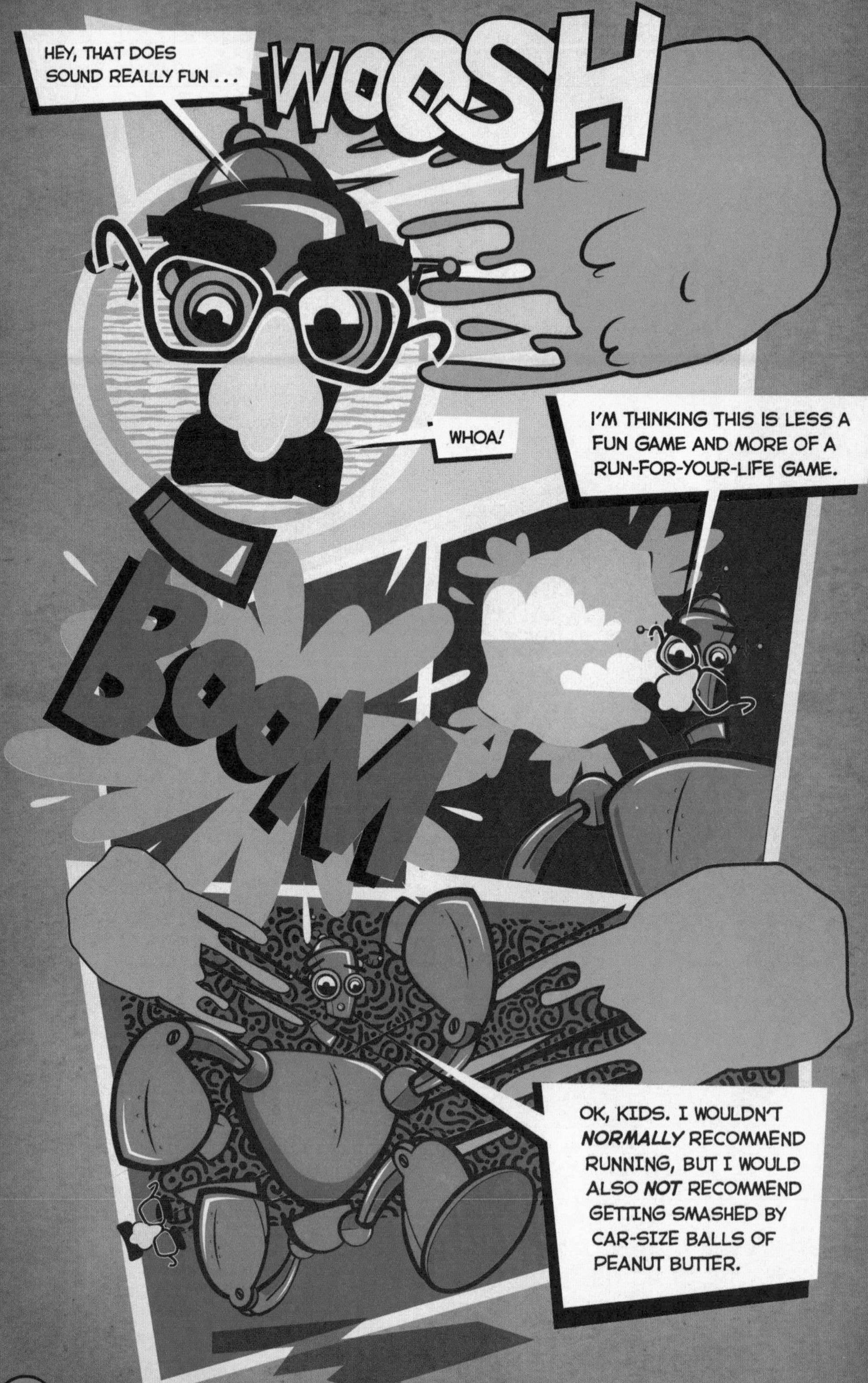
HEY, THAT DOES SOUND REALLY FUN . . .
WOOSH
WHOA!
I'M THINKING THIS IS LESS A FUN GAME AND MORE OF A RUN-FOR-YOUR-LIFE GAME.
BOOM
OK, KIDS. I WOULDN'T *NORMALLY* RECOMMEND RUNNING, BUT I WOULD ALSO *NOT* RECOMMEND GETTING SMASHED BY CAR-SIZE BALLS OF PEANUT BUTTER.

MONSTER TAG DODGEBALL

COME ON OUT SO WE CAN PLAY A SUPER FUN GAME OF MONSTER TAG DODGEBALL!
IT MIGHT BE FUN, BUT I AM FEELING PRETTY INCLINED TO RUN FOR MY LIFE FOR THE TIME BEING.

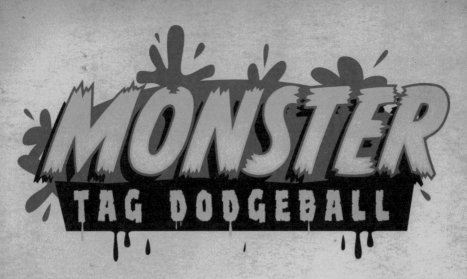

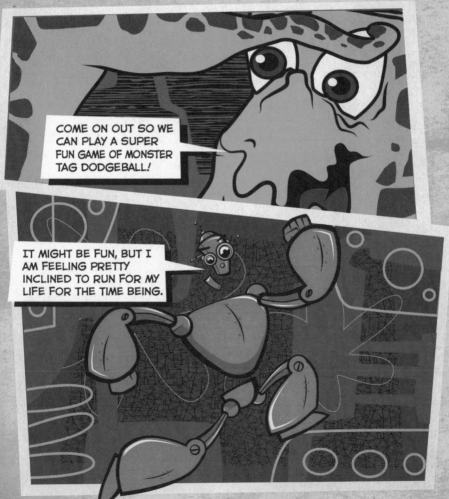

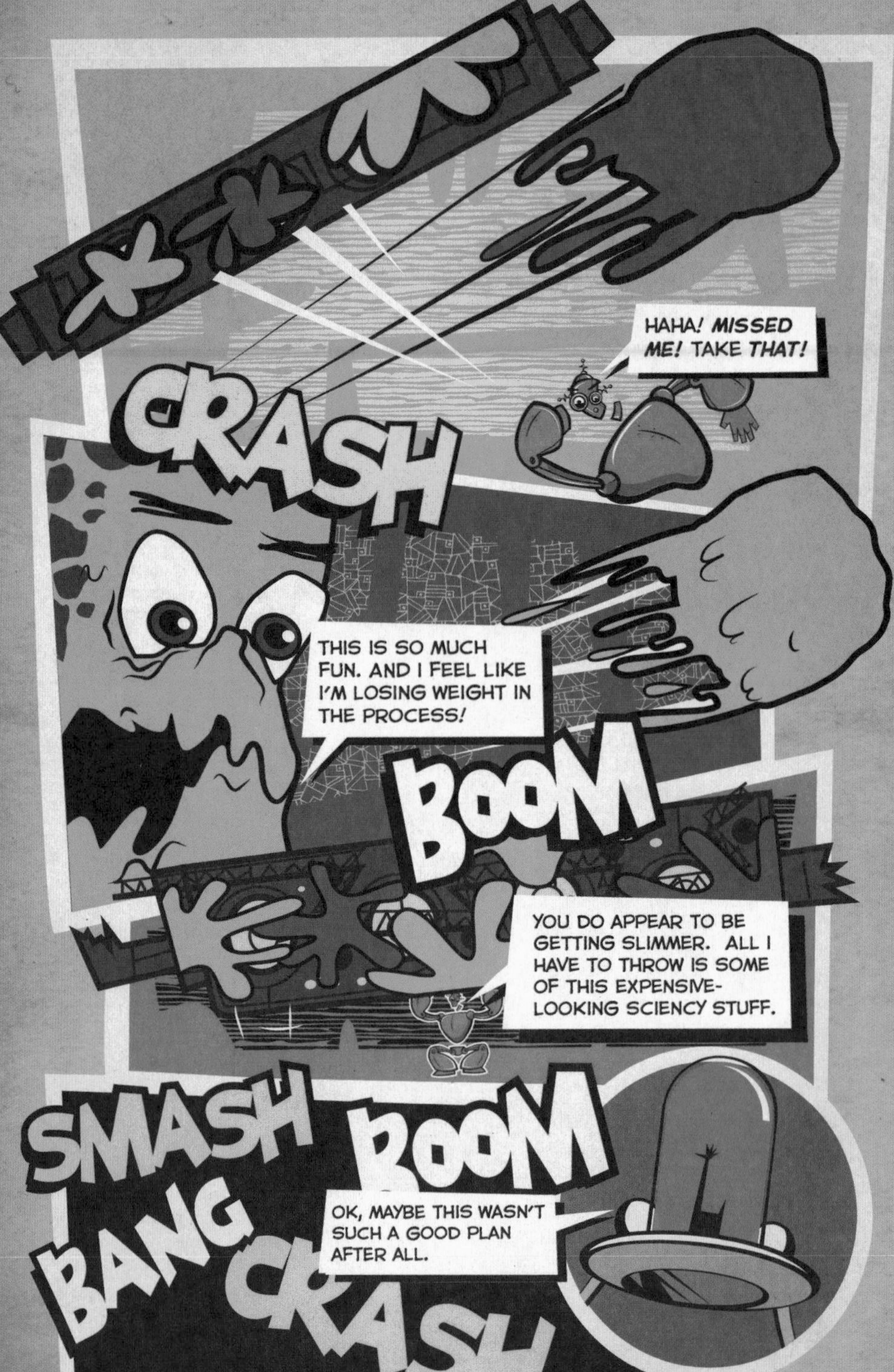
CRASH
HAHA! MISSED ME! TAKE THAT!
THIS IS SO MUCH FUN. AND I FEEL LIKE I'M LOSING WEIGHT IN THE PROCESS!
BOOM
YOU DO APPEAR TO BE GETTING SLIMMER. ALL I HAVE TO THROW IS SOME OF THIS EXPENSIVE-LOOKING SCIENCY STUFF.
SMASH
BOOM
BANG
OK, MAYBE THIS WASN'T SUCH A GOOD PLAN AFTER ALL.
CRASH

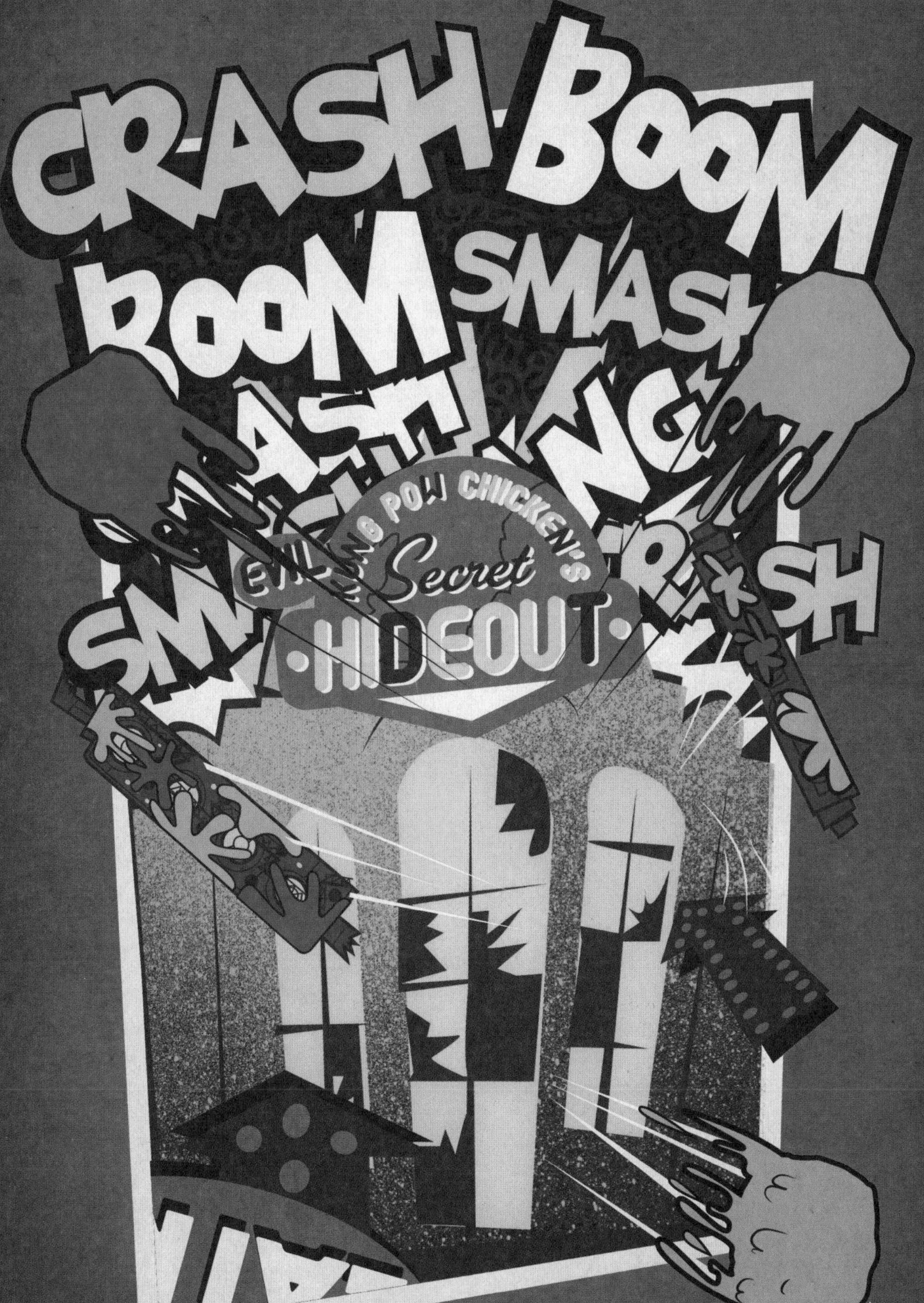
CRASH BOOM
BOOM SMASH
EVIL
POW CHICKEN'S
Secret
HIDEOUT

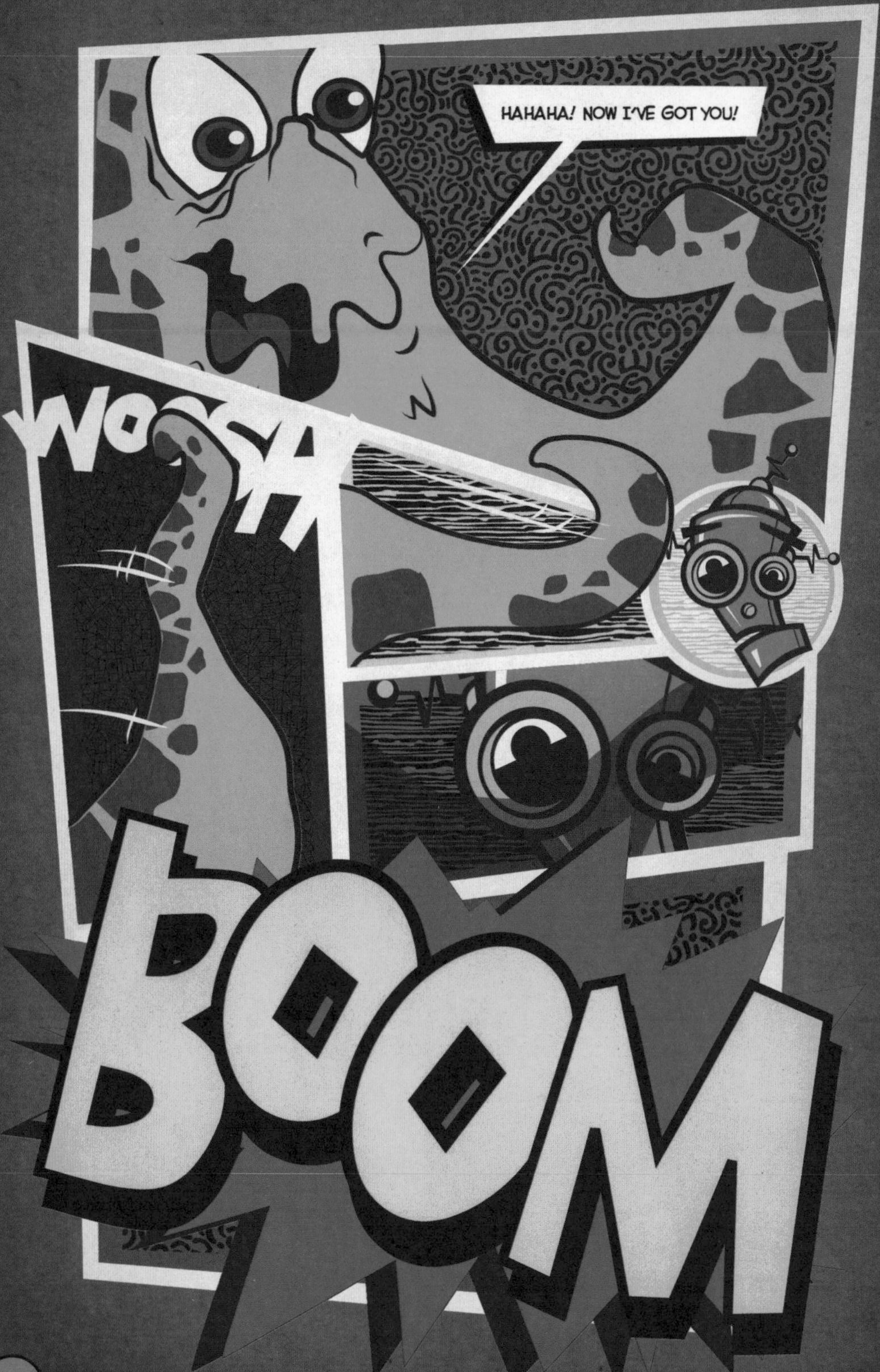
HAHAHA! NOW I'VE GOT YOU!
BOOM

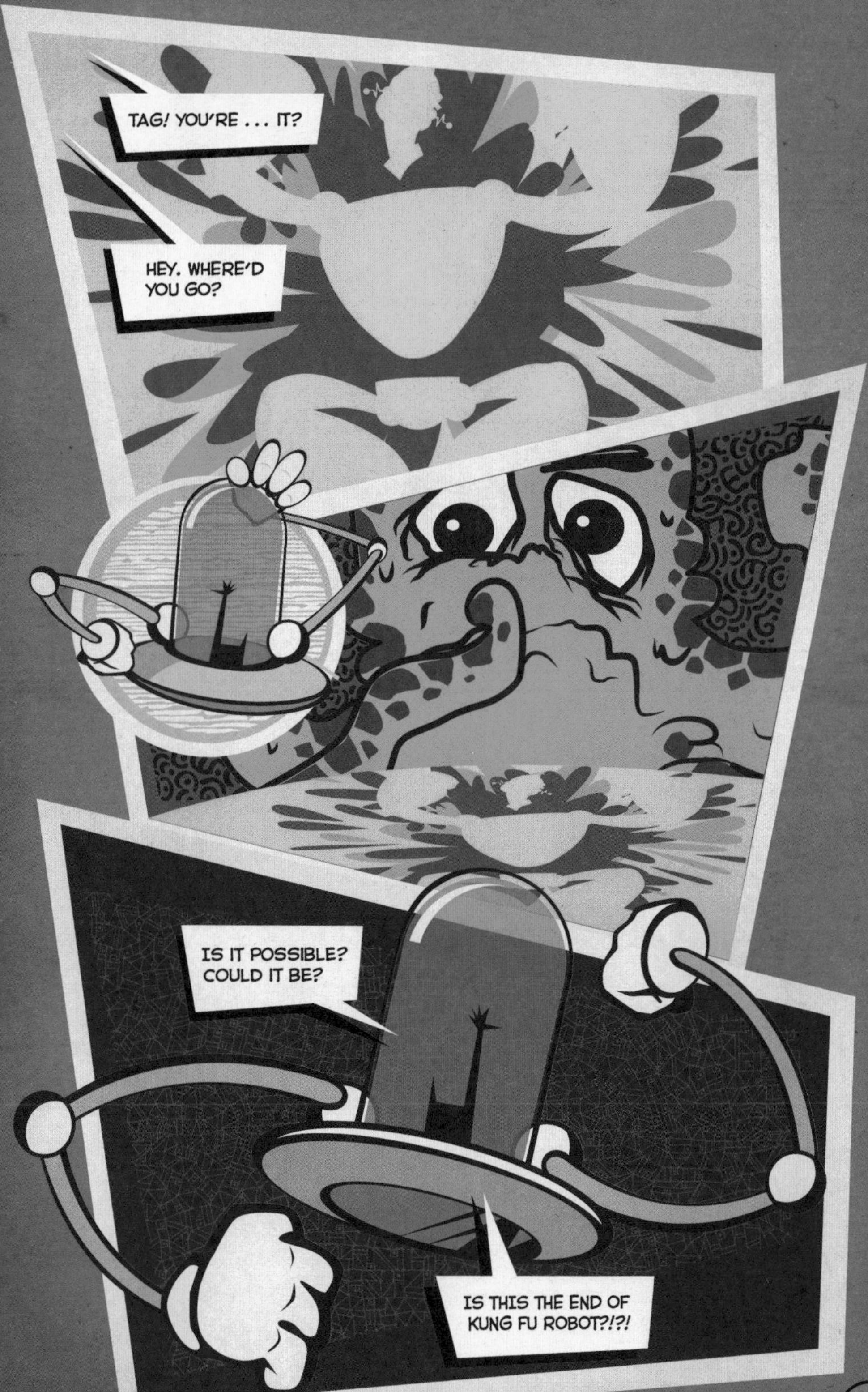
TAG! YOU'RE . . . IT?
HEY. WHERE'D YOU GO?
IS IT POSSIBLE? COULD IT BE?
IS THIS THE END OF KUNG FU ROBOT?!?!

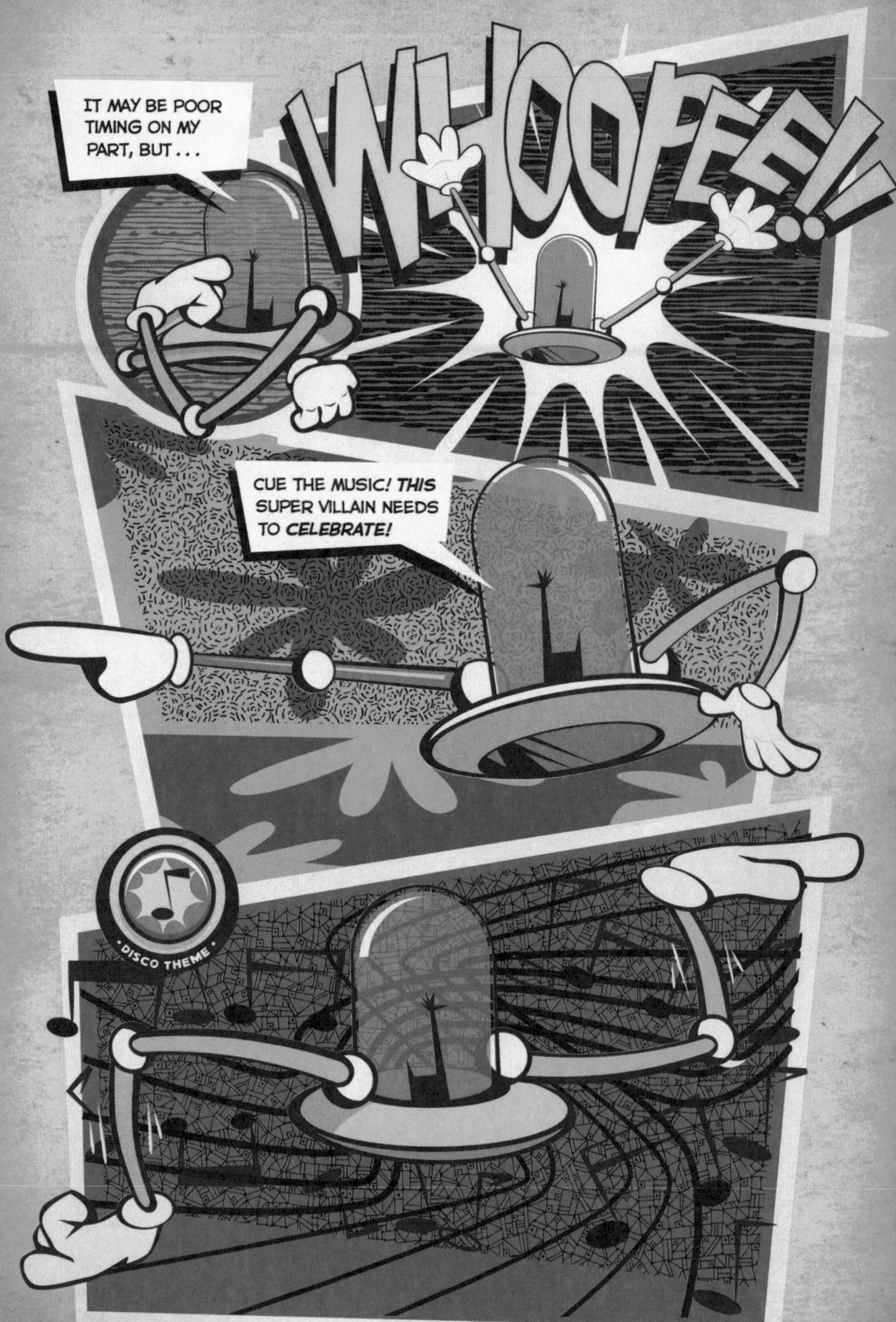
IT MAY BE POOR TIMING ON MY PART, BUT . . .
WHOOPEE!!
CUE THE MUSIC! THIS SUPER VILLAIN NEEDS TO CELEBRATE!
DISCO THEME

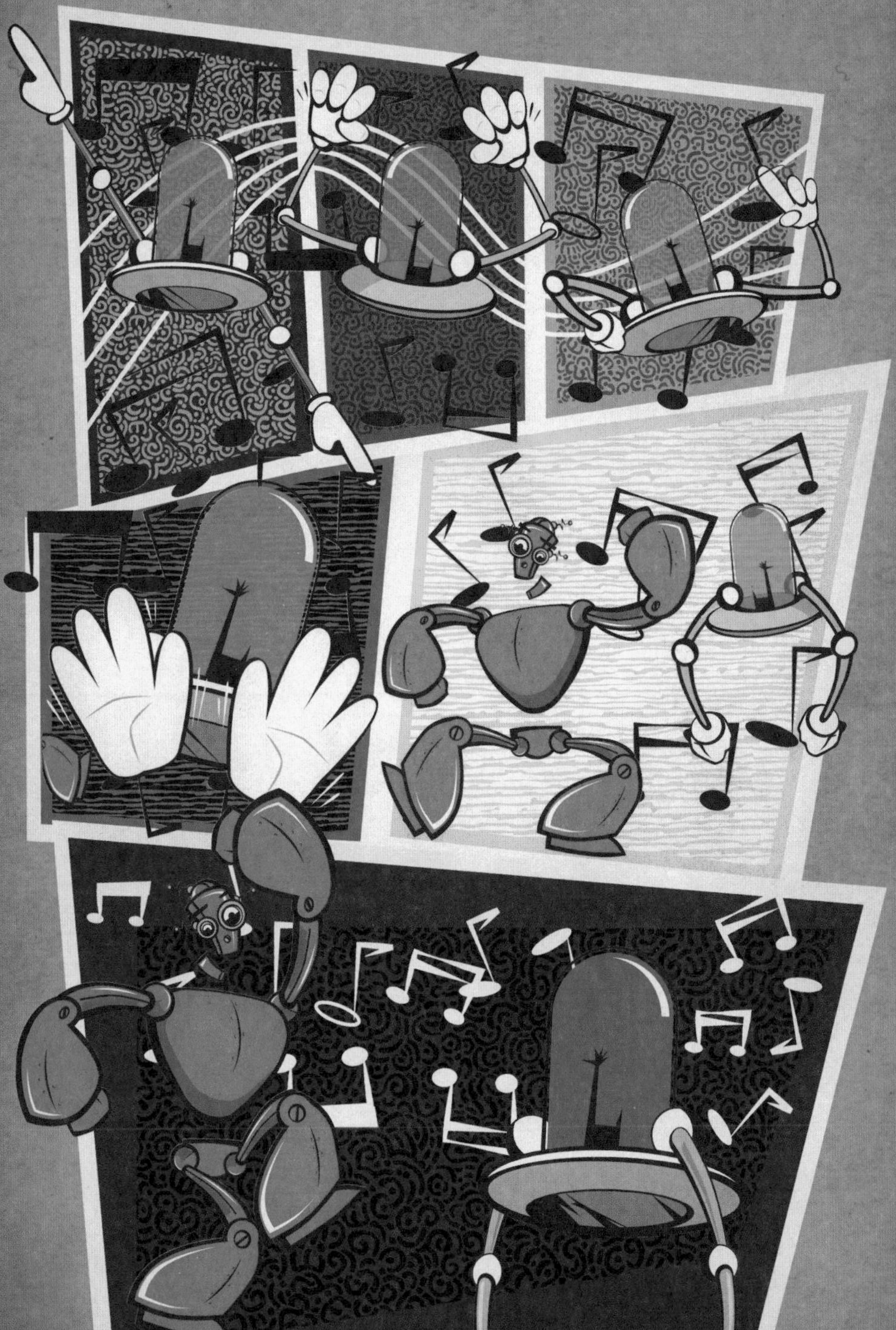

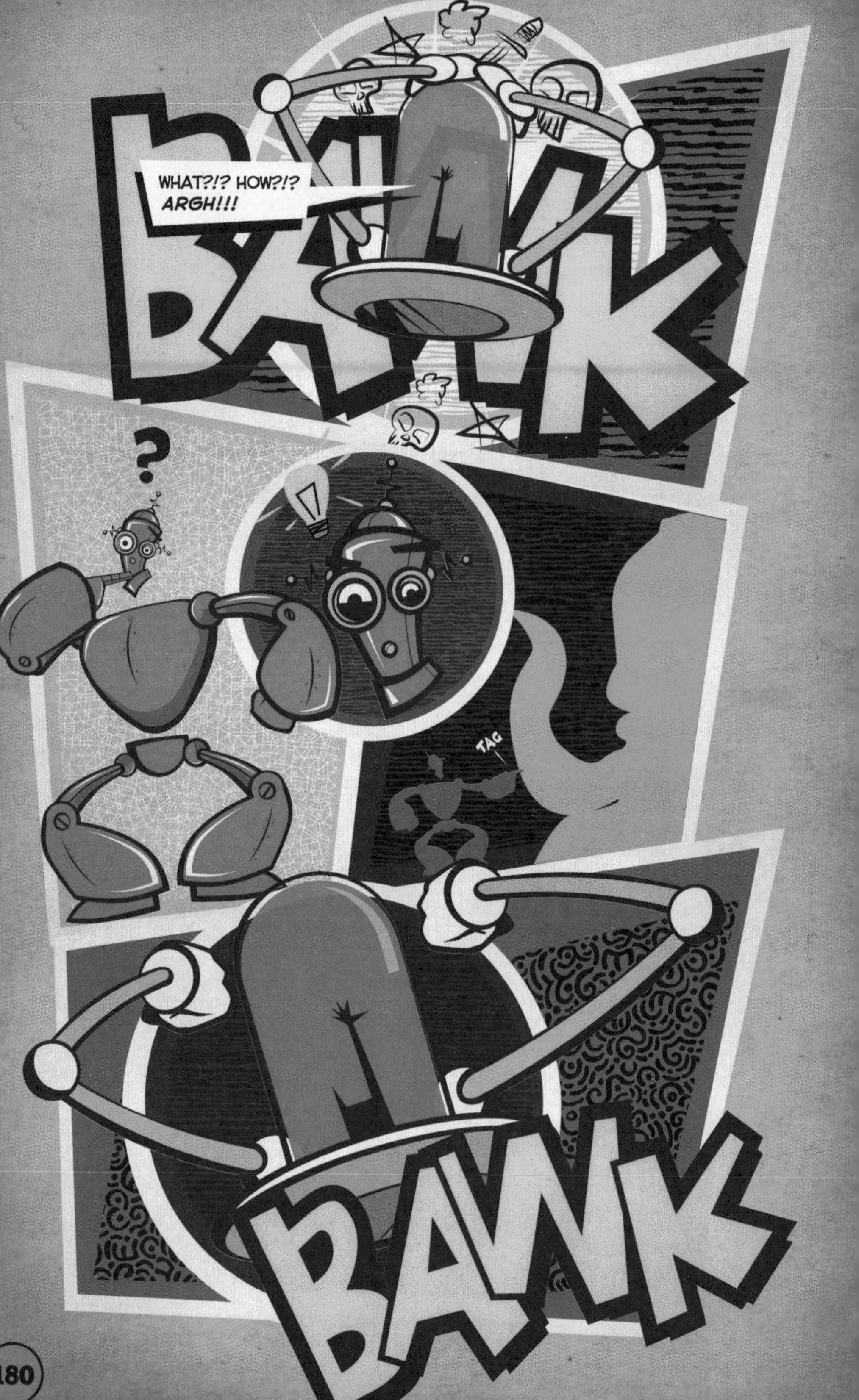
BANK
WHAT?!? HOW?!?
ARGH!!!
?
TAG
BANK

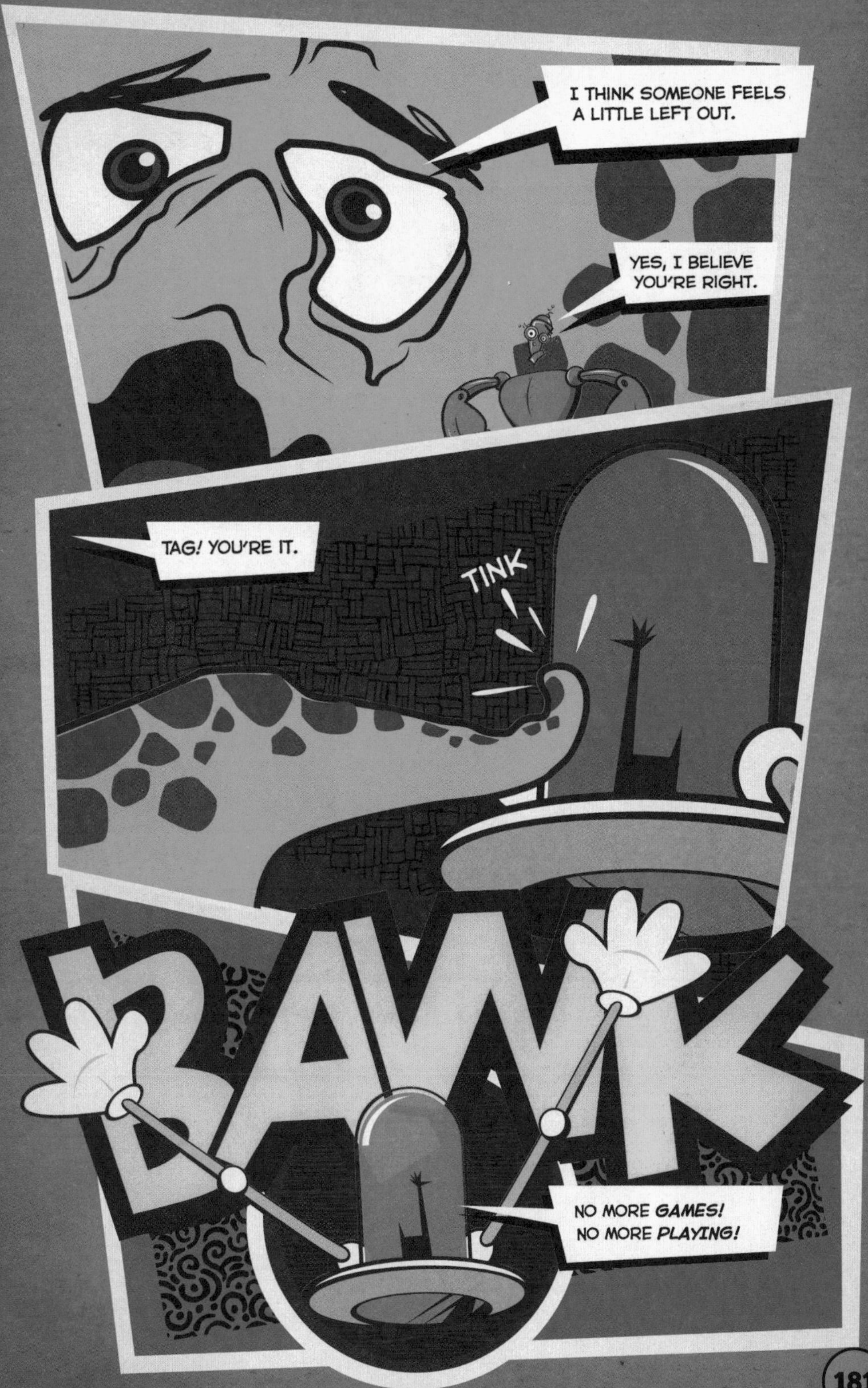
I THINK SOMEONE FEELS A LITTLE LEFT OUT.
YES, I BELIEVE YOU'RE RIGHT.
TAG! YOU'RE IT.
TINK
BAWK
NO MORE GAMES! NO MORE PLAYING!

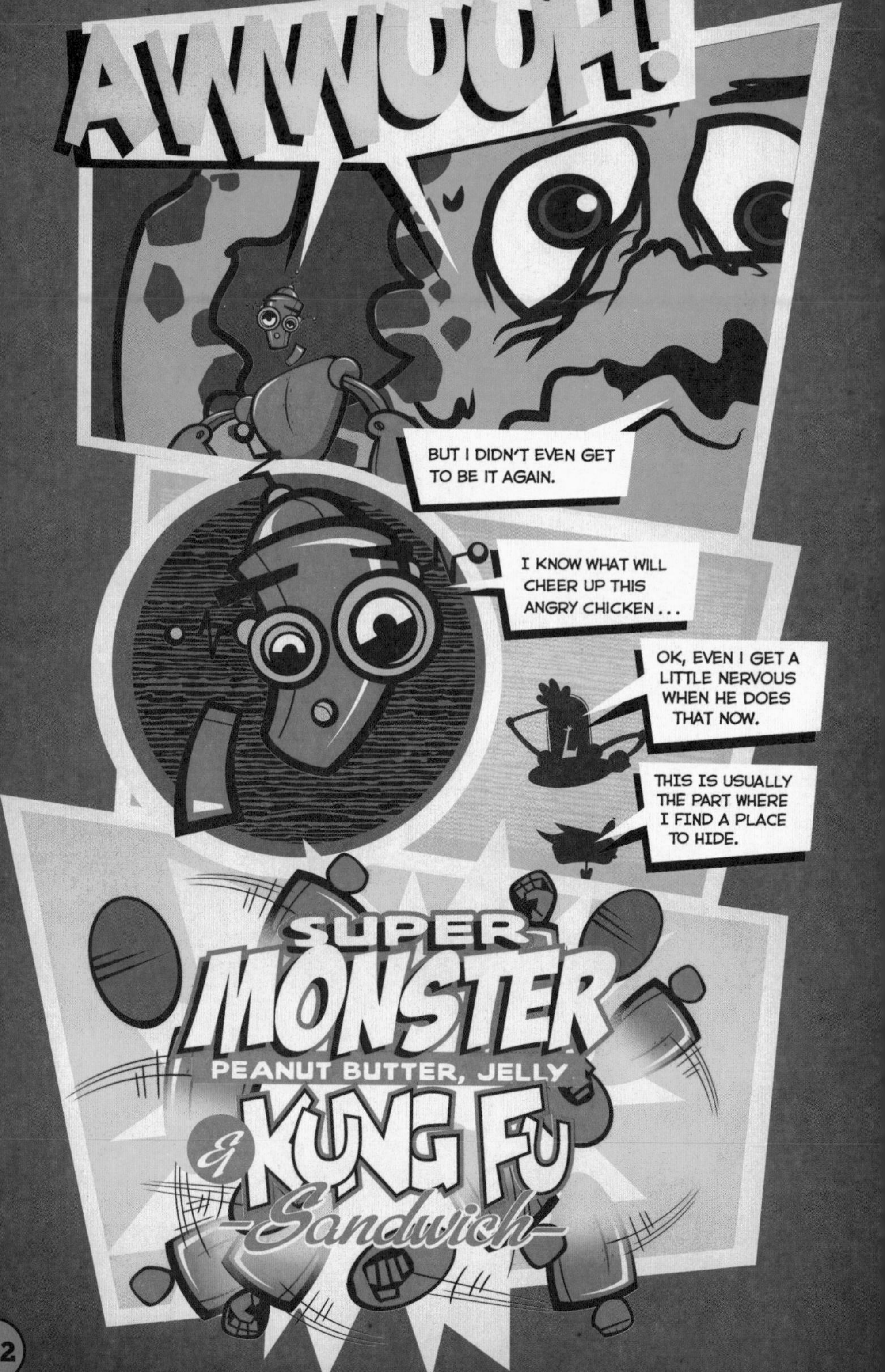

AWWUUH!
BUT I DIDN'T EVEN GET TO BE IT AGAIN.
I KNOW WHAT WILL CHEER UP THIS ANGRY CHICKEN . . .
OK, EVEN I GET A LITTLE NERVOUS WHEN HE DOES THAT NOW.
THIS IS USUALLY THE PART WHERE I FIND A PLACE TO HIDE.
SUPER MONSTER
PEANUT BUTTER, JELLY
& KUNG FU
Sandwich

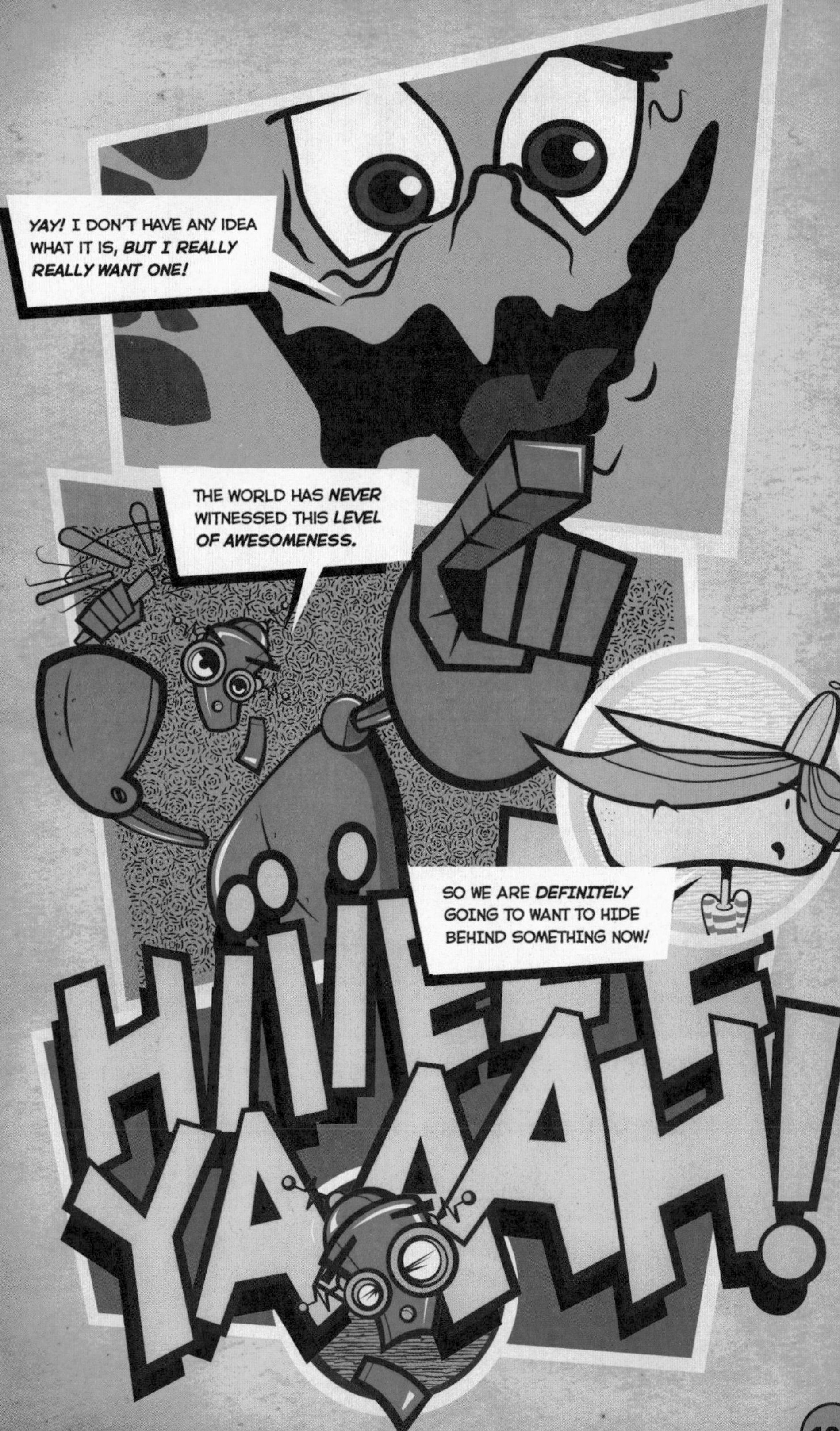
YAY! I DON'T HAVE ANY IDEA WHAT IT IS, BUT I REALLY REALLY WANT ONE!
THE WORLD HAS NEVER WITNESSED THIS LEVEL OF AWESOMENESS.
SO WE ARE DEFINITELY GOING TO WANT TO HIDE BEHIND SOMETHING NOW!
HIIIEEE YAAAH!

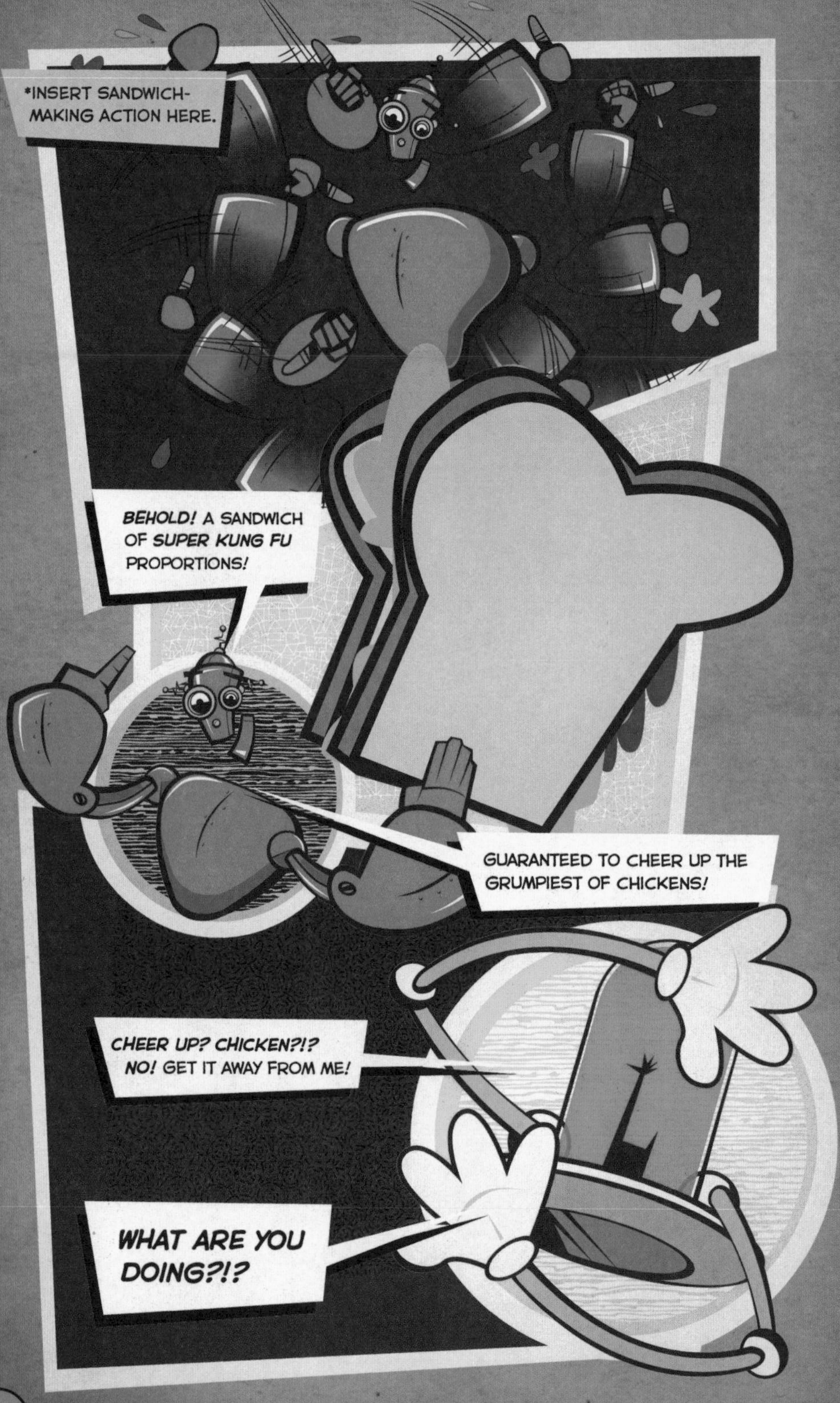
*INSERT SANDWICH-
MAKING ACTION HERE.
BEHOLD! A SANDWICH OF SUPER KUNG FU PROPORTIONS!
GUARANTEED TO CHEER UP THE GRUMPIEST OF CHICKENS!
CHEER UP? CHICKEN?!? NO! GET IT AWAY FROM ME!
WHAT ARE YOU DOING?!?

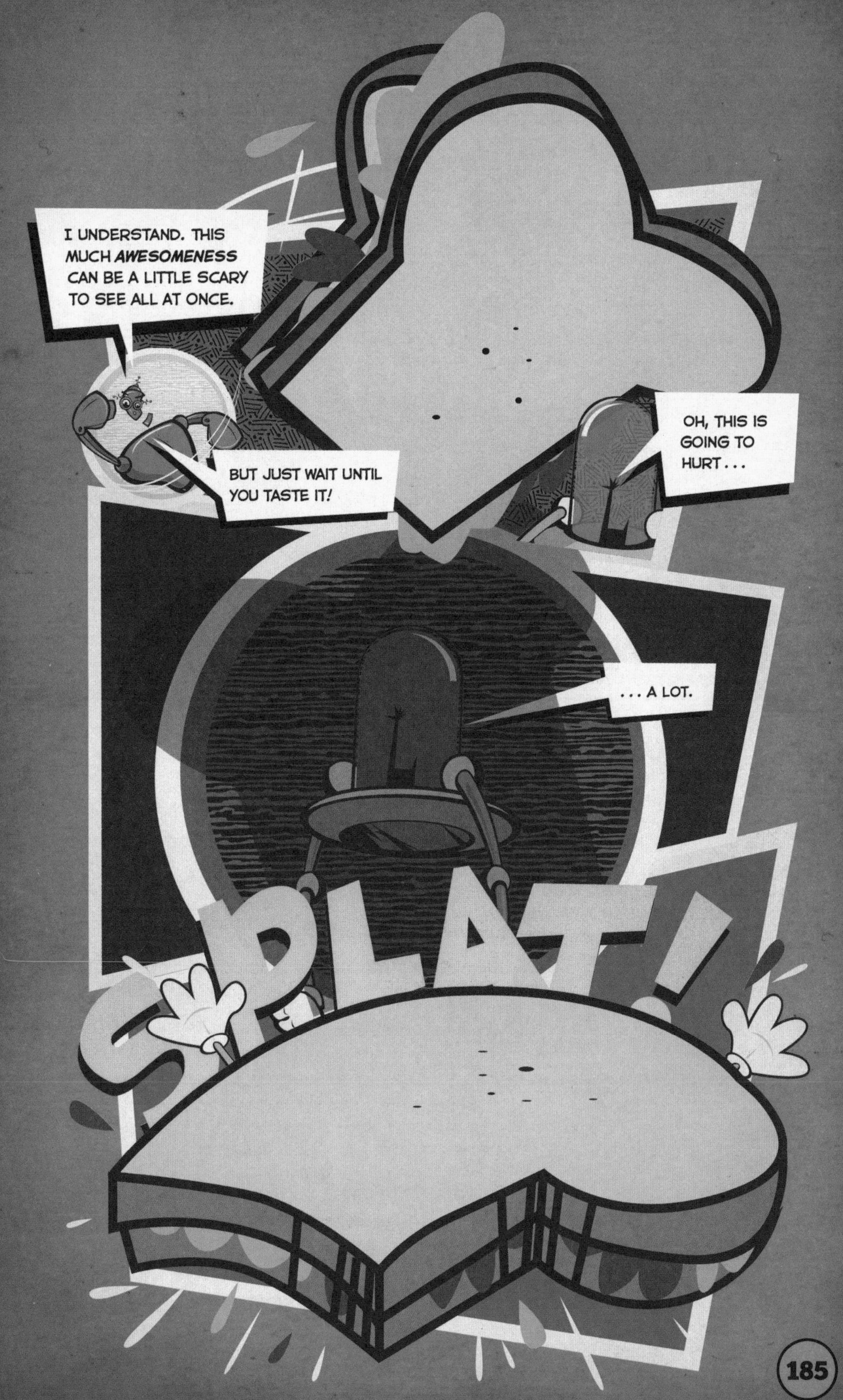
I UNDERSTAND. THIS MUCH ***AWESOMENESS*** CAN BE A LITTLE SCARY TO SEE ALL AT ONCE.
BUT JUST WAIT UNTIL YOU TASTE IT!
OH, THIS IS GOING TO HURT . . .
. . . A LOT.
SPLAT!

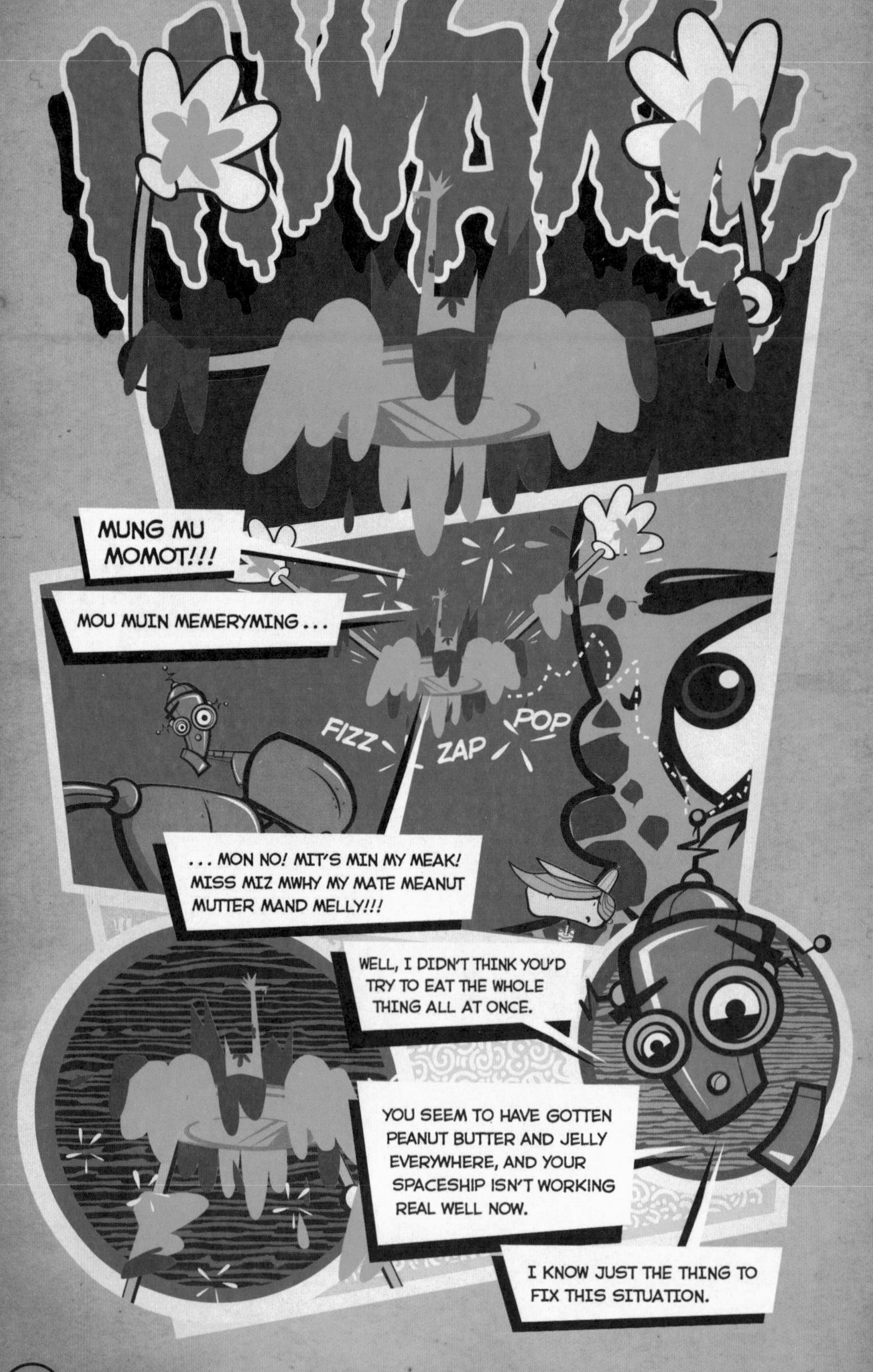
MUNG MU MOMOT!!!
MOU MUIN MEMERYMING . . .
FIZZ
ZAP
POP
. . . MON NO! MIT'S MIN MY MEAK! MISS MIZ MWHY MY MATE MEANUT MUTTER MAND MELLY!!!
WELL, I DIDN'T THINK YOU'D TRY TO EAT THE WHOLE THING ALL AT ONCE.
YOU SEEM TO HAVE GOTTEN PEANUT BUTTER AND JELLY EVERYWHERE, AND YOUR SPACESHIP ISN'T WORKING REAL WELL NOW.
I KNOW JUST THE THING TO FIX THIS SITUATION.

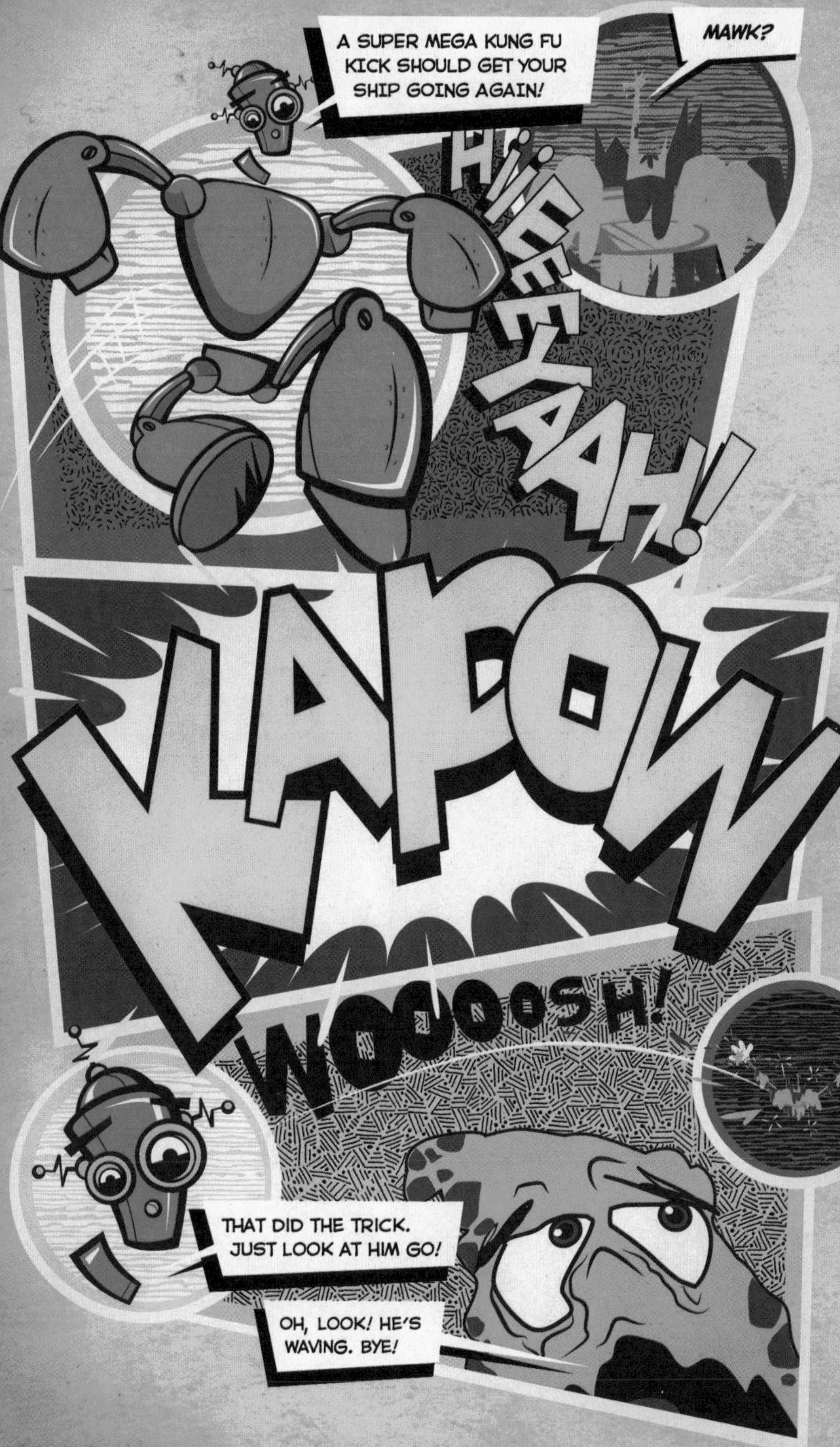
A SUPER MEGA KUNG FU KICK SHOULD GET YOUR SHIP GOING AGAIN!
MAWK?
HIIEEEYAAH!
KAPOW
WOOOOOSH!
THAT DID THE TRICK. JUST LOOK AT HIM GO!
OH, LOOK! HE'S WAVING. BYE!

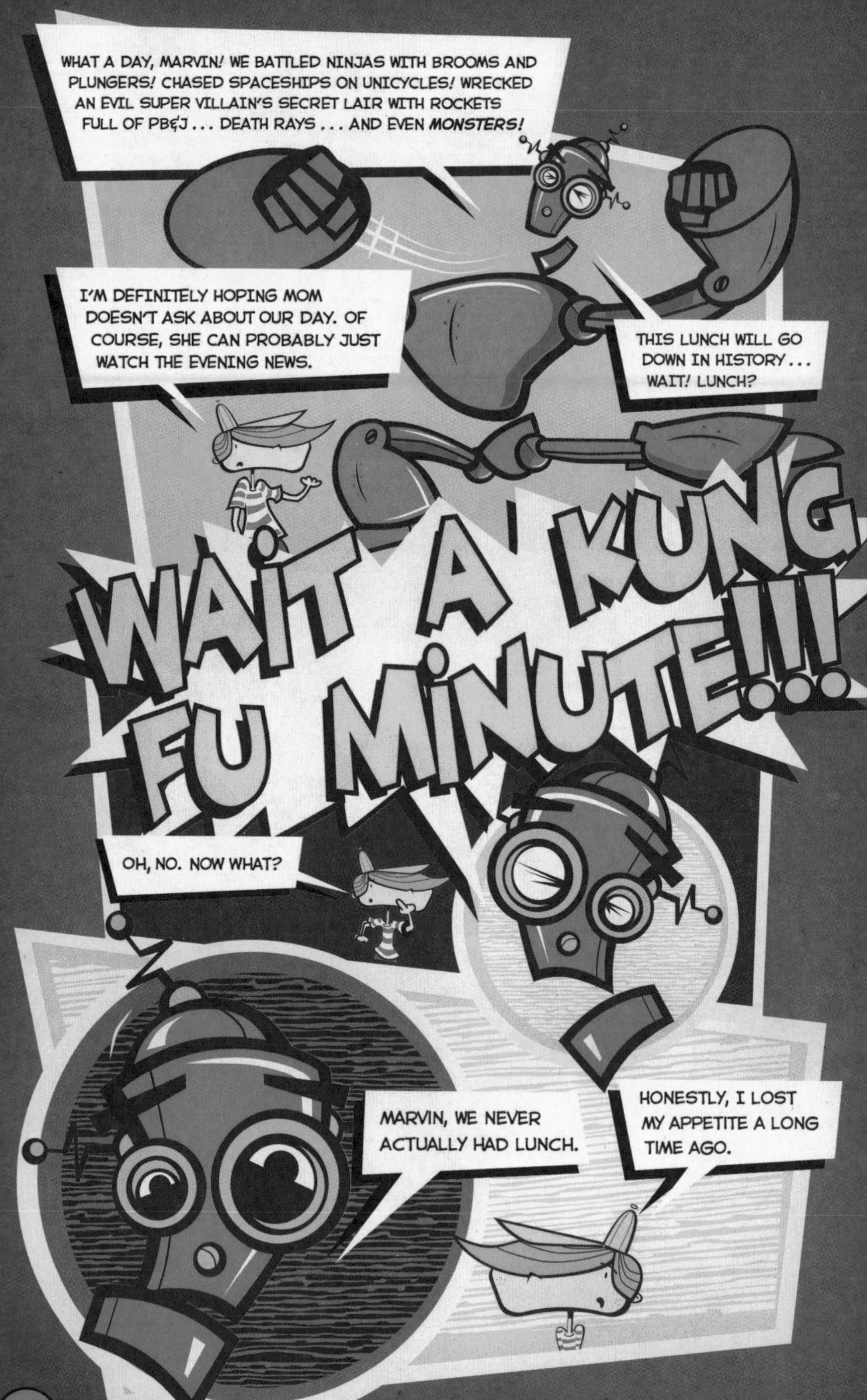
WHAT A DAY, MARVIN! WE BATTLED NINJAS WITH BROOMS AND PLUNGERS! CHASED SPACESHIPS ON UNICYCLES! WRECKED AN EVIL SUPER VILLAIN'S SECRET LAIR WITH ROCKETS FULL OF PB&J . . . DEATH RAYS . . . AND EVEN MONSTERS!
I'M DEFINITELY HOPING MOM DOESN'T ASK ABOUT OUR DAY. OF COURSE, SHE CAN PROBABLY JUST WATCH THE EVENING NEWS.
THIS LUNCH WILL GO DOWN IN HISTORY . . . WAIT! LUNCH?
WAIT A KUNG FU MINUTE!!!
OH, NO. NOW WHAT?
MARVIN, WE NEVER ACTUALLY HAD LUNCH.
HONESTLY, I LOST MY APPETITE A LONG TIME AGO.

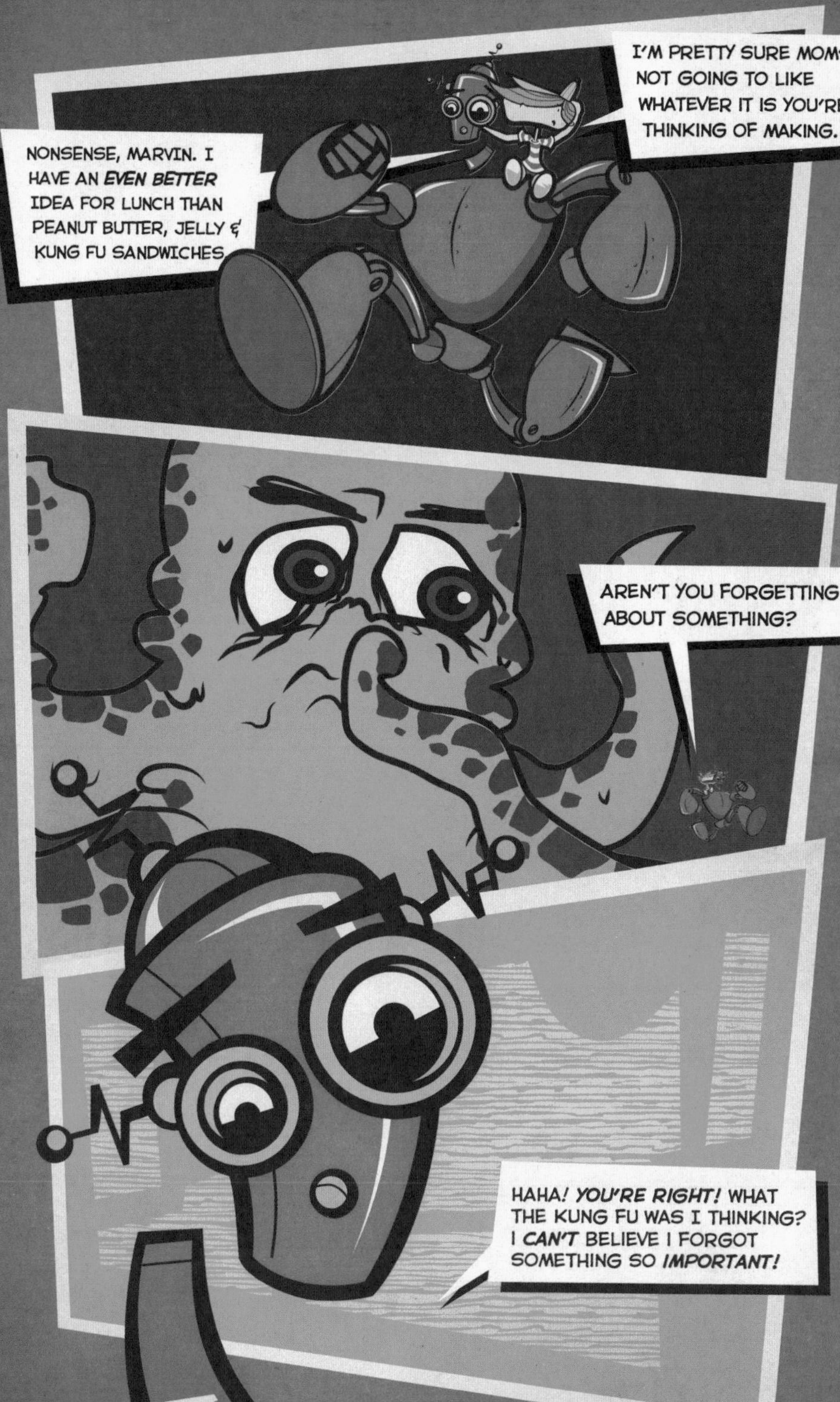
I'M PRETTY SURE MOM'S NOT GOING TO LIKE WHATEVER IT IS YOU'RE THINKING OF MAKING.
NONSENSE, MARVIN. I HAVE AN *EVEN BETTER* IDEA FOR LUNCH THAN PEANUT BUTTER, JELLY & KUNG FU SANDWICHES
AREN'T YOU FORGETTING ABOUT SOMETHING?
HAHA! *YOU'RE RIGHT!* WHAT THE KUNG FU WAS I THINKING? I *CAN'T* BELIEVE I FORGOT SOMETHING SO *IMPORTANT!*

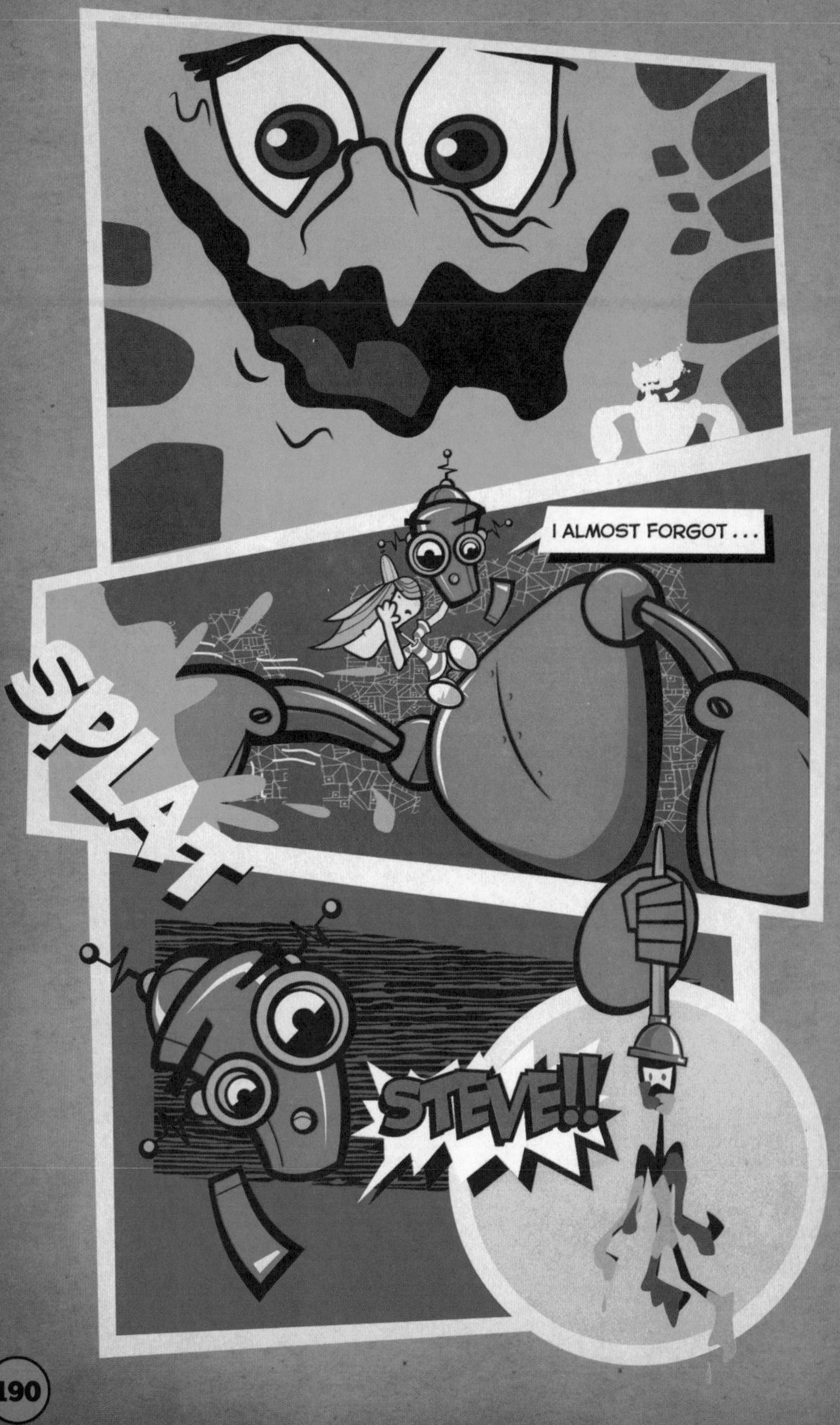
I ALMOST FORGOT . . .
SPLAT
STEVE!!

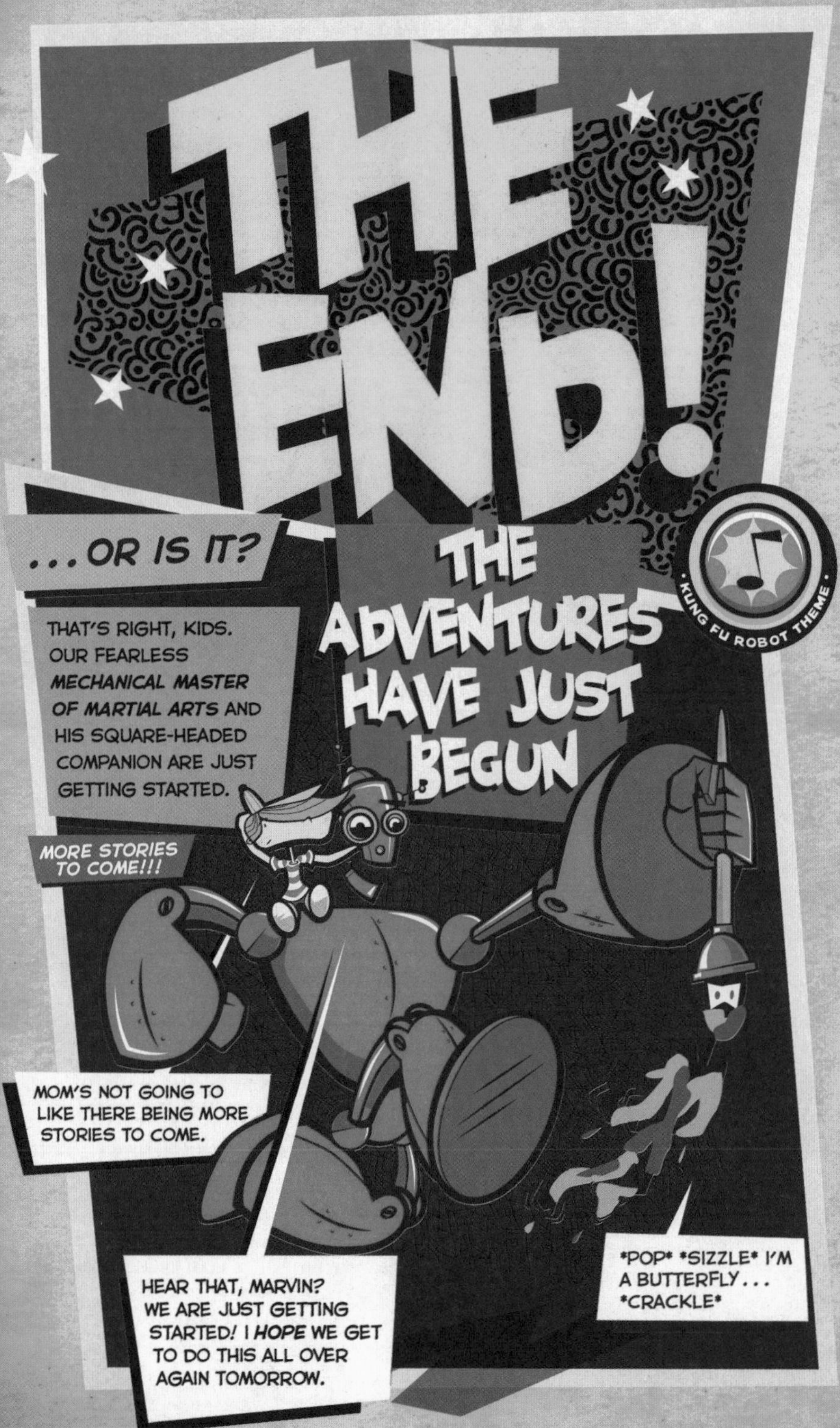

THE END!
. . . OR IS IT?
THAT'S RIGHT, KIDS. OUR FEARLESS *MECHANICAL MASTER OF MARTIAL ARTS* AND HIS SQUARE-HEADED COMPANION ARE JUST GETTING STARTED.
THE ADVENTURES HAVE JUST BEGUN
KUNG FU ROBOT THEME
MORE STORIES TO COME!!!
MOM'S NOT GOING TO LIKE THERE BEING MORE STORIES TO COME.
HEAR THAT, MARVIN? WE ARE JUST GETTING STARTED! I *HOPE* WE GET TO DO THIS ALL OVER AGAIN TOMORROW.
POP *SIZZLE* I'M A BUTTERFLY . . . *CRACKLE*

MORE TO EXPLORE

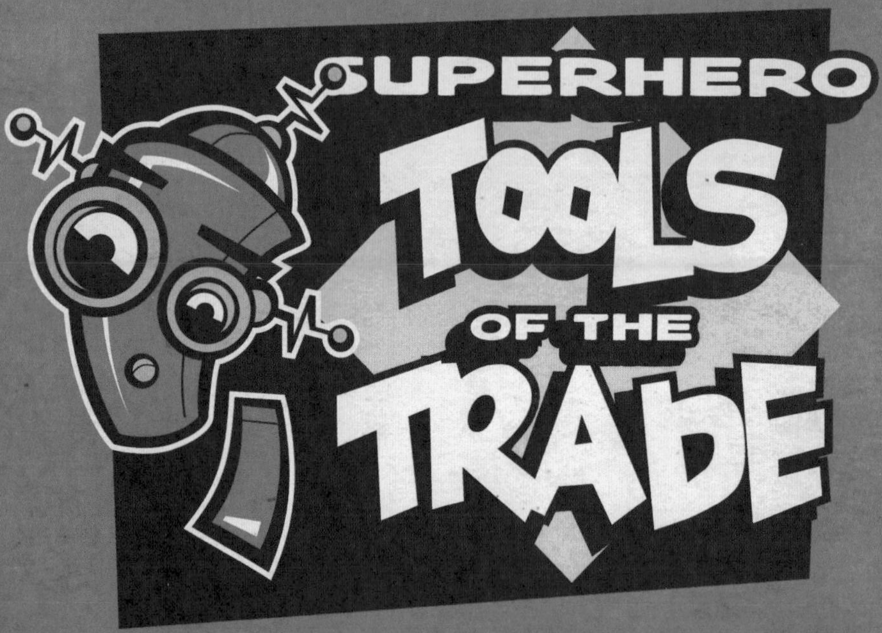
SUPERHERO
TOOLS
OF THE
TRADE

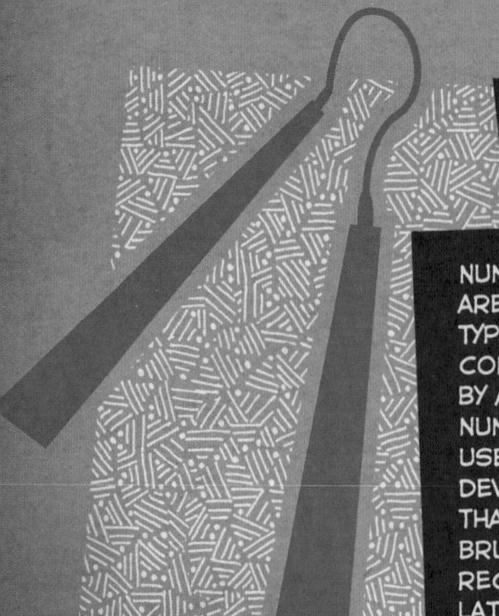

NUNCHUKS

NUNCHUKS (ALSO KNOWN AS NUNCHAKU) ARE A TRADITIONAL MARTIAL ARTS WEAPON. TYPICALLY THEY CONSIST OF TWO STICKS CONNECTED TO EACH OTHER AT ONE END BY A SHORT CHAIN OR CORD. HISTORICALLY, NUNCHUKS MORE OFTEN HAVE BEEN USED AS A TRAINING DEVICE TO HELP DEVELOP HAND/EYE COORDINATION RATHER THAN A WEAPON USED IN ACTUAL COMBAT. BRUCE LEE, ONE OF THE MOST WIDELY RECOGNIZED MARTIAL ARTISTS FROM THE LATE TWENTIETH CENTURY, WAS INCREDIBLY ADEPT AT NUNCHUKS.

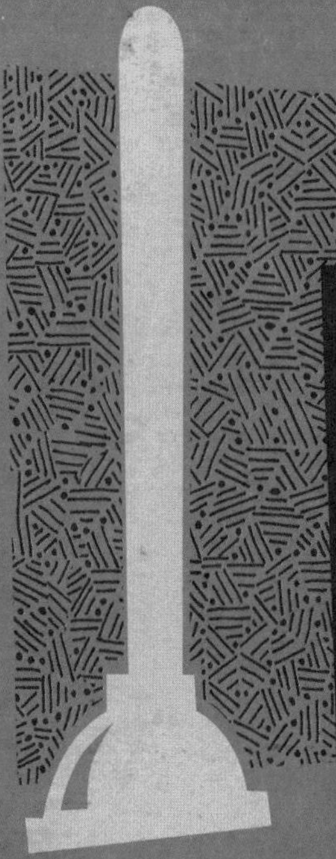

PLUNGER

WHILE THE EXACT DATE AND IDENTITY OF THE INVENTOR OF THE PLUNGER ARE NOT CLEAR, ITS USEFULNESS IS VERY WELL KNOWN. ASIDE FROM ITS MORE OBVIOUS FUNCTIONS IN THE WORLD OF PLUMBING, DID YOU KNOW THAT MUSICIANS HAVE LONG USED THE SUCTION CUP PORTION OF THE PLUNGER TO TRANSFORM THE SOUND OF CERTAIN BRASS INSTRUMENTS? THE MOST RECOGNIZABLE USE OF THIS TECHNIQUE IS IN COMBINATION WITH A TROMBONE TO MAKE THE CHARACTERISTIC "WAH WAH" SOUND OF ADULTS SPEAKING IN THE *PEANUTS* CARTOONS.

UNICYCLE

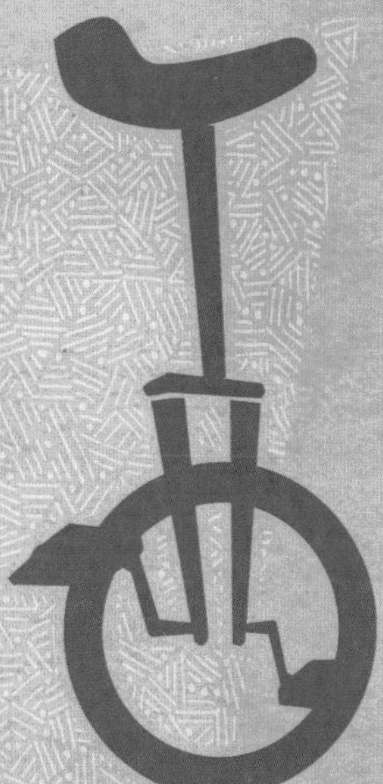

THE HISTORY OF THE UNICYCLE GOES BACK TO THE LATE 1800S AND THE FIRST BICYCLES. THOUGH OFTEN ASSOCIATED WITH CIRCUS AND STREET PERFORMERS, THE UNICYCLE HAS BEEN ADAPTED FOR MOUNTAIN BIKING, OBSTACLE-BASED TRAIL RIDING, FREESTYLE/TRICK RIDING, AND EVEN LONG DISTANCE RIDING.

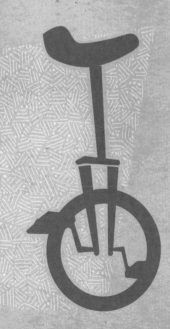

BROOM

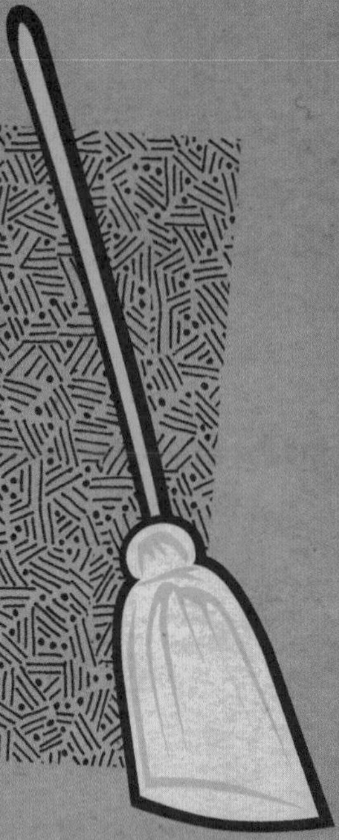

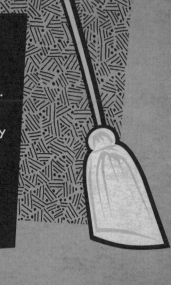

BROOMS HAVE BEEN USED AS A HOUSEHOLD CLEANING IMPLEMENT FOR CENTURIES, GOING ALL THE WAY BACK TO WHEN BRANCHES WERE HARVESTED FROM SMALL SHRUBS AND USED FOR SWEEPING. THE MODERN MANUFACTURE OF BROOMS STARTED AROUND THE EARLY 1800S THANKS TO A MASSACHUSETTS FARMER BY THE NAME OF LEVI DICKENSON, WHO IS CREDITED WITH INVENTING ONE OF THE FIRST BROOM-MAKING MACHINES. WHILE BROOMS HAVE NEVER BEEN CONSIDERED A WEAPON IN TRADITIONAL KUNG FU, THE LONG HANDLE COULD LEND ITSELF TO USING CERTAIN BO STAFF TECHNIQUES.

TAPE

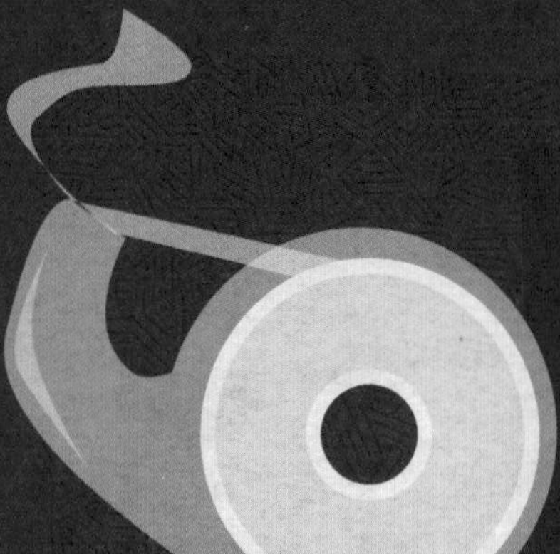

PRESSURE-SENSITIVE TAPE— TAPE THAT USES A SELF-STICKING ADHESIVE AS A BACKING TO PAPER, THIN PLASTIC FILM, CLOTH, OR EVEN METAL— HAS BEEN AROUND SINCE THE MID-1800S. IT WAS DEVELOPED BY HORACE DAY, A SURGEON, AS A MEANS OF CLOSING WOUNDS AND SURGICAL INCISIONS. TODAY, TAPE CAN TAKE MANY DIFFERENT FORMS, FROM PAINTER'S OR MASKING TAPE TO GIFT WRAP TAPE TO THE UNIVERSALLY ACCLAIMED DUCT TAPE.

SUPERVILLAIN TOOLS OF THE TRADE

MINIONS

A MINION IS A LOYAL SERVANT OR TRUSTED FOLLOWER OF ANOTHER PERSON. OFTEN USED BY SUPER VILLAINS AS INDISCRIMINATE, AND USUALLY UNINTELLIGENT BRUTE FORCE OR LABOR, MINIONS HAVE EARNED A REPUTATION AS BEING FANATICAL IN THEIR FOLLOWING, OFTEN TO A FAULT. MINIONS, HOWEVER, DON'T ALWAYS HAVE TO BE EVIL OR MALICIOUS. ON OCCASION, AN INDIVIDUAL MINION HAS BEEN KNOWN TO BREAK FROM HIS OR HER COLLEAGUES AND OFFER HELP TO HEROES IN NEED IN WHAT IS SOMETIMES KNOWN AS A CRISIS OF CONSCIENCE.

ROCKETS

A ROCKET IS A FORM OF AIRCRAFT OR SPACECRAFT THAT OBTAINS THRUST— AND THUS FLIGHT—FROM A ROCKET ENGINE. ROCKETS OFTEN RELY ON AN INTERNAL COMBUSTION ENGINE AND MULTIPLE STAGES TO ATTAIN LONG DISTANCE FLIGHT AND EVEN ESCAPE EARTH'S ATMOSPHERE. BY EXPELLING ITS EXHAUST AT HIGH SPEED IN THE OPPOSITE DIRECTION IN WHICH IT TRAVELS, A ROCKET IS AN EXCELLENT EXAMPLE OF NEWTON'S THIRD LAW: FOR EVERY ACTION, THERE IS AN EQUAL AND OPPOSITE REACTION.

MONOLOGUES

BLAH BLAH BLAH EVIL STUFF BLAH BLAH DIABOLICAL PLANS BLAH BLAH BLAH RULE THE WORLD BLAH BLAH BRUSSELS SPROUTS BLAH BLAH BLAH I'M SO EVIL BLAH BLAH BLAH BLAH ...

AN OFTEN-EMPLOYED TECHNIQUE OR TROPE OF COMIC BOOK-STYLE STORYTELLING, THE EVIL DRAMATIC MONOLOGUE—ALSO KNOWN AS GLOATING—IS A CLASSIC BEHAVIOR OF SUPER VILLAINS. IT'S TYPICALLY USED AS AN OPPORTUNITY TO REVEAL THE DASTARDLY PLANS OF A STORY'S ANTAGONIST EITHER DIRECTLY OR INDIRECTLY TO THE STORY'S HERO, AND THUS THE READER OR AUDIENCE AS WELL. TYPICALLY AN EVIL MONOLOGUE CAN GO ON FOR A PROLONGED PERIOD OF TIME, WHICH OCCASIONALLY PROVIDES AMPLE OPPORTUNITY FOR A HERO TO TAKE ACTION, ESPECIALLY IF SAID HERO IS CONFINED OR RESTRAINED.

EVIL PLANS

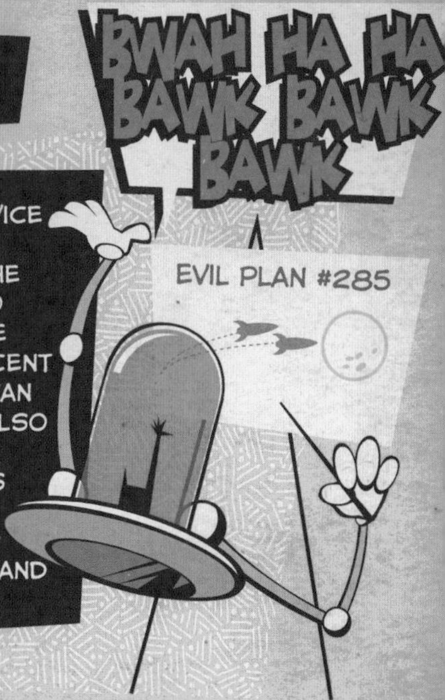
BWAH HA HA BAWK BAWK BAWK
EVIL PLAN #285

AN EVIL PLAN IS THE DRAMATIC DEVICE IN A COMIC BOOK-STYLE STORY BY WHICH CONFLICT IS CREATED BY THE STORY'S ANTAGONIST IN ORDER TO IMPOSE HIS OR HER WILL UPON THE WORLD AROUND THEM. BOTH INNOCENT BYSTANDERS OR SUPER HEROES CAN BE THE TARGET OF AN EVIL PLAN, ALSO KNOW AS A PLOT, SCHEME, OR MANIACAL MACHINATION. EVIL PLANS ARE ALSO THE TYPICAL SUBJECT OF A MONOLOGUE DELIVERED BY A SUPER VILLAIN IN A MOMENT OF DRAMATIC AND GLEEFUL GLOATING (SEE IMAGE).

SECRET LAIR

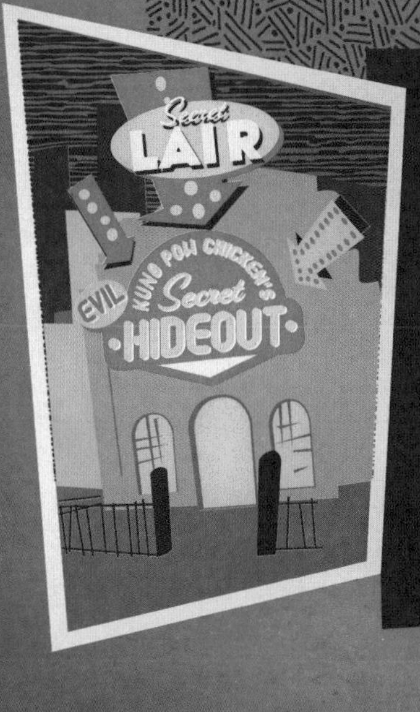
Secret LAIR
EVIL KUNG POW CHICKEN'S Secret HIDEOUT

A SECRET LAIR IS THE PRIVATE—AND USUALLY HIDDEN—DOMAIN OF EITHER A SUPERHERO OR SUPER VILLAIN. ALSO KNOWN AS A HIDEOUT, HIDDEN BASE, OR HEADQUARTERS, THE LOCATION FOR A GOOD SECRET LAIR OFTEN RELIES ON REMOTE PLACEMENT OR DRAMATIC SURROUNDINGS AND ELABORATE SECURITY MEASURES. REMOTE ISLANDS, UNDERWATER OR UNDERGROUND CAVERNS, ICY FORTRESSES, ACTIVE VOLCANOES, CITY SEWERS, DISTANT PLANETS, OR HIGHLY GUARDED BUILDINGS HAVE BEEN OFTEN DEPICTED AS IDEAL SETTINGS FOR SECRET LAIRS.

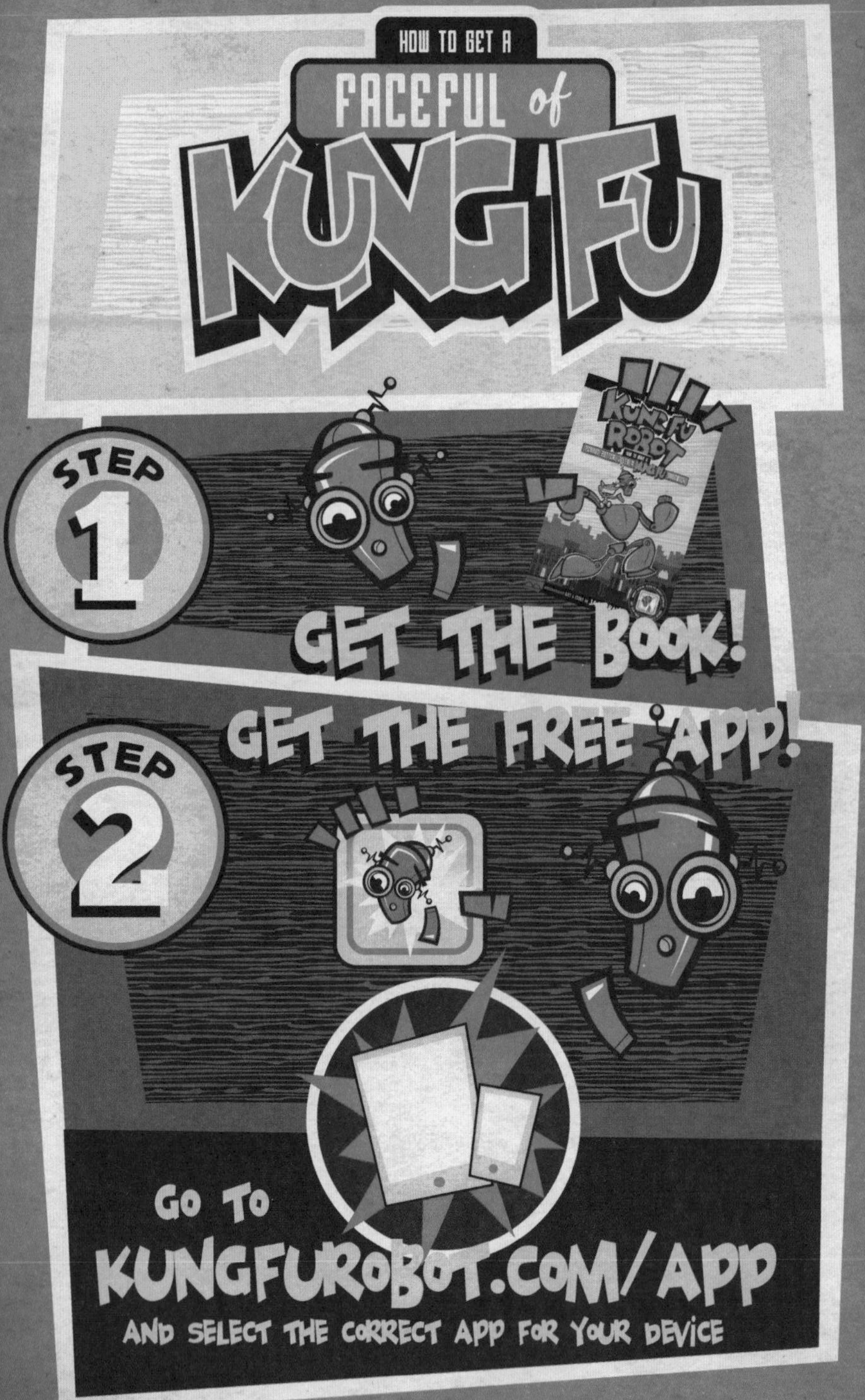

HOW TO GET A
FACEFUL of
KUNG FU
STEP 1
GET THE BOOK!
STEP 2
GET THE FREE APP!
GO TO
KUNGFUROBOT.COM/APP
AND SELECT THE CORRECT APP FOR YOUR DEVICE

USE THE SUPER KUNG FU VISION FEATURE

STEP 3 SCAN THE BOOK

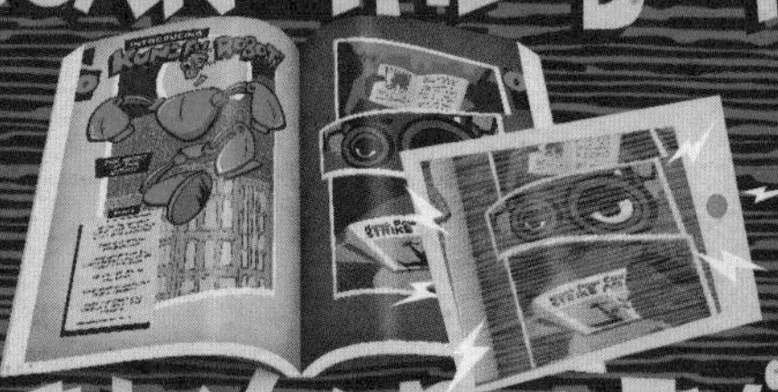

WITH YOUR DEVICE

STEP 4 GET A FACEFUL OF KUNG FU!

FIND AND UNLOCK ACTIVITIES, GAMES, AND OTHER FUN DIGITAL FEATURES

LAUNCHING IMAGINATIONS

KIDROCKETSTUDIOS.COM

Kid Rocket Studios // 2101 Broadway Boulevard, Suite 11, Kansas City, MO 64108
816.474.6333 // info@KidRocketStudios.com